PRAIS

"Readers looking for a good historical mystery/romance or a historical with a little more kink will enjoy *The Duke Who Knew Too Much*."—*Smart Bitches, Trashy Books*

"*Her Husband's Harlot* is a pleasing, out of the ordinary read."—*Dear Author*

"Grace Callaway's book is the first in her 'Heart of Enquiry' series, and this excellent brew of romance and intrigue and emotion is also *Stevereads* best Romance novel of 2015."—*The Duke Who Knew Too Much* named the #1 Best Romance of 2015 by *Stevereads*

"I discovered a new auto-buy author with [*M is for Marquess*]... I've now read each of Grace Callaway's books and loved them—which is exceptional. Gabriel and Thea from this book were two of the best characters I read this year. Both had their difficulties and it was charming to see how they overcame them together, even though it wasn't always easy for them. This is my favorite book of 2015."—*Romantic Historical Reviews*

"Erotic historical romance isn't as plentiful as many would think, but here you have a very well-written example of this genre. It's entertaining and fun and a darn good read."—*The Book Binge*

Regarding the Duke

Book Three

GRACE CALLAWAY

PROLOGUE

ALMOST THERE. KEEP MOVING. DON'T LET THEM CATCH YOU.

Heart pounding, nine-year-old Anthony Hale trod through the streets of Mayfair, keeping his head down and gaze vigilant beneath his tattered cap. He didn't dare run for fear of rousing suspicion. In this playground of the rich and powerful, he stuck out like a runty black sheep among plump, fluffy lambs, his soot-stained clothes betraying his profession as a climbing boy. The last thing he needed was for one of the blue-bloods taking their morning constitutionals to summon a constable. He tried to appear casual, as if he were on his way to clean another chimney... when in fact he was running for his life.

I own you, you li'l bugger. Roger Wiley's menacing face flashed before his eyes. *If I catch you runnin' away again, you'll wish you was dead.*

The scars on Anthony's back drew taut at the memory of his last flogging by the master sweep. He'd been feverish for days afterward, his blood soaking into the flour sacks that served as mattresses in the windowless cellar where all the climbing boys slept. It had been his second attempt to escape, and Wiley had made an example of him. Now none of the other children dared to step out of line. They were resigned to their fates—unlike Anthony.

He had a different path to follow. A promise to keep...and a destiny to fulfill.

He heard again his mother's desperate last words. *I won't make it off this ship, my dear boy, but promise me you'll find Anthony De Villier. He's your father...your last hope. You're so handsome and clever, I know he'll take you in. If he doesn't believe you, give him this.* She'd pulled a piece of knotted leather from beneath her bodice, upon which dangled a magnificent bloodstone ring. The thick shank was made of gold, the shoulders carved in a scroll design. The ring's black-and-red-flecked stone was carved with the ornate initials, "A. D."

Keep it safe until you see De Villier. Until then, tell no one, my son... trust no one...

Anthony had been stupid; he hadn't heeded his mama's words. He'd thought he could trust the Wileys, fellow passengers on the ship who'd pretended to be Good Samaritans. When his mother died the day before reaching London, he'd sobbed in Drusilla Wiley's arms. She and her husband Roger, a master sweep, had taken him to their home in St. Giles.

At Drusilla's gentle persuasion, Anthony had confessed his purpose for coming to London.

Promising to help him find his father, Drusilla had asked to see the ring, and he'd given it to her. She and Roger had promptly locked him in the cellar—where Anthony had found himself face-to-face with a score of dirty, hungry, terrified boys...

For three years, he'd lived the nightmare of being one of the sweep's "apprentices." He'd cleaned stinking, suffocating stacks from dawn until dusk; by night, he'd toiled in the sweep's other trade, committing burglaries and petty theft. He'd proven himself to be the fastest and cleverest of his peers, bringing in the most loot and artfully dodging the Charleys. He supposed this was the only reason Wiley had let him live after his two attempted flits.

As valuable as Anthony was, he knew that if Wiley caught him this third time, he would not survive. This was his last chance. His last hope...and he'd finally arrived.

He stared up at the imposing mansion built of cool grey stone. Rows of windows with rounded tops gleamed in the morning sunlight. Grand columns flanked the entryway, the steps leading up to the door so clean that you could eat off them.

"Crikey," Anthony murmured. His father lived in a bleeding palace.

Casting a furtive glance around, he took out the handkerchief he'd nabbed from an unsuspecting passerby. Spitting in the fine linen, he used it to rub his face, removing as much soot as he could. Smoothing his unruly black hair beneath his cap, he climbed the steps and stood on tiptoe to reach the heavy brass knocker shaped like a lion's head. Three raps, and the door opened to reveal a stern-faced butler.

"Deliveries around back," the man barked.

As the door began to close, Anthony jammed one worn boot into the door's path.

"What in God's name—" the butler thundered.

"Please, sir, I need to see Mr. De Villier," Anthony said desperately. "It's a matter o' great import—"

"Who are you to utter the master's name? Move, you dirty cur, or I shall send for a constable!"

Calculating his options, Anthony made his face contrite. "You win, guv, but you've got my foot trapped in this 'ere door."

With a huff, the butler eased the pressure on the door—and Anthony charged into the wooden barrier. The door slammed into the butler, who landed on his arse with a startled curse, and Anthony dashed into the house.

His holey soles slid against the gleaming marble floor, but he kept his balance, racing through the antechamber with its dripping chandelier, past the wide staircase that wound up toward the upper floors. He dodged a swearing footman, almost collided into a maid who screeched, her cleaning bucket crashing to the ground.

This time of day, a rich cove would likely be in his private sanctuary. Anthony's experience cleaning the chimneys of fine homes helped him to guess the present layout. He sprinted down a painting-lined hallway, passing the billiards room, music room, library, finally arriving at a closed door.

The study...voices coming from inside.

He reached for the door handle. His fingertips touched the smooth metal knob—and the next instant he was yanked back by the collar. He struggled, kicking out, his curses muffled by his captor's hand.

"Got the li'l bugger," the footman said. "What do you want me to do with him, Mr. Laraby?"

Appearing behind the footman, the butler said with a scowl, "The guttersnipe broke into a gentleman's home; he's undoubtedly a burglar in the making. It's off to Newgate for him. Lock him in a cupboard while I summon the authorities."

The footman began to drag Anthony away from the study. From his only chance for survival.

He bared his teeth, sinking them into the footman's palm. Swearing, the servant jerked his hand away, and Anthony shouted, "Anthony De Villier, I'm your son! My mama was Seraphina Hale—"

The footman backhanded him, making him see stars. "Shut your filthy gob, you rabid mongrel—"

"Bring him here," an imperious voice commanded.

His vision clearing, Anthony saw that a tall, well-built gent now stood in the open doorway of the study. The man's hair was the shade of bleached wheat, the clipped waves gleaming around his handsome, chiseled features. In contrast, his eyes were the black of coal and the only feature he and Anthony had in common.

Anthony's heart thumped against his ribs. *This toff...he's my father?*

"Beg pardon for the intrusion, Mr. De Villier," the butler said hastily. "This brat barged in from the street, and I was about to contact the magistrates—"

"I'll deal with it," De Villier said.

"But, sir, he's a street urchin. There's no telling what he could do—"

De Villier looked at Anthony. "Did you come to do harm, boy?"

"N-no, sir."

"Follow me." De Villier turned and walked back into the study.

An instant later, the footman's grip loosened, and Anthony jerked free. He followed De Villier's broad back into the study, turning briefly to stick his tongue out at the glowering servants. Hah. Soon they would be answering to him...and the notion filled him with impossible hope.

Have I come home...at last?

"Close the door behind you."

At De Villier's command, Anthony shut the heavy door, gawking at the opulent space. He'd cleaned the chimneys of many a fine house but never had he seen a study as grand as this one. It even *smelled* rich, a mix of oiled leather, fine tobacco, and lemony beeswax polish. The shelves that reached from the floor to the soaring ceiling were filled with books—a luxury denied Anthony for the past three years, although his mama had taught him his letters. His boots sank into a carpet softer than anything he'd slept on.

Tall windows stood to the right of De Villier's massive mahogany desk, the long velvet drapes pulled back to offer a view of the gardens. De Villier seated himself behind the desk. Anthony remained standing on the other side, belatedly remembering to doff his cap.

"You have something to say to me?" De Villier had his head idly propped against his left hand, his elbow resting on the arm of his studded wingchair. Once, Anthony had found a gentleman's magazine in a rubbish heap, and this cove looked like one of the bleeding fashion plates.

Now's your chance. Tell 'im who you are.

Twisting his cap, Anthony said in a rush, "My mama was Seraphina Hale. I was born in a village in Tuscany, lived all o'er Italy 'til I was six. Mama told me my father died afore I was born, so it was just the two o' us. We got by all right. Mama was a fine singer, see, and 'er performances kept a roof o'er our 'eads and food in our bellies. But one day, she started to cough and couldn't stop." The memory flashed of his beautiful mother withering away in a dirty cot, blood-stained handkerchiefs strewn around her like crimson petals. With ease borne of practice, he tucked away the grief. "She told me it was time that I knew the truth: that 'er 'usband wasn't dead but 'ad left 'er—and 'e didn't know about me...'is son."

"And you believe that *I* am this husband and father?" De Villier drawled.

Anthony gritted his teeth at the indifferent response. When Mama had told him about his father, he'd been angry: what sort of faithless whoreson would abandon his own wife? And why hadn't his mama gone after the cad and demanded that he provide for her and their unborn child?

Pride and passion led to my downfall, Anthony, his mama had whispered. *Don't be like me.*

"Mama said that you are," he said in flat tones. "When she learned that she was dying, she sold all we 'ad to get passage to London. We arrived 'ere three years ago, but she died afore we made it to shore. 'Er last words to me were to find you."

She died because you left 'er to fend for 'erself and your son, you black-guard. Because she worked 'erself to the bone and couldn't afford a decent doctor. Because she spent everything she 'ad to get me 'ere to you.

"Three years ago?" De Villier lifted his brows, which were oddly dark like his eyes rather than fair like his hair. It gave him a hawkish, predatory look. "It took you that long to find me?"

Anthony reined in his rising fury. "On the ship, Mama and I were 'befriended' by a sweep named Wiley and 'is mort. After Mama died, the Wileys said they would 'elp me. They lied." He gestured at his sooty clothes. "For the past three years, I've been one o' their climbing boys."

Among other things. He thought it best to keep his criminal activities under wraps.

De Villier's gaze turned considering. "You have proof of your connection to this Seraphina Hale? To me?"

For the umpteenth time, Anthony cursed himself for being a gull and handing over the signet ring to the Wileys. Risking his life more than once, he'd snuck into the Wileys's rooms in the flash house to look for his lost treasure. He'd never found it. No doubt the Wileys had pawned the ring years ago, disposing of the stolen goods...and Anthony's future along with it.

If living in the stews had taught him anything, it was this: an eye for an eye. Anthony had an excellent memory, never forgot a wrong. He would get his justice...eventually. He wasn't the same fool he'd been at six. Now he understood the importance of self-control, discipline, biding one's time.

The Wileys betrayed me, stole my legacy, and one day they'll pay for it.

But the time for retribution was later. For now, he had to convince De Villier that they were kin. Even if he despised the bastard, he would swallow his pride for the sake of survival. Like an alley cat, he didn't give a damn whose hand fed him as long as he got food in his belly. Once he was strong and powerful, he would get his due.

"Mama gave me a ring, sir. Made o' gold and set with a blood-stone in the center." Encouraged by the flicker in those dark eyes, he forged on. "The bloodstone was carved with the initials 'A. D.' There was an inscription inside the band too."

Was it his imagination, or did the blighter sit up straighter?

De Villier said slowly, "What did it say?"

"It wasn't in English." Anthony's mama had shown him the Latin, told him the meaning. "*Numquam obliviscar*, it means—"

"*Never forget*," De Villier said in a low voice.

Hope burgeoned inside Anthony; he gave a vigorous nod.

"You have this ring?"

"The Wileys stole it from me," he admitted.

De Villier regarded him dispassionately. "Then you have no proof."

A cold droplet trickled down his spine. "I ain't got the ring, but I described it, didn't I?" From Wiley, he'd learned that pleading was futile, the strategy of the weak. He kept his voice strong and steady. "You can't deny you know what I'm speaking o'—"

"I do."

Relief burst in him. "So...you believe me? That I'm your son?"

De Villier lifted his right hand, the one that had been below Anthony's line of sight, onto the desk. Shock barricaded Anthony's breath: he stared in disbelief at the heavy gold ring, the crimson-flecked black stone that bore those distinctive initials.

"I d-don't understand," he stammered. "'Ow do you 'ave the ring...?"

"Wiley," De Villier said.

Wiley gave it to him? Before Anthony could make sense of it, a side door opened—and Roger Wiley entered the study. At the sight of the sweep's cruel features, self-preservation overrode shock, and Anthony bolted toward the main door. He didn't make it, the familiar beefy hand catching him by the scruff, lifting him clear off the ground.

He yelled for his life, punching and kicking out. Wiley's fist slammed into his jaw. Metallic pain flooded his mouth, the blows coming again and again, pounding the fight out of him. Finally, he slumped to the ground, curling up against the onslaught, the truth more agonizing than bruises and shattered bones.

De Villier knew about me...this whole bleedin' time...

"That is enough." De Villier's voice came from above him.

"Beg pardon, sir," Wiley replied. "What do you want me to do wif the bugger?"

"Your job was to keep him away. That was the deal."

"Brat's slippery as a lamprey. From now on, I'll keep 'im chained night and day—"

"No. I want a permanent solution."

"Do you mean...?"

"I don't want to see him again."

De Villier's command penetrated the red waves of agony. Anthony forced himself to sit up, to look at his sire.

"I 'ave your blood," he gasped out. "You would murder you own son?"

De Villier's eyes were as cold and dark as the Thames. "A powerful man isn't blinded by sentiment."

Anthony's survival instincts wouldn't let him die this way. He tried to get on his feet, pain forcing him back on his knees. Using his hands, he dragged his broken body away from the danger.

De Villier abandoned my mama, and she suffered, died because o' 'im. 'E paid the Wileys to abuse and imprison me, work me like a slave. And now the bastard wants me dead...my own father—tears rolled down Anthony's face, despite his vow not to show weakness—*...'e's my enemy. I'll never forget...*

"Where do you think you're going?" Wiley snarled.

Anthony crawled doggedly on. The vicious kick caught him in the ribs. He heard the snap of bones, the helpless cry of an animal claimed by the dark.

1830, TRAVERSTOKE, COUNTRY ESTATE OF CURTIS
BILLINGS

MISS GABRIELLA BILLINGS DASHED INTO THE MOONLIT
courtyard. Her slippers took her down one of the graveled paths,
away from the laughter of the guests and strains of the orchestra
floating from the ballroom. She sought the sanctuary of hedges
that lined the quadrangle. White marble statues of Greek gods
gleamed in the darkness, seeming to offer protection from the
outside world.

Under the watchful eye of Diana, Gabby couldn't keep her
emotions in any longer. All through supper and the dancing afterward, she'd kept a brave face, never letting her smile slip even in
the face of subtle—and not so subtle—snubs. Years of experience
had taught her that her best defense in such situations was to
keep her expression cheerful and feign ignorance. To simply
pretend that she didn't understand the underhanded insults. If she
didn't give others the satisfaction of seeing their barbs hit home,
then sooner or later they would leave her alone.

The strategy, while effective, was not without its cost. It

required all of her willpower to keep her manner bright as the slights pierced her skin, their poison trickling into her lifeblood. Now her strength deserted her, tears leaking down her cheeks.

Father spared no expense in throwing this house party. All for your sake. Yet you've managed to become the outcast...of your own dashed fête.

She looked up at the sky, and even the stars, in their bright glory, seemed to be mocking her.

What's wrong with me? she thought in despair. *Why can't I fit in? Why must I be the object of incessant ridicule?*

"Good evening, Miss Billings."

Gabby started at the smooth, cultured baritone. She swiped the backs of her gloved hands across her cheeks and pinned a smile in place before turning around. Her heart stuttered when she saw who was standing a few feet away.

Adam Garrity was one of her father's business associates and the most ruthlessly elegant man she'd ever met. His coal-black hair was immaculately slicked back, his somber tailoring fitting his lean, virile figure like a glove. She guessed that he was a dozen years older than her own age of two-and-twenty, but his austerely handsome features defied such banalities as age.

She'd met him for the first time that afternoon when he'd arrived unannounced to the house party. Such was Garrity's power that her papa, one of the wealthiest and most influential bankers in London, instructed her to have the best suite readied for their unexpected guest's use.

"Whatever Garrity wants, Garrity gets," Father had told her in no uncertain terms. "You must ensure that his stay is nothing short of perfection, Gabriella."

All her life, she'd wanted desperately to please her papa, and this occasion was no exception. He'd spent an exorbitant amount on the party, renovating the sprawling country estate and providing first-rate entertainment and refreshments for the guests. He'd even provided her with a luxurious new wardrobe and dazzling jewels to match. All because he wanted her to make an aristocratic catch.

And you're failing miserably at it...the way you've failed at everything.

Realizing that she still hadn't answered the esteemed guest, she pushed aside her woes.

"Good evening, Mr. Garrity," she said. "Are you, um, looking for something?"

"I've found what I'm looking for."

She blinked, not certain how to respond. If he was with any other female, his comment might be construed as flirtatious. But since he was with *her*, he was likely being literal.

"You wanted a breath of fresh air in the courtyard?" she asked.

His gaze remained steady on her face. During their introductions earlier, she'd been struck by the intensity of his presence. His exquisite manners were paired with a predatory stillness. He didn't say much, didn't need to: it was as if he was simply waiting for one to make the wrong move. If life were a staring contest, Adam Garrity would always emerge victorious, the very last to blink.

She'd seen other guests scurry away from him, unable to bear his compelling authority. She, herself, found him fascinating. She'd recently read *Arabian Nights' Entertainments*, and he could have stepped out of the pages of her imagination. He was exactly how she pictured Shahriar, the mighty sultan whose betrayal by his adulteress wife led him to wed and execute a new bride every day...until the brave and beautiful Scheherazade captivated him with her stories, turning him from his dark path.

It wasn't just Mr. Garrity's inky hair and hard eyes, the cruel yet sensual curve of his mouth that reminded her of an ancient Persian king. It was his aura of power. That bone-deep male confidence bordering on arrogance that aroused a strange awareness in her...

"I wanted to know that you are well, Miss Billings," he said. "I saw you leave the ballroom."

That he'd noticed her absence was surprising enough. That he was concerned about her well-being and had made the effort to find her was downright shocking. Her pulse fluttered.

"You are ever so kind, sir," she said breathlessly. "But I am quite well, as you see. The ballroom was just, um, a bit stifling."

More accurately, it had been the smothering condescension of some of the guests that had made her flee. That and the fact that her dance card was nearly empty. Her potential suitor, the gruff and unapproachable Viscount Carlisle, had done his duty, partnering her in a quadrille, but his expression had betrayed his impatience with the task. Carlisle's interest in her was motivated by his financial circumstances, but as her father had succinctly put it, "Beggars can't be choosers, girl."

Is it wrong that, for once in my life, I want a choice? she thought dejectedly.

Her dreams were simple: all she wanted was a husband to love. He didn't have to be handsome or rich, just nice and understanding. A comfortable sort of man who wouldn't mind her flaws and who would enjoy spending time with her, doing ordinary things. She wanted to make a home with him and bear his children. To have a place where she would feel safe and always belong.

"Perhaps you would care for a stroll, Miss Billings?"

Mr. Garrity's invitation reclaimed her attention. Her jaw slackened; surely a man as important as he was wouldn't think her worthy of his time? The realization struck her: he must be acting out of obligation because he was her father's colleague.

"That's ever so considerate of you to ask, sir," she said earnestly. "But it's unnecessary. I'm sure you have much more important matters to attend to."

"None more important than what I'm attending to now."

She tilted her head, not following. "What are you attending to?"

"You, Miss Billings," he said simply.

"Oh." The startled sound popped from her lips.

His gallantry flooded her with a foreign, pleasurable warmth. Her heart pounding, she hoped the moonlight hid her furious blush. She didn't need red cheeks to go with her red hair.

Then her common sense chimed in. As tempting as it was to spend time in the company of this charismatic man who deemed her worthy of his attention, the current circumstances wouldn't permit it. Social rejection at one's own party was bad enough; she didn't need to add ruination to the list of her night's accomplishments.

"I'd like to stroll with you, sir, ever so much, but I have no chaperone—"

"I've made arrangements." He raised his hand, snapped his fingers.

A pair of burly guards emerged from the shadows onto the graveled path, an auburn-haired matron between them. Gabby recognized Mrs. Sumner, one of the guests. Over supper, she'd been a bit intimidated by the widow's bold and provocative manner. Although, Gabby thought ruefully, she could stand to learn a thing or two from Mrs. Sumner's ease with the opposite sex.

Flirtation, like most social skills, wasn't Gabby's forte.

"Mrs. Sumner has volunteered her chaperonage," Mr. Garrity said.

"I'm glad to be of service, Mr. Garrity," Mrs. Sumner called out in simpering, deferential tones.

With a wave of his hand, Mr. Garrity sent the guards and widow retreating back to a discreet distance. Then he offered Gabby his arm. "You have my word that this will be a short, perfectly respectable interlude. Shall we?"

"You think of everything, don't you?" Gabby asked, bemused.

"I want you to know that your reputation is safe with me." The stars reflected in his eyes, which were darker than the sky and so deep that she had the sensation of losing herself in ever-lasting midnight. "That you, Miss Billings, will always be safe with me."

Mesmerized, she felt her fingers lift of their own accord, landing on the plush sleeve of his jacket. He led the way along the path. Given her short stature, she often had to hurry to keep up with others, which added to her general aura of inelegance. Yet with Mr. Garrity steering her, she seemed to float along, perfectly in step.

"May I compliment you on your fine looks this eve, Miss Billings?"

Now Gabby was aware of her frumpiness. It wasn't the fault of her white silk gown, which was *au courant* with its fitted bodice, billowing sleeves, and full, flounced skirts. The problem was her. Her figure always strained seams in the wrong places, causing a surfeit of rumpling and bunching. Even stays weren't a solution. While tight lacing reduced her fleshiness in one place, it made her bulge unbecomingly in others. Voices from finishing school assailed her, reminding her of her many short-comings:

"Look at Gabriella...she's a walking sausage stuffed in a corset."

"And her manner? I've never heard anyone chatter so much about so little."

"My mama says nothing is more common than red hair and freckles."

Gabby shut out the painful memories of rejection. She told herself that it was kind of Mr. Garrity to compliment her. To take notice of her at all.

"You're ever so nice to say so," she said, her voice trembling.

"First you say I'm kind. Now I'm nice?" He lifted his brows. "Have a care, Miss Billings, lest you do irreparable damage to my reputation."

The humor glinting in his eyes was a balm to her ruffled nerves.

"Well, *I* think you're both," she said impulsively.

"What you think is what matters to me, my dear Miss Billings."

The endearment and intensity of his regard made her heart thump against the cage of her ribs. She found it difficult to breathe. And not just because of her corset.

Don't be a ninny. He's obviously just taking pity on you. Doing the pretty because he's a friend of Father's.

"You, um, don't care what others think?" she managed.

"I'm a busy man. The opinion of others is a distraction that I don't have time for."

How she admired and envied his confidence.

"I wish I could be like you," she said. "I wish the opinions of others didn't matter."

"Is that why you were crying?"

His acuity took her off guard. She pulled back on instinct, yet his hand closed over hers, keeping her on his arm. Not with force —she could have pulled free—but his touch had an engrossing warmth, one that made her grow still. His heat seeped through her satin gloves, the sensation of being trapped by his long fingers setting off quivers in her belly.

"You need hide nothing from me, Miss Billings," he said. "If we are to further our acquaintance, it would be best for us to be honest with one another."

Stunned, she came to a halt. "You wish to further your acquaintance with *me?*"

His brows lifted. "Why does that surprise you?"

"Because you're..." *Handsome as a prince. And rich and powerful. Why would you want to get to know* me? "You're my father's business associate," she finished lamely.

He studied her. "Do you find me old, Miss Billings? Too old to be your friend?"

The idea was laughable. He radiated virile energy, the essence of a man in his prime.

"No," she blurted. "Definitely not."

His lips gave a faint twitch. He had a beautiful mouth, she thought. Thin, firm-looking lips with a wicked curve to the bottom one.

What would it be like to be kissed by that mouth?

The shockingly wanton thought burst into her head. She shoved it out just as quickly, told herself that it was idle curiosity. She'd never been kissed and feared that no one would ever *want* to kiss her.

"I'm glad to hear it," he said solemnly. "Now tell me what caused your tears."

He was so strong and unflappable. The desire to unburden herself was irresistible.

"I'm a horrid hostess," she admitted. "A complete failure."

"How so?"

She appreciated his bluntness. That he didn't try to placate or minimize her worries. As he continued navigating them along the garden path, it felt natural to tell him everything.

"I'm ill-at-ease at large gatherings. When I'm nervous, I tend to chatter. About the inanest topics." She paused, then with a shrug confessed, "I'm supposed to make a good impression on Viscount Carlisle. He needs a wife with a dowry, you see, which is the one attraction I do have. Father would be ever so pleased to have a title in the family. But the problem is that I find Lord Carlisle rather, well, intimidating. And, as I've said, when I'm anxious I go on about the most nonsensical things."

"I'm certain your conversation was as charming as you are."

"At supper, I went on about bonnets and gloves for an entire *hour*," she said grimly.

Instead of looking horrified—as Viscount Carlisle had during her lengthy soliloquy about frippery—Mr. Garrity slanted her an amused look. "What is it about Carlisle that you find intimidating?"

"He doesn't talk *back*, for starters. Nor does he smile, at least not at me," she explained. "Worst of all, he's overly *large*."

A strange sound escaped Mr. Garrity.

"Are you all right, sir?" She peered at him anxiously.

"You don't like, er, large men?"

"I prefer my companion to be a more manageable height. Being vertically disadvantaged, I'd rather not get a crick in my neck every time we dance or stand together." She gave him an admiring look. He was a shade under six feet, every inch of him fit and well-proportioned. "You, for example, are the perfect height. Not too tall, not short, just right."

"I'm glad I meet with your approval," he murmured.

Something in his tone made her skin tingle. She realized how brazen she was being, commenting on his personal attributes. What in heaven's name was wrong with her?

"I meant no offense—"

"And I took none. Now about Carlisle," he said smoothly. "Are you upset that he hasn't come up to scratch?"

"Oh no," she said honestly. "I'd be ever so relieved if he *didn't*. We don't suit at all."

"Then why did you call yourself a failure?"

She swallowed, not knowing if she could share this latest humiliation aloud.

"You can trust me."

Compelled by Mr. Garrity's quiet command, she confided the awful events in a rush.

"At supper, one of the guests said that a lady...she must guard her secrets as closely as her jewels. And I asked, what if a lady doesn't have any secrets? Because I'm ever so boring, you see, and not mysterious at all."

"There's nothing boring about you, Miss Billings. Your candor is both rare and charming."

Her heart thumped giddily. "That's ever so kind of you to say, sir."

"I'm the soul of kindness, it seems. Go on."

Entranced by his unwavering attention, she'd lost her train of thought. "Um...where was I?"

"You'd made the comment about a lady not having secrets."

"Oh. Right." She drew a breath, deciding that discretion was the best policy; she need not name names. "To my comment, one of the guests replied, 'Then she has no choice but to rely on her jewels.' Then he complimented me...on my necklace."

The guest had been Lord Parnell, a young rake known for his rapier wit. His cut had been clear, slicing deep into the heart of her woes: because Gabby lacked any alluring charms or mystique, she had to rely on her money to attract a husband.

Gabby lowered her head in embarrassment. The necklace in question felt as heavy as an albatross around her throat. It wasn't as if she didn't *know* her own shortcomings; she didn't need to have them pointed out in a public fashion. During the dancing after supper, Parnell and his cronies had watched her with smirks on their faces, sniggering to one another, and she'd known they were making fun of her.

"Who said this to you?"

The lethal edge in Mr. Garrity's voice made her look up. To her surprise, his jaw was taut, and his eyes were *smoldering*, embers heating up the cold black.

"Who said this?" he repeated.

"It doesn't matter—"

"I beg to differ. No one insults you without consequences."

"I'm all right, truly." His chivalry suffused her with wonder. "But thank you...for caring."

He stopped. Curled a finger beneath her chin. His touch rendered her incapable of motion or speech; even her worries about propriety and her reputation faded. He was like the sun and she a planet drawn into his powerful orbit. For a wild moment, she lost herself in his magnetic heat.

"If anyone else is a nuisance, promise that you will come to me," he said.

Her breath puffed from her lips. He stood so close. Close enough for his scent to tickle her nostrils, a virile mix of exotic spice and clean male. Heat bloomed inside her, her knees melting.

He increased the subtle pressure of his finger on her chin. His strength seemed to flow into her from that single point of contact. "Give me your word, my dear."

No man had ever offered to be her champion. To defend and protect her.

Her voice hushed with wonder and amazement, she said, "I promise."

Satisfaction flared in his eyes before his gaze hooded.

"Good." He dropped his hand. "For the sake of your reputation, you'd best go back inside."

She hadn't even noticed that they were once again near the main building. Although she didn't want the magical interlude to end, she knew he was right.

"Good night, Mr. Garrity," she said with a tremulous smile. "I shan't ever forget this evening."

He bowed. "Adieu, Miss Billings."

She floated back toward the house.

"If you insult Miss Billings again—if you even look askance at her —you will answer to me." Adam kept the target of his displeasure pinned against the wall of the stables. "Do I make myself clear?"

"Crystal," Lord Parnell gasped.

"From here on in, you and your cronies will ensure that her dance card is full. Except for the waltzes; those are mine. Otherwise, you'll do the pretty, and you'll do it well."

"Y-yes, sir. Anything you say, sir."

The scent of urine wafted into Adam's nostrils. With distaste, he saw the dark spot spreading over the front of Parnell's trousers. The lily-livered bastard had no problem destroying a young woman's confidence to further his own popularity, yet he hadn't even tried to fight back against Adam. Like any bully, Parnell was a coward who only preyed upon the vulnerable.

Having dealt with this despicable sort all his life, Adam knew how to deal with them. There was only one thing a bully respected: a bigger bully.

Releasing the blackguard with a hard shove, Adam opened and closed his hands, feeling the burn of his well-used fists. These days, he didn't dirty his hands much, but this was a matter of honor. His soon-to-be-bride's honor.

Recalling Gabriella's sweet departing smile, he felt a surge of satisfaction.

Everything is going according to plan. Soon she'll be mine. And I'll be one step closer to getting my vengeance.

Numquam obliviscar—never forget.

"Shall I finish up here, sir?"

This came from Kerrigan, one of Adam's personal guards. A giant with a shaved head and an eye patch, Kerrigan had a special hatred of toffs who hurt young women. Adam felt the same way. And Gabriella, with her poignant sweetness, stirred his protective instincts in a way no woman had for a long, long time.

Adam straightened the lapels of his jacket. "Avoid the face. Leave no visible marks."

Kerrigan grinned, cracking his knuckles.

The last thing Adam heard as he left the stables was Parnell's terrified whimper.

❧ 2 ❧

TEN DAYS LATER

"You wanted to see me, Miss Billings?"

At the deep, silky tones, Gabby spun around. She'd been nervously studying one of the gilt-framed landscapes in the gallery whilst waiting for Mr. Garrity's arrival. She'd chosen this room for the privacy it offered. The cross-shaped chamber was situated in a low-traffic corner of the East Wing. And, if other guests happened to come by, she had the excuse that she was showing Mr. Garrity some of the paintings.

Now he was here. Garbed in an impeccable suit of charcoal superfine, he looked like a sleek jungle cat juxtaposed against the chamber's green walls. She, on the other hand, felt like a plump pigeon in her sprigged white muslin.

"Beg pardon, I didn't hear you come in," she blurted.

Above his pristine maize-silk cravat, his mouth curved. "Old habits, I'm afraid."

Despite the pressing concerns she had to address, she couldn't help but ask, "Why would you have the habit of moving so silently?"

"Because I once ran with a gang in the stews, and my survival depended upon stealth."

It took her a moment to digest the revelation, which had been delivered with his usual equanimity.

"You were in a gang?" she said stupidly. "In the *stews?*"

Looking at the elegant, powerful man before her, she found the notion unbelievable. Since he'd first approached her in the garden, she'd spent time with him every day. No one had seemed to take notice for murder had taken center stage: one of the performers hired to entertain the guests had been found dead in the library. But now the mystery of the acrobat's death had been solved—thanks to the investigative prowess of Gabby's friends, the Kents—and the murderer brought to justice.

Just as one catastrophe ended, however, another had cropped up. This time, the intrigue involved one of the house guests, Mr. Wickham Murray. Apparently, Mr. Murray owed a substantial sum to Mr. Garrity, and others were characterizing the latter as a ruthless cutthroat.

Given what Gabby knew of Mr. Garrity, she could not believe this to be true.

Normally, she wouldn't interfere in the affairs of others, but Mr. Murray was ever so nice. Moreover, he was soon to be the brother-in-law of Gabby's dear chum, Miss Violet Kent, who'd made a surprising love match with Viscount Carlisle, Mr. Murray's older brother, over the course of the house party.

A lot had happened in ten days.

Not least of all the fact that Gabby had fallen head-over-slippers in love with the man of her dreams. Actually, Mr. Garrity left all her girlish expectations in the dust: she couldn't have even *imagined* a man as wonderful as him. While others might find his self-assurance daunting, she felt calm and protected in his presence. With his fierce intelligence and perceptiveness, she was certain that he saw all her flaws, but he didn't seem to mind them. He treated her ever so kindly, his chivalry the stuff of fantasy.

And there was no denying that he was the most handsome man she'd ever met.

But now the party was ending, and she didn't know when she would see Mr. Garrity next. *If* she'd see him again. She shut out that depressing thought. The important thing, she told herself, the reason that she'd sent a note asking for him to meet her here, was to discuss the situation with Mr. Murray. She was certain that, if Mr. Garrity but understood Mr. Murray's difficult situation, he would show mercy on the young gentleman.

"I grew up in the streets of St. Giles. I survived by any means possible," Mr. Garrity said calmly. "All of that is far behind me. But I thought it best you should know."

She stared at him, heart hammering, thoughts of Mr. Murray's plight overshadowed by Mr. Garrity's startling revelations. In their prior encounters, Mr. Garrity hadn't revealed much about himself. He'd asked *her* many questions, however...and seemed genuinely interested in her replies. In fact, he was the only man of her acquaintance who seemed to enjoy her chatter.

Now, for the first time, he was sharing something about himself. No etiquette lessons had taught her how to respond to such astonishing, intimate facts. In truth, nothing in her life had prepared her for a man like Adam Garrity.

"Does that disgust you?" he asked.

"*No.*" Horrified that he'd misinterpreted her silence for condemnation, she said in a rush, "Heavens, not at all! You could never disgust me. I...I just never thought of you as anything but the man you are now."

He raised a brow. "And what sort of man is that, Miss Billings?"

"Powerful. Rich. Elegant and ever so handsome." *Lord above, please tell me I didn't say that last part aloud.*

"I am, of course, gratified by your assessment." The devilish glint in his eyes confirmed that she had, indeed, blurted her thoughts like a moonstruck ninny. "It gives me hope, my dear."

Her pulse quickened. "Hope for what?"

"I wish to inform you of some facts," he said, not answering her question. "I believe honesty to be the essential ingredient in any successful union, which is why I must be truthful with you."

A successful union? Does he mean...what I think he means?

Although he'd paid her attention these past few days, she hadn't dared to believe that a man as worldly and charismatic as he would ever view her in a romantic light.

Hope bubbled through her like uncorked champagne. Giddy, breathless, she could only nod.

"I do not, as a rule, discuss my past. I will do so this once, in order for you to have the necessary facts to make an informed decision. After that, I will consider the matter addressed and laid to rest." He paused. "Does that suit you, Miss Billings?"

"Yes," she said speedily for fear that he might change his mind.

"Perhaps you would care to sit?"

He led her to a velvet bench situated in an alcove. Arranging her skirts, she peered up at him. From her angle, his dark masculinity was contrasted against the snowy plasterwork flowers that adorned the domed ceiling. With his inky, slicked-back hair and slashing brows, he looked like an angel fallen from that heavenly field.

Exciting and earthly...a bit dangerous.

"I am a self-made man, Miss Billings, in every respect. My mother died when I was six; I never knew my sire, who abandoned her shortly after they were married and before my birth." His tone was devoid of emotion. "I've been making my own way in the world since I can recall. In my twenties, I started a business providing funds to those in need. One, in truth, not unlike your father's bank. I have since grown and diversified that enterprise. I own properties throughout England as well as holdings in various industrial projects." He paused. "Do you have any questions thus far?"

Um, only about a million?

She said the first thing that came to her mind.

"Was it difficult...being so alone?" Her heart ached for all the hardship he must have endured and from such a young age.

He dealt her a level stare. "Solitude has never been a problem for me, Miss Billings."

"You are saying that you prefer that state?" she asked with a frown.

"I wouldn't call it a preference, no. Merely a condition that I've come to accept." His mouth ticked up at one corner. "Until you came along."

Gabby's hand fluttered to her bosom. "M-me?"

"You, Miss Billings." His eyes were like a brazier, dark and smoldering. "I am five-and-thirty, my dear, and my thoughts have, of late, turned to the future. I hope I do not sound immodest when I say that I have achieved the majority of the goals I set forth for myself as a young man. I have wealth, property, and the freedom to live life on my own terms. What I do not have is someone to share it with. Someone with whom I can build a family. Someone who will give me sons to whom I may pass on my legacy."

Her heart was beating so fast that she feared it might burst from her chest. It was as if he'd plucked her dreams out of her head, presenting them as his own.

"Since I have come to know you, Miss Billings, I've become convinced that you are the one I seek." He studied her intently. "May I dare to presume that you might have a similar preference for me?"

"Oh, Mr. Garrity, I do. Ever so much," she said in an aching whisper.

The slow curving of his sultan's mouth touched upon the nerve of her deepest romantic yearnings.

"Before I ask you an important question, there is something else I must address," he said.

"Anything," she breathed. "Anything at all, sir."

Although his expression didn't change much, she saw the way his smile reached his eyes. It was subtle, faint lines crinkling around his dark gaze, but it was there. And she loved that she could make him smile.

I love him, she thought joyfully.

"It concerns the notion of love."

Wariness smothered her giddy state. "What...what about it?"

"I know that the concept of a love match is much in fashion with modern young ladies. Too much novel reading, I daresay. But I am an old-fashioned fellow and, more to point, one who values honesty. If I am to wed, I would want there to be no illusions between me and my wife."

"Illusions?" Gabby said in a small voice.

"I don't have much use for sentiment, Miss Billings. Being a practical man, I believe that actions speak louder than poetry ever could. In sum, I have no use for romantic love."

Her hopes deflated like a hot-air balloon that had suddenly run out of fuel. Her heart plummeting, she chastised herself for being stupid. For hoping that any man could ever fall in love with her. This was Adam Garrity, for goodness' sake. He could have anybody he wanted. He'd only chosen her because...

You're convenient. An heiress.

She forced the words out of her tight throat. "You're proposing a marriage of convenience?"

"Christ, no."

His adamant reply made her blink. And, dash it, hope once more. "Then what are you...?"

"I'm proposing a marriage based on mutual respect and shared goals. I am seeking a spouse who is loyal, virtuous, and worthy of trust."

I can give you what you want, her heart cried. *Be what you want.*

Swallowing, she forced herself to address her doubts. "And do you also wish for a wife who will bring a substantial dowry?" *Do you want me simply because I'm an heiress?* "If that is the case, you ought to know that—"

"Your fortune is in a trust. A separate estate that is governed by a trustee and that your future husband may not touch," he said matter-of-factly. "If your father should pass, your inheritance will also go into said trust, to be dispersed by the trustee for your benefit and that of your children. Am I missing anything?"

Her jaw slackened. "How...how did you know...?"

"As we become more intimately acquainted, you will find that I am not a man who leaves matters up to chance. When something is important to me, I make certain to have all the facts. And to make any necessary provisions to get what I want."

Some might think that his declaration sounded cold-blooded.

To Gabby, it was the essence of romance.

"And you want...*me?*" she whispered in disbelief. "Even without my money?"

"I have no need of your money." His eyes were mesmerizing whirlpools, drawing her in. "What I am in want of is a wife who will be a true and steadfast partner in our life together."

Longing halted her breath. And that was before he went down on one bended knee, engulfing her trembling hand in his large, warm one.

"I will speak to your father, of course," he said in husky tones, "but first I must know your wishes. Is my suit favorable to you, Miss Billings?"

Yes, her heart sang. *Yes, yes, yes.*

He doesn't believe in love, her head reminded her.

She summoned her courage. "You said you valued honesty, so I feel I must be candid with you."

His eyes gleamed. "It is my wish that you always will be."

"I don't know if I can have a marriage without affection. I understand your views on romantic love, sir, and I respect them, but I'm not certain I can be as...as indifferent." Heat scorched her cheeks; she lowered her gaze to the gold buttons of his waistcoat as she carried on. "I may develop feelings, ones that you will find inconvenient. I shan't be able to stop myself." *I'm already falling in love with you.* "I don't know that I'll be able to be the sensible, cold, detached sort of spouse that you want."

Miserably, she looked at him. And was surprised to see the crinkles around his eyes.

"I could never find you inconvenient, my dear," he murmured.

"But you don't want love." She shook her head. "And if I were to...to..."

"I would cherish whatever feelings you chose to bestow upon me. Take care of them as I will take care of you." He rose, pulling her with him. Her head spun at how closely they now stood together, only a sliver of space between them. "While I may not believe in romantic love, I do think that affection is a desirable quality in marriage. I will be faithful to you, protect you, see that you want for nothing. You will not find me a cold husband."

He lifted his hands to her jaw, tipping her head back. Anticipation shivered through her as she read the intent in his eyes: he was going to kiss her. Her first kiss. Worries wormed into her head. *Am I going to do this right? How is one supposed to kiss? Goodness, my breath—what did I eat last?* Then his lips descended, landing on hers, gently, ever so gently.

His kiss was warm and firm, dissolving her doubts in a wave of honeyed heat.

The taste of him was foreign, deliciously male. He kissed the way he did everything else: with absolute authority...and it made her relax into the new, exciting sensations. The prickling of her skin, throbbing of her pulse points. The flutters and trembles deep inside her. Most of all, the dizzying, ground-shifting pleasure. When her knees wobbled, he caught her easily against him.

Because he was Adam Garrity. He wouldn't let her fall. In his arms, she felt a security she'd never felt before.

Held against his virile strength, she shivered with delight. Everything about him felt so *right*. When his tongue swept across her lips, it was only natural to part them. To let him in where no man had been before. He coaxed her to mate her tongue with his, and the sinuous, slick dance caused the tips of her breasts to tingle, a strange, molten feeling awakening at her core. A sudden gush of wetness between her thighs made her squirm—and she felt something very hard and very large poking into her midsection.

What does Mr. Garrity have in his pocket? came the nonsensical thought.

Abruptly, he ended the kiss. He exhaled sharply, and Gabby was fascinated by the tinge of color on his slashing cheekbones. A strand of ebony hair had strayed from the rest and now dangled over his noble forehead. The tiny imperfection made him look even more handsome.

He shoved the hair into place. "Bloody hell."

His muttered words and the way he looked at her—as if she were some sort of odd creature he'd never encountered before—pierced her pleasant state. Icy reality crashed over her. Had she kissed him incorrectly? Had she disappointed him?

"Did I...do something wrong?" she said haltingly.

His gaze softened. He lifted his hand, rubbing his thumb briefly over her bottom lip, which felt puffy from his kiss. Then his brows drew together, and he took his hand away.

"On the contrary, Miss Billings, you did everything right. Too right." He cleared his throat. "I hope your wish is not for a long engagement."

As his meaning sank in, she was swamped with sudden joy. *He wants to marry me. I'm going to be Mrs. Adam Garrity!*

"I will leave that up to you and Papa," she said shyly.

"Excellent. And I must commend you on your timing, my dear," he murmured. "Your setting up this rendezvous saved me the trouble of trying to get you alone."

She suddenly remembered why she'd sent for him in the first place.

"Mr. Murray," she blurted.

The warmth in Mr. Garrity's gaze flickered out. He regarded her with eyes as flat and black as coal. "What about him?"

"That's why I wanted to see you. Not the only reason why," she added hastily, seeing his darkening countenance. "The others were saying that you've called in his debt."

"This is a business matter. And I fail to see why you are so concerned for Murray."

"He's a friend—or, at least, a friend of a friend. He's a chum of Miss Violet Kent," she explained, "and Violet has been so good to me. In fact, I'm indebted to all the Kents, who took me under their wing during my seasons."

"I am acquainted with the Kents." Mr. Garrity's tone was rather dry.

"Then you know that they are good people. And once Violet weds Viscount Carlisle, Mr. Murray will practically be one of their family. Couldn't you extend your generosity to him just a while longer? Give him a chance to make good on his debts?" she pleaded.

Mr. Garrity gave her a brooding look. "You do understand that I don't run a charity."

"But these are exigent circumstances. And I know you are a kind and honorable man. That's what I told the Kents."

"Did you indeed?" He smiled without humor. "And what did they say to that?"

Garrity is one of the most dangerous and ruthless men in all of London.

"I, um, can't recall exactly. But won't you please, this once, grant Mr. Murray a boon...for my sake?"

"You are asking me to do this for you," he said without inflection.

She wondered if she'd gone too far. But she couldn't let her friends down, not after all they'd done for her. Squaring her shoulders, she said, "Yes."

"I'll speak with Murray. Work something out with him."

"You *will*? Oh, Mr. Garrity, you are ever so good and noble and kind—"

"On one condition."

"Anything," she said happily.

"From here on in, when we are in private, you will call me Adam."

"Oh, all right...Adam," she said shyly. "And, um, do call me Gabby. Everyone does."

"Gabriella." His possessive rasp made her ordinary name sound beautiful and exotic. "I will speak to your father today, if that suits."

"Yes, please," she said over her thumping heart.

His eyes burned with that dark fire, and she knew he was going to kiss her again. She trembled in anticipation. As his mouth claimed hers, her last thought was, *Adam Garrity, you're going to be my husband...my everything.*

PRESENT DAY, 1838

Seated at his desk, Adam Garrity listened as Wickham Murray, his right-hand man, relayed the preparations for the meeting that was to take place that evening. "Meeting" was a euphemism: theirs would be a rescue mission, one that entailed doing battle with Erasmus Sweeney, one of London's newest and deadliest cutthroats.

Adam wasn't worried. Not only had he been around longer than Sweeney, he was deadlier.

A man couldn't rise from the stews and end up where he was without being ruthless. Moneylending wasn't an easy business but it was a profitable one, when done properly.

Adam did it properly.

As Murray discussed the firepower they'd be bringing, Adam gazed around his study. Surveying the fruits of his labor gave him a sense of gratification. When he'd had this townhouse built, his instructions to the architect reflected his general philosophy in life.

I want the best.

Adam's study was as large as many ballrooms, the walls covered with polished oak boiserie panels imported from Paris and hung with gilt-framed mirrors and landscapes. Three large Aubusson carpets padded the journey across the parqueted floors. In addition to the desk, there were two seating areas: one by the marble fireplace, above which hung portraits of Adam's wife and two children, Fiona and Maximillian, and the other by the tall bookcases that lined the opposite end of the room.

To the right of Adam's desk, immaculate windows soared from floor to ceiling. He'd insisted on having abundant light. He'd lived too many years in the dark.

Although he had properties flung across England and beyond, this London house was the jewel in his crown. The seat of his power that came from decades of sweat, blood, and merciless discipline. Anyone who dared to threaten his authority had better beware...Sweeney included.

"I approve the plans, Murray," he said dismissively. "That will do."

"You're certain you wish to interfere in this business with Sweeney?" Sitting on the other side of the desk, Wickham Murray lifted his brows. "It is not our fight, after all."

It was a measure of Adam's respect for the other that he allowed the questioning of his command. Murray had come a long way since he'd begun working for Adam eight years ago. Back then, the younger man had been a spoiled fop who'd owed Adam a great deal of money. Ten thousand pounds, to be exact (when it came to money and retribution, Adam was *always* exact).

When Murray couldn't cough up the sum, Adam had been persuaded to let the other work off the debt. Murray had surprised him by proving to be more than a feckless Adonis. With his gentleman's comportment and blue-blooded connections, he'd helped to spread Adam's empire into the highest echelons.

As any cent-per-cent worth his salt knew, no one was as short of the ready as the aristocracy. Ladies hiding gambling debts from their husbands, lords concealing expensive mistresses from their wives...the *ton* was a moneylender's oyster. Murray, with his gilded brown hair, raffish good looks, and effortless charm, had been particularly successful with the gentler sex. The interest on the vowels that Murray had collected from desperate matrons alone had paid off his debt within two years.

Being a fair man, Adam had released the other from his employ; Murray had stated his desire to stay on. Adam had renegotiated the terms to give the other a stake in whatever business he brought in. The arrangement had lined both men's pockets. Murray had brains as well as brawn and, unlike most gents, wasn't afraid to dirty his hands.

Fine by Adam. Having lived the first half of his three-and-forty years in squalor, he preferred to delegate unpleasantness. From guards to footmen to maids, he retained a legion of employees to keep his life—and that of his family—untroubled and running smoothly.

"Sweeney intends to cut me out of my share," he said. "He's shown disloyalty to Tessa Kent and therefore to the order of the underworld. Such disrespect cannot be tolerated."

Murray's hazel eyes narrowed, conveying his understanding. While outsiders might view the underclass of London as unruly and unorganized, anyone who made his living in this world knew better. The hierarchy here was as steadfast as that found in the finest London drawing rooms. Perhaps more so, for it was the only thing that kept chaos at bay.

Known as the "King of the Underworld," cutthroat Bartholomew Black ruled London's darkest streets, enforcing its rules and administering justice when necessary. He was aided by powerful "dukes" who oversaw specific territories; Adam was known as the "Duke of the City" since his power flourished in the financial center of London. Tessa Kent was the "Duchess of Covent Garden" and, moreover, she was Black's beloved granddaughter.

Like Adam, Erasmus Sweeney ran a usury business. Adam had no liking for the uncouth bastard, but they had a common interest: the Duke of Ranelagh and Somerville owed them each fifty thousand pounds. His Grace, also known by the moniker "Ransom," had somehow gained the favor of Tessa Kent, who'd brokered an armistice, allowing the duke extra time to recover a treasure that would pay off his debts. Adam had agreed to the deal because it was always wise to curry Mrs. Kent's favor and that of her grandfather's. The extra twenty percent interest he'd be getting was naught to sneeze at either.

Sweeney, too, had agreed to the temporary truce. Then he'd reneged. He'd violated the agreement by kidnapping Ransom's young daughter and demanding the entirety of the duke's newly discovered fortune—including Adam's portion—in exchange.

If there was anything Adam despised, it was a man who lacked honor.

His distaste must have showed, for Murray rose, muttering, "I'll make the necessary arrangements for tonight."

A soft knock on the door prevented Adam's reply. His wife entered, and as he rose to greet her, he couldn't stop the familiar stir of warmth inside him. Gabriella wasn't beautiful in a conventional sense: her unabashedly red hair, golden freckles, and generous curves didn't feature on current fashion plates. Yet the moment Adam had laid eyes on her, he'd been struck by a stunning sense of recognition.

He was possessed of a singular memory (a handy ability for he never forgot a debt) and could recall the past with vivid clarity. At that first meeting with Gabriella, he'd flashed back to his earliest years. He'd been five at the time, living in Florence with his mama, and she'd had the rare day off from performing. As an artist, she was a lover of beauty, and she'd taken him to a grand gallery called the Uffizi. In that palace of treasures, he'd seen a painting of a woman so beautiful that it had stopped his boy's breath, his knees growing weak.

I see you've lost your heart to Venus, Mama had said with a smile. *You have good taste, Anthony. This is the work of the great painter Titian.*

He'd never been back to Italy, hadn't seen the painting again. But he saw the Venus of his memory every day in his wife. The same Titian hair and glowing lush curves, the same sweetly expressive eyes.

There were differences, of course, the main one being that Gabriella lacked the goddess's come-hither confidence. To him, this was a boon. His past had taught him the perils of loving a woman who was too aware of her own charms.

For an instant, he saw Jessabelle on the last night of her short life, tossed like another piece of rubbish in the alley behind the pleasure house. He saw the surprise on her angel's face as she lay there, the vermin gathering around her, drawn to the dark stain soaking through her tawdry dress. Crystals had glittered like tears on the golden demi-mask still dangling from her neck.

I'm sorry, luv. I was lonely... Her fading whisper. *Forgive me?*

He'd forgiven her but not himself. She'd died because he'd failed to protect her from the recklessness and excesses that were part of her nature. Because he'd asked her to marry him despite knowing that his ambition was a demanding mistress. Because he'd forgotten the lesson he'd learned at age nine:

A powerful man isn't blinded by sentiment.

Love was a distraction he couldn't afford, not while he still had his vengeance to achieve. Not only did love weaken a man, he couldn't see any benefit to the emotion: all it resulted in was pain. His mama had loved a man who'd abandoned her and tried to murder their son. Adam had loved a woman who'd betrayed him, her death leaving him with nothing but guilt and regret. Hell, even his mama's love for him had led to suffering; in her naïve efforts to save him, she'd delivered him into the hands of the devil.

No, love, that fickle, deceptive emotion, couldn't be trusted. He'd learned from his past, adapted accordingly. Self-control and cool-headed logic had led to his success in business, and he'd applied those principles to relationships as well. He felt a surge of satisfaction as his wife's sky-blue eyes immediately searched him out. He'd made a rational, intelligent decision marrying her eight years ago.

As he'd made his views on love clear from the outset, there were no false expectations to muddy their union. Gabriella gave him no trouble for she was sweetly biddable and eager to please. She was the opposite of a flirt: a wallflower who was shy, insecure, and a bit nervy. She tended to chatter when she was anxious. And when she was not anxious. She was loyal, trusting, and tender-hearted, willing to see the best in others while being overly attuned to her own flaws.

She was also endearingly unaware of her own charms. She favored frocks that hid more than they revealed, and that was fine by him. He didn't need other men to get an eyeful of what lay beneath those frills and flounces: those pleasures were for him alone.

Moreover, there were pragmatic benefits to his marriage. Gabriella's father, Curtis Billings, was a banker known equally for his discretion and flexible morality. He was as rich as Croesus, and Gabriella was his only child and heir. Yet money hadn't been the reason why Adam offered for her. Billings Bank had another, more vital role to play. Once his father-in-law was dead—and given the man's ailing health, the day wasn't far off—Adam would have the means to execute the last piece of his long-awaited vengeance.

Numquam obliviscar. Never forget. An eye for an eye.

One by one, Adam had served retribution to those who'd wronged him. Only his ultimate enemy remained: Anthony De Villier. Up until now, De Villier's wealth and success had made him difficult to destroy, but the tides had finally started to turn.

In recent years, De Villier had become obsessed with the railways. Not only had he waged expensive campaigns to gain the necessary Acts of Parliament to build routes from London to various cities, he'd claimed that his company, Grand London National Railway or GLNR, would soon be unveiling the world's fastest locomotive. The steam-powered engine that would revolutionize travel had proved to be a brilliant selling point: the price of De Villier's stock was soaring. From aristocrats to bricklayers, everyone was investing in GLNR.

Yet Adam had inside information. According to his well-placed source, De Villier's engineers couldn't produce the promised locomotive. Between constructing the railways and the development of the much-touted engine, De Villier had been bleeding money, taking out huge loans in secret, his debts beginning to outpace even his considerable wealth. Soon, his Achilles' heel would be exposed...and Adam would deal the killing blow.

He could have ended De Villier with a bullet, but that wouldn't satisfy his honor. He needed to take away the only things the bastard cared about: the wealth and social standing for which De Villier had abandoned his wife and sent his son to perdition. Then, and only then, would Adam have the peace he'd been searching for all these years.

"Pardon my interruption, sirs." Gabriella's breathless voice returned him to the moment.

"You are always a welcome and charming distraction from work, Mrs. Garrity," Murray said with a bow.

When Gabriella blushed, brushing her hands over the abundant skirts of her blue gown, Adam felt his jaw clench. He forced the muscles to relax. He knew Murray meant nothing by it; flirting was second nature for the rake. All the same, Adam didn't like anyone dallying with what was his.

Gabriella was most definitely his.

He crossed over to her, taking her hand. Her gaze flew to his, and primal satisfaction filled him as her pupils darkened, her plump, naturally red lips parting as he brushed a kiss over her soft knuckles. Her fingers trembled in his grasp...the way she trembled in his bed.

Although Adam had made it a habit not to be taken by surprise, he had to admit that his wife's physical effect on him had been most unexpected. After all, he prided himself on self-discipline and didn't believe in indulging in excessive appetites of any sort. A man ought to be in control of his impulses, not the other way around. Yet from the start, sweet, guileless Gabriella had made him inexplicably...randy.

At first, he'd chalked it up to the novelty of having a wife at his beck and call. But his carnal desire for her had only grown stronger and more distracting over time. Right now, for instance, his brain sizzled with the notion of bending her over his desk. Of tossing up her fussy skirts and exposing her delightfully rounded bottom, which might be too generous for fashion but was absolute perfection for bedding. As, indeed, was the rest of her.

He saw his hands on the pale quivering mounds of her arse, parting them to expose her delicate sex, the piquant red nest and silky pinkness. He knew she would be hot and wet and ready for him; she always was. An accommodating wife through and through.

But he wouldn't take her here. Or in any place other than their proper marital bed.

And only at the regularly scheduled time.

He wouldn't repeat his past mistakes. Jessabelle had delighted in inciting his carnal, animalistic side. His passion for her had clouded his judgement and led to her death. No way would he risk anything happening to Gabriella.

From the outset, he'd taken pains to safeguard his marriage, swaddling it in layers of routine, propriety, and restraint. He would protect his innocent lady from the darkness of his world and within himself. With Gabriella, he would never lose control, never let sentiment prevent him from thinking clearly and acting in her best interests.

He dispelled the fantasy of taking his wife on his desk. He'd had plenty of practice reining in his arousal over the last eight years. It wasn't pleasant, but it was necessary.

He released her hand. "Did you want something, my dear?"

Her curly lashes swept up against her curving auburn brows. He hid a smile at the shy, honest desire shining in her rounded blue eyes. His spouse possessed not an ounce of coyness, another quality he liked. She couldn't hide her feelings any more than she could fly. He always knew where he stood with her...which was a refreshing change from the scheming and machinations he was accustomed to in every other aspect of his life.

Not that he minded scheming and machinations. They were his specialties.

"I, um, wanted to see if Mr. Murray would care to stay for luncheon," Gabriella said. "Chef Pierre is preparing your favorite duck confit, as well as the usual courses. The soup is asparagus, I believe, and for dessert there's trifle, the one with the chocolate and brandied cherries you showed a preference for last week and a selection of cakes—"

"Murray will not be staying, my dear." Adam cut her off before she recited the entire menu. The rush of words betrayed her anxiety, and although he knew the cause of it, he wouldn't discuss the matter with her in front of company. That would wait until they had privacy. "He has preparations to make for this eve."

Taking the hint, Murray said ruefully, "As tempting as your invitation sounds, Mrs. Garrity, I fear I must be on my way."

As Murray's tawny head bent over her hand, Adam felt his molars grinding again. He didn't know why the younger man's gallantry bothered him; perhaps it was that Murray was close to Gabriella in age, and there'd always been an ineffable bond between them. Adam couldn't forget that, all those years ago, Gabriella had pleaded on Murray's behalf, asking Adam to let the fellow work off his debt.

The pair murmured some private good-byes, and jealousy twisted Adam's gut. Which was ridiculous. He told himself that his reaction was simply proprietary: he didn't share. What was his was his. And Gabriella was his wife, the mother of his children. She belonged to him.

If she needed reminding, however, he'd be happy to oblige her. Surely, he thought broodingly, it was his husbandly duty to stake his claim...even if it meant altering the schedule. A small deviation from routine wouldn't hurt.

Indeed, it would be quite pleasurable.

After Murray finally departed, Gabby turned to Adam. "When will you be ready to dine, sir?" She tilted her head in question, a flame-red curl sliding into her eye.

Before she could brush it aside, he did it for her. He trailed his fingertips over her silky, rounded cheek, feeling the rising warmth of her blush. Her eyes were wide and slightly glazed, like that of a doe confronted by danger. Only his little spouse didn't want to flee. Her ripe breasts rose and fell with an enticing jiggle that no modest, high-necked bodice could conceal, and he'd wager his empire that, beneath all those layers of fabric, her cherry-red nipples were already hard and budded.

Anticipation simmered in his blood.

Hiding a private smile, he offered her his arm. "I'm ready when you are, my dear."

❧ 4 ❧

LATER THAT AFTERNOON, GABBY WAS SEATED AT THE ROSEWOOD table in her sitting room with the housekeeper, Mrs. Page. It was their weekly meeting to review the household accounts. Typically, Gabby enjoyed her chats with the silver-haired lady, but at the moment her mind was elsewhere. Specifically, it was on her husband and the dangerous mission he would be embarking upon tonight. The mission that *she* had convinced him to take on.

Her fingers knotted in her lap. *Have I sent Adam into mortal danger?*

"I have your approval for the new bed linens, Mrs. Garrity?"

Gabby nodded absently. "Mr. Garrity prefers silk sheets, from that mill in France."

"Yes, ma'am."

As Mrs. Page continued to go down the list, worry churned in Gabby. She looked longingly at the tray of refreshments. The housekeeper had brought along a plate of iced cakes, which looked ever so tempting, but Gabby was determined to reduce (part of her never-ending self-improvement plan). In point of fact, she'd started a slimming regimen just this afternoon.

She resigned herself to sipping plain black tea from her Sèvres cup. It wasn't nearly as comforting as that lemon sponge layered with jam and whipped cream would be. Or that marzipan-covered genoise. She stifled a sigh. How she wished she had delicious flavors to concentrate on, something to distract her from the dark swell of her thoughts.

It had started yesterday, when Tessa Kent had stopped by. Gabby had become friends with Tessa because her husband Harry Kent was the brother of Gabby's dearest friends, the former Kent sisters (the ladies were now all married to aristocratic husbands who adored them). Tessa's visit had not been social in nature. She'd come to tell Gabby about a terrible plight: Glory, an eight-year-old girl, had been kidnapped. The villain, a man named Sweeney, had threatened to *kill* the girl if her father, the Duke of Ranelagh and Somerville, didn't pay the ransom. Tessa had grimly shared her belief that Sweeney intended to murder his young hostage either way.

Gabby had been horrified. Her first thought had been of her own children, Fiona and Maximillian, her heart squeezing with a mother's panic. She'd asked Tessa if there was anything she could do to help.

Tapping her finger against her chin, Tessa had said, "There *is* something. Talk to Mr. Garrity. Convince him to join our rescue mission."

Gabby had gone directly to Adam and hadn't been surprised when he'd agreed to help. He was a good man and the most accommodating of husbands. At dawn, the two of them had gone to Tessa's house to plan Glory's rescue. Gabby had been glad to assist...until Adam had said that he would *personally* participate in the dangerous battle.

She'd frozen in panic.

On one level, it was stupid of her. It wasn't as if she didn't know what her husband did for a living. As a business, money-lending did not come without risks; it wasn't for naught that Adam had a coterie of guards that regularly accompanied him and the family on outings. Nonetheless, when Adam went off to work, her mental picture was of him in his lavish offices near the Bank of England and the Exchange. Running his empire from behind his very large and elegant desk.

In truth, she'd blocked from her mind the dangers of his trade. When he'd stated that he and his team would surround the dock and prevent any possibility of Sweeney escaping with Glory, reality had struck her with a terrifying blow. She'd expected Adam to be a general, planning and directing the rescue from the safety of an encampment, not some foot solider leading the charge on the battlefield. What if he got hurt, shot...or something *worse* happened?

He was her world. The center of her universe. She loved him with all of her heart and couldn't bear for anything to happen to him.

Of course, she couldn't disclose her worries during the strategy session. To do so would undermine Adam in front of their friends, and she knew how much his pride meant to him. She'd bided her time, anxiously devouring a plate of cakes in Tessa's drawing room (hence the newly instituted reducing plan). By some miracle, she'd managed to hold back her concerns until the carriage ride home, when they'd burst from her. She couldn't remember how far she'd gotten—perhaps to their poor, grieving, fatherless children—when Adam had tipped her chin up.

"Don't worry your head about it, my dear," he'd said.

"Not worry? How can I not worry? You're my husband—"

"Precisely. As your husband, you will trust me in this. All will be well."

In the face of his implacable control, her arguments had withered like unready grapes on a vine. Yet her worry had continued to grow after they arrived home and he disappeared into the study with Mr. Murray. To distract herself, she'd gone to check on the children. Fiona and Max were preparing for the play that they, along with their young friends, would be performing this evening for their respective families. Given the circumstances, Gabby had wanted to call off the event, but Adam had said there was no reason to disappoint the children, and it was best to carry on as usual.

After Mr. Murray left, she and Adam had sat down for lunch. She'd tried again to bring up her fears, yet the presence of the servants had precluded her from making inroads. As had her husband's obvious disinclination to discuss the matter. And by obvious, this was what he'd said: "Let's not discuss the matter now, my dear."

Not wanting to annoy him, she'd dropped the subject.

"I'm afraid we have a staffing concern."

The housekeeper's somber tone returned Gabby to the moment. "Yes, Mrs. Page?"

"It's about Nell. We'll be needing a replacement for her soon."

Nell was Gabby's lady's maid of three years, a chatty, friendly blonde with a true talent for dressing hair. Nell had a follower named Tom, a cabinetmaker's apprentice who'd been saving up for years to marry her. Tired of waiting, Tom had recently hit upon the idea of investing his meager earnings in a railway venture founded by the wealthy industrialist Anthony De Villier.

Gabby knew of De Villier and not just because his success was the talk of the town. Her father's business, Billings Bank, counted the industrialist amongst its most important and illustrious clients. Papa had been an early supporter of De Villier and took great pride in the other's achievements.

Thinking of her papa caused a band to tighten around Gabby's chest. Her formerly indomitable parent had taken ill, and his physician had recently diagnosed him with a wasting disease that was likely to progress. Even so, he refused to rest, still going off to the bank every morning despite her pleas and the doctor's advice to the contrary.

Her father had always been a driven man, with exacting standards for himself and everyone else. His mind, once made up, was nigh impossible to change. Nonetheless, when he attended the children's play this eve, perhaps she could convince him to cut back his work hours…

Realizing that Mrs. Page was awaiting a response, she tucked away her concerns with a skill borne of practice. She'd been plagued by worries all her life, another one of her oddities. Perhaps it was because she'd never known a mama's soothing love (her mother had died giving birth to her). Or because she hadn't had any siblings or childhood friends with whom to air out these feelings. Or because she'd endured years of social ostracism, her peers at finishing school gleefully pointing out all her faults.

Whatever the cause, her head was a repository of anxious thoughts.

Since her marriage, she'd worked on improving herself, on becoming a wife worthy of Adam. What man wanted to be married to a woman who was constantly fretting? She was proud of the progress she'd made in managing her worries. When she couldn't block them out, she'd learned to organize them so they wouldn't feel as overwhelming. It was akin to sorting frippery into boxes to prevent the mess from spilling everywhere and into everything. How could one function with the chaos otherwise?

She'd created different categories for the thoughts she stored away. *Worries About My Looks*, *Concerns About the Children*, and *Scary Thoughts in Social Situations*, to name a few. Her favorite was the *Bin of Blissful Ignorance*, to which she'd consign all her troublesome thoughts if she could. She dumped her worry about her father, along with her concerns for Adam's safety, into the *When Men Refuse to Listen to Reason* box—one that was frequently overflowing—and shut the lid.

She forced a smile. "Is Tom ready to make an honest woman out of our Nell?"

"He's proposed, although the engagement may be a long one. Tom is using his profits to purchase *more* shares, you see. Young people these days." Mrs. Page shook her head, her neat silver twist gleaming. "In my day, we didn't wager our hard-earned savings on a fortune-making scheme."

"I'm happy for Nell. What do you think she would like for a wedding gift?" Gabby mused.

"Isn't that like you, ma'am, to always be thinking of others?" Mrs. Page gave her a fond look. "But lest you forget, you will need to start looking for a new lady's maid, and the sooner the better."

Gabby wrinkled her nose. Prior to Nell, she hadn't had good luck with lady's maids. Transforming herself into a fashionable wife had been a second area of self-improvement, one with significant challenges. Nonetheless, she'd remembered the advice given to her by a schoolmistress: "If you cannot improve upon the defect, then you must do your best to hide it."

There was naught Gabby could do about her hair or freckles (fading solutions only irritated her sensitive skin and didn't remove the offending specks). She had, however, given her wardrobe a complete refurbishment. Eschewing close-fitting silhouettes, she opted for garments with concealing necklines, roomy bodices, and full skirts. She requested extra ruffles, flounces, and trimmings to hide her excessive curviness (let's face it, two pregnancies hadn't helped matters in that regard). The end result might not be precisely *de rigueur*, but the extra layers of armor made her feel more secure.

She didn't know if her efforts pleased Adam; he seldom made comments of an intimate nature. Oh, he complimented her wifely accomplishments, such as her decorating skills and the menus she planned, her patience with the children. And, she thought with a rush of heat, he never shirked from his conjugal duties.

At the same time, he was also private and reserved, and she told herself that some distance in a marriage was a good thing. Indeed, it might make the heart grow fonder. The last thing she needed was for him to look too closely at her flaws and wish that he'd married someone better.

Her thoughts were proving draining. Her gaze wandered to

the plate of cakes, the perfect pick-me-up. The fluffy golden sponge beckoned, its layers of snowy whipped cream and ruby jam mesmerizing.

I'll make you feel better, it called to her. *Fill you with sweetness and delight...*

Her fingers trembled, her hand reaching out...

The imperious knock made her jerk, her hand dropping into her lap.

Adam? she thought in surprise. *What is he doing here?*

"Come in," she said quickly.

Her husband entered, and all thoughts of cake vanished from her head. He was far more delicious. His larger-than-life presence dwarfed her spacious sitting room, his masculinity pronounced against the primrose silk walls. Whenever he was around, he absorbed her senses as black absorbs all light. Every fiber of her was attuned to him.

At their first meeting, he'd reminded her of Schahriar, the sultan from *Arabian Nights' Entertainments* (minus the wife-killing tendencies) and that fanciful image of him had deepened over time. She pictured him wearing flowing robes, strolling through his palace the way he was strolling toward her now. With the casual confidence of a man who knows he is master of all he surveys.

The hairs on her skin tingled as she took in the subtle flexing of sinew beneath his clothes...not exotic robes, of course, but English tailoring, somber and precise. Restrained power infused his every movement, his very being. His utter control and self-discipline awed her: she would never understand in a million years why a man like him had chosen her to be his wife.

"May I have a word with you, Mrs. Garrity?" he asked.

Dear heavens. Even after eight years of marriage and two children together, his silky baritone made her feel like a bride on her wedding night.

"Of course," she said breathlessly.

Mrs. Page discreetly departed.

Adam took the housekeeper's vacated seat. His gaze settled on Gabby, and she shivered at the intensity of his regard. His irises were so dark that they melded with his pupils, giving the impression of fathomless darkness. His eyes could be as cold as a winter's night or hotter than an iron brand left in the fire.

Others might be intimidated by her husband's keen scrutiny, but strangely she wasn't. Perhaps it was because he'd always been honest with her and seen her for who she was. He'd married her because he'd wanted a virtuous wife, a devoted mother to his children, and a gracious hostess to his friends and associates. And, Gabby thought with trembling pride, he'd made the right choice because she *was* all of those things. Being Mrs. Adam Garrity was the only thing she'd ever been good at, an honor she tried her utmost to live up to every day.

"Did I forget that we had a meeting on the schedule?" she asked.

Adam smiled...and, oh, how she loved that faint curving of his hard, sensual mouth. Instead of softening him, it made him look even more virile. More deliciously sinful.

"This wasn't on the schedule, my dear," he said.

She was relieved that she hadn't forgotten something on the daily calendar. Years ago, Adam had come across her in a state of distress. It had been soon after the birth of their son Maximillian, and she'd been beset by inexplicable doldrums. Up until then, she'd taken pride in her ability to create a comfortable domestic sphere for her family but, in a blink, everything had changed.

Motherhood, household management, and the many social duties expected of the wife of a successful businessman became overwhelming. She'd felt like she was her children's favorite juggler at Astley's Amphitheatre, keeping ten balls in the air at once. She'd tried to hide her bouts of tearfulness, but her husband had caught her sobbing...over a spilled cup of tea, for goodness' sake.

Adam hadn't rejected her for being odd, the way the girls at finishing school had. Nor had he told her to buck up and gain control of herself, which had always been her father's advice. He hadn't even told her to save her tears for a private time as her schoolmistress would have done.

Instead, he'd just...listened. Without comment. He'd sat beside her as she'd sobbingly—and a tad nonsensically—confessed that she was a terrible juggler who was dropping balls *everywhere*. After she'd ceased to be a watering pot, he'd dried her tears, made love to her (which proved to be a powerful remedy for worry), and tucked her into bed.

The next morning, she'd awoken to find a schedule on the pillow next to her. It clearly highlighted the priorities of her day. Periods were also designated for rest and leisure activities, two things that, left to her own devices, she tended to forget.

It was better than any love note she could have received. To her mind, his actions conveyed his affection louder than words ever could. From that day on, she received a daily schedule written in his bold hand, and she cherished them for what they were: reminders of his care for her.

"What is it that you wished to speak with me about?" she asked curiously.

"It isn't what *I* wish to talk to you about. It is what you have to say to me."

"Me? But what do I have to..." Seeing his lifted brows, she trailed off. Merciful heavens, but the man knew her well. Perhaps better than she knew herself.

She expelled a breath. "I'm an open book, aren't I?"

"It's part of your charm, my dear."

"You won't think it's charming when I pester you about tonight's meeting again," she warned.

He flicked an invisible speck of lint from his grey trousers. He was a valet's dream. Unlike her, he had nothing to hide and never got rumpled or stained. His charcoal frockcoat and plum waistcoat, like all his garments, fit flawlessly on his lean, muscular frame.

"It seems my assurances have not allayed your worries," he said. "I would not wish to leave the house with you in an unsatisfied state."

At the possible innuendo, her core fluttered. Her thighs pressed together against a sudden lick of heat. But no, he couldn't be making conjugal overtures...it was the afternoon, for heaven's sake. Not to mention Friday. When it came to marital activities, as with everything else, Adam followed a precise routine.

He arrived at her bedchamber on Wednesdays at nine o'clock in the evening. He made love to her until she was too weak to move...to even *think*. Afterward, he returned to his own room. An alteration to the schedule occurred only if she had her monthly flux, in which case he would postpone his visit to the following Wednesday, or if either of them was feeling unwell (and by either of them, she meant herself because her husband was never in anything but robust health).

In their eight years of marriage, there'd only been one exception to this routine. That Saturday night a few months ago when Adam had returned home drunk, a state she'd never seen him in before or since. He'd shown her a side of him she'd never witnessed before. The mere thought of his unleashed carnality—and her own shockingly *un*virtuous behavior—made her shiver now, with confusing pleasure...and painful doubts.

Luckily, the spirits had wiped his memory of that night. He seemed to have no recollection of what had transpired between them. And she told herself she was glad. She'd shoved that episode into the mental bin labelled *Let Sleeping Dogs Lie*, and there was no reason to dig it out...not when she had more pressing anxieties to deal with.

"Couldn't you let your men handle the exchange tonight? Why can't you wait in the carriage? What if there's fighting and gunfire and—"

"I can handle myself in a fight." His lips twitched as if he was amused.

Amused...when his life was at stake!

"That's not the point," she insisted. "Why take unnecessary risks?"

"I thought you wanted me to help your friends."

"Not at the expense of your own well-being!"

He raised his brows. "Why are you so concerned, my dear?"

"Because I can't stand the thought of you getting hurt." Her throat swelled with the power of her feelings. "Because I love you. You're everything to me."

In the next instant, he was on his feet, stalking toward her with thrilling purpose. That was another wonderful quality of Adam's: although he didn't take stock in romantic love, he didn't seem to mind if *she* professed her feelings. Which happened frequently because she simply couldn't hold them back. Nor did she want to.

Her breath whooshed from her lungs as he lifted her, as effortlessly as if she were made of thistledown. Her hands landed on his shoulders, his bunched power quivering through her fingertips. His scent—expensive spice mingled with his own clean male musk—entered her nose, an elixir that amplified her craving for him. Her indelicate hunger for her husband.

Because she couldn't help herself, she asked, "What are you doing?"

His eyes gleamed. "Since words don't seem to be enough, I'm providing husbandly reassurance through other means."

"But it's not Wednesday," she blurted.

"We'll make an exception."

She had an instant to catch his wolfish smile before his mouth claimed hers.

SHE WAS DROWNING IN ADAM'S KISS, AND SHE *LOVED* IT. HER worries and insecurities faded as a wave of passion swept her up. As she surrendered to her husband's masterful touch.

He set her down by her tester bed, her spine fitting against one of the posters. His hands framed her jaw, holding her still for his kiss. His mouth possessed hers with firm, arousing authority. She parted her lips for his tongue, moaning as he plundered her softness. As he licked inside, saturating her senses with his masculine flavor. As he took of her...because she was his.

Beneath the demanding flame of his kiss, she melted into pure sensation. Her back molded against the hard poster and her front against her even harder husband. Good Lord, but he was potent. His hands began moving down her spine, undoing her with devastating efficiency. He stripped her layer by layer, the weight falling from her, pooling at her stockinged feet.

He lifted his mouth from hers, and the loss of contact broke her reverie. Awareness jolted her: it was *daytime*. Only the under curtains were drawn, the afternoon light filtering through the filmy material, tinting the room with a golden glow. And she wore not a stitch—well, except for her white silk stockings and shirred garters adorned with satin rosebuds.

Which meant she was utterly *exposed* to Adam.

Her chest heaved with growing panic as he took a step back, his fathomless gaze roving over her nudity. In the past, he'd always made love to her in the dark or by firelight, both of which were far more flattering to one's figure. Of course, he could feel her excessive fleshiness...but feeling wasn't the same as *seeing*.

Her hands flew to cover herself—only she didn't even know *where* to place them. Her breasts? Her hips? Her belly? Goodness, her hands weren't *big* enough to conceal all that needed to be concealed. She settled for crossing her arms and squeezing her thighs together.

"Oh, *please* don't look at me," she pleaded.

His dark slashing brows drew together. "Why not?"

"Because it's not bedtime...and you can see me," she whispered.

"I assure you it's nothing I haven't seen before."

"Not like this." Her cheeks flaming, she dropped her gaze. "It's different...in the dark."

He curled a finger under her chin, bringing her eyes back to his.

"The lighting has no impact on your beauty," he murmured.

She swallowed, searching his austere features for any sign that he was humoring her. She saw none, yet her mind told her that he had to say such things because he was a kind and caring husband. A true gentleman. He wouldn't lie to her...yet his words could be interpreted in more than one way, couldn't they? Perhaps he meant that lighting couldn't alter her looks for better or worse—because she was a lost cause.

Why, oh why, did I eat that dashed plate of cakes at Tessa's?

"Could we draw the drapes?" she asked fretfully.

"No." His firm reply startled her. "You're not to hide yourself from me."

Her breath puffed through her lips as his long-fingered hands circled her wrists, pulling her hands to her sides. Her cheeks grew hotter as his gaze settled on her breasts, which jiggled inelegantly with each rise and fall, the engorged peaks nearly the same vulgar shade as her hair.

"You're lovely, Gabriella," he said. "And you're mine."

She couldn't look away from the possession smoldering in his eyes. She trembled as his touch coursed down her throat, the slope of her shoulder, her upper arm. When the backs of his fingers brushed the jutting curve of her breast, she reacted with instinctive modesty, her arms crossing over her bosom.

"What did I say about hiding yourself?" he inquired.

Tension crackled in the space between them. This strange, magnetic attraction had been there from the moment they met. That she'd been drawn to Adam was no surprise, but the fact that *he* had felt a reciprocal pull never ceased to amaze her. Over time, this sensual charge had grown even more intense...to the point where just being in the same room as him could make her feel as if she'd touched an electrifying machine.

The thought of the unknown dangers he would be facing tonight only amplified her feelings. Fear and desire made her blood rush. She felt as if she might burst out of her skin with worry and wanting and love.

"You said not to," she said over her fiercely thudding heart. "Hide myself, I mean."

"Then be a good wife and put your hands on the bedpost behind you."

Her limbs moved to obey his quiet command. As her fingers gripped the thick, carved pole, heady anticipation enveloped her. She didn't understand this strange new game they were playing. Yet she was in his thrall, the heated approval in his sultan's eyes turning her thoughts to ashes.

"How pleasing you are," he murmured.

For once, she was bereft of words. The touch of his lips on her collarbone dissolved her capacity for speech altogether. His kiss followed that delicate slant to her throat, his tongue sweeping over her throbbing pulse. Gabby tightened her grip on the pole, the position thrusting her breasts forward, and she moaned when he cupped the rounded mounds in his elegant hands, nuzzling the deep crevice between. The budded tips strained for his attention, yet he did not touch them with his fingers or lips.

"Please, Adam." The words left her in a gasp.

He lifted his head. "Please what, my dear?"

"You know," she said shyly.

She knew he did. After all, he attended to her there during every Wednesday night visit.

"I'd like for you to tell me."

She blinked at the novel and altogether scandalous command. "I can't say it *aloud*."

His hard, sensual mouth slowly curved. Gilded by the afternoon light, her husband was even more attractive—more dangerously virile. She couldn't conceal anything from his keen gaze, and she had the distinct feeling that he liked that. She felt as if he were leading her through a new dance...and she didn't know the steps.

Yet she trusted Adam. He led flawlessly and had never, not once, let her fall. In his arms, she'd found the safety she'd always craved.

"We've been married for eight years," he murmured. "Surely you've no secrets left to hide?"

"I don't have any secrets," she said with quivering honesty.

Wickedness glinted in his eyes. "Then tell me what you want."

She bit her lip, her fingers curling around the ridged wood. Could she do that? Now that he'd planted the idea in her head, impulsive words bubbled in her throat.

Desperately, she tried to keep them corked. "You'll think me wanton."

"I hope you're right." His gaze turned even more carnal. "Tell me, Gabriella."

"I'd like you to kiss me...on my breasts," she said faintly.

Could one die of mortification? How would he react to her shockingly forward request?

His nostrils flared, the dark maelstrom of his gaze churning her insides with trepidation and excitement.

"It would be my pleasure, my sweet wife."

Adam knew that he was playing with fire.

His initial plan had been to remind Gabriella of his claim via a pleasant afternoon bedding. Having calculated the odds, he'd decided that the deviation from their usual schedule was acceptable. After all, even proper couples on occasion engaged in marital activities outside of nighttime.

Then he'd seen his wife in the light: all her charms displayed in lush, trembling splendor. Her sweet uncertainty had caused an odd constriction in his chest, and he'd had the desire to reassure her. To protect what was his. Yet when she'd obeyed his command to not hide herself, her small, white hands curling around the dark poster, his desire had morphed into another sort altogether.

With startling swiftness, their love play had veered into the territory of his deepest fantasies.

Dark, erotic games flashed in his head. The kind of temptation he hadn't indulged in since his marriage. Never would he despoil his innocent Gabriella with the depravity of his old life. He knew the price of being governed by passion, and he would never expose Gabriella to that risk.

Yet his wife was naked, her flame-colored tresses tumbling over her shoulders, her pretty blue eyes bright with need. Her creamy tits beckoned with each luscious rise and fall, their pomegranate tips calling to his tongue. Not to mention, she'd asked him so nicely for her pleasure.

Animal instincts warred with logic.

As long as you stay in control, there's no harm in having a little fun, he reasoned. *Don't let things get too far; keep it suitable for the marital bower.*

Satisfied with his decision, he cupped his wife's breasts, enjoying their firm heft. Bending, he kissed the rounded tops; her skin flowed like silk beneath his lips. He sampled her generous curves, hiding a smile as her breaths turned fitful. He spiraled his tongue slowly toward the peak of one breast, teasing her nipple into plump ripeness but not yet tasting the fruit.

"Adam, *please*," she begged in a breathy voice.

Christ, she made him hard.

He toyed with the idea of playing with her some more, but his pounding erection convinced him otherwise. He drew her nipple into his mouth, sucking with firm pressure. Her cries of pleasure heated his blood, seed swelling in his stones. The wet friction of his tongue made her moan and squirm delightfully against the bed pole. He switched his attentions to her other breast, licking and flicking, while also enjoying the view of the twin he'd left behind, the rosy nipple so wet and stiff.

Her moans rose in that familiar but no less delightful cadence. His wife's responsiveness was more powerful than any aphrodisiac. When they made love, her nervy energy turned into a sweet, feminine passion that tested the limits of his restraint. He put a hand between her soft thighs, a growl of approval rising in his throat.

She was drenched. Dripping with honey.

He wanted her even wetter.

He stepped between her legs, widening her stance while keeping her trapped against the bedpost. Claiming her mouth in a searing kiss, he fondled her pussy, his thumb finding her love-knot. He circled the slick bud—once, twice, then she went off like a Roman candle. She let out a keening cry, and he consumed the sound, its reverberation pushing a spurt of pre-seed from his cock.

Lifting his head, he stared at his wife's passion-flushed face, her adoring eyes—and lust darkened his vision, forbidden images flooding his mind.

Of her against this bedpost, her wrists bound above her head.

Of her on all fours upon the mattress as he took her hard from behind.

Of her kneeling at his feet as he fucked her sweet mouth.

Stay. In. Bloody. Control.

With force of will, he locked away his dark urges.

"Be a good wife and lie on the bed," he said.

She obeyed, her fingers nervously twisting the silk coverlet. She likely had no idea of the picture she made. That juxtaposition of innocence and wanton decadence. Her dreamy eyes paired with those flushed, surging tits. Her prim white stockings and garters framing her spicy cunny wet with spend.

She was Venus, and she was his.

He began to strip, not giving into haste. Gabriella was watching him, her accelerated breaths conveying that she liked what she saw. When he removed his trousers, her eyes widened as she took in the extent of his arousal. He couldn't blame her: his cock was incapable of discretion where she was concerned. He was monstrously erect, the crown fat and swollen purple, the vein bulging on the underside of his long, thick shaft.

When she wetted her lips with her tongue, he nearly groaned.

Rein it in. She's your wife, for God's sake. Bed her properly—not like some damned animal.

He got on the bed and climbed atop her, taking his weight on one arm. With his other hand, he fitted his cock to her opening and sheathed himself in one thrust. Pleasure scalded his insides as his wife's snug, dewy passage enveloped him; it took all his willpower not to take her hard and fast. To resist pounding into her quim, his balls smacking her nether lips with rough possession that she would feel the next day.

Setting his jaw, he took her in a steady, disciplined, spousal rhythm. He would not come until she did again. Gritting his teeth, he turned to an old trick, mentally naming kings of England to distract from the prodigious pleasure of his wife's tight cunny.

Edward I, Edward II...ah, God...Edward III...

Fortunately, he didn't have to go past the House of York. She was writhing beneath him, her fingers gripping the bedsheets, and he knew she was close. He bent, closing his lips around her nipple, sucking rhythmically with his thrusts. With a wild cry, she climaxed again, the ripples of her pussy massaging his shaft...and finally he let go.

He bit back his groan, shuddering as his seed shot from him, as her spasms sucked him of every pulsing drop.

Regaining his breath, he withdrew from her. She mumbled something drowsily as he tucked her beneath the bedclothes. From experience, he knew that the aftermath eased her into slumber—and sure enough, a wisp of a snore escaped her. His lips twitched...and then he firmed them.

He dressed with his usual efficiency. But he didn't leave right away, his wife's loveliness holding him as surely as her body had. Making him linger.

Bathed in golden light, Gabriella looked like an innocent goddess, her auburn lashes fluttering against her creamy, gold-speckled cheeks. He had the urge to stretch out beside her—not to sleep, for he wasn't one for idle napping—but just to...watch over her. To guard his wife as she dreamed the dreams of the blameless. To vicariously experience the innocence that he, himself, had lost a lifetime ago.

As his fingers reached to brush the errant red curl from her cheek, his mind chided him.

Don't get distracted. Maintain your discipline. You've stops to make before the business with Sweeney tonight.

He dropped his hand. Straightening his lapels, he left the room.

❧ 6 ❧

ADAM CONTINUED WITH HIS REGULAR FRIDAY SCHEDULE, making his first stop at his office.

The building was located in London's financial hub, close to the Bank of England. The tasteful interior with its wood paneling and elegantly subdued décor told patrons that this was a legitimate business and not some shady, back alley operation. Indeed, Adam considered his trade no different from that of a bank or joint-stock venture. Seated in his opulent suite on the third floor, a view of the bustling city behind him, he was proud of how far he'd come...and knew how hard he'd fight to keep what was his.

Even when the work was bothersome.

"Please, sir, you know I wouldn't ask it of you, but it is a matter of life or *death*."

The dramatic declaration came from Lord Evanston, the rumpled, bleary-eyed lordling who occupied the chair across the desk from Adam's. Since the cull made a visit at least once a month, the seat probably bore his arse print by now.

"That's what you said last month," Adam said. *And the month before that.*

"But it truly *is* an emergency. Just last night my grandmama died and the poor thing hadn't a feather to fly with. Being a good grandson, it falls upon me to give her a proper burial."

Evanston's pious look was at odds with the rouge stains on his collar, the alcohol fumes he emitted with every word. Bloody hell, it was three in the afternoon, and the cove was already in his cups. In his early twenties and new to London, Evanston was a feckless but amiable fop. He had a large inheritance waiting in the wings, but for now he had to get by on a stipend...which was where Adam came in.

"Strange." Leaning back in his chair, Adam steepled his fingers. "Here I was thinking that a man could only have two grandmothers. This is the third one you've killed off."

"Did I say grandmama? I meant grand-aunt." Evanston's smile was beatific. "One who was *like* a grandmother to me."

"Get out, Evanston, before I have Kerrigan toss you out."

Most men were rightly afraid of Adam's head guard, a nearly seven-foot mountain of muscle whose shaved head and eyepatch added to his aura of intimidation.

"Kerrigan wouldn't do that," Evanston said affably. "He and I are old friends by now."

Adam was certain that Kerrigan had fantasies of making a human projectile out of Evanston. And he knew this because the taciturn guard had growled more than once, "Give me the word, sir, and I'll bounce that cull out of here like a bloody ball."

Adam hadn't given the word because Evanston was a good patron who always paid his debts in the end and with heavy interest. Also, the young lord was so cheerfully annoying that, when tossed, he'd probably bounce off a wall and hit Kerrigan in the face. In truth, the diversification in Adam's business meant that he didn't need to take on much risk in the moneylending department. He only worked with the *crème de la crème* of clients, relying less on muscle to get his due and more on his ability to make a good speculative investment.

Evanston was such an investment, even if he needed to be reined in on a regular basis.

"No more credit until you pay off your debt. Entirely," Adam said sternly. "Now begone."

"Thank you for the advice, sir." Evanston scrambled to his feet and bowed his way out. "See you next month!"

Shaking his head, Adam skimmed over a report from his man-of-business and dictated a letter to one of the clerks. Then he gathered his things and proceeded to his next stop.

At five o'clock, Adam's carriage glided to a stop in front of a large, four-story Italianate building on a tiny lane in Covent Garden. His driver, Thompson, had required no instruction to bring him here for it was part of his routine. For years, he'd made this monthly Friday night visit.

"Wait here, Thompson," Adam said as he alighted. "My visit will be short this eve."

"Yes, sir."

Adam headed for the private entrance at the rear of the property. The guard there greeted him deferentially, unhooking the velvet rope barrier to let him in. Adam headed up the stairs reserved for workers; along the way, he passed several whores wearing short sateen robes, their faces painted and hair still tied in rags. He nodded coolly to their cooed hellos.

Reaching his destination on the third floor, he knocked.

The door opened, revealing a tall, statuesque blonde, dramatically framed by the scarlet boudoir behind her. She was dressed in a black corset made of leather, her arms encased in black satin gloves and legs in black silk stockings. A coiled leather whip dangled from one hand.

"Adam," Jeannette Wilde said in rich, sultry tones. "You're early tonight."

"I can't stay long," he replied.

Her red lips curving, she widened the door. "Then don't just stand there, love. Come in."

7

THAT NIGHT, THE SKY WAS DARK AND CLEAR ABOVE THE Thames, the air bearing the crispness of autumn. A constellation of lights winked along the shore, and there was a disorientating seamlessness between water, land, and sky. Due to the lack of fog cover, Adam ordered his men to drop anchor a safe distance away from the warehouse where the battle with Sweeney was to take place.

As the boat rocked, Adam steadied himself against the railing, memories flooding him.

Don't fight it, you li'l bastard. I'm just following your father's orders. I'll drown you like a kitten—you won't feel a thing.

Wiley's menacing laughter muffled his own desperate pleas. He felt those icy dark waves closing over his head, the brine gargling his cries. He fought to free his hands and legs from the binding rope, the bricks in the sack dragging him down, down, into the suffocating deep...

Keep your eyes on the target. You cannot change the past, but you can make sure those who are responsible pay for their sins. Take care of the business at hand.

Inhaling deeply, he shut out the memories.

"How many guards, Kerrigan?" he asked.

Standing at the prow of the lighter, the guard had a telescope aimed at the warehouse. "From the lamps, I'd count maybe a dozen guards doing the rounds."

Adam consulted his pocket watch. "There's half an hour until the exchange. Keep monitoring."

"Yes, sir."

As he was about to close the cover of the watch, Adam paused, seeing the inscription inside.

On the occasion of our seventh wedding anniversary. Your loving Gabriella.

He rubbed his thumb over the script. A familiar warmth unfurled, chasing away some of the chill. He frowned at himself. It wasn't like him to get distracted, yet his thoughts had grown increasingly unruly. At unexpected times, he found himself ambushed by thoughts of Gabriella...and his old life. If he were honest with himself—and he made it a policy to be—he could trace this phenomenon back to a few months ago, when The Gilded Pearl, an infamous brothel, had gone up in flames, taking with it a piece of his revenge.

Cold rage rushed into his veins. *She got off too easily. She deserved to suffer more.*

He snapped the pocket watch shut. What was done was done. And if the punishment hadn't quite compensated for the crime, he reminded himself that the most important part of his vengeance was yet to come.

The moment was nearing when De Villier's financial jugular would be exposed. The blade was in Adam's hand, and he couldn't wait to strike. To have his justice at last...and with it, peace.

Stay in command. The prize is nearly yours.

Footsteps sounded on the steps from the lower cabin, and Murray emerged onto the deck. Like Adam, he wore a caped greatcoat. The wool warded off the damp chill, and the pockets were convenient. Adam had a pair of pistols stowed in his and a blade in each boot for good measure.

You could take a man out of the stews but not the stews out of the man.

Murray joined him at the side of the boat, looking across the black water. "Any movement?"

"Not yet. We don't go in until we see Mrs. Kent's signal," Adam said.

Per the plan, Tessa Kent would send up a firework to let Adam and his men know to row in and charge the dock. Their job was to prevent Sweeney and his gang from escaping via the water—by any means necessary.

"This could get messy," Murray commented.

"We have enough firepower to take on the Royal Navy." Adam lifted his brows. "If there's to be a mess tonight, it will not be on our side."

A pause. "Do you ever tire of this?"

"Of what?"

"The fighting. The bloodshed and mayhem."

"It's life." *All I've known.* "Success doesn't come without a price."

"So you've always said."

Silence stretched. Undercurrents of tension bobbed along with the boat. After years of working with Murray, Adam knew the other was brooding over something.

"If you have something to say, say it."

"Many a fellow would envy your wealth." Murray's hands closed around the railing as he glanced at Adam. "You know that, don't you? How lucky you are?"

Although Adam didn't know where the non sequitur was leading, he was certain that it wasn't in a direction he preferred. He did not speak of personal matters with his employees. Indeed, he could count on one hand the men who had the courage to speak to him so freely. He both respected Murray's familiarity and found it irksome.

"Luck had naught to do with it," he said coolly. "But, yes, I'm aware that my hard work has paid off."

"How much is enough?"

"Beg pardon?"

"When will you decide to simply enjoy what you have?"

When I look De Villier in the eyes, and he knows that the man who destroyed him is the son he tried to murder. The son of the woman he abandoned to poverty and indignities. Then—and only then—will I be at peace.

Adam lifted his brows. "What makes you think I do not?"

Murray straightened from the railing. His shoulders went back, as if he was bracing for something unpleasant. "On the way to the pier tonight, you made a stop."

It took an instant for the other's meaning to sink in. When it did, Adam felt a blast of icy rage.

How bloody dare he. *Who does he think he is questioning my private affairs?*

"And when did it become your business to spy on your employer?" he clipped out.

"It's not my business, I know that." Murray raked a hand through his hair. "Goddamnit, Garrity, I'm the last man who should be telling another how to run his life—"

"On this, we are in perfect agreement."

"But do you know what your wife said to me? Before I left this afternoon?"

The notion that the other knew something about Gabriella that Adam did not was incensing. Adam flashed back to the way Murray's tawny head had dipped toward Gabby's. The way the too-handsome rake had murmured intimate good-byes...to *Adam's* wife.

"I do not enjoy guessing games," Adam said, his hands curling.

"Promise me you'll look after Mr. Garrity. I couldn't bear it if anything happened to him."

The words struck Adam like fists of sunshine. Warmth exploded through his chest, a confounding contrast to his cold rage. He exhaled sharply, reminding himself that what went on between him and his wife was no one's business. Least of all his employee's.

"I am capable of looking after myself," he said in glacial tones.

"That's beside the point." Murray shook his head. "You're a lucky bastard to have a wife as devoted as Mrs. Garrity. And to throw that away on—"

"On what?" Adam said with pounding fury.

"On whatever it is you do at Mrs. Wilde's Club," Murray said flatly.

Red flashed across Adam's vision. Not being a fool, he'd realized that his visits to Jeannette's establishment would not go unnoticed. Although his employees were discreet, gossip always found a way to surface. He didn't give a damn what others said or thought about his visits to the bawdy house. What he did care about was Murray's bloody *temerity*. The bastard had some nerve accusing Adam of infidelity and casting himself in the role of Gabriella's protector.

Gabriella is mine.

"You presume to lecture me on my marriage?" he said with lethal softness.

"Mrs. Garrity has been kind to me. I don't want to see her get hurt."

As Murray faced him squarely, like some bleeding knight fighting on Gabriella's behalf, rage decimated Adam's self-control.

"My wife's welfare is none of your damned business." Adam fought to keep his voice even—and the impulse to plant a facer on the bastard. "The same applies to my private affairs. Remember your place, Murray, or I'll have to remind you."

Before Murray could reply, a blue light streaked like a comet across the sky.

"The signal," Kerrigan shouted. "Hoist the anchor, lads! We're going in!"

8

"IT'S COLD IN HERE," CURTIS BILLINGS GRUMBLED FROM HIS cozy seat by the fire. "Is your husband too much of a skinflint to heat this palace of his?"

Gabby kept her smile patient despite the fact that her father had been complaining about something or other since his arrival to see the children's play. They were in the spacious sitting room of the nursery, fires roaring in the double hearths. The other guests, the Strathavens and the Actons, whose children would also be performing, were milling about. Being good friends and considerate guests, they were giving Gabby space to deal with her father's cantankerous mood.

"Would you like more blankets?" she asked. "I could have some fetched—"

"I'm already wrapped up tighter than an Egyptian mummy," her papa said.

He wasn't wrong. His thin frame was engulfed by the warm woolen layers. Even though Gabby visited her father at least once a week, she'd been surprised by how gaunt he'd become, the sunken hollows of his cheeks and pallor of his skin. The few remaining strands of his grey hair clung like seaweed to his age-speckled pate.

With thrumming worry, she said, "Perhaps you'd like something to eat? Chef Pierre has a wonderful soup—"

"I ate before I came." He harrumphed. "A good, sturdy English meal."

"Something hot to drink, then. I'll get you a nice cup of the posset—"

"I don't need posset," he said crossly. "I need a minute with you. Sit down."

Flummoxed, Gabriella obeyed. She couldn't recall the last time her father had voiced a desire to spend time with her. Or if he'd ever done so. Growing up, she'd always longed for his presence, but the bank had demanded most of his time. Now he was finally here...and might soon be taken away from her.

Sorrow and dread tightening her throat, she placed a hand over his. "I'm here, Father."

He pulled his hand away to adjust the blankets, clearing his throat. "Where is your husband?"

"He had, um, urgent business tonight," she mumbled.

Father looked around the nursery, his brows rising as he took in the large, curtained stage at the other end of the room. "Are you certain that he's not just avoiding the circus?"

Gabby could see what he meant. Fiona's play had become quite the production.

Ever since Gabby, the Strathavens, and the Actons had taken their collective offspring to see a performance at Sadler's Wells, the children had been bitten by the theatre bug. Fiona, Gabby's seven-year-old, had been particularly enamored of the experience and had declared her intention to stage her own productions.

Accordingly, Gabby had gone to the toy shop and returned with one of the popular toy theatres. The shopkeeper had claimed that the miniature stage—the size of a dollhouse and designed to fit upon a tabletop—was all the rage amongst youngsters. Children, he said, adored cutting out characters from printed paper-board and staging plays from various playbooks written for tots.

Fiona, as it turned out, was not most children. Although she took after Gabby in coloring with her red hair and blue eyes, her precociousness and ambitious nature clearly came from her father.

"The toy theatre is too *small*," she'd decreed when Gabby had presented her with the gift over breakfast, which was the one meal the family usually shared together. "It's for babes—like Maximillian."

Across the table, her younger brother had predictably scowled.

"I'm not a babe," he'd muttered at his coddled eggs.

"You're only five, and I'm seven," Fi pointed out in lofty tones. "And everyone knows that boys take longer than girls to grow up. Taking that into account, you're more like three. It's a fact of nature; there's naught you can do about it."

Faced with Fi's poise and rather daunting logic, Max—who'd inherited his papa's dark coloring and his mama's shyness—had turned pleading brown eyes to Gabby. Her heart had melted seeing his flushed, chubby cheeks and quivering bottom lip.

"It's not nice to tease your brother," Gabby had said.

"It's not teasing if it's the *truth*." Tossing her auburn ringlets, Fiona had turned to Adam, who'd remained absorbed in his newspaper during the exchange. "Besides, a gentleman is supposed to be strong. He isn't supposed to cry, is he, Papa?"

"A gentleman must be master of himself," came Adam's reply. "Self-discipline before sentiment. Always."

Max's eyes sheened. Gabby didn't think he fully understood what his father meant, but the stern tone was enough of a repri-mand. He quickly blinked, then lowered his head, shoveling in a bite of eggs.

"And if one is going to do a thing, one should do it properly," Fi went on triumphantly. "Isn't that what you always say, Papa?

Please may I have the real thing...instead of this silly toy Mama bought?"

Adam had lowered his newspaper long enough to give his first-born an indulgent look and his usual response to her requests. "Whatever you'd like, poppet."

Fiona's carte blanche had resulted in the footmen building the present stage, which took up a third of the large sitting room. Behind the closed blue velvet curtains, the whispering and giggles of the would-be performers could be heard as they readied for their show.

Gabby wished Adam was here. In fact, she wished he was anywhere but where he presently was. The worry she'd been keeping at bay surged, her fingers lacing tightly in her lap.

"You must keep a firmer rein on the children. On my hellion of a granddaughter especially," her father lectured. "You're far too soft, Gabriella. Who will look after you when I'm gone?"

"Oh, Father, please don't talk of—"

"I won't be here forever," he muttered. "But whatever Garrity does, he cannot get his hands on your money. Thank God I set up that trust to protect you and the children."

Before Gabby could reply, a gong sounded five times. Five minutes until the show started.

"Go attend to your guests, Gabriella." Due to his illness, her father had abrupt spells of fatigue. He yawned, his eyelids suddenly drooping. "I'll watch the play from here."

Seeing that he was nodding off, she tucked the blankets more securely around him and went to join her friends in the row of chairs facing the stage. They'd saved her the seat between Polly, the Duchess of Acton and Emma, the Duchess of Strathaven, the dukes occupying the chairs beside their respective ladies.

"Is your papa all right, Gabby?" The soft inquiry came from Polly, who was ravishingly pretty with golden-brown hair and aquamarine eyes. She was also sweet and sensitive, with an uncanny knack for guessing what one was feeling.

"He's fine. He was just asking about Mr. Garrity," Gabby admitted.

Earlier, she'd told her guests that Adam was off on a mission with Tessa and Harry Kent. She hadn't felt right withholding that information since Harry was the duchesses' brother. Not wanting to cause undue concern, however, she'd kept the details to a minimum.

"I do wish Harry had informed us about this 'meeting' tonight," Emma, the Duchess of Strathaven said.

Gabby had met Emma a decade ago, before the other's marriage to the tall, dark, and wickedly handsome Strathaven. She would be forever grateful to Em for befriending her at a party; to this day, the duchess was one of the most sensible, kind, and down-to-earth ladies of Gabby's acquaintance.

"The mission came up at the last minute," Gabby said quickly. "I'm sure he would have told you otherwise."

"If Harry had let us know, we could have lent a hand," Emma muttered.

"That is precisely why your brother didn't say anything, pet," Strathaven said dryly.

Emma frowned. "I don't follow."

"Harry's quite capable of handling his own affairs and a private fellow by nature. Not to mention, he has married into one of London's most formidable families." The duke quirked a dark brow. "Can you blame the man for avoiding his meddling sisters?"

"I don't meddle." Emma narrowed her tea-colored gaze at her husband. "I simply offer my assistance where it's warranted."

"You involved yourself in a murder investigation where the main suspect was an absolute stranger. Then you proceeded to torment and entice him in equal measure. And I should know," Strathaven said, his jade eyes gleaming, "since I was that stranger."

Although her cheeks were pink, Em said determinedly, "You have to admit you needed my help, Alaric."

"Oh, I needed you all right," her duke drawled softly. "Still do, as a matter of fact."

Gabby hid a wistful smile. This sort of bantering was typical amongst her friends. Acton, a dark-haired Adonis with midnight blue eyes, took this as his cue to whisper something in *his* duchess's ear. Polly turned charmingly rosy, her hand fluttering to rest on her midsection. Although the swell was not yet visible, she'd confided to Gabby that she and her duke were expecting their second child next summer.

Surrounded by the openly affectionate couples, Gabby felt a queer pang...which she quickly relegated to her *Do Not Mope Over* box. She was lucky to have a husband like Adam, who was a generous provider and took splendid care of her and the children. During his proposal, he'd been frank about his stance on romantic love, and she'd agreed to his terms.

She told herself that she was perfectly content with having a husband who was faithful and caring. It would be foolish to long for more, especially given her own paucity of charms. It was enough that Adam accepted her and never made her feel stupid or gauche when she couldn't hold back her professions of love. He was the best of husbands.

And he could be at this minute facing down a cutthroat.

Desperate fear spread through her. Her gaze flew to the cart of refreshments that the butler had wheeled in. Perhaps she could take the edge off by nibbling on one of the choux pastries stuffed with hazelnut cream...

A series of piano chords cut through her thoughts. Miss Thornton, the children's governess, had taken her seat before the instrument at the side of the stage, and her crisp crescendo of notes heralded the start of the play.

"Ladies and Gentlemen!" From behind the curtains came a high, melodic voice, which Gabby recognized as belonging to Lady Olivia, the Strathavens' eldest. "Thank you for attending this premier performance of an original work. Prepare yourself for a tale of tragedy and triumph and a spectacle for the ages."

She paused for Miss Thornton's suspenseful trills.

"You will witness one girl's journey from downtrodden scullery maid to celebrated princess. Before your very eyes, you will see her transformation. Our heroine will impress you with her metamorphosis from caterpillar to butterfly..."

"Did you teach Livy that word?" Strathaven murmured to his wife.

"Which word? There are rather many to choose from in this introduction," Em whispered back.

Her husband's lips twitched. "Our daughter has inherited your brains, no doubt about it."

"...and now, without further ado," their offspring announced, "I invite you all to sit back and immerse yourself in the magic of the theatre. May I present to you the scintillating story of *The Princess and the Dancing Slippers!*"

The next hour raced by. Gabby was enthralled by the children's creativity and talent. Fiona was spectacular in her lead role as Princess Gianna, and Lady Olivia sparkled in her various turns as the bosom chum, evil queen, and stable boy. Lord Christopher, Strathaven's heir, excelled as the knight in shining armor (made of tin pans tied together with string). Even the Actons' tot, young Lord Stephan, did a credible job as the dragon, smashing towers of toy blocks with a loud roar.

The only mishap was when poor Max forgot his cue to enter. Cast in the non-speaking role of a tree, he was supposed to appear when Princess Gianna danced her way—thanks to the magic slippers—into the Forest of Mystery. But apparently he developed a case of stage fright, and Fiona could be heard saying in a furious undertone, "Hurry up, dunderhead! You're supposed to be on!"

He scrambled onto the stage. His pudgy face was shiny with sweat beneath his crown of twigs, his leafy branches trembling. Gabby let out a secret sigh of relief when his part was over and applauded him vigorously as he dashed off the boards.

When the performance ended, the audience jumped to their feet, clapping enthusiastically and crying "Bravo!" and "Encore!" Everyone came out to take their bows...everyone except Max, Gabby noticed with a stab of worry.

As the young actors disappeared behind the curtain to change out of their costumes, Polly touched her arm. "Do you think Maximillian is all right?"

"The poor dear," Gabby said in a low voice. "He does try, you know."

"I thought he did a wonderful job." Emma elbowed her husband. "Don't you agree, Strathaven?"

"Absolutely. Max nailed the part of the tree." The duke paused. "He was, er, very leafy."

"And he's been so supportive of the others during the rehearsals," Em added. "Christopher has benefited greatly from Max's encouragement."

"Stephan as well," Polly chimed in.

The children approached in an excited stampede.

"How did you like it?" Lady Olivia demanded of her parents.

"It was an exceptional production, poppet." Strathaven ruffled her raven ringlets, and she beamed with pleasure.

"What about me?" Standing beside his sister, Lord Christopher looked expectantly at his parents. "Was I good as the knight?"

"You were entirely convincing, lad," his papa assured him.

"I particularly enjoyed the part where Princess Gianna danced her way to freedom," Emma said. "It was a wonderful twist that it wasn't the knight who rescued her in the end, but her belief in her own magic."

"That part was Fiona's idea," Lady Olivia said graciously.

"Well done, Fiona," Strathaven said.

"Thank you, Your Grace." Fi's gaze was downcast.

Seeing the other children flanked by their loving parents, Gabby could guess the cause of her daughter's subdued state. She knew how much Fiona had wanted Adam to see the play: the girl had been talking about it for weeks.

"You were wonderful, dear." Gabby injected extra brightness into her praise. "You all were."

Fi traced the ground with the toe of her dancing slipper. "I wish Papa was here to see it."

"He wanted to be here ever so much," Gabby said quietly. "But he got called away on an important matter."

"He *always* gets called away."

Of course, Gabby's father had come over just in time to catch his granddaughter's statement. Not wanting to add to her papa's animosity toward Adam or air the family laundry in front of guests, Gabby said, "You can tell Papa all about it later. Now have you seen Max?"

Fiona's chin jutted out, her blue eyes flashing. "Max, Max, Max! He's all you care about."

Caught off-guard by the outburst, Gabby didn't know how to respond.

"Is that any way to speak to your mama, young lady?" Father cut in. At his reproving frown, his granddaughter lowered her gaze. "You must apologize. At once."

Fiona's bottom lip trembled.

"It's late," Gabby said quickly. "I'm sure Fiona spoke out of turn because she's tired. Isn't that so, dear?"

Casting a nervous glance at her grandpapa, Fiona gave a small nod.

"I think we've had enough drama for one evening." Polly came over, putting a gentle arm around Fiona's stiff shoulders. "Why don't we take refreshment with the children while you find Max, Gabby?"

"Thank you." Gabby summoned a smile. "He and I will be back in a minute."

She hurried behind the stage, where the children's governess was tidying up the props and costumes.

"He's in his bedchamber, ma'am," Miss Thornton said quietly. "He said he wants to be alone."

With a nod of thanks, Gabby headed to the adjoining room and knocked on the door.

"Go away," came Max's muffled voice.

"It's me, dear," Gabby said lightly. "We're having refreshments now. Don't you want to celebrate with your friends?"

"No. I don't want to see anyone. *Go away*."

Hearing the hitched breaths that punctuated the words, Gabby turned the knob and went in.

Her son was sitting on the floor beside his bed, his arms around his raised knees. He'd thrown off his crown of twigs but was still wearing the brown burlap tunic that had been part of his costume. At her approach, he raised his head, and her chest ached to see his tear-splotched face. She went and sat next to him on the floor—rather awkwardly, given the bulk of her petticoats.

He dashed the back of his hand across his small face, smudging tears and snot. "I said I want to be left alone."

"Sometimes I feel that way too." Rummaging in the hidden pocket of her skirt, Gabby found a rumpled handkerchief and handed it over. "But in the end I feel better after I talk about it."

Clutching the linen, Max blurted, "I ruined the play."

"No, you didn't. The play was ever so good. All the parents thought so—"

"I was the only one who didn't get it right. I never get *anything* right."

Gabby's heart squeezed. "That's not true, dear."

"I'm not like Fiona." Tears swam in his dark eyes. "Papa loves her best because she's good at everything."

"Oh, Max." Gabby put an arm around her youngest's slumped

shoulders, and he didn't pull away. "You and Fi are different, as siblings often are. But that doesn't mean one is better than the other. Papa loves you both equally. *I* love you both."

"You have to say that because you're my mama," Max sniffled.

"I'm saying it because it's true," Gabby said firmly. "You and Fiona are both my angels, and I'm the luckiest mama in the entire world."

"Truly? You truly think that?"

"Truly, my dearest."

Max let out a hiccupping sigh. "I'm glad Papa wasn't here tonight to see me make a hash of things. And to see me blubbering like a babe. You won't tell him, will you, Mama? Promise me you won't."

After a hesitation, Gabby said, "I promise. But there's no shame in making a mistake, my lamb. Everyone does...*I* do, certainly. It's part of life."

"Papa and Fiona never make mistakes."

"They do. They're just more..."—she struggled to find the right words—"poised about it."

"Why can't I be like them, Mama?" Max said glumly.

The pain in her child's eyes made her throat swell. "Because you are yourself, Max. You're a good boy, and that is what counts."

"I hope you're right." He didn't sound convinced.

"I'm positive that I am. Do you know what else I know?"

"What?"

"You'll feel better if you join the others for refreshments." She ruffled her son's dark curls, dislodging a few stray leaves. "Cook made your favorite lemon cake."

Rising, she held out her hand. After a quivery sigh, Max reached out, his small fingers curling around hers. Together they went to join their guests.

9

FROM THE PROW OF THE ANCHORED BOAT, ADAM MONITORED the situation on the dock. The fighting had just started; as far as he could tell, neither side had the upper hand. Mayhem ruled the night with gunfire, smoke, and the shouts of brawling men.

In other words, just another day at the office.

Murray emerged from the fray, jumping onto the boat's deck. Gunpowder streaked his clothes, a shallow cut upon his cheek.

"What's causing the delay?" Adam asked.

"Sweeney's got an army," Murray said through harsh breaths. "They outnumber us."

Adam removed a pair of pistols from his pockets. Cocked them.

Murray's brows inched up. "*You* are going in? Are you certain you want to do that?"

The other's incredulity grated on Adam's nerves. Hell, he'd started in this business whilst the other had been toddling around in nappies on a country estate somewhere. Although he didn't often dirty his hands these days, he had full possession of the skills he'd honed in the streets. There was no bloody reason for

Murray to treat him as if he were some ancient relic incapable of handling himself in a fight.

"To get the job done properly, I'll have to do it myself," Adam said shortly.

He leapt onto the dock, heading into the heart of the melee.

Through the smoke and grappling figures, he spotted Kerrigan. A brute had Adam's guard pinned to the ground, a blade poised above the other's neck. Adam took aim and discharged his pistol; the brute slumped to the side, and Kerrigan shoved him off, sitting up and gasping. Before Adam could go over, he was tackled from behind, his used pistol skittering across the dock.

Adam rolled with his opponent, using momentum to gain the upper hand. He plowed his gloved fist into the other's face, the crunch of bone a visceral satisfaction. He evaded the other's clawing hands, landing punch after punch. When he stood over his vanquished foe, bloodlust flowed hotly through his veins.

Leading the charge, he dispatched another pair of villains, one with his pistol, the other with the blade he unsheathed from his boot. *Just like old times.* His mind was crystal-clear, cold, focused as his muscles burned pleasantly from use. He took on attackers from left and right, leaving a trail of incapacitated enemies in his wake.

Finally, chest heaving, he arrived at the side of the dock, assessing the situation. He and his men had gained the upper hand now; the enemy either lay fallen or were running off with their tails between their legs. In the distance, he heard the shouts of victory from Tessa Kent's army, who'd charged the front of the warehouse.

Another victory...and another step closer to my vengeance.

For Tessa was now in his debt. She owed him for his part in the conquest tonight, and he would be calling in that favor when the time came. While he eviscerated De Villier financially, he might request the use of Tessa's men to dismantle De Villier's railway foundry brick by brick...best not to leave any loose ends, after all.

As heady triumph filled him, his thoughts veered unexpectedly toward Gabriella. He flashed to an image of her innocently sleeping in her bed, and the heat in his blood reached a boiling point. There was no better way to discharge the aftermath of battle than fucking.

He wondered if he could allow himself to break his own rules twice in one day. He probably shouldn't. But the notion of burying himself in his wife's tight, wet quim, losing himself in her sweetness—

A movement caught the corner of his eye. A man coming out of nowhere, running toward him, pistol glinting...

Christ.

The thought exploded in his head as gunfire ripped through the night. The punch of the bullet made him stagger, his feet losing purchase. Suddenly, he was falling backward through the air. His head struck something, pain erupting, red splattering his vision. He heard a splash, felt the cold downward drag. Before panic could claw its way to the surface, icy blackness closed over him.

10

AFTER TUCKING THE EXHAUSTED CHILDREN INTO BED, GABBY went to her chambers.

Although she was physically tired, sleep eluded her. She lay awake, watching shadows chase across the embroidered vines of the canopy. She'd left the lamp on, a behavior carried over from her childhood. Back then, she'd been afraid of the dark, convinced that monsters lurked in the wardrobe and beneath the bed. She'd wake up in the middle of the night, bathed in sweat, nameless dread pounding in her heart.

The phantom worries followed her into adolescence and womanhood. The truth was she'd never been a sound sleeper. Indeed, the only thing that seemed to help was when Adam made his weekly bedtime visits. After making love to her, he would stay until she fell asleep.

She always slept well on Wednesday nights.

Thinking of her husband caused the tide of worry to rise ever higher. She glanced anxiously at the Ormolu clock on her bedside table.

It's nearly two in the morning. Where is he? Something's wrong, I can feel it...

At the sound of voices, she bolted upright against the pillows. Relief filled her as she heard footsteps coming up the stairs. She jumped out of bed, dragging on a wrapper.

Adam's back. She hugged the knowledge to herself. *Everything is all right.*

She heard a knock on her bedroom door and dashed over, flinging it open.

Nell stood there. The maid's apple-cheeked face was unusually somber.

Gabby's giddiness fizzled. "What's happened? Where's Mr. Garrity?"

"He's back, ma'am. With Mr. Murray. There's a physician with them—"

Gabby didn't wait to hear more. She was already running, fear propelling every step. She burst into Adam's suite. Mr. Murray and a sandy-haired man whirled around at her approach...but her gaze was focused on the figure lying on the bed.

Adam. His face bone-white. He was so still...*too still.*

His chest surged, and a hitched sob broke from her lips.

She stumbled to the bedside, putting a trembling hand on her husband's jaw. She felt the scrape of his night beard against her palm, the terrifying chill of his skin. An angry, swelling cut spanned his right temple. His hair stuck in damp whorls on his forehead, and his clothes were sodden.

Her gaze caught on the torn fabric on his right side. On the lethal-looking dark stain.

"What happened?" She forced the words from her numb lips.

"He was shot—not fatally," Mr. Murray said hurriedly when she gasped. "Mrs. Garrity, this is Dr. Abernathy. He's been attending to your husband."

"Good evening, ma'am." The sandy-haired fellow bowed.

"You're not Dr. Abernathy," she said with a frown.

Dr. Abernathy, who'd attended to the family's ailments for years, was a crusty Scotsman, with beetled brows and greying sideburns. This man looked to be in his early twenties...at *most*. His handsome boyishness might turn female heads, but it didn't inspire Gabby's confidence in his degree of experience.

"Dr. Douglas Abernathy, at your service. My father, the Dr. Abernathy with whom you are acquainted, is attending a birthing in Hampshire." The young physician's manner was competent and brisk, his Scottish brogue less pronounced than his father's. "I examined the patient in the carriage. The good news is the bullet itself didn't cause too much damage. A flesh wound to the right side, with no organs or bones hit. I was able to staunch the bleeding."

She took in the information with fervent gratitude.

"The next step is to properly clean and dress the wound," the doctor went on.

At that moment, footmen arrived with pitchers of steaming water, towels, and an empty cart, setting up the equipment per the physician's orders. Dr. Abernathy unpacked his leather satchel onto the cart, laying out the instruments of his profession with the precision of a boy lining up toy soldiers.

He used a pair of pinchers to pick up what appeared to be a large darning needle, passing it back and forth through the flame of a candle. "The task ahead is rather grisly, I'm afraid. Perhaps you'd care to wait outside, ma'am?"

"I'm staying." Swallowing, she asked, "You've, um, done this before?"

Dr. Abernathy went to scrub his hands thoroughly in the washbasin, using water from a steaming ewer. "I've recently returned from six years of medical training at the University of Edinburgh, practicing at the city's largest hospital."

That was reassuring, at least.

"Tell me how I can help," she said.

"Your job will be to keep your husband calm whilst I clean his wound with a saline solution. I've given him some laudanum, but it won't ease the pain entirely. After that I'll stitch him up—"

Adam's moan caused Gabby to whirl around. She gently brushed the hair off his forehead.

"Everything's going to be all right, my love," she said softly. "You're home now."

His lashes lifted, revealing his dark and glassy gaze. She could tell that he wasn't seeing her.

"Won't drown...not a bleedin' kitten..." he mumbled.

Dr. Abernathy wheeled the cart to the other side of the bed. "Keep talking to him, ma'am."

"You're safe, darling." She forced the words over the lump in her throat. "We'll have you right as rain in no time."

Wielding a pair of scissors, the physician expertly snipped at Adam's garments. The fabrics fell away readily until he reached Adam's shirt. Gabby's breath lodged at the sight of the massive crimson bloom on the linen. When Dr. Abernathy tried to pull the shirt away from the wound, Adam jolted with vicious force, nearly throwing Gabby from the bed.

"Mr. Murray, if you'd secure the patient's left arm. And you two,"—Dr. Abernathy nodded at the footmen—"one at his legs, the other over here at the right arm. All of you hold him as still as you can. Mrs. Garrity, keep him distracted."

Nodding, Gabby remained by Adam's side, giving Mr. Murray enough room to do his part. Brushing her trembling fingers through her husband's thick hair, she channeled her strength and began telling the story from the children's play. The physician moistened Adam's shirt, easing the linen away while Adam jerked, groaning. At the sight of the gaping, oozing crater of flesh, a buffle-headed sensation swept over her.

"You're doing fine, Mrs. Garrity." Mr. Murray's voice grounded her. His brow was sheened from the effort of holding her husband still. "Now what happened when Princess Gianna found her dancing slippers?"

Somehow, Gabby managed to continue her tale. As the physician rinsed and cleaned the lesion, she babbled on about mysterious forests, magical castles, and triumphant princesses. The needle flashed, pulling the tattered edges of skin together, darning flesh as if it were a torn stocking. Tamping down nausea, she kept talking until finally, *finally* the doctor completed his handiwork.

"It's done, my love," she said shakily.

Adam didn't reply; he'd lost consciousness.

"It's for the better. His body needs rest to heal." Dr. Abernathy uncapped a glass jar, removing its grayish-brown contents with a spoon. Carefully, he smeared the gruel-like substance over the stitched flesh.

"What is that?" Gabby asked queasily.

"A healing poultice made from moldy bread and honey. To minimize the risk of infection." With Mr. Murray's help, the physician wound a bandage around Adam's torso and covered him with a blanket. "My work is done for now. I'll be by to check on the patient tomorrow."

Gabby gave him an anxious look. "How long will it take for my husband to recover?"

At Dr. Abernathy's somber expression, her stomach plummeted. He drew her away from the bed, Mr. Murray joining them.

"The bullet wound should heal in a fortnight," the physician said quietly. "But there is another concern."

"What concern?" she blurted.

He and Mr. Murray exchanged looks.

Her voice rose. "What aren't you telling me?"

"When Garrity was shot, the force of the bullet knocked him off his feet." It was Mr. Murray who replied, his tone grim. "He hit his head and fell into the water. I saw this from the other end of the dock. I don't know where that shooter came from, thought we had the enemy under wraps. I ran over, dispatching the assailant and diving in after Garrity. He wasn't breathing when I got him out. But I was able to pump the water from his lungs and revive him."

Gabby clutched her hands tightly.

"Your husband is a fit man in his prime, which bodes well for his recovery," Dr. Abernathy said. "As we cannot predict the future, we must concentrate on what we can do for him in the present. There'll likely be a fever, and our immediate job will be to keep him as comfortable as we can."

A million thoughts skirled in her head, but she knew he was right. She had to remain calm. She couldn't let herself become overwhelmed or paralyzed by fears about the future.

Adam needs me now.

Drawing her shoulders back, she asked, "You will leave instructions for my husband's care?"

"Of course, ma'am." The physician looked relieved, as if he'd been expecting her to fall apart. "And I'll be by to check on him on the morrow."

"I am obliged, sir."

After the physician departed, Gabby returned to Adam's side. His eyes were closed, the wound on his temple pronounced against his ashen skin. A deep divot formed between his brows, his jaw taut. Beneath the blanket, his chest rose and fell in rapid, shallow surges. It seemed impossible that her potent, vital husband could be this vulnerable. She took his hand in both of hers, willing some of her own strength into him.

Please God, she prayed, *see my husband well. I'll do anything... anything at all...*

"Everything will be all right," Mr. Murray said gruffly.

"Yes." Forcing back tears, she said, "Thank you, sir, for your heroism this night. We owe you more than we can ever repay—"

"If Garrity wants to thank me, he can do it himself." Mr. Murray attempted a smile, which came out rather lopsided. "He has the toughest hide of anyone I know. He'll pull through."

Gabby fought the quiver in her throat. In her soul.

She had to be strong—for Adam's sake.

"I know he will," she said.

He has to. Please God, he has to.

THE DARKNESS WAS WINNING.

Adam fought it, but the freezing depths pulled him deeper and deeper. Fear suffocated him, filling his lungs, weighing him down like bricks dragging him to his watery grave.

No, I won't die like this. Like a bloody drowned kitten. Won't give him the satisfaction...

He was weary and cold...so bleeding cold...but something in him wouldn't give up. Pain burned, yet he resisted yielding to oblivion. He struggled on through searing flame and bone-cracking chill. For an infinity, he fought gravity's pull, striving for the surface. For survival.

Sink or swim, sink or swim, not going to sink...

Just as the last of his strength was leaving him and he knew he could fight no more, he saw a glimmer...a shaft of light piercing the darkness...

"What've you found, Mr. Garrity?" Even distorted by water, the girl's voice was bubbly and sweet, like lemonade mixed with champagne. "Is it a treasure?"

"Ne'er know what gifts the Mother Thames will bring," a man's voice replied. "Whate'er it is, it's heavy, that's for certain."

Adam felt a jerk as he was pulled upward. The depths grew lighter and lighter, voices clearer and clearer...

"Bloody 'ell! 'Tis a lad."

"Is 'e dead?" came the girl's trembly voice.

"Give us some room, dove, and we'll see."

Weight descended on Adam's chest, the pressure on his broken ribs forcing a cry from his lips.

"That's right, boy. Cough it up," the man said. "Swallowed 'alf the Thames, you did."

He choked, brine spewing from his mouth and nose. He vomited and vomited until his throat was raw. When he was empty, he tried to open his eyes, the lids crusted together with the salt of the river and his own tears. His lashes came unstuck, and he blinked as he saw the face of an angel. A girl with blonde ringlets haloed by light.

"You ain't dead," she said in that sparkling sweet voice.

"Wh-where am I?" he croaked.

"On a lighter wif me and Mr. Garrity. We were scavenging for goods but found you instead." She tilted her head. "I'm Jessabelle. Who're you?"

"Jessabelle," he murmured. "I...I'm..."

His teeth chattered. Cold and heat flashed through him simultaneously, his limbs shaking. Darkness replaced the images and voices, a whirlpool of nothingness beckoning. He felt a gentle hand upon his forehead, calming him as oblivion claimed him once more.

Gabby jerked her fingers from her husband's brow. His skin was hot; as Dr. Abernathy had predicted, a fever had set in. For the past three days and nights, she'd kept vigil, dozing in fits by Adam's side, waking to his incoherent moans. Although Mrs. Page and Nell had offered to keep watch so that Gabby could get some rest, Gabby had refused to leave him.

She'd replaced one cool compress after another as each became steamy with his feverish heat. Using a spoon, she'd painstakingly fed him water and soothed his chapped lips with salve.

Mostly she'd prayed and prayed and prayed.

But what made her pull away now wasn't the burning flame of Adam's skin. Shaking, she rose from her chair and went to rinse a compress at the washbasin, another worry joining all the rest.

Who is Jessabelle? Why is my husband calling this woman's name?

Adam had never mentioned a Jessabelle before. Gabby would know, wouldn't she, if her husband had a female acquaintance... one with whom he was apparently so familiar that he would utter her name in the throes of delirium? And if Gabby didn't know this woman, why would Adam keep the knowledge from her? Unless...unless...

No, stop it. He promised he would be faithful to you...and Adam is a man of his word. He's never lied to you.

"Jessabelle...*don't go*..." This time, Adam's voice had a raw, guttural, *tormented* quality to it.

Virulent heat built inside Gabby as if she'd caught her own fever, one born of suspicion and doubt. She couldn't stop her mind from wandering back to a few months ago. To that time when she'd found Adam thoroughly foxed in his study. It was the one and only time she'd ever seen her husband drunk...and free of his usual restraint.

Shocked, she'd asked him if something was the matter.

And he'd slurred, "Someone important died. In a workplace fire."

When she'd tried to ask him more, he'd put a stop to her questioning by kissing her. By doing unspeakably intimate things that made her blush and quiver just to think of them. Afterward, he'd passed out, and the next day he'd recalled nothing of what transpired between them that night...which was probably just as well. She still didn't know what to make of that dark, animalistic side of her husband.

Or of her own shamefully wanton response.

The next morning, she'd read in the papers that a massive fire had consumed a notorious brothel called The Gilded Pearl. Stunned by the coincidence and unable to contain her suspicions, she'd gone to Adam. Asked him if the person he'd lost—if the person he'd gotten drunk over—had had something to do with this house of ill repute.

He'd denied having a mistress or lover.

Faced with his frigid displeasure and her own pounding anxiety, she'd let the matter drop.

But now all her doubts came boiling to the surface. Was this Jessabelle the one who died in the bawdy house fire? Who was she to Adam, why was he moaning her name with such anguish...?

Do you really want to know?

Fear churned her insides.

As she wrung the towel over the basin, she told herself that Adam wouldn't lie to her. He'd said that he had no mistress, and she had to believe him. Because if she couldn't trust her husband —the man she loved with her heart and soul—then what sort of marriage did she have?

I will be faithful to you, take care of you, see that you want for nothing.

He'd given her his word: that had to be good enough for her.

Besides, she reasoned, Jessabelle could be anyone...not necessarily a lover. Not even necessarily someone important. Who knew what a fever could do to one's mind, the hodge-podge of memories it might unearth? Perhaps in his delirium, Adam was recalling a childhood friend or a maidservant or...even an animal.

Why, Jessabelle would be an excellent name for a cat—or, better yet, a *cow*. Picturing a giant black-and-white beast with swollen udders comforted Gabby.

"Gabriella..."

Adam's voice broke her reverie. She hurried back to his bedside. His head was turning agitatedly on the pillow, his brows pulled together and features sheened with sweat.

"I'm here, my love," she said soothingly.

She laid the rinsed towel upon his brow. Her pulse quickened at the contrast between the cool cloth and his burning skin. Dear God, when would this fever abate? She chastised herself for worrying over the mysterious Jessabelle while her husband's health was in a precarious state.

"Don't go," he muttered. "Don't leave me..."

"I'm not going anywhere." Her throat tight, she cupped his bristly cheek. "I'm right by your side, my darling, where I'll always be."

The lines on his face eased. He mumbled something, his words slackening into incoherence as he drifted off. As he entered some restless state between wakefulness and sleep.

Returning to the chair by his side, Gabby kept watch and prayed.

HE OPENED HIS EYES, BLINKING GROGGILY.

As his vision adjusted to the dimness, he found himself staring up at green pleats...a tester bed? Matching green silk curtains hung at the sides, tied back with tasseled cords. His gaze jerked beyond the bed to the high-ceilinged chamber filled with dark furnishings and Persian rugs. There were gilt-framed paintings on the walls. A fire flickered in a marble hearth.

It was a palatial suite, fit for a king.

Where the bloody hell am I?

He tried to sit up—agony shot through his right side. He gasped, falling back, his head landing on soft pillows. When he regained his breath, he took stock of himself. He patted the site of the pain; beneath the sleep shirt was a thick wad of bandaging...had he been injured? In addition to the stabbing in his torso, he felt a throbbing on the right side of his head and touched the spot gingerly. Christ, there was an egg-sized bump on his temple.

Cautiously, he scanned the rest of his body, moving limbs, wiggling toes. When everything seemed intact and accounted for, he exhaled...and winced. Each breath felt like knives scoring the back of his throat. A thought emerged through the fog in his brain.

Water...I need water.

Carefully this time, he leveraged himself upward, grimacing as the contracting muscles burned in protest. There was a chair next to the bed, a small table with an empty glass. He scanned the room and saw a pitcher sitting on a half-moon console several feet away.

Gritting his teeth, he pushed aside the blankets and slowly swung his legs over the side of the bed. *That wasn't so difficult, was it?* His feet touched the carpet, thick soft wool squishing between his toes. Buoyed by his success, he stood, panting slightly from the piercing sensation in his side. *You can do it, a few more steps...*

He took a step—and a strange, floaty feeling overcame him. A buzzing filled his ears. His knees buckled, the carpet flying up at him with dizzying speed. He landed with an agonizing thud.

Pain blackened his vision. "Bloody *fuck*."

"Dear *heavens*. Oh, my poor darling, let me help you!"

He managed to catch his breath...only to lose it again as he looked up.

A goddess was rushing toward him: Venus in the flesh.

Her flame-red hair cascaded over her ruffled pink dressing gown. Her cheeks were rounded and smooth, freckles sprinkled across her little nose like specks of gold leaf clinging to alabaster. She got down on the floor beside him, easing his head onto her lap. And his pain was momentarily forgotten as he looked up into eyes bluer than heaven.

"Are you hurt? Oh, my dearest, why didn't you wait for me? I only left for a moment to check on the children. They've been climbing the walls of the nursery, ever so eager to see you." Words flowed from her cherry-ripe lips in a seemingly endless stream; dazedly, he thought he'd be content to lie here forever, his head upon the soft bank of her thighs, her voice as soothing as a meadow brook. "No, you mustn't try to get up by yourself. Here, lean against me: let's see if we can get you sitting up first."

She helped him, propping his head against her bosom, and even in his current state he felt a flicker of lust. Christ, but she was perfectly formed. Beneath the silk and ruffles, her tits were large and firm; as he turned his head, his cheek brushed against the enticing bump of a nipple.

He looked wonderingly at her.

"Who are you?" he asked.

Her sky-blue eyes got even huger. "You...you don't recognize me?"

He flashed to an image...of a painting or real life? In his foggy state, he didn't know. But he knew the image was of her, this woman, her naked curves lush and glowing. In one hand she held roses as red as her hair and nipples; her other hand was positioned over her sex, her delicate fingers hiding what he somehow knew was a wet, hot, and decadent pussy.

Beneath his sleepshirt, his cock throbbed along with his head.

"You do know who I am...don't you?" she said haltingly.

Some goddess-like wench I've tupped before? But her manner wasn't that of a lightskirt. Confused, he shook his head—and wished he hadn't. The room started to spin again.

"I'm Gabriella," she said in a tremulous voice. "Your wife."

This gorgeous creature was his *wife?* Bugger him, he was *married?*

Why don't I remember her? He tried to think, couldn't with the room whirling like a blasted dervish. A hammer pounded against his skull, and another realization detonated in his brain.

Amidst the spinning darkness, words scraped from his throat. "Bloody hell, who am *I?*"

The last thing he saw was her rounded eyes before blackness swallowed him.

∽

"You are saying my husband's state is *normal?*" Gabby asked in disbelief.

It was two hours later, after Dr. Abernathy had arrived and completed a thorough examination of Adam. Leaving her husband under the watchful care of Mrs. Page, Gabby was meeting with the physician in the upstairs parlor. She needed privacy to discuss her concerns.

"Not normal per se. But not abnormal given Mr. Garrity's injuries." Seated across from her, the physician looked more earnestly boyish than ever. His sandy hair had an unruly cowlick, and beneath his square chin, his cravat was a trifle askew. "Your husband was shot, knocked unconscious, and nearly drowned. Given all that, he's doing remarkably well."

"*Well?* He doesn't know who he is! He doesn't recognize me"— she clapped a hand against her chest—"his wife of *eight years.*"

"I understand how stressful this must be, Mrs. Garrity."

For some reason, the physician's tone, which was no doubt meant to be soothing, rubbed her nerves the wrong way. It must be her lack of sleep, the constant worrying. But, truly, how could this... this *man-child* understand what it was like to have a spouse who didn't remember anything of one's marriage—or anything at all?

She bit her lip and said nothing.

"I've attended other cases involving a near-drowning," he went on. "In many of them, there was some memory loss, related to the deprivation of air, I believe. Several patients had no recollection of their histories, nor the circumstances surrounding the accident itself."

Trepidation slithered down Gabby's spine. "Is this memory loss...permanent?"

"Not necessarily." The physician leaned forward, his grey eyes somber. "Several of my patients made full recoveries, regaining all their memories, knowledge, and abilities. With your husband, I would expect a positive prognosis, given his brief period under the water and his excellent general health. Indeed, the wound on his side is healing even better than expected. Shouldn't trouble him at all in a fortnight or so."

With burgeoning relief, she asked, "How long will it take for him to regain his memories?"

"I cannot say for certain, nor can I make any guarantees. But I will say that for my patients who recovered fully from amnesia, the recuperation period took from days to a year."

A year of Adam not knowing who he is? Panic drummed in her chest. *Not knowing who I am, who the children are?*

And, dear God, what about Adam's business? It was his life's work, his pride and joy. While other men might try to hide their roots in trade, Adam was proud of the empire he'd built out of nothing.

"How will he function in his current state?" she burst out.

"Oddly enough, the loss of memory, in my experience, did not seem to bother the patients over much. Perhaps they were preoccupied by the task of relearning the world and themselves; they exhibited an openness, a curiosity and adaptability...not unlike that of children. They took their initial limitations in stride." Clearing his throat, Dr. Abernathy added, "Their families, on the other hand, suffered more during this phase, for they had full recollection of how the patient used to be prior to the accident. They had to grapple with old expectations and fears about the future."

"You do not know my husband, sir." Gabby shook her head. "He is a driven man, one of great ambition. He will not take kindly to anything that keeps him from his work."

"He will have no choice but to accept his recovery as it comes," the physician said bluntly.

"What can I do? There must be something..."

"What the patient needs most is time and peace to heal. The best thing you can do, ma'am, is to minimize his exposure to stressful circumstances. First and foremost, his work must be delegated for now."

"Mr. Murray is looking after his business affairs." Dear Mr. Murray—she and Adam owed so much to him. "I'm certain he will be willing to continue doing so."

"Excellent. As for the domestic sphere, you must set firm limits if the patient insists upon doing too much too soon. He could have undone my handiwork with that fall he took this morning," the physician said sternly. "He's lucky that no further damage was done."

"I'll keep a better eye on him," she promised.

The other's expression softened. "If your husband is as driven as you say, your job will not be an easy one. But he cannot force himself to recover more quickly or to remember the past. Attempts to do so will only cause harm and perhaps a regression. What he needs is rest, and his memories will hopefully return in due course."

"What about the children? They are rather...lively," she said with a frisson of worry. "Will their visits be too taxing for my husband?"

"I shouldn't think so. Indeed, interacting with family and friends may aid the recovery of Mr. Garrity's memories," Dr. Abernathy assured her.

She straightened her shoulders. "I'll do everything in my power to aid his recovery."

"Your devotion is admirable." The young doctor paused. "May I ask how you are faring, ma'am?"

Faced with the unexpected question, Gabby didn't know how to answer. She hadn't thought about herself; she'd been entirely wrapped up in Adam.

"I'm fine," she said self-consciously.

"How much have you been sleeping, Mrs. Garrity?"

Dr. Abernathy's scrutiny made her squirm in her chair. She realized that she must look a fright, unwashed and wearing stained clothes. She'd waved off Nell's efforts to create a proper coiffure in favor of an expedient braid. Her eyes felt heavy, and she knew they must be puffy and shadowed by fatigue.

"I, um, don't know exactly. But I'm sure I dozed off here and there," she said awkwardly.

"And the last meal you've eaten?"

Goodness, when had that been? Consumed by anxiety, she'd lost her appetite entirely.

"Perhaps breakfast...yesterday," she confessed.

"I must advise you to take better care of yourself, madam." Dr. Abernathy's tone was firm yet gentle. "The caregiver's journey is as arduous as that of the patient, and you must prepare yourself for the travails ahead. Who do you turn to in your hour of need?"

Adam, came the immediate answer. *He's my world...my everything.*

"Family members, perhaps?" the doctor prompted.

"I have my father, but he has been unwell of late." Guilt pricked her; in the week since Adam's injury, she hadn't looked in on her papa. "I don't wish to burden him further."

"Friends, then. People you could turn to for assistance?"

The Kents and their spouses had all paid visits to offer support. As had the Duke of Ranelagh and Somerville and Maggie Foley, Glory's grateful parents. Given her frazzled state, Gabby hadn't entertained the well-wishers for long, but they'd been kind and understanding, offering to help in any way they could. As grateful as Gabby was to have true friends, she'd never been good at asking for help. Moreover, Adam was a man who valued privacy, and the few times she'd confided her domestic concerns to others, she'd experienced a niggling sense of unease, as if she were betraying him.

She knew that things were different this time. She couldn't handle this situation alone.

"I have friends who would help me," she said.

"Then do not hesitate to call upon them. Or me." The doctor rose.

"Thank you." Recalling her churlish thoughts earlier, she added, "You've been a blessing during this difficult time. Truly, sir."

He bowed then surprised her by taking her hand between both of his. His grip was strong, lightly callused. "Have a proper meal, Mrs. Garrity, and a nap afterward. Doctor's orders."

She managed a smile. "I shall try."

"Do more than try, ma'am," he advised. "You have a long battle ahead, and you'll need all the strength you can muster."

13

ADAM CAME AWAKE, AND THE FIRST THING HE NOTICED WAS the absence of fog: his head was as clear as a newly washed window. He saw the green pleats of the canopy, registering that he was in that strange, lavish bedchamber again. Not a dream, then? He turned his head on the pillow: there she was, the red-haired Venus, dozing in a chair beside the bed.

No...not Venus.

She'd claimed that she was his *wife*.

He sat up slowly, discovering the pains were still there, though duller and less insistent. Propping himself up against the pillows, he just looked at her. Her long auburn lashes quivered against her creamy cheeks, her generous bosom rising and falling, the ruffles on her pink dressing gown stirring like leaves in a breeze. Her hair was a sleek waterfall of fire.

She wasn't part of some fever-dream. This fancy place wasn't either.

Why can't I remember anything?

Searching his mind for memories was like running through a dark, winding alleyway. No light to guide him, nothing to find, crashing into wall after wall. Frustration built as did the ache in his head. *Who am I? How did I get here?* As he tried to remember, the pounding increased at his injured temple, spreading to the back of his skull. An agonizing haze began to descend.

He needed something for the pain. Couldn't afford to lose his senses again.

A word flickered in the misty recesses of his mind.

The goddess: she'd given him her name.

"Gabriella," he said hoarsely.

Her eyes flew open, as if she'd only been floating on the surface of sleep. Her pure blue gaze focused on him, widening, and she rose in a flurry of pink, hastening to his side.

"Adam, you're awake," she said tremulously. "How are you feeling?"

Adam...is that my name? Why don't I remember it? Why don't I remember you?

He stared at her, uncertain how to answer.

"I...I'd like water," he said at length.

"Of course. You must be ever so parched." As if his wish were her command, she spun around, heading to the half-moon console that held a pitcher and array of glasses, chattering all the while. "It's been nearly two days since you lost consciousness...the second time, I mean. You were feverish for three days prior to that. I tried to give you water with a spoon, but most of it dribbled out. I was ever so worried, but the physician said your body needed the sleep to heal." She came back with a full glass, her smile so dazzling that he had to blink. "Here, let me help you with this."

She placed the glass at his lips, and he drank greedily. The cool citrus-infused beverage slid over his dry membranes, soothing the ache.

"Not too fast, my darling." She slowed the flow of liquid. "You must take things slowly at the beginning. Dr. Abernathy's orders."

"Who's Dr. Abernathy?" he asked.

Twin lines appeared at the inner edges of her brows. "You don't remember him?"

He wondered if this was the time to tell her. Looking into her clear, cornflower eyes, he felt a clench of fear. Gabriella was his only anchor in this strange place. What if he told her he didn't remember being this Adam, her husband? What if he *wasn't* Adam and this was all some bizarre mistake?

His gut told him that he didn't belong in this world of comfort and luxury. It felt too foreign: this beautiful room...this beautiful female. If he'd had to make a wager about himself, he'd lay down money that his origins were less refined. Even in his present state, there was a covetousness in him, a thieving hunger for the finer things that surrounded him. They felt as if they didn't belong to him, as if they could be ripped away at any moment...

Out of nowhere, a tunnel of darkness closed around him, choking his lungs with the memory of smoke and soot. He coughed and coughed, the water rushing back up.

"There, there." Gabriella blotted his face with a scented handkerchief, seemingly unconcerned that he'd puked all over the expensive coverlet. "Feeling better?"

"I don't...I don't remember anything."

The words left him reflexively, like a final emptying heave that he couldn't contain. Seeing the spasm on Gabriella's face, he wished he'd kept his mouth shut. She was his light in the gloom; he couldn't afford to lose her. With a certainty that he couldn't explain, he knew that she was the key to his survival...at least until he could figure out who the bloody hell he was.

"Dr. Abernathy is the physician who attended to you," she said gently. "You were shot, my darling, then hit your head and fell into the Thames. If Mr. Murray, your business associate, hadn't rescued you, you could have..." Her eyes glimmered with an emotion that caused his heart to stutter. Visibly collecting herself, she went on, "The doctor said that memory loss is not unusual, given the trauma you suffered. But you're not to worry, Adam.

Given rest and time, your memory will come back. The most important thing is that you mustn't push yourself too hard."

"My name is Adam?" he pressed. "You are certain of this?"

You're certain that I am your husband?

"You are Adam Garrity." The pride in her voice was unmistakable. "One of the most successful businessmen in all of London. You and I have been married for eight years. We have two children, Fiona and Maximillian."

Christ...I'm a father?

Reeling, he stammered, "H-how old are they?"

"Fiona is seven, Max five. They're chomping at the bit to see you." She brushed her fingertips against his jaw, the tender touch quickening his pulse. "You can see them when you're ready."

He didn't know if he was ready to face the small humans he'd apparently sired. Being a father was too much to contemplate on top of everything else. Questions tumbled through his brain.

And Gabriella—she had the answers.

"Do I have other family? Parents? Siblings?" he asked.

She chewed on her plump bottom lip. Her mouth was a deep, natural coral. "You weren't one to speak about the past. I'm afraid I don't know very much."

"Tell me what you know," he said urgently.

"Your mama died when you were young. Your father had left her soon after their marriage, and you never knew him." As he absorbed that information, she said hesitantly, "You grew up in the streets of St. Giles, and I believe you were part of a...gang."

The fact that the news didn't come as a shock was telling. Indeed, it *felt* right. As he'd suspected, he hadn't been born into his present circumstances, a silver spoon stuck in his mouth. His survival instincts were too keen, as if he'd had to fight for everything his entire life. Even now, in this uncanny situation, he had an alley cat's mentality.

Land on your feet, assess for danger, and claim your territory.

"You've risen above your origins." Gabriella sounded a bit

defensive, as if she'd misinterpreted his silence for shame. "You're a self-made man and a great success."

"What sort of business am I in?" He scanned for any memory of his so-called success and came up empty. The notion of being a merchant or professional man just didn't sit right.

"The business of loaning funds," she replied.

Her meaning sank in.

"I'm a bleeding *moneylender*?"

"Amongst other things." She primly folded the handkerchief into a neat square. "You believed in what you termed 'diversification.' Your holdings include many properties and investments in industrial ventures and the like. I don't know all the details—you preferred to keep business matters out of the domestic sphere—but I'm sure Mr. Henry Cornish, your solicitor and man-of-business, could fill you in. And Mr. Wickham Murray, your trusted right-hand man, has been looking after the moneylending side of things in your absence."

It struck him that he, Adam Garrity, was not merely plump in the pocket, he was as rich as Croesus. Properties and investments? *Diversification?* Only a toff who was truly wealthy (and, let's face it, a might pretentious) would use a word like that. As for the fact that he'd made his fortune through usury...it didn't bother him.

Not one bloody whit.

A moneylender didn't force people to take his money. He was doing a service and at no small risk for those who borrowed from cent-per-cents were not what one would call a reliable sort. If some cull wanted to hand over his vowels, who was Adam to complain?

As he'd suspected, he wasn't a man of refined sensibilities. He might not remember his past, but he felt one driving principle within himself, its rhythm as ingrained as that of his heart.

Survive, survive, survive.

"Who shot me?" he demanded.

"It's a long story." She bit her lip. "Dr. Abernathy said you weren't to be stressed."

"I'll be more stressed if I don't know who put a damned hole in my hide."

Hesitating, she said, "You were helping our friends defeat a villain named Sweeney. He was holding the young daughter of the Duke of Ranelagh and Somerville ransom, and you were part of the rescue mission. In the battle, you were shot by one of Sweeney's henchmen. But Mr. Murray dispatched the shooter, and Sweeney is now in custody and a danger no longer." Softly, she added, "Glory, the young girl, was saved, in no small part due to your heroic efforts."

Hmm. He couldn't quite fathom himself being a hero, but if she said it happened, then it must have. Who was he to question his own valiant behavior? All he knew was that he could get used to that look in her eyes: as if he'd hung the moon and the stars in the sky for her.

At the same time, the gears were slowly turning in his mind, working off the rust. He'd rescued the daughter of a duke, had he? Then the cove owed him a favor. He began to contemplate the sort of boons he might ask from His Grace...

One didn't do something for nothing. That was the way of the world.

As he schemed, the throbbing in his head increased, along with his assorted aches and pains.

Gabriella's head tilted alertly. "Where does it hurt, my darling?"

"My head...and other places," he said, grimacing.

"Dr. Abernathy left some willow bark. It tastes dreadful but will help with the pain. Would you like it?"

He nodded, and she went over to the console again, returning with a small paper packet and another glass of water. He tossed back the yellowish-white powder, gulping water to wash down the bitter tang. He sank into the pillows, struck by a wave of exhaustion.

"The physician said you mustn't overdo. Healing takes rest and time." Gabriella's fingertips flitted over his forehead, the muscles relaxing at her touch. "Do you think you could manage some beef tea and toast?"

At the mention of food, his stomach gave a growl of interest.

A smile tucked into her cheeks. "After you eat, we'll have Quinn help you with your ablutions."

"Who's Quinn?"

"Your valet."

Bleeding hell, he had a *valet*. He really had died and gone to heaven.

It struck him fully for the first time. Although he had been shot and nearly drowned and his memory was dashed to smithereens, he was alive. And not only was he alive, look at where he'd ended up. And who he'd ended up *with*.

As he watched Gabriella go to pull the bell, her pink robe hugging her curvaceous arse, an undercurrent swirled beneath the tides of pain and fatigue. Aye, he was a survivor—and too practical a man to question the good fortune that had fallen into his lap. If he couldn't remember his past right now, then so be it. The present held plenty of attractions he wanted to explore.

Aye, he'd step into the shoes of that lucky bastard Adam Garrity...whoever he was.

14

THE NEXT MORNING, GABBY WENT TO THE NURSERY TO collect the children. Their governess could have brought them to Adam's suite, but Gabby wanted to speak with them first. They were waiting for her, freshly changed and ready for their visit with their father. Fiona looked charming in her snowy frock with a pink satin sash, the full skirts swishing over her pantalettes. Matching pink bows sat atop the twin clusters of her glossy red ringlets.

Max was in a blue tunic suit, his unruly black forelock defying any comb. Crumbs from breakfast clung to his knee-length shirt and loose trousers. Gabby gestured subtly at the affected areas, and he hastily brushed them off.

"Before we visit Papa," Gabby began, "you must remember that he has been through an ordeal and—"

"We're not to pester him." Fiona rolled her eyes. "Mama, you've reminded us of this at least a *hundred* times."

"It's important, dearest. Your father is doing ever so much better, but he's having a bit of a problem with his memory, and you mustn't take that personally. The doctor said it is part of the healing process."

After his examination yesterday, Dr. Abernathy had declared Adam's progress most satisfactory: a little over a week and the wound was healing nicely. Gabby had been grateful when he'd instructed Adam to be patient during his convalescence for her husband had, predictably, already started chafing at his loss of memory.

Since waking up yesterday afternoon, he'd bombarded her with a multitude of questions, wanting to know everything about himself. She'd done her best to give him answers while not feeding into his desire to do too much too quickly. It was an exhausting task, akin to trying to keep a panther on a leash.

"Has Papa forgotten us forever?" Max asked in a small voice.

"No, my lamb." Straightening his collar, Gabby gave him a reassuring smile. "But it may take a while for him to recall all the details. In the meantime, you must be patient with him and, above all, do not disturb his peace—"

"You went through this already, Mama," Fiona said impatiently. "Max might have a sieve for a brain, but I don't."

"I do *not* have a sieve for a brain." Max's cheeks turned red.

"Bacon, then," his sister retorted.

"I am not bacon-brained!"

"You're bacon all over. This little piggy went to market…" Fiona chanted.

"Don't call me a pig!" Max shouted.

"Children," Gabby began.

They ignored her, tossing arguments back and forth like a ball. Her temples pounded, the muscles tightening at the base of her skull. Worry and lack of sleep had taken their toll, and she felt like an old blanket, fraying at the edges. She tried again to capture her children's attention; their voices only got louder.

"Fiona and Maximillian, for heaven's sake, stop bickering."

The words burst from Gabby, and she didn't know who was more surprised, she or the children. Although she felt a jab of guilt for her sharp tone, her authority was respected for once. The pair quieted, staring at her with rounded eyes.

She regained her composure. "Fiona, stop teasing your brother. Max, don't take the bait so readily."

The children looked at each other, then at her, chorusing, "Yes, Mama."

"All right." She exhaled, trying to ease the tightness in her head. "Let us proceed."

She shepherded her offspring toward Adam's suite, pausing when Max had to race back to the nursery to fetch something he'd forgotten. He rejoined them, huffing and carrying a book, then he and his sister skipped ahead while Gabby tried to calm her nerves. As relieved as she was that Adam was safely on the mend, a host of other worries swarmed.

When would he regain his memories? How would he be with the children, whom he didn't remember? What could Gabby do to aid his recovery? And most of all...

Who in God's name is Jessabelle?

It felt churlish of her to obsess over the unknown female, bovine or otherwise, when there were bigger and more pressing concerns. But she couldn't help it. No matter how she tried to stuff her suspicions into the *Let Sleeping Dogs Lie* bin, they refused to be quarantined. The identity of Jessabelle had taken on a monumental sense of importance, for reasons she didn't completely understand. But it would not leave her alone, festering like a sliver that she could neither remove nor ignore.

She simply *had* to know. But could she risk adding to Adam's strain during this precarious time? And even if she found the courage to ask him...would he remember?

Arriving at her husband's door, she forced herself to concentrate on the visit at hand. This meeting between Adam and the children had to be handled delicately. She didn't know how Fiona and Max would respond to the changes in their previously larger-than-life papa.

With a ready smile on her face, she knocked and opened the door. "Good morning—"

Fiona flew past her. "Papa! Oh, Papa, I've missed you ever so much!"

The girl ran toward the green brocade sofa where Adam was reclined, propped up against pillows. Gabby's breath held when it looked like Fi might fling herself at him, heedless of his injury... but she stopped just short of the sofa.

Her red ringlets tipping to one side, Fiona said tremulously, "Are you hurt, Papa?"

"I'm doing better." Adam stared at his daughter, clearly trying to think of what to say next. "Thank you for asking."

On the surface, he looked more like his old self. Quinn had given him a shave and arranged his ebony hair into its usual slicked-back style. Over his sleepshirt, he wore his maroon dressing gown lined with black silk. With the exception of the yellow bruises on his temple and the visible bulk of the bandage beneath the robe, he appeared almost normal.

His tentativeness, however, was new. His throat bobbed, his gaze flicking between Fiona and Max, who'd come to stand just behind his sister. Gabby couldn't fathom what it must be like for Adam, seeing his own flesh and blood and having no recollection of them.

"Now that you've seen me, don't you remember me, Papa?" Fiona's voice had a tell-tale quiver that hurt Gabby's heart. "You *do* know me, don't you?"

Seeing the flare of panic in Adam's gaze, Gabby cut in. "Now, dear, remember what I said."

"I'm not pestering Papa." Fi's bottom lip wobbled, her precocious poise slipping. "I'm asking a question."

"That's fair, Fiona." Adam cleared his throat. "The truth is that I don't remember you, your brother, or your mama. Or much of anything before the accident," he said frankly. "The doctor says the hit to my head shook things up a bit. But I'm hoping that as my injury heals, the memories will return as well."

Fi stared at him. "How long will it take?"

"No one knows for certain." He paused. "Although I've been thinking...if you and your brother are willing to help me, my memories might return more quickly."

"How can we help?" Fi wanted to know.

"You can remind me of the things I used to know. The details of my old life might help me to remember the past," Adam said earnestly, as if he'd given the matter some thought. "You children have a wealth of information you could share with me."

Fiona looked taken aback; Gabby couldn't blame her. The Adam before the accident had always been in command, of himself and the universe around him. He was their confident and invincible leader, and everyone had followed along, trying to keep up.

This Adam was doing something the old one had never done: he was asking for help.

As Fiona clearly struggled with how to respond to the changes, Max stepped forward.

"Um, hello, Papa. I'm Maximillian, and I'm five." He gave a shy bow. "Everyone calls me Max...well, except you. You don't like pet names, in case you don't remember."

Adam looked puzzled. "Why don't I like pet names?"

"I don't know why." Max's shoulders hitched. "You just don't. You always call Mama by her full name, not Gabby like her friends do. And you always call me by my full name, although I wouldn't mind if you wanted to call me Max."

"I appreciate that, Max." Adam's tone was grave, but his eyes glinted with humor. "And thank you. This is precisely the sort of detail that might help me remember more of the past."

"You're welcome. I understand what it's like to forget things." Flushing, Max held out the book that he'd gone back to the nursery to fetch. "I thought this might help pass the time."

"That's thoughtful of you." Adam took the leather-bound volume, reading the embossed title aloud. "*Oriental Tales, Being Moral Selections from the Arabian Nights' Entertainments Calculated Both to Amuse and Improve the Minds of Youth.*" His lips twitched as his gaze met Gabby's. "That's a mouthful, isn't it?"

A clerk at Hatchard's had recommended the book to Gabby, saying that it was a popular choice for children. She'd been surprised to find that her favorite tales had been adapted for the nursery—minus the wife-slaying and other scandalous parts, of course. Selected stories, including *The Adventures of Sinbad the Sailor* and *Aladdin's Wonderful Lamp* had been rewritten to high-light particular moral lessons, in the manner of Aesop's Fables.

"The stories are jolly good," Max told him. "You always come to the nursery on Thursday nights to read one to Fiona and me. Maybe if you read the book now," he added with growing excite-ment, "it might help you remember reading it before?"

Adam looked intrigued, flipping through the pages. "Capital suggestion, Max. I'll try it."

Max beamed.

"I have a suggestion too," Fiona burst out.

Adam looked up from the book with a quizzical smile. "Yes?"

"I could play the pianoforte for you. You always like it when I play. You hired Maestro Bellucci from Italy to tutor me, and I'm one of the best pupils he's ever had, he said so himself." While immodest, Fi's claim wasn't inaccurate. Being her father's daugh-ter, she excelled at everything she did. "I've been practicing a sonatina by Maestro Clementi. Let's go to the music room, and I'll play it for you!"

"Papa's hurt. He can't walk," Max pointed out.

"Who asked you?" Fiona narrowed her eyes at her brother. "Papa's not an invalid. He's already out of bed, and if he needs help, the footmen can carry him down the stairs."

"That is a lovely idea, my dear," Gabby said, trying to defuse the situation. "But Papa needs rest. Later, when he's better—"

"But I want to play for Papa *now*." A storm gathered in Fi's blue eyes. "If he can't go down, then the footmen can bring the piano up."

"You know the first footman has a bad back." As much as she loved her daughter, Gabby wished the girl would think more of others. "It's not considerate, dear, nor is it practical to ask the servants to haul a heavy instrument up the stairs."

Hands curled, Fi yelled, "You always side with Max!"

As Gabby strove to hold onto her patience, Adam's baritone cut through the tension.

"Your mother has the right of it," he said in a tone that brooked no argument. "While I appreciate your offer to play, it'll have to wait until I'm better and can manage those stairs on my own."

Gabby's jaw slackened. The old Adam had cossetted Fiona, indulged her every whim. To hear him gainsay her wishes was nothing short of startling.

Fiona's wide eyes confirmed that she, too, was shocked.

Cheeks flushing, she mumbled, "All right, Papa. I'll play for you later."

"I look forward to it," he said evenly.

Seeing the deepening lines around his mouth, Gabby knew that he was getting weary.

"Say your goodbyes, children. Papa needs his rest," she said. "You can visit again later."

Fiona and Max made their farewells, and Gabby was about to escort them out when Adam's voice stopped her.

"Gabriella. Would you stay a moment, please?"

"We'll see ourselves back to the nursery," Fiona volunteered.

She took Max's hand, and the pair scampered off.

Closing the door, Gabby returned to Adam. He indicated that she should share the sofa with him, and she perched carefully by his feet, not wanting to jostle him. As she met his gaze, she felt a quiver in her belly. He was so familiar and yet he was looking at her like a stranger might. His frank appraisal affected her breathing like a quick tug on her corset strings.

"Do you need more willow bark?" she said into the silence.

"A hammer does seem to have taken up residence in my skull." His look was rueful. "How did you know?"

"You've lost your color. And you get these lines around your mouth."

"You're observant."

Flushing, she said, "Not really. I just notice things."

"That's the definition of being observant, pet." He sounded amused.

Flustered by the casual endearment—one he'd never used with her before—she said, "I'll, um, fetch the willow bark—"

"Wait, I wanted to ask...how did I do?"

She tilted her head.

"The children," he clarified. "How do you think that went?"

Touched that he cared, she answered, "You handled them very well. Fiona especially."

"I'm glad you think so." He rubbed the back of his neck. "The girl...our daughter, I mean. She's a handful, isn't she?"

"You've always been proud of her spirit and ambition," Gabby said, a bit defensively.

"Combined with her beauty, she'll wreak havoc on male hearts when she grows up. I'll have my hands full warding off her suitors." He slid her a look. "Takes after you, I suppose."

Gabby blinked. Was he saying that he thought *she* was a beauty who captivated men? While she knew that Adam held her in high esteem, he'd never been one for frivolous compliments or flirtation. His last comment, along with the earlier endearment, made her feel uneasy...as if she didn't know him.

How well do *you know him?* The question escaped from one of her mental boxes.

"I...I've never wreaked havoc in my life," she said awkwardly.

"I doubt that. You must have been popular as a debutante. How did I manage to snatch you up before someone else did?"

Not knowing how else to answer, Gabby gave him the truth. "You were the only one who offered for me."

"I was?" His brows inched up. "Were all the gents around you blind?"

She didn't know how to answer that.

"I don't know how to answer that," she said.

"Never mind. Worked out well for me, and I don't need you having second thoughts."

His slow smile pumped her heart, warmth rushing through her veins. This man had Adam's charisma and intensity, *and* he was less reserved. His undeniably virile interest filled the room, and she felt caught between longing...and fear.

She was acutely reminded of the one other time Adam had acted this way toward her. That time when she'd found him drunk and agitated over the death of some mysterious woman. That night had opened up Pandora's box. Even though she'd slammed a lid on the doubts, kept them at bay for the last few months, they were now rattling to get free.

The words catapulted from her. "Who is Jessabelle?"

Dear God, I can't believe I just asked him outright.

It was too late to take it back.

"I don't know." Adam gave her a blank look. "Am I supposed to know?"

Her throat dry, she said, "While you were feverish, you said her name. Twice. I don't know anyone named Jessabelle and just wondered..."

She trailed off, not wanting to sound like a jealous fishwife. If the mention of Jessabelle had triggered no response in Adam, then maybe Jessabelle wasn't important after all. Gabby was making a mountain out of a molehill, working herself into a frenzy over nothing.

"It's not important." She rose, smoothing her skirts. "I'll fetch your willow bark. Your head must be aching dreadfully by now."

As she walked past him, he caught her hand. "You'll come back to me? Talk with me some more?"

"Yes, of course," she said, her pulse thrumming. "If you wish it."

"I wish it." He brushed his lips across the back of her hand. The tender abrasion ruffled up her spine, goose pimples prickling her skin, the tips of her breasts tingling. But it was the raw male hunger in his eyes that arrested her breath. "I'm ready to get on with my life, Gabriella. *Our* life. And I don't want to waste any time."

15

A FEW MONTHS EARLIER

As the longcase clock chimed one in the morning, Gabby paused outside her husband's study. He'd arrived home earlier than usual this evening, and he'd seemed unlike his usual self. Dark turbulence had swirled in his eyes; when she'd asked him what was the matter, however, he'd denied that anything was wrong. Then he'd locked himself in the present room.

Hours later, she still hadn't heard him come upstairs, and concern had made her don a wrapper over her nightgown and come in search of him. Now she saw the light flickering beneath the door of the study and heard the sounds of heavy movement within. Which was also unusual. Adam possessed a predatory grace; indeed, he routinely startled her with his stealth.

Then she heard the familiar resonance of her husband's voice. Filtered through the heavy wood, the words were muffled and indistinct. Puzzled, she wondered who he could be talking to at this late hour; no guests had arrived...was he talking to one of the staff? But surely all the servants were abed.

Curious, she rapped on the door.

A minute passed. When no one answered, she tried the knob. The smooth brass turned in her hand, and she let herself inside.

Entering her husband's domain always sent a tingle of pleasure through her. The vast space suited Adam with its dark masculine elegance and air of tasteful luxury. The rich scents of leather, tobacco, and a hint of Adam's own delicious spice teased her senses. Her gaze went to the massive desk at the far end of the room, where her husband was usually found.

He was not there.

"There was a fair maid named Faye, whom I came upon one day. And she in turn came upon me, her bubbies white and bouncing free..."

The unmistakably bawdy tune, sang in her husband's voice, slackened her jaw. It came from the seating area by the flickering hearth. She hurried over, her astonishment deepening at the scene that greeted her: Adam was lying on the studded leather sofa, his eyes closed as he belted out the lewd ditty. Her usually immaculate husband was in his shirtsleeves, his feet bare. His throat was exposed, his dark chest hair visible in the open vee of his collar.

His cravat lay in a crumpled ball on the carpet beside him. Next to his discarded neckwear was an empty glass and a nearly empty decanter, the crystal facets glinting in the firelight.

"What on earth?" she said in bemusement.

Adam's eyes opened. The intensity of his dark stare was diluted by the fact that it was out of focus. He blinked up at her... then smiled lazily.

"'Ello there, my beauty," he said in slurred tones.

"Hello." Flummoxed, she asked, "Um, what are you doing?"

"Drinking. Brandy," he clarified. "Join me?"

He gestured grandly at the decanter, knocking it over and scattering the few remaining drops across the Aubusson.

She hastened to pick up the bottle, placing it safely out of his reach. Standing by the side of the sofa, she looked down at her husband. His face was flushed, his expression languid. A strand of inky hair had escaped its restrained style to curl upon his brow.

She recognized that unruly forelock for he'd passed it on to their son.

Kneeling, she tenderly smoothed aside the stray hair. "How much have you had to drink, darling?"

"Dunno." His wide shoulders hitched against the cushions. "Not enough?"

He sounded so hopeful that she had to fight a smile. "A decanter of brandy is definitely enough. What has gotten into you, Adam? You're not one to overindulge."

In fact, she'd never seen her husband foxed. He might enjoy a glass of wine with supper and a postprandial spirit with a cigar but, unlike many gentlemen, he stopped there. He approached drinking like he did everything else: with absolute control.

"Ain't overindulging. Can 'old my alcohol." His garbled accents undermined the credibility of his claim. "Back in the day, I could drink anyone under the table. Everyone thought I 'ad a 'ollow leg. Won more than one drinking contest in my time—that's 'ow I began to build up my stake, y'know."

She *didn't* know. Aside from his proposal, when he'd told her that he'd been part of a gang in his youth, Adam rarely referenced his past. Any questions she'd asked him had received curt replies. The number of facts she knew about her husband's history could be counted on one hand. She'd always been curious to know more about his past, however, and now he was volunteering information about himself. What harm could it do to find out more about the man she loved?

"What did you need stakes for?" she asked.

"To start my own business, o' course. Weren't going to stay under another man's thumb even if 'e saved my life. Ne'er could convince ol' Garrity that petty thievery and scavenging weren't no way to get rich," he muttered.

"Garrity?" Surprise percolated through her. "But I thought you didn't have any living relations whilst you were growing up."

"'E weren't my relation. Thought 'e was a father to us all,

though. Thought that since we was all 'is children, we ought to act like brother an' sister." He shook his head drunkenly. "But we wasn't siblings, was we?"

Gabby's nape tingled. "Who are you referring to? You...and who else?"

Adam stared at her, his gaze hooded. The firelight licked lovingly over his features, deepening the hollows beneath his slanting cheekbones and the fathomless pools of his eyes. The scruff of his night beard added to his air of virile wickedness.

"It doesn't matter." He righted his accent the way a gentleman might a slipping hat, clamping it back in place. "The past is irrelevant."

Gabby could not agree. She felt as if she were teetering on the edge of discovery. As if she were suddenly looking down into a dark abyss where the unknown lay in wait. Perhaps she'd always sensed its existence. In the sunlit contentment of her marriage, it was easy enough to ignore; but at night, when all was still and dark, it slithered through her dreams, sending tremors through the foundation of her happiness.

Secrets, secrets, secrets, it whispered.

She'd never gathered the courage to peer into the darkness. Yet now the danger was staring her in the face; she couldn't ignore it.

"It does matter. To me." She forced herself to stand her ground, not easy when her husband was eyeing her with an odd glint in his eyes. "Adam, who was she? This woman, who wasn't like a sister to you?"

Why haven't you mentioned her before? Did you care for her? Did you...love her?

Gabby's heart trembled; with bated breath, she awaited her husband's answer.

"You're the prettiest piece I've ever laid eyes on, you know that?" He gave her a leering grin. "Did well for myself, I did."

Although flustered, she persisted, "Who is she? Is she…is she why you're in this state?"

Was this mysterious woman the cause of her husband's inexplicable behavior?

A spasm hit Gabby's chest.

"No," he said solemnly. "In this state on account of you, love."

She frowned. "You got foxed because of me?"

"Not talking about being foxed—which I'm not," he said with an edge of belligerence. "Talking about this."

Her gaze followed the sweep of his hand. Her breath jammed when she saw what he was gesturing at. The thick, straining ridge in the front of his trousers was unmistakable.

Goodness, he was…*aroused?*

A wave of heat swamped her, making her feel light-headed. Yet she couldn't let him distract her, not when they were engaged in this important conversation.

Despite the flare of heat in her cheeks and elsewhere, she forged on. "I've never seen you in your cups before. What has happened, Adam? Tell me, please."

He sat up, pulling her to stand between his splayed thighs. "I love it when you blush. It spreads like a sunrise over your cheeks, your throat." His knuckles followed the trail of his words, a hot graze against the side of her face and neck, above the lacy ruffle of her high-necked nightgown. "I'd wager that beneath those layers your tits are a pretty pink, too."

When he casually cupped one of her breasts, wetness trickled between her thighs. Her head spun…with an uneasy mix of desire and misgiving. Who was this man? *Her* Adam had never been one to display his affection so boldly; their intimacy was always scheduled and carried out within the confines of their marital bed.

Yet here he was *fondling* her in his study. Her breaths came fitfully as he continued to stroke her breast. His other hand slid behind her back, holding her steady against his torturously pleasurable touch. Her nipple poked out rudely, the taut outline visible through the layers of her nightclothes.

"Ripe as a cherry," he said in a guttural voice. "You make my mouth water, love."

Hanging onto the last vestiges of her sanity, she choked out, "Adam, you must answer my question. Why did you drink so much this eve?"

His fingers paused upon her breast, although he didn't release her.

"If I answer your question,"—his glazed, hungry gaze made her heart bounce against her ribs—"will you be a good wife and let me have my way with you?"

After an instant, she nodded.

"Someone important died today. In a workplace fire."

"Dear heavens," she exclaimed. "Who?"

"No one you need concern yourself with," he muttered. "The past is over and done with. None of it matters—nothing matters but this..."

His hand pressed between her shoulder blades, drawing her closer. A gasp left her as his lips closed around the bud he'd teased into stiffness. He suckled her through the layers of silk and lawn, unleashing a wave of molten heat. She knew she ought to question him further about his startling revelation: who had died in the fire? And why was he so agitated over the loss that he'd gotten inebriated? Yet her willpower lessened with each decadent drag of his mouth.

Goodness, what Adam was doing, with his lips and tongue...

When he withdrew his mouth, she whimpered. Standing between his spread knees, she felt like a harem girl showing off her wares to an all-powerful sultan, and her intimate muscles fluttered at the naughty fantasy. If only she had the charms and wiles of Scheherazade...if only she had the power to win her husband's love...

"Take off your robe," he said thickly.

The very idea was wicked. And rather...titillating. Could she be so wanton as to disrobe here, in this public place where her husband conducted his business?

The burning demand in his gaze made up her mind. Her trembling fingers went to the sash of her robe. Her efforts at harem-girl-like grace were foiled when she couldn't unknot her belt, which she'd tied rather hastily. She tugged and tugged until finally the silk noose loosened. Grateful to be free, she forgot to be alluring and shrugged off the garment.

Adam's dark gaze roved over her. "The nightgown as well."

She stared down at the battalion of pearl buttons standing guard along the front of her voluminous nightgown. *Good Lord.* Without her lady's maid to help her, the act of getting undressed could very well take a thousand and one dashed nights. So much for captivating her husband. With an inward sigh, she reached for the top button; wedged tightly in its hole, the pearl refused to budge.

"Allow me."

Adam's long fingers wrapped around hers, her belly quivering as he took over. Even soused, he was dexterous, his fingers deftly undoing her. He whipped the garment over her head, tossing it to the floor. A heartbeat later, she found herself lifted and sitting astride him. The position was novel, astonishing...and utterly depraved.

She was naked, he fully dressed. Her knees braced his trouser-clad thighs, his manhood an iron bar pressing into her belly. His hand cupped her nape, bringing her face down to his, their noses almost touching. She was mesmerized by the flames of unbridled lust in his eyes. While she'd undoubtedly seen—and felt—his arousal before, it had never been quite like this. *He* had never let his desire for her show in so raw and primal a manner.

It had never occurred to her that she might get past his wall of control. That she had the ability to stir him up was as shocking as it was...*thrilling.*

"Kiss me, Gabriella," he demanded.

Overcome with the need to please him, she did. The kiss was hot, heady, spiced with brandy and desire. When his tongue stroked the seam of her mouth, she let him in eagerly, his masculine flavor saturating her senses.

How delicious he was, this husband of hers.

His mouth left hers to explore her cheeks and jaw. When he found the rim of her ear, she shivered, squirming as his tongue investigated the delicate shell. Her fingers dug into his muscular shoulders as he licked the sensitive lobe, then sucked upon it.

"You're like a sugar plum." His words entered her ear, sending thrills straight to her woman's place. "A sweet treat meant to be savored."

She moaned as his lips coursed down her throat. His stubble grazed her skin, making her feel hot and prickly everywhere. Heavens, she didn't know how much more stimulation she could take. When he lightly bit the tender junction of her neck and shoulder, she jerked in surprise. Moisture gushed between her thighs.

"Christ, your pussy is soaking through my trousers," he said with guttural approval.

Shock percolated through her. Her husband had *never* used such language in her presence before. And he'd certainly never been ungentlemanly enough to point out the dampness of that part of her anatomy. Embarrassment threatened to swamp her, and she made to pull away, but his hands clamped on her hips.

"I bloody love how wet you get."

His voice rasped down her spine, setting her nerves afire. And that was before he pulled her sex snug against his bulging erection. Even through the cloth, she felt the turgid proof of his desire, his huge shaft pulsing against her moist cove.

"Rub yourself against me." His hands guided her hips in a gyrating motion that made her arch with pleasure. "That's right, love, slide up and down against my cock. Rub your sweet pearl against my prick until you come."

Her head spun as her naughty vocabulary grew by leaps and bounds. A proper lady would have been offended...but she was aroused. Shockingly so. The fires of passion incinerated her capacity for thought: she was all sensation as she rubbed her pussy against the thick ridge of her husband's cock. She slid up and down, angling her hips so that the exquisite friction stimulated that sensitive peak...her *pearl*, now that she had a word for it.

The ascent to bliss made her pant. Then her husband's lips closed around her nipple, and the fierce suction sent her soaring. She climaxed with a cry, floating on the winds of rapture.

Then the world spun; suddenly she was on her hands and knees on the sofa, and the first hot swipe of his tongue against her convulsing flesh made her gasp.

"*Adam.*" She twisted her head back in shock. He was upon bended knee on the carpet, his hands holding her thighs apart, his ravenous eyes upon her quivering sex. "Wh-what are you doing?"

"I'm eating your cunny, licking up all this sweet cream," he said in dark, hungry tones. "Then I'm going to fuck you hard and fast until we come together."

Before she could formulate a response, his mouth was once again upon her sex. Her eyes widened then shut tightly as the foreign sensations poured through her. He'd never done this before. And she'd never imagined that a man could...that a man would want to...and in this lewd position...

Soon her senses became too overwhelmed. Her upper body collapsed onto the sofa, but Adam's hands kept her bottom held indecently high. Her cheek and palms resting against the leather cushion, she surrendered to the swirling possession of his kiss. Everything became a dream: a wanton twilight moment where there were no fears or consequences.

Adam's tongue plundered her from behind, licking and lashing her drenched pussy, his night beard abrading her trembling thighs. His grunts conveyed his enjoyment of what he was doing, his fingers working her pearl to a feverish pitch. He left no part of her unexplored, not even the tight, secret pucker she knew only for another purpose, and she sobbed with the ecstasy of her own surrender.

When he took her at last, his cock filled her so completely that it pushed the air from her lungs. She came, or perhaps she simply continued coming for the waves that rocked her were unending. Bliss inundated her, more and more bliss pouring through her as her husband took her in a primal frenzy. His hard hips slammed against her bottom, growls rising from his throat as he drove his big shaft into her.

Again and again. Harder and harder still.

And she begged for more even as she came and came and came.

Finally, he stopped, embedded in her, his heavy stones grinding against her swollen folds.

"You're mine. You belong to me," he growled. "Say it."

"I...belong to you," she moaned.

"Then take me. All of me."

He pounded into her, his thickness straining the limits of her passage. He groaned, his fingers biting into her hips as his liquid heat jetted inside her, over and again. Inundating her with pleasure.

It was too much, not enough.

"I love you," she whispered.

Then she swooned.

~

The next evening, the knock on her bedchamber door set off a mix of emotions in Gabby.

Fear, heartbreak...anger.

All day she'd been waiting to see her husband. Last night, when she'd recovered from her swoon, Adam had been passed out beside her on the sofa. Shaken by their animalistic coupling, she'd fled to her own bedchamber.

She'd needed time to think. To gather the courage to face her husband.

He'd been drunk: what was *her* excuse for behaving like the veriest wanton?

Surely no proper lady would have allowed her husband to take such liberties in the study. Nor would they encourage him to do the things that Adam had done...with his mouth...down *there*...

Heat scalded her cheeks. In all their years of marriage, he'd *never* done that. He was a proper gentleman; what had triggered him to act in so depraved a manner? Would he regret it in the morning? Sweet heavens, would he blame her for encouraging it?

Fretful, ashamed, and indecently aroused, she'd hidden in her bedchamber until she heard him leave for his offices. Finally, her growling belly had prompted her to ring for breakfast; debauchery apparently worked up one's appetite. Nell had delivered the tray, along with the morning paper. As Gabby scanned the front page, the buttered toast had suddenly turned to sawdust in her mouth.

FIRE DESTROYS HOUSE OF ILL REPUTE.

The article had reported the gory details of a fiery explosion that had incinerated The Gilded Pearl, a brothel in Covent Garden, and claimed the lives of several dozen victims.

Someone important died. In a workplace fire.

Adam's admission had echoed in her head. The coincidence was too great to be ignored. Had the person whom he had lost—and gotten drunk over—been...a whore?

All day Gabby had struggled with that abominable possibility. Even last night, her intuition had told her that something was wrong, that she ought to find out more about who had died, about why Adam was acting so strangely. Now Adam was here, and she had no choice but to confront him with her new suspicions.

You cannot sweep this into the Bin of Blissful Ignorance. Wide, dilated eyes stared back from the looking glass of her dressing table. *You must find out the truth.*

Inhaling, she rose and called, "Come in."

Adam entered. He was his usual elegant self, his lean muscularity accentuated by his formal evening wear. A diamond stick pin glittered in the snowy folds of his cravat as he approached her.

"I came to bid you good night before heading to bed," he said.

When he leaned in to kiss her cheek, she evaded him.

His head lifted, tilting slightly. "Is something the matter?"

Although his tone was neutral, she saw the wary glint in his eyes...as if he were bracing for trouble. Why would he feel that way, unless he was guilty of something?

The knots in her tightened. As calmly as she could, she lifted the newspaper from her vanity and handed it to him. Brows drawn, he took it. The moment he scanned the front page, she saw the flare of recognition, lines deepening around his mouth.

"There was a fire yesterday." She couldn't keep her voice from shaking. "A brothel called The Gilded Pearl burned down, killing dozens. But you already knew that...didn't you?"

He tossed the paper onto a nearby table. "What, precisely, are you implying?"

"Did you visit that place?" she burst out. "That woman who died—whom you got drunk as a wheelbarrow over—was she some *prostitute* you bedded?"

"Don't be silly," he said.

His clipped tone fueled her anger and fear. As did the fact that he didn't deny that the person who died had been female.

"While I may admit to occasional bouts of silliness," she said, "I am *not* stupid. You tell me someone important to you dies in a workplace fire. The very next day, I learn that a dashed *brothel* has burned down. Answer my question, Adam: are you mourning a lightskirt?"

"I'm going to say this once. I have never been unfaithful to you, nor will I disrespect our marriage vows. Ever," he said evenly.

Chest heaving, she stared at him. Oh, how she *longed* to believe that he held their vows as sacred as she did. With a sharp pang, she realized that the root of her insecurity came from the fact that she loved her husband with every fiber of her being...a feeling that was not returned.

He told you from the start that he didn't believe in love. You have no right to ask it of him now. Be content with his affection—with the safety and protection he's given you.

"I have your word?" she asked, faltering.

He held her gaze, his expression stony. "Upon my honor as a gentleman."

She knew his honor meant everything to him. Even when people disparaged her husband because of his profession, no one ever doubted that he was a man of his word.

Relief trickled through her. An awkward silence followed during which she underwent a fraught debate in her head. Should she beleaguer him about the identity of the mysterious woman... or should she try to heal the breach caused by her unwarranted suspicions?

As she struggled to decide, Adam spoke first.

"Last night," he said. "Did anything happen?"

Fire crept up her face. "What, um, are you referring to?"

"You were right in saying that I overindulged. It is not my habit, as you know." He cleared his throat, looking as discomfited as she'd ever seen him. "I woke up in the study with a blasted megrim and no recollection of last night...except that you were possibly there with me. At some point. Am I mistaken?"

Sweet heavens...he doesn't remember what happened.

Dumbly, she stared at him. In his tense features, she saw no sign that he recalled what he'd done with her. What she'd done with him.

"I was there," she croaked.

"Did I do or say anything to offend?"

Other than fucking me? With your cock...and your tongue? Whilst I came and came like a harlot and begged you for more?

Mutely, she shook her head.

"I'm glad for it. If I did say anything—do anything—to distress you, you would let me know?"

Distress hadn't been the emotion she'd felt: that was the crux of the problem. Adam had married her because he wanted a proper wife, one who was virtuous and good. She couldn't stand for him to discover that, in addition to her other faults, she was a trollop. Panic twisted her insides as she imagined his disapproval.

He never has to know. Don't ruin your marriage over this. Hide, hide, hide.

"Gabriella?" Adam was scrutinizing her, his jaw taut.

"Yes," she mumbled. "I would let you know."

Lines eased from his brow. He cleared his throat again. "Nasty stuff, brandy. I shan't overdo it again. Now I'm off to bed. Early meeting on the morrow. Good night, my dear. Sleep well."

He leaned to kiss her on the cheek, and this time she didn't pull away. His spicy maleness filled her senses, and for one charged moment, her inner barriers seemed to collapse. She had the urge to do something utterly mad: to throw herself at him, be a slave to his every wicked desire...

Her hands clenched at her sides as he gave her a husbandly peck. Tucking a stray tress behind her ear, he smiled faintly before exiting to the adjoining chamber.

Her heart beating like a wild trapped thing, she watched the door close between them.

❧ 16 ❧

PRESENT DAY

ADAM FELT THE SCRAPE OF HONED STEEL AGAINST HIS THROAT.

Since it had been preceded by a steamy warm towel wrapped around his face and the application of rich and luxuriously scented shaving soap with a soft brush, he relaxed in the chair. His eyes closed as Quinn, his personal valet, began removing his night beard with deft strokes.

I could get used to this.

It was three weeks after he'd awakened with amnesia. Physically, he was healed, the knitted flesh giving him hardly any trouble at all. It joined the faded collection of scars he'd found on himself, badges of honor worn by any man who'd apparently come from where he had. He still didn't remember his old life, but he'd reached an undeniable conclusion: there was nowhere else he'd rather be than where he was now.

He lived a gentleman's life, one of casual and undeniable extravagance. Not only were his personal needs catered to by professionals—Quinn being one amongst his army of servants—but he lived in a house with twenty-eight rooms...and this was no exaggeration. As soon as he'd started walking on his own, he'd wandered through and *counted*.

He'd taken an inventory of the household goods too. The silver plate alone could probably buy a small kingdom, and he'd made sure to tell Burke, the dried-up old stick of a butler, to do a regular accounting. Although Burke had responded as all the staff had to Adam's requests, with a deferential "Yes, sir," the ancient retainer hadn't liked being lectured on his responsibilities.

Too bloody bad. Adam might have lost his memory, but he wasn't going to have more stolen from him. As far as he could tell, he lived like a king, and he was going to keep it that way.

Land on his feet. Assess the danger. *Claim his territory*.

Now that Adam was well on the mend, he had three priorities. The first was getting back to work. Dr. Abernathy had advised Adam not to return to the office for another week. Since the doctor had helped to save his life and to avoid another gently scolding lecture from his wife, Adam had agreed...but that didn't mean he hadn't started getting the lay of the land.

Henry Cornish, his man-of-business, would be coming in a couple of days with a full summary of Adam's holdings. He wanted to know, down to the penny, the extent and nature of his fortune. Wickham Murray, his right-hand man, had made weekly visits during his recuperation, and Adam had taken those opportunities to grill the other about the moneylending business.

To Adam's amusement, Murray had become as tight-lipped as a clam whenever Gabriella came in to check on things; clearly, Murray had also been treated to one of her lectures on Adam's need for rest. Adam would have smiled but didn't want to risk getting nicked by Quinn's sweeping razor.

When it came to protecting those she cared about, his soft kitten of a wife had claws.

Not being a fool, Adam was well aware that his greatest fortune wasn't his earthly goods: he'd been given the gift of a family. Something that, from what little he knew of the past, he hadn't had before. Something that he knew he wanted now. Once he got over the shock of learning that he was a father, he'd made it a priority to get to know his children. He'd found it no chore for his daughter and son were charming tots.

Fiona was a headstrong chit who did indeed tickle the ivories like a maestro (she'd insisted on playing the piano for him the very minute he'd made it down the stairs). Indeed, she seemed to excel at everything she did, from dancing to singing to playwriting. Adam couldn't deny that he liked her ambitious spirit...even if, at times, he needed to curb it. It was oddly gratifying to see a part of himself in his daughter, who also had the blessing of her mama's beauty.

Max, on the other hand, looked like Adam, but had his mama's good-hearted nature. He was always thinking of others, trying his best, yet he lacked self-confidence. The lad needed less coddling and more toughening up. Adam planned to coach the boy in some manly sports. Boxing would be a good start.

Adam was discovering that his body remembered things that his mind did not. Take sparring, for instance. He'd tried a few moves. The jab, hook, uppercut...his muscles coordinated with practiced ease. He was confident he could give a good accounting of himself in a fight. Those faded scars on his manicured hands hadn't come from shuffling papers around on a desk.

His body recognized more than fighting moves. When he was around Gabriella, his entire being reacted with instantaneous hunger: to her scent, the inviting curve of her neck, the unique, bubbly cadence of her speech. While he had no conscious memory of making love to her, his body could *feel* hers: her soft, firm tits overflowing his palms, the sweetness of her lips against his...her hot, wet pussy gripping his cock.

Now that his wound was healed, his body had started clamoring for other things. Which led him to his most important goal: getting his marriage back on course. And by on course, he meant getting his wife into bed.

Every time he looked at Gabriella, he felt a surge of lust and possessiveness he couldn't deny. And why should he? He had a wife who was beautiful, tender, and loyal. She attended to him with a devotion that he knew in his gut he'd never experienced growing up as a guttersnipe. And she'd given him a pair of fine children to boot.

And yet...there was a distance between them. An invisible wall. Despite her attentiveness and wifely care, Gabriella shied away from the physical aspect of their marriage.

He didn't know what to make of it.

He'd tried to bridge the gap between them. To communicate his interest in resuming bedroom activities with her. He'd given her compliments, letting her know how attractive he found her, thinking she would take the hint.

She'd responded like an uncomfortable virgin.

Last week, she'd been pouring him tea, an everyday ritual she performed that never failed to get him into a lather. What aroused him was her attention to detail, the graceful precision with which she prepared his beverage: each cup she served him was the perfect balance of creamy, bitter, and sweet, just the way he liked it. When he expressed his approval of her efforts, she'd looked pleased.

Then he'd taken it a step further, commenting on the pretty color of her eyes and said eyes had widened in obvious distress. An awkward silence had fallen as she dropped her gaze, fumbling with the tea service while he wondered what the hell he'd said wrong. Yesterday, he'd tried another compliment, telling her that her hair was brighter than roses, and her face had turned the same shade to match. To his terror, her bottom lip had wobbled as if she might burst into tears.

If he told her what he thought of her breasts and arse, she'd probably expire on the spot.

Not a man to give up, he'd tried other means of sparking their marital flame. Last evening, for instance, during a game of charades with the children, Adam had positioned himself next to his wife on a sofa. Less than two feet separated them yet that distance felt as vast as an ocean. As Fiona nearly tore her hair out pantomiming to Max (Adam couldn't blame her: the poor lad had been utterly confused despite her excellent acting out of falling rain and tying a bow to represent the word "rainbow"), Adam decided to test the waters by sliding an arm casually around Gabriella's waist.

She'd jolted as if she'd touched an electrifying machine. Cheeks crimson, she'd jumped up, startling them both. She'd mumbled about having to attend to something and all but ran from the room.

He didn't know how to read her reactions. Had he offended her delicate sensibilities? Was she shy...or a cold-natured sort of female? Given her warm, generous spirit and sensual looks, he had a hard time believing the latter to be true. Perhaps she was worried, then, that he wasn't ready to resume his husbandly duties? But he was communicating quite clearly that he was ready.

Was her reticence related to their past? Not having any memory of their sexual history was the damnedest thing. What had their marital bed been like before? He couldn't imagine that he could have been around his wife and not tupped her at every available opportunity. In every room, on every surface of this bleeding mansion, if he'd had his way.

Yes, he was more than ready to get intimately reacquainted with his wife. The problem was getting Gabriella on the same page. He felt like a bridegroom fumbling about on his wedding night...Good God, he hoped he hadn't been a fumbler. Could that be why his spouse was so shy about sexual matters? Had he not satisfied her in bed?

"Is the shave satisfactory, sir?"

With a shudder, Adam relinquished that unwelcome theory and opened his eyes. He saw no nicks or redness in the looking glass. When he touched his jaw, he found it as smooth as a well-made bed.

"Very," he said. "Don't know how you manage such a close shave cutting with the grain, Quinn."

"Experience, I expect, sir. The shaving soap from Truefitt & Hill helps as well. You had them blend this custom formulation for you."

No wonder he found the spicy scent so pleasant.

As the valet removed the towel from around Adam's neck and began to pack up the assorted implements, Adam studied himself in the mirror. He was a decent-looking chap, had all his teeth. His form was fit and muscular. It wouldn't be immodest to say that women would find him attractive. Moreover, he was sure he was a man of sexual experience. He knew what pleased him...and knew he enjoyed a woman's pleasure as well.

Stuck in bed, with Gabriella hovering so close, he'd entertained quite a few fantasies. The notion of burying his face between her thighs, for instance, gave him an instant cockstand. He had a loin-firing curiosity to know if the hair on her mound was as lovely and pure a shade as the fiery locks on her head. If she tasted as sweet as she looked. If she was as talkative during sex as she was in daily life, if she would beg him with hot, breathy words to make her come...

He regained his focus. He was no namby-pamby idiot. What little he knew of his history painted him as a man who knew what he wanted and went after it. He'd built himself an empire and had his own personal blend of shaving soap, for Christ's sake.

By comparison, how difficult could it be to get Gabriella—*his wife*—to resume conjugal relations with him? In his gut, he knew that getting her in bed wasn't just about slaking his lust. It was about establishing his claim, of making her his in the most primal way so that neither of them had any doubts about whom she belonged to.

It was about making this marriage *real* because, Christ, he wanted it to be.

The solution struck him: he would plan an intimate night for them. He'd set the scene for a romantic interlude. Supper, flowers, a musical serenade—and a *gift*. Everyone knew that trinkets were the way to a female's heart, and he was as rich as Croesus, wasn't he?

"Is there anything else, Mr. Garrity?" Quinn inquired.

"Yes, actually. Do you know where I purchased jewelry for my wife in the past?"

"You have accounts at all the finest jewelers, sir. But for special occasions, you favored Rundell, Bridge, & Co. Shall I send for them?"

Adam cocked his head. "The jeweler will come to me?"

"Given your patronage over the years, I'd suspect Misters Rundell and Bridge would set up shop next door if you ask them to."

At least I did one thing right.

"Have them come this afternoon, when Mrs. Garrity is out visiting her father," Adam said. "The gift is to be a surprise. And send Burke up. I want to discuss tomorrow night's supper with him."

"Very good, sir."

As Quinn departed, Adam continued to plot out his plan...to seduce his wife.

IN THE DRAWING ROOM THE FOLLOWING AFTERNOON, GABBY poured tea for her three guests. To her right, Tessa Kent, a slight, raven-haired beauty shared a divan with Emma, the Duchess of Strathaven (and Tessa's sister-in-law). Maggie Foley, a cinnamon-haired widow and the future bride of the Duke of Ranelagh and Somerville, occupied the curricle chair to Gabby's left.

"You're always a wonderful hostess, Gabby, but you needn't have gone to the trouble," Emma said, waving at the cart and sideboard laden with cakes, sliced fruits, and a cold collation. "You already have your hands full looking after your husband."

"Swift Nick appreciates the feast," Tessa said.

Her poppy-colored carriage dress was cut to conceal the swell of the babe she was expecting next year, and curled up against the barely detectable bump was Swift Nick, her beloved pet ferret, whose dark mask of fur and searching gaze gave it the look of an inquisitive bandit. She broke off a piece of cheese for Swift Nick, who snatched and gobbled the morsel.

Tessa's choice of pet was as unique as she was. For despite her delicate exterior, she was a force to be reckoned with. Her grand-father was a powerful cutthroat who ruled the London underworld and, as the Duchess of Covent Garden, Tessa did her part to bring order and justice to the territory she oversaw. It spoke volumes that even a man as influential as Adam respected her authority.

"It was no trouble. And Mr. Garrity's ever so much improved," Gabby said. "Indeed, he's chafing at the doctor's instructions to stay in the house, which is how I know he's on the mend."

"When Strathaven's injured foot kept him confined to the house, he was like a caged tiger." Over the rim of her teacup, Emma's brown eyes were knowing. "The staff went into hiding."

Since Adam had been prowling around the house, poking his nose in everyone's business, Gabby had a feeling that her own servants would have liked to do the same. Poor Burke, in particular, had been mortally offended when Adam questioned his accounting of the household silver. She'd spent no little time smoothing the ancient butler's ruffled feathers.

Despite his impatience with his own recovery, Adam was improving at lightning speed. Day by day, he was stronger, more commanding, more like his old self. Yet he was also...different.

Thinking of the changes sent a wave of foreboding through Gabby. She didn't know what to make of them. Of the fact that her husband was, in some ways, a stranger. The awareness reaffirmed that she might not know him at all, a notion that pained her heart.

"I'm so very glad to hear that Mr. Garrity is feeling better." Maggie's hands curled in her olive satin skirts. "Ransom and I owe him more than we can ever repay."

In the other's emerald eyes, Gabby saw sincerity and no little guilt. She knew it was because Adam had been hurt whilst helping to rescue Maggie and Ransom's daughter, Glory. Although Maggie and her duke were newly engaged, Maggie had divulged that they'd had a brief affair some years earlier, Glory being the result of it. It was only recently that the lovers had reunited and His Grace had discovered that he had a daughter.

While Gabby had known Emma forever and Tessa for a few months, she'd only recently become acquainted with Maggie. Normally, she'd be intimidated by a woman as beautiful as Maggie, but the other's no-nonsense manner had put her at ease. Maggie's late husband had apparently been an older, ailing gentleman, and she'd run his fossils shop for many years, even digging for bones herself along the Dorset coast where she'd lived. One had the sense that Maggie's life hadn't been easy, yet she'd persevered and now she was to marry the man of her dreams.

Gabby didn't want anything hanging over her new friend's happiness.

"There is to be no talk of debt," she said firmly. "Mr. Garrity was happy to oblige."

"He's a hero. And I know that you and your family have suffered on my daughter's behalf. If there is any way for Ransom and me to return the favor," Maggie said solemnly, "you must let us know."

Gabby nodded, taking wifely pride in hearing Adam called a hero. The nature of his business hadn't always sat well with her friends, and more than once, he'd been cast in a villainous light. What they didn't understand was that Adam wasn't evil or cruel: he was a man of honor who simply believed in getting his just due.

In the past, she hadn't been able to persuade her friends of her husband's generosity and goodness any more than she could convince him that they were worthy of his trust. For her sake, both parties had tolerated one another. Perhaps the silver lining to the recent crisis was the setting aside of old differences. During Adam's recuperation, her friends and their husbands had come to pay their respects to him, and the exchanges had been warm and genuine on both sides.

"How is Garrity's noggin, by the by?" Tessa forked up a bite of treacle tart as Swift Nick watched alertly from her lap. "Have the loose screws settled back into place?"

"*Tessa.*" Emma nudged her sister-in-law.

"What?" Tessa's sooty lashes swept up over her jade-green eyes. "Gabby already told us he was having problems in that area. I just wanted to know if his memory had returned."

"Not yet." Gabby summoned a smile. "But Dr. Abernathy said it would take time."

"How are the children adjusting to Mr. Garrity's condition?" Maggie asked.

"Better than expected—far better, actually," Gabby admitted. "Before the accident, he wasn't home as much, and Fiona and Max are enjoying having more of his company. And vice versa."

The truth was that Fiona and Max had been following Adam around as if he were the Pied Piper, and he didn't seem to mind. Prior to the injury, he'd worked long hours at the office. When at home, he'd been preoccupied with his many business dealings, and his interactions with the children were limited to scheduled times. His behavior was not unusual for gentlemen of their class. By any standard, he was a good father.

Since the accident, he'd become an exceptional one.

He'd been a captive and enthusiastic audience to Fiona's many recitals. He'd read to both the children...and helped Max to read a few lines of a story *by himself*. Recalling the shining look of accomplishment on her son's face, Gabby felt her heart squeeze.

"And you, my dear?" Emma's voice drew her back. "How are you managing?"

"Oh, I'm fine."

"Really?"

Emma's scrutiny made her squirm a little in her seat. In addition to being a duchess, Emma was also an amateur investigator. She'd learned from the best as her eldest brother Ambrose Kent operated a famous private enquiry firm. Now Em was turning those keen observation skills on Gabby.

"Perhaps I'm a bit peaked," Gabby confessed.

"Swift Nick could fit into the bags under your eyes," Tessa said.

Aghast, Gabby covered her cheeks with her hands. "Do I look that horrid?"

"Not horrid, just tired," Tessa said bluntly. "Have you been sleeping?"

"Yes, but not well." She sighed. "Whenever I close my eyes, I start to think..."

"About what, dearest?" Emma asked.

Faced with the concern of her friends, Gabby said haltingly, "About what could have happened. About the future..."

To her horror, her voice cracked. She heard her schoolmistress's voice. *Hide your flaws...*

"I'm so...sorry," Gabby said, fighting the surge of heat behind her eyes.

"My poor dear." Emma came over in a rustle of plum taffeta. Her hand moved in soothing circles over Gabby's back. "Let it all out."

The permission opened floodgates. Suddenly, Gabby was sobbing.

She cried and cried and cried until she couldn't anymore.

"There, now. How do you feel?" Emma murmured.

Taking the handkerchief her friend held out, Gabby blew her nose.

"Tired but better. And embarrassed," she added in a small voice.

"There's naught to be embarrassed about. We all need a good cry now and again." Maggie leaned forward in her seat. "And you've had the weight of the world on your shoulders."

"Why don't you tell us about it?" Tessa suggested. "Maybe we can help."

Gabby didn't know if it was the strain of recent weeks or her friends' empathy, but she found herself talking. Hesitantly at first, then with increasing alacrity, she shared her fears and worries. How long would Adam's amnesia last? What if he *never* recovered his memory? Was she doing enough to help him?

"And he's *different*," she concluded.

Tessa's brow furrowed. "Different in a good or bad way?"

"Not bad," she said after a sniffle. "Just different. Sometimes I feel as if he's...a stranger."

"Perhaps if you could give us an example?" Maggie suggested.

"I think he's been *flirting* with me," she said in a mortified rush.

Silence blanketed the room. A giggle escaped Tessa, which seemed to have a domino effect on Emma and Maggie. Soon the three of them were pealing with laughter.

"What is so amusing?" Hurt and bewildered, Gabby said, "I'm *serious*."

"I'm sorry," Emma gasped. "It's just that...well, flirting, it's quite *normal* between husband and wife, isn't it?"

"Between you and your husbands, perhaps." Gabby twisted the damp linen in her hands. "But Adam is not the flirting sort. He's direct and honest; he'd never pay a compliment if he didn't mean it."

Tessa's fine brows drew together. "What makes you think his compliments aren't sincere?"

"He told me my hair reminded him of roses," Gabby said miserably. "And that my eyes stole the blue out of heaven."

Looking confused, Tessa said, "That's good...isn't it?"

"If it were *true*. But I've got carroty hair and ordinary eyes." Her cheeks hot, Gabby said fiercely, "My Adam, the one before the accident, would never tease me so horribly!"

"Did she compare her hair to carrots?" Maggie raised her brows at Emma and Tessa. "And she thinks her eyes are *ordinary*?"

"That's Gabby." Emma sighed. "She refuses to see that she's beautiful."

"You're only saying that because you're my friends and ever so kind," Gabby said with as much dignity as she could muster. "But the truth is my looks don't matter to me because I had a husband who saw beyond them. Whose honesty I valued more than flummery—"

"Hold up," Tessa interrupted. "Are you saying that the old Garrity *never* told you that you were beautiful?"

"Not in so many words. That is, he told me he found me pleasing," she added hastily when Tessa's visage darkened, "and how proud he was to call me his wife, but he wasn't one for romantic notions. He was quite forthright about it when he offered for me."

"Every man should tell his wife she is beautiful," Tessa declared.

"At least once a day," Emma agreed.

"Communication is important in a relationship." With a rueful smile, Maggie said, "Ransom and I are discovering this for ourselves."

Fatigue pounded at Gabby's temples. Every marriage was built differently, and her friends didn't understand the sort of union that she and Adam had constructed. Perhaps not all the doors had been open between them, but the walls of privacy had made her feel safe. She'd always had a place to retreat, to hide. Their arrangement had worked...hadn't it?

She pushed aside the niggling doubts. She didn't want to besmirch Adam in her friends' eyes, nor did she want to argue with them. The truth was that she, herself, didn't quite understand why she was upset over his compliments.

"Perhaps the crux of what is bothering you isn't the flirting per se, but the fact that your husband seems changed?"

Maggie's insight reverberated through Gabby, shaking loose a fresh wave of tears.

"I love him." She dabbed at her eyes. "What if I've lost him—who he *truly* is—for good?"

"But he's here, dear, isn't he? And doing better day by day." Reaching over, Emma patted Gabby's hand. "And pardon my saying, but the changes in him do not sound terrible. Your husband now takes more interest in the children and expresses an attraction to your person. That is no cause for distress, I daresay."

"Besides, how do you know that this *isn't* the real Adam Garrity?" Tessa's head tilted thoughtfully. "Perhaps he secretly thought you were beautiful all along but never said it. Perhaps this new version is the real one and the previous one was fake."

"Why would he keep his admiration of Gabby a secret?" Emma asked.

"How am I supposed to know?" Tessa shrugged. "I'm not Garrity. I'm just giving him the benefit of the doubt since he got shot doing me a favor."

"But your hypothesis is even worse," Gabby said morosely. "For it would mean that I never knew my husband at all."

As she said the words, she felt a frisson of fear. A chill that snaked up her spine and stirred the hairs on her nape. That ended up as a whisper in her ear.

Jessabelle.

Had she *ever* known her husband? What secrets had he kept from her?

That, she saw with a flash of insight, was the true cost of having walls in her marriage. They provided security and a place to hide, yes...but they also allowed secrets to take root. Doubt and suspicion could flourish in the wake of those secrets, spreading like ivy and overrunning happiness.

"Gabby, you're so pale," Emma said. "Are you quite all right?"

"Have some tea, my dear." Maggie made up a fresh cup and passed it to her.

She took a fortifying sip of the beverage, liberally doctored with sugar and cream. The warmth that flowed through her came not only from the tea but also her friends' care. Even after all these years, she had to remind herself that she was no longer the outcast she once was. These beautiful, sweet ladies were her friends. Time and again, they'd supported her without judgement.

A few months earlier, after she'd confronted Adam about the

fire at The Gilded Pearl and he'd denied having a mistress, she'd confided her suspicions to Emma and Tessa. She'd tried to respect the privacy of her marriage and hadn't told them everything, only that she feared that her husband had had an intimate connection to a victim of the brothel fire. Talking to them then had helped her to reflect upon matters and allay some of her worries; perhaps it would also help her now.

"I think Adam may have had a mistress," she said in a quavering voice.

She told them about Jessabelle. And her fear that Jessabelle was the "someone important" who'd perished in the bawdy house fire.

"A name's not much to go on." Tessa rubbed her ferret's belly with contemplative strokes. "Jessabelle could be anyone...even a pet."

Hearing it from someone else was ever so relieving.

"I thought the name had a rather bovine ring to it," Gabby said eagerly.

"Not to mention he uttered the name in the throes of a fever. It could mean anything—or nothing." A line formed between Emma's brows. "When you asked him about it, he had no recollection of this name?"

"None whatsoever," Gabby confirmed.

"Then there's no way of knowing who this Jessabelle is, is there?" Maggie mused.

"Actually, there is one way," Tessa said.

All eyes turned to her.

"I could find out the names of all who died in the fire. See if there was a Jessabelle."

"You can do that?" Maggie asked as dread percolated through Gabby.

"I'm the Duchess of Covent Garden," Tessa said simply. "I can get a complete list of names...if Gabby wants me to."

"Do you want her to, Gabby?" Emma asked.

It struck Gabby how tired she was. Not just physically, but emotionally. She was tired of hiding from the truth, of living with doubt. She'd come to a crossroads in her marriage: she couldn't move forward if she was mired in the quicksand of the past.

A part of her feared that she was betraying her husband. Yet wasn't she betraying their marriage if she had the means to discover the truth and lacked the courage to use it? Besides, if she was to believe in Adam's vow of fidelity, then this had to be some sort of misunderstanding. If she could clear it up, then the ghost of Jessabelle would haunt their relationship no longer.

"Yes." She straightened her shoulders. "I must know the truth."

"Leave it to me," Tessa said.

The door opened, and Gabby's heart thumped as Adam strode in. He was fully restored to his former self, lean and elegant in a blue frockcoat, his biscuit-colored trousers tucked into gleaming boots.

He bowed to the group. "Ladies, I hope I am not intruding on your charming conversation."

"Um, no." Gabby licked her lips nervously. "Not at all. We were just talking about...um..."

"My ball," the ever quick-witted Tessa supplied. "The one I'm throwing in honor of Ransom and Maggie's engagement. It's in a fortnight, and you're both invited, of course. I was getting your wife's advice since she's the consummate hostess and tip-top when it comes to decorating and refreshments. Whereas I, myself, can't tell the difference between a rose and a potato."

Adam looked amused. "Next time I see your husband, I'll remind him of that. Advise the fellow not to throw away blunt on expensive bouquets."

"Harry already knows I prefer confections to flowers." Smiling, Tessa rested her hand for a moment on her belly. "Especially nowadays."

Gabby had been taking in the exchange, silently thanking

Tessa for the reprieve, when Adam turned back to her. His dark gaze honed in upon her face.

"Is everything all right, pet?" he asked.

Aware of her friends' fascinated stares, Gabby said, "Y-yes. Why do you ask?"

"You look tired. And I fear I am to blame." He approached her as if the rest of the world ceased to exist, and it was only the two of them in this room. He brushed his thumb along her cheekbone, his eyes probing. "Poor wife, always helping and looking after everyone. Who is looking after you?"

Mesmerized by his warm concern, she swallowed. "I-I'm fine."

"You ought to have a nap. If I had my way," he murmured, "you'd stay the day in bed."

The male interest in his eyes was blatant and unmistakable. Who *was* this man who'd taken the place of her reserved husband? Wariness and longing trembled through her.

"I have errands to run later," she began.

"Errands can wait. I want you to have a lie-down so you'll be rested for tonight."

She blinked, trying to remember the schedule. "Do we have an event tonight?"

"We do, and it's a surprise."

Intrigued, she asked, "What kind of a surprise?"

His mouth twitched. "If I told you, it wouldn't be a surprise, would it?"

"We must be on our way." Emma's bright announcement broke the reverie.

Gabby had forgotten her friends' presence entirely. Blushing at her rudeness, she pleaded, "Please, do stay—"

"Listen to your husband, dear. We know our way out." Emma led the group to the door.

"Get some rest, Gabby," Maggie said with a warm smile.

As the ladies exited, Gabby heard Tessa add with a catch of laughter, "I have a feeling you're going to need it."

18

WHEN GABBY AWOKE, SHE WAS DISCONCERTED TO DISCOVER that it was nearly nine o'clock in the evening. After her friends departed, Adam had insisted she take a nap. She couldn't believe she'd slept the entire afternoon and then some. Getting out of bed, she rang for Nell.

As she sat at the dressing table, she saw that she did indeed look more refreshed. The sleep had helped, as had the talk with her friends. And if she felt a prick of guilt that she'd enlisted Tessa's help in discovering the identity of Jessabelle, she pushed it aside. She was doing the right thing, taking steps to discover the truth. Her suspicions were likely worse than facing reality head-on, and they were preventing her from moving forward in her marriage.

The changes in her husband were perturbing enough. She couldn't manage those *and* simultaneously be worried about whether or not he had a lover—not without becoming a candidate for Bedlam anyway. She'd reached full capacity when it came to worry; no more would fit into her mental categories. Something had to give. Besides, in her heart she trusted Adam: he'd told her he was faithful. Which meant Jessabelle, whoever she was, was just a mix-up, and the sooner the matter was cleared up, the better.

Nell arrived with a cheery smile. "Feeling better, ma'am?"

"Much better, thank you." She yawned, then said sheepishly, "I'm feeling rather peckish. Would you have Cook prepare a tray?"

"Oh, no, ma'am. You have to get dressed and come down. There's a surprise waiting for you."

Gabby had forgotten all about Adam's surprise. "What does Mr. Garrity have planned?"

"We'll get you ready, and you'll find out," Nell said, a merry twinkle in her eyes.

Bemused, Gabby allowed the other to dress her in a sapphire evening gown. It was one of her favorites, with a modest square neckline and plenty of ruffles and trimmings on the bodice to hide any unsightly bulges. The skirts were full and flounced, all the better to obscure her lower half.

Nell hummed as she worked on Gabby's hair. She expertly tamed the red tresses into a bun at the back and braided the sides, looping the plaits over Gabby's ears.

Sensing the other's good spirits, Gabby asked, "Have you had news from your beau?"

"Indeed, ma'am." Dimples appeared in Nell's apple-round cheeks. "The value of my Tom's shares in Grand London National Railway continues to rise. He says that after the unveiling of the new steam-powered locomotive next month—which Mr. De Villier claims will be the world's fastest—the prices will soar sky-high. We'll have enough money to get married and buy ourselves a home, we will."

"I'm ever so happy for you," Gabby said sincerely. "Although I will miss you dreadfully."

"And I you. You're the kindest mistress I've ever served, and if it weren't for my Tom, I'd be reluctant to go." Nell put the finishing touches on Gabby's coiffure, winking at her in the looking glass. "But never mind me, ma'am. You have your own gentleman waiting for you."

Entering the dining room, Gabby stopped short.

The austerely elegant room had been transformed...into a romantic paradise.

Dozens of beeswax candles cast a warm and cozy glow over the cavernous space. Huge bouquets of hothouse blooms were everywhere, the scent of roses and greenery perfuming the air. The best table linens and silver had been laid out on the long dining room table, two place settings clustered intimately at one end.

In the midst of it all was Adam. Dressed in formal black and white, he was the epitome of elegant virility. She couldn't take her eyes off him as he drew near.

"What is all this for?" she asked in amazement.

"We're celebrating." Candlelight flickered in his eyes.

"Your recovery, you mean?"

"That too. But mostly we're celebrating you."

"Me?" Her hand fluttered to her breast.

"You, my dear." He took her trembling hand and kissed it. "You've seen me through a difficult time. I want you to have a respite from the burdens you've been carrying."

As if on cue, the soothing strains of a quartet floated in from the adjoining room.

"You hired musicians?" she asked stupidly.

"I've been told I'm rich." He flashed one of his new, easy grins which made her pulse race.

Feeling as if she'd wandered into one of Fiona's faerie tale plays, she allowed Adam to seat her at the table. Burke arrived with champagne; popping the cork, he filled their flutes with golden bubbly liquid.

Adam lifted his glass. "Here's to you, pet."

Shyly, she touched her glass to his and took a sip. Although she didn't indulge often, champagne was one of her favorites. This vintage was delicious, crisp and icy cold, the bubbles tickling her nose.

"I'm fond of champagne," she admitted.

"I know."

She blinked. "You remember?"

"Unfortunately, no." Above the pristine folds of his cravat, his lips curved in a rueful smile. "But hopefully my research will compensate for my lack of memory."

The fact that he'd made such an effort made her insides melt like a Gunter's ice on a hot summer day. His "research" extended to the rest of the meal, she soon discovered. The first course was also one of her favorites: a bite-sized golden coquette of potatoes and shallots, topped with a spoonful of caviar and a dollop of crème fraiche.

The pairing of the crispy, melt-in-the mouth potato with the salty pop of roe was divine. Noticing the intent way Adam was watching her eat, she blushed.

"This is delicious," she said. "Thank you for arranging such a lovely supper."

"You're welcome. I have something else for you." He placed a flat velvet box on the table. "A small token."

Now this was the Adam she knew. Her husband had always been generous when it came to material things. And she'd appreciated his gifts because they were symbols of his affection for her.

"How kind of you, but you needn't have," she said, lifting the lid. "*Oh.*"

She couldn't help but gawk at the stunning diamond bracelet. The gems were set in white gold and fashioned to resemble a glittering vine. The detail in the metalwork showed flowers in various stages of bloom.

"Do you like it?" he asked.

"The craftsmanship is exquisite," she breathed.

"Let me help you with it." Lifting the piece, he draped the diamonds over her wrist. The bracelet was a cool contrast to his warm touch as he secured the clasp. "There you are. It suits you very well."

His expression reminded her a bit of Max's when he'd read a sentence aloud by himself. He looked so boyishly pleased with himself that she had to smile.

"Thank you ever so much," she said.

"It is I who should be thanking you for your care this past month."

"As your wife, it is my duty to care for you."

"Duty?" he murmured. "Is that why you've tended to me?"

Her heart thumping, she said, "Well, no...not only that. I mean to say, I am your wife. Obviously, I..." *I love you, I've always loved you...but do I know you?* "That is, my feelings go beyond mere duty."

"Our relationship is something I want to discuss with you," he said smoothly. "You've been most patient and obliging with my many questions. I hope you will forgive me for asking more. These being of an intimate nature."

Reaching for her champagne, she took a nervous gulp. "Yes, of course."

He took the bottle from the ice-filled silver bucket and refilled her glass. "Were we happy?"

She blinked at the unexpected query. "Yes, of course we were. Very happy."

"And we were comfortable with one another?"

Her cheeks pulsed with sudden heat. Comfortable wasn't a word she'd ever apply to her husband, then or now. It was hard to be entirely relaxed around a man who was so accomplished and commanding...so *male*. Compared to him, she felt as insignificant as a pebble next to a mountain. The recognition struck her: as much as she adored her husband, she'd never felt like she was his equal.

"Is everything all right?" Adam was looking at her, his brow furrowed.

Her throat tight, she was saved from answering by the arrival of the soup, which was her favorite...of course. Even with amnesia, Adam was flawless.

"Lobster consommé." She fixed her gaze on the clear broth. "How wonderful."

"Gabby, did I say something wrong?"

"You called me Gabby." She lifted her head in surprise. "You've *never* called me that."

"Right...I don't like pet names. I forgot." He ran a hand through his hair—another mannerism that didn't belong to the husband she'd known. "It's the damnedest thing, not remembering who I used to be."

His obvious frustration filled her with empathy. As confusing as all this was for her, it must be even more so for him not to recall anything of their past.

"You've made so much progress in a short time," she soothed. "You must be patient. The rest will come back soon enough."

"And if it doesn't? What if I'm never again the man you were once married to? The husband and father I used to be?"

The vulnerability in his expression arrested her. Lines were carved around his mouth, his eyes stark as a winter's night. The old Adam had been entirely self-composed. An island unto himself. But this Adam—the husband who was with her now— showed his emotions. He had fears, same as her. He *needed* her, and the realization was accompanied by a shock of tenderness.

"Then we will simply have to get to know one another anew," she said tremulously. "*For better or worse.* Those were the vows we exchanged on our wedding day."

"I want to know you, Gabriella." His baritone had a rough edge. "More than anything."

On impulse, she reached out and touched his arm. "You may call me Gabby, if you prefer."

"I do prefer it." His hand closed over hers, his grip warm and strong. The smoldering need in his gaze shook her to the marrow. "Gabby, will you tell me about yourself...help me to remember who you are?"

He was asking for something he'd never asked of her before. The one thing that was more difficult than anything for her to give. She'd spent most of her life trying to hide, and now he was asking her to walk out into the light. Her heart pounded...yet she couldn't look away from the yearning that transformed his austerity into something even more irresistible. Even more compelling.

He's your husband, the man you love.

When he released her hand, she reached for her champagne and took a steadying sip.

With a tentative smile, she asked, "What do you wish to know?"

❧

As Adam led Gabby up the stairs back to her room, he was cognizant of two facts.

The first was that his wife was more than a trifle disguised. In truth, he was at fault for her tipsy state: to ease her nervousness, he'd refilled her champagne time and again during supper. At first, she'd seemed reluctant to talk about herself, but once she got into the flow of conversation, she lost her self-consciousness bit by bit.

He'd led her along with questions. What was she like as a girl? What was her family like? What were her favorite hobbies?

Once she relaxed, he broached more intimate topics. How did the two of them meet? What was their courtship like and how did he propose to her? Who were her suitors before him? (Married or not, it was always good to know one's competition.)

He'd listened in rapt fascination as, like the Persian queen in Max's book, she wove a spell with her stories. Her accounts were so uniquely *her*, sparkling with the colorful, artless gems of her observations. She was intelligent, amusing, and often self-deprecating. He'd had to hold back a snort when she described their first encounter as that of a sleek panther (him) coming upon a plump pigeon (her).

She spoke candidly of being the only child of a father who spent the bulk of his time at his bank. Adam's chest tightened when she didn't blame Billings for his absence but *herself* for not being the son he'd wanted or an accomplished daughter. She described herself as a "carroty-haired, pudgy, and bran-faced" girl during her adolescence. Although she didn't get into the details, other than to say that she "wasn't popular" with her peers, he saw the pain in her expressive eyes.

He was beginning to see the source of his wife's shyness. To understand that beneath her sweetness and self-effacing humor lay a core of aching insecurity. And he was rocked by a strong surge of protectiveness.

They reached the top step, and she stumbled, giggling. As he caught her against him, he thought grimly of the second conclusion he'd arrived at tonight.

The man he'd been in the past had been a right *arse*.

Halfway through the second bottle of champagne, Gabriella had confided that they'd *never* spoken like this before. That the "old Adam" had believed in moving forward and leaving the past where it was. And being "ever so honest," he'd apparently told her from the start that he didn't believe in sentimental notions of romantic love.

Flummoxed and disgusted in equal measure, he, the present Adam, couldn't fathom spewing such nonsense. He'd only known Gabby for a month, and already he knew that she was a rare treasure. God's blood, she was the kind of woman that any cove with the good fortune to find would hold onto with both hands and fight to the death to keep.

He'd taken a blow to the brains, but he still *had* brains.

"This was ever so much fun." Snuggled under his arm, Gabby smiled dreamily up at him. "We should do this more often. I don't know why we haven't."

Because I used to be an ass, apparently?

How had he allowed her to harbor such misconceived notions about herself? A woman like Gabby should see herself as a queen. She should know that she was beautiful, one of a kind. And if she didn't, then it was his damned duty as her husband to convince her of her worth. Just as she conveyed *his* worth through her attention to his every need, her tenderness as she'd nursed him, and her unconcealed pride in him and his accomplishments.

He tucked her closer, guiding her to the door of her bedchamber. "We'll do this as often as you like, sweetheart."

"Sweetheart...that's lovely." Twin lines appeared at the inner edges of her eyebrows, making her look like a puzzled faerie. "You never used to call me endearments. You don't prefer them."

"Well, I prefer them now," he said firmly.

He led her inside, where her maid was waiting.

"I'll take care of Mrs. Garrity. You may go," he said.

The maid's hesitation showed her concern for her mistress. All the servants, he'd noticed, were protective of Gabby. She had that effect on people: they cared about her because she was so bloody *nice*. And her genuine regard didn't distinguish between whether you were from the stews, middling classes, or the upper echelons.

"Mrs. Garrity will need help getting changed." The maid bravely held her ground.

"That's ever so good of you, Nell, but I'll manage." Gabby plopped onto her turned-down bed with a drunken lack of inhibition. "It's late, and I'm certain you're sleepy. Me, too, actually."

At her huge, unladylike yawn, Adam had to hide a grin.

The maid departed. Alone with his wife, who was now singing a children's lullaby off-key, Adam thought ruefully that things had not gone as planned this evening. He'd wanted to seduce Gabby with an intimate dinner; instead she was utterly foxed. And the ache in his groin was momentarily surpassed by another ache... higher up. In the vicinity of his heart.

Grabbing the nightgown that hung on the dressing screen, he strode over to the bed.

She looked up at him with heavy-lidded eyes. Her cheeks were charmingly flushed, and her hair had come undone, tendrils of fire trailing across the linen sheets. She was the very picture of wanton innocence.

That image flashed in his head again: the reclined goddess, clutching a bouquet of roses...a painting, it had to be. Where had he seen it?

Seeing that his wife was falling asleep, he shook off the puzzling memory. "Time to get you ready for bed, pet."

She stretched languidly. "I'm already in bed."

If it were any other woman but his guileless bride, he might have thought she was flirting with him. God knew her sultry smile hit him in his cock. Even as his member throbbed with interest, he reminded himself that not only was she foxed, she was far more vulnerable than he'd first realized. He would not take advantage of her.

"Up you go." He hoisted her to her feet, catching her when she swayed. He steered her hands onto the bedpost. "Hold on while I undress you."

He made quick work of the tiny buttons on the back of her frock. Tossing aside the blue velvet, he started on her corset strings. God's blood, the knots were tight. How did she breathe with this blasted thing on?

When he freed her from the heavy cage of whalebone and stiffened fabric, she sighed with pleasure. "You're even faster at this than Nell."

She was looking at him over her shoulder, the pose unintentionally and unbearably erotic. Especially since he'd just rid her of her petticoats and all she was wearing was a fine linen chemise and white silk stockings. In the firelight, her shift was nearly transparent. He swallowed as he took in her generous backside. Her rounded hips were made for a man's hands to hold onto, her lush, peach-shaped arse the perfect cushion for his pounding hips.

Christ, she would tempt a saint—and he was no saint. He was a sex-starved husband who'd been lusting after his wife for weeks. His erection threatened to tear through his trousers.

She's soused. Get yourself under bloody control.

"Sit on the bed," he said hoarsely. "I'll help you with your stockings."

Obediently, she plunked herself back onto the mattress. He knelt on one knee and, taking a deep breath, reached beneath her shift to her garter. His throat convulsed as his fingers brushed her smooth, silky thighs. As he worked on unhooking the garter, her chemise slid up, bunching at her hips, giving him a glimpse of her thatch, which was—God help him—the same fiery shade as the hair on her head.

With a shuddering breath, he focused on the exquisite torture of rolling her stocking down her shapely leg and over her delicately arched foot. Lust gripped his stones, the pressure shooting up his cock. A drop of wetness leaked from the tip.

Then he had to repeat everything with her other leg.

"This is ever so kind of you," she said with a tipsy giggle.

"That's me. Kindest man alive. Let's change you into your nightgown."

Her hands stretched obediently upward. With a prayer for willpower, he pulled the chemise up and over her head.

Bloody. Fucking. *Hell.*

He didn't know if a man could spontaneously combust but he was about a hair's breadth from doing so. From unloading his cannon like an untried lad. Just from *looking* at his naked wife.

He expelled a ragged breath. "You're magnificent."

With a snort of laughter, she fell backward onto the bed. She grew silent, her eyes closing, and he wondered if she'd passed out. The only thing she had on was the diamond bracelet and her plain gold wedding band, and satisfaction mingled with lust as he saw those symbols upon her, marking her as his.

Just as he was about to tuck her in, she lurched up on her elbows.

She peered at him through her lashes. "Are you going to make love to me?"

Bloody hell, yes, his brain shouted.

"Not tonight, sweetheart," he forced himself to say.

"I didn't think so." She collapsed onto the mattress again, yawning languorously. "It's not Wednesday, after all."

"What does that matter?" he asked, confused.

She curled onto her side, mumbling drowsily, "You only make love to me on Wednesdays. That's the schedule."

He had a schedule for making love to his wife? What kind of godforsaken *idiot* had he been?

Dumbfounded, Adam stared at his naked, dozing spouse, emotions tangling inside him. Yearning, desire, and more. A recognition that it would take more than a simple seduction to get his marriage back on course. If he wanted this relationship to be real, then he had to get re-acquainted with his wife and vice versa...or perhaps they would be getting to know each other for the first time.

While he couldn't change the past—hell, perhaps it was for the better that he couldn't recall what a fool he'd been—he did have power over the future.

Reaching for the coverlet and blankets, he tucked them securely around Gabby. He kissed her brow; she murmured something, looking so sweet and beautiful that it was difficult to leave her.

But he did, his mind on his next move.

19

THE NEXT MORNING, GABBY STOPPED OUTSIDE THE CLOSED door of Adam's study.

She raised her hand to knock, pausing at the last second. A part of her was tempted to just sweep the events of last night—whatever they happened to be—into the darkest depths of the *Bin of Blissful Ignorance* and go on her merry way. That is, directly to the kitchen, where she would ask Chef Pierre for an entire cake and a fork.

A new and wiser voice told her that cake wasn't the answer. Nor was the *Bin of Blissful Ignorance*, which, frankly, was overflowing. There was no hiding from the fact that she'd awoken without a stitch on and with no memory of how that had come to be. The only thing she did know was what Nell had told her this morning: "The master took care of you last night, ma'am."

Adam took care of me...in what manner?

Gabby's marriage had enough uncertainty; her nerves couldn't handle any more.

Sweet heavens, get it over with. Just as her fist was poised to knock, the door opened. She scooted back with a startled squeak, dropping her hand to her side.

"Good morning, my dear," Adam said.

Framed by the doorway, he was the picture of elegant masculinity. His dark hair gleamed in its restrained style, his chiseled features radiating vitality. He was in his shirtsleeves, his silver-grey waistcoat hugging his trim torso, his dark trousers perfectly fitted to his sinewy legs.

"I, um, don't wish to bother you—" she began.

"You could never be a bother, pet." Was that a knowing glint in his eyes? His slow smile caused her belly to flutter. "After last night, however, I didn't think you would be up this early."

After last night. Pulse leaping, she was about to reply when she heard another voice.

"Good day, Mrs. Garrity."

Henry Cornish, Adam's portly man of business, was standing behind him. Adam had once told her that the solicitor's jolly manner and penchant for eye-catching waistcoats—his current one was a florid shade of puce—came in handy during negotiations. Opponents often underestimated him...until it was too late.

He was one of Adam's long-standing retainers, and Gabby had always liked him.

"Hello, Mr. Cornish," she said with a smile. "I didn't realize you were here."

"I was on my way out, ma'am. It is a pleasure to see your husband back on his feet, all thanks to you, I understand." He winked at her. "Nothing like a pretty wife to get a man on the mend, eh?"

Gabby blushed.

"If you're done flirting with my wife, Cornish," Adam said mildly, "I'll remind you that I want a report on the underperforming assets as soon as possible."

"I'll have it ready within the week, sir." With a bow, Cornish departed.

"Underperforming assets?" Gabriella asked.

"Cornish and I spent the morning reviewing my portfolio."

Adam ushered her into the study. "As impressive as it was, I noticed that several businesses—banks, mostly—have been reporting losses on a consistent basis. According to Cornish, when he brought up the idea of selling them in the past, I refused. He's going to look into whether I knew something about these businesses that doesn't show up on the profit ledger."

"Should you be working?" she asked worriedly. "Dr. Abernathy was quite specific that you should wait at least another week. The strain—"

"The strain of knowing that I'm losing money and not doing anything about it is more likely to cause a relapse than a few hours with Cornish." Adam led her to the seating area by the hearth. "Shall I ring for tea?"

"No." She bit her lip, torn between her wifely duty to remind him to rest and the need to address what had brought her here in the first place. "I won't bother you for long."

"As I've said, pet, you could never be a bother. Come, sit."

As her bottom made contact with the studded leather sofa, she flashed to another time she'd been here, her cheek pressed against this same cushion as Adam had put his mouth on her and taken her from behind. Heat swirled from her core, spreading through her limbs, burgeoning under her skin.

"You look warm." Adam took the seat beside her. "Is the fire too high?"

"It's fine." Clearing her throat, she told herself to get it over with. "I'm afraid that I, um, had too much champagne last night. The evening was rather a blur."

His brows lifted. "How much do you remember?"

"Um...nothing after the truffle soufflé."

"At least you remember the soufflé." His lips twitched. "I understand that the chef went to great lengths to prepare that dish."

Unable to bear the suspense any longer, she blurted, "Did something happen last night?"

"A number of things, I should say."

"After supper, I mean. Did we..."

"Yes, my dear?"

She let her fears out in a rush. "How did I end up in my bed without any clothes on?"

"Well, I helped you up the stairs and removed said clothes."

"After that, did we...um...you know..." She wetted her lips.

His gaze on her mouth, he said, "You're referring to conjugal activities?"

"Yes," she nearly shouted.

"Then no, we didn't."

Before she could enjoy the relief, he said, "Should I be offended that you thought you might not recall that I made love to you?" He cocked a brow. "Was my lovemaking forgettable in the past?"

Her cheeks flamed. "No...no, of course not."

"Did you enjoy being in my bed?"

Her heart was beating so fast she feared it might burst from her chest altogether. She couldn't look away from the heat in his eyes, the smoldering question that demanded an answer.

"Yes." The admission whispered from her lips.

He cupped her jaw, his thumb tracing the smooth edge to the point of her chin. Then it skated lower, over the quivering arch of her throat. His touch rested upon her pulse, just above her lace-trimmed chemisette, as if measuring its wild beat. Her gaze dropped to his mouth, the harsh yet sensual curve filling her with yearning.

She missed Adam's kisses. A month's worth of kisses that, since their marriage, she'd never gone without. His cologne, that subtle alchemy of man and spice, fed her hunger, and she could almost feel the firm pressure of his mouth on hers, the taste of him upon her tongue...

"I want to take you somewhere," he murmured.

"Where?" she asked dazedly.

"Outside of London. According to Cornish, I own a host of properties in the countryside."

She tried to wrest her senses from the grip of wanting. From her husband's animal magnetism.

"Buying estates was a hobby of yours," she managed. "You've collected so many that we haven't stayed at half of them."

"That's one hell of a hobby." Smiling wryly, he said, "What about the hunting lodge in Hertfordshire? Have you been?"

She recalled the cozy, Tudor-style manor. "Yes, I visited several times to oversee its refurbishment. We kept saying that we would bring the children, but there never seemed to be the time."

"For this trip, I'd like to take you alone. We'll go for a few days and have privacy to get reacquainted. The children will be fine here under Miss Thornton's capable watch."

I'll be alone with Adam. In the country. No distractions, just him...and me.

Her insides quivering like an aspic, she said, "What about your injury? I'm not sure you ought to be travelling—"

"My wound is fine, sweetheart. But I have other aches that only time alone with my wife can heal." He took her hand in his. "What do you say, Gabby? Will you go on this journey with me? Give us a chance to get to know one another again, as we are now?"

Reasons not to go burst through her head like released doves. The children, his health, her father...and so on and so forth. Yet looking into the dark mirror of her husband's eyes, she saw them for what they were: excuses.

Excuses because she was afraid of the burgeoning intimacy between them, the changes that were exhilarating and frightening at the same time. Changes that threatened to tear down the walls of the past. The walls that had felt safe, yes, but that had also established a distance between them. Was she ready to get to know her husband without the security of retreat?

After Adam's close brush with death and the ensuing weeks of uncertainty, she realized she was tired of being afraid. Tired of hiding. Whatever lay in the journey ahead, she would explore it... by her husband's side.

"Yes," she said, her voice trembling. "I want to go with you."

Blatant approval blazed in his eyes. He brought her hand to his lips, and her entire being shivered with anticipation.

"I'll make the arrangements," he said. "We'll leave the day after tomorrow."

20

AFTER AN EXTENDED FAREWELL WITH THE CHILDREN, ADAM whisked his wife off two mornings later. He'd chosen the hunting lodge in Hertfordshire because it offered both proximity to and seclusion from London. He'd come to see that his amnesia was not the only barrier between him and Gabby. He didn't fully understand the workings of his marriage, and he wanted this time alone with her so that they could get reacquainted without the distractions of everyday life.

Or, in truth, they might be getting acquainted for the first time.

Looking at his wife seated on the opposite side of the carriage, Adam felt a hot stirring that wasn't just about lust. Beneath her brown velvet toque, her hair was an autumn blaze in the sunlight. Knowing the bounty that lay beneath her fussy, frilly russet carriage dress necessitated a discreet adjustment of his trousers to ease the tightness, but his attraction to her was more than physical.

She was nibbling on her bottom lip as she looked out the window, watching the sharp angles of the city fade to the flowing curves of the countryside. Thus far during the trip, she'd assiduously avoided his gaze. Yet he could sense her mood, that heady mix of uncertainty and anticipation, and it filled him with equal parts of tenderness and lust.

How a woman could be so unaware of her beauty and worth was beyond him. He had no clue why the old Adam Garrity had eschewed romantic notions. Yet when Gabby spoke of his old self, it was always with pride and adoration, to the point where he sometimes felt jealous...of himself.

Ridiculous, but there it was.

He was her husband now, and he wanted her to see him for who he was. To want him as a woman wants a man...and to fall in love with him. The way she'd grabbed hold of his heart since he'd awakened.

Three weeks into this marriage and he was already certain that he had the wife of his dreams. He didn't have to know the past to know that he wanted her. And he hadn't even kissed her yet. He might not remember who he'd been, but he did know himself now. The soul-deep hunger and possessiveness he felt for the woman across from him. He was driven and ambitious; his natural tendency was to take command. When he wanted something, he went after it.

He wanted his wife. More than anything.

"Penny for your thoughts?" he asked.

Gabby's gaze flew to his. "Oh...I was, um, thinking of Fiona and Max. I hope that they won't miss us too much." Her smile was rueful. "And that they won't run amok while we're gone."

"They gave me their word they would behave."

"You mean you bribed them with the promise of presents." She wrinkled her nose in that way of hers that he found adorable. "You do spoil them, Adam."

"It's my intention to spoil their mama as well."

Tell-tale roses bloomed in her cheeks. She was thinking about what lay ahead in the next five days for them. Particularly, he guessed, in the intimate realm.

"Nervous?" he asked gently.

"No. Well, yes. Maybe a little?" Twin furrows worked between her curving auburn brows. "I don't know why I'm all aflutter. It seems ever so silly."

"If it helps at all, I have a touch of nerves myself."

"You do?" She tipped her head to the side. "But you're never discomfited by anything. At least, you weren't before the accident."

"Every man is bothered by something." *For instance, the thought of eating your pussy while you scream my name gets me into a lather.* "Perhaps I just didn't show it."

"Perhaps." She gave him a doubtful look. "Why do you have nerves now?"

He decided to be direct. "Because I feel like a bridegroom on his wedding night."

Her cheeks turned even pinker. "We've been married for eight years."

"None of which I remember. This is all new to me, and I want to do everything right. To be a good husband and father."

"You've been wonderful with the children," she said instantly. "They adore you, perhaps now more than ever. You've helped to build Max's confidence ever so much. And Fiona's too, in a way. I think that the more time she spends with you, the less she feels she needs to gain your attention through her accomplishments."

He felt he'd made inroads with the imps, and he was glad his wife agreed. Yet he didn't want her to dodge the issue of how he'd fared with *her*.

"And you, Gabriella? Have I been a good husband to you?" he said intently.

She bit her lip. "Well, yes. Of course."

"But I haven't been a true husband to you since the accident, have I?"

She squirmed against the plush green squabs, her voluminous

skirts rustling. Her gaze dropped to the vicinity of his waistcoat. "You've been ill."

"Look at me, Gabby."

His groin heated when she immediately raised her eyes to his. His gut told him that she liked having him be in control, liked relinquishing her worries and inhibitions under his command. As his was a dominant nature, he found her sweet capitulation more than a little arousing.

"I'm not ill now," he said. "And I find myself quite eager to resume my husbandly duties."

Her lashes swept higher. "Here? Right...now?"

"Here and now." He patted his lap. "Come here, sweetheart."

Her gaze darted to the window, the view of the rolling farmlands. "But anyone could see..."

He didn't give a damn what cows and clodhoppers thought of his marital activities. For her modesty's sake, however, he reached over and twitched the curtains closed.

He patted his lap again. "Come here."

To his everlasting satisfaction, she crossed over to him. The motion of the carriage made her sway, and he caught her by the waist, guiding her down onto his thighs in a flurry of taffeta and petticoats. Her pretty toque fell unheeded to the floor.

Her hands on his shoulders, she protested, "I don't want to hurt you. I...I'm too heavy. Your injury—"

"I'm recovered. And I don't want to hear another word about you being anything but what you are: perfection itself. You will trust me in this and all things."

He infused his tone with sternness, to allay her worries and assuage a need in him to assert his will. For the past month, he'd played the part of an invalid, one that had had its benefits— mainly the sweetness of having his wife fuss over him—but it wasn't his preferred or natural role. Perhaps that was why he'd had trouble connecting with her on a sensual level: he'd been too tentative, too lenient when she'd avoided intimacy.

He needed something different now. And, his instincts were telling him, so did she.

"This is where I ache, Gabby." He captured her hand, bringing it to the placket of his trousers. Pressing it over the unapologetic bulge of his erection. "I'm harder than a steel pike for you, sweetheart."

The gentle spasm of her hand injected pleasure through his veins. He didn't miss the increased cadence of her breath, her breasts rebelling against the restraint of whalebone and fabric. Her eyes were wide, a little dazed, that of a doe who doesn't know whether to run or stay. When he took his hand from hers, her palm didn't budge. It remained quiescently, obediently where he'd positioned it. All of this spoke volumes about what his wife truly wanted.

And it made him harder than ever, his cock straining beneath her touch.

He tipped her chin up. "I want something from you."

"What...what do you want?"

She wetted her lips, a nervous, enticing habit. He wondered if she knew that her body gave her away. The flick of her pink tongue over her bee-stung lips. The expanding well of her pupils. The excited flutter at her wrist that sent butterfly reverberations through his rigid prick.

She was as hot and bothered as he was. He could practically see the wicked scenarios forming in her head: the favors she imagined he might ask of her. His intuition told him that his naughty minx would be quite willing to fulfill any one of those fantasies... because they would also be hers.

He was tempted. Christ, he was.

What he wanted, however, was more than a quick fuck in the carriage. He wanted to start afresh with his wife. To lay his claim on her so thoroughly that she would never doubt that she belonged to him, as he was now. Now and forever. He wanted this bonding to imprint itself upon his own mind as well: if and when his memory returned, he wanted his old self to never again take for granted the gift he'd been given.

To that end, he'd spent a great deal of energy strategizing how to go about seducing his wife body, mind, and soul. Hence, this trip and the intimate game he was about to initiate.

"Kiss me, Gabriella," he said.

Her widening eyes made him speculate whether he'd asked that of her before. To initiate rather than be a passive recipient. Right now, he wanted to know that this was about her desire as much as his...and he wanted her to know it too.

A heartbeat passed.

Timidly, sweetly, she brought her mouth to his.

God's blood, her lips were as plush as they looked, fitting perfectly to his firmer edges. Even though he knew this wasn't their first kiss, it was *his* first taste of his wife since he'd awakened. And her kiss was everything a woman's kiss should be: soft and demure, a hint of wantonness in the way her mouth shaped so readily to his.

Her kiss spoke of a longing to please that aroused him utterly. He could tell she wasn't used to being in command, for she was attuned to his slightest reactions, her instinct to follow his lead. When he tested this by running his tongue along her mouth's sweet seam, she parted her lips immediately, welcoming him into her honeyed, feminine heat.

His wife might be shy, but she was no novice. She was a temptress, a goddess who seduced through the art of yielding. It called to his deepest carnal fantasies, and he took what she offered as his due.

One arm around her waist, his other hand at her jaw, he held her still for his plundering. He delved into her cavern, his tongue claiming her warm, satiny treasure. He tasted her moan, felt it in the throbbing insistence of his groin. Her hand still cradled his cock, now so hard that it threatened to rip through the thin wool barrier. He flexed his hips, pressing his erection into her touch, letting her know her effect on him, as was her due.

He slanted his mouth over hers, deepening his penetration. Thrusting into her wet hole and luring her tongue to play with his. She whimpered, squirming delightfully against him, the shy rub of her tongue threatening his self-control.

It would be so easy to toss up her skirts. To take her then and there, sheath his turgid, aching prick in his wife's pussy—the pussy that belonged to him and that he'd yet to claim.

But that wasn't his plan.

He lifted his mouth from hers. It took a moment for her eyelids to slide up, revealing her gloriously disoriented gaze. It made him want to kiss her again, but there was something else he wanted too. Something essential. Something that took precedence over the fire she ignited in his loins.

Rubbing his thumb over her kiss-swollen lips, he gave his second command. "Now tell me about a past kiss."

Her long lashes fluttered up. "Wh-what?"

"This is what I want from you, Gabriella: to be my wife in body and mind. As my amnesia has robbed me of our past conjugal bliss, you will be my memory," he told her. "For the duration of our trip, for every physical pleasure we share, you will share a story of it from our past. Our first time, our best time, even our worst…I will leave it up to you what you wish to tell me."

"I don't know if I can say such things *aloud*."

As charming as he found her maidenly modesty, he wouldn't let it stand between them.

"You can because I'm your husband and you're my wife," he stated. "I wish there to be no secrets between us. Moreover, your memories of our past might trigger my own and hasten my recovery."

As she chewed on that and her tempting bottom lip, he went on, "There is no guarantee when or if my amnesia will resolve. But I'm not going to let the future of our marriage be dictated by that uncertainty. You have my word that I will guide us through this journey, Gabby, but it would be a damned sight easier if I knew what baggage we're carrying. Will you give me what I ask? Your honesty, loyalty, and commitment as my wife?"

"Yes." Her instant reply filled him with satisfaction. "I...I'll do my best."

"Which kiss will you tell me about? Our first, best, or worst?" he prompted.

God help him if he'd ever bollixed a kiss. Or anything else. Yet if he had, he wanted to know.

"Since we've never had any bad kisses," she said softly and to his profound relief, "I suppose I could, um, tell you about our first time."

"I'm all ears, sweetheart," he said with simmering anticipation.

Each bump and sway of the carriage seemed to add to Gabby's state of overstimulation. It wasn't just the kissing, which in and of itself had set her nerve endings afire, but also the *talking* about the kissing. When Adam had asked her to speak of their past intimacy, she hadn't known if she could. Never in her life had she spoken of such things. Never had he asked it of her.

Yet the husband with her now was not the same man she'd married. Nor was she the same woman, she realized with a small shock. The years of marriage had changed her, and these past weeks in particular had cracked open her deepest fears: of losing the man she loved, who'd made her feel safe and protected, who'd given her a place to belong.

Walking through fire had made her realize that although her marriage had satisfied the needs of the girl she'd been, the woman she was now yearned for more. Her dreams...they'd somehow changed along the way. She wanted more than security from her husband, wanted things that were risky and terrifying. Wanted these things so badly it hurt.

Despite the crisp chill outside, the inside of the carriage felt steamy. Sitting on her husband's lap, Gabby was flushed with humid heat as she recounted their first kiss in the gallery after he'd proposed.

"Did you like my kiss?" he murmured.

"It was my first." Her candor was rewarded by the flare of possessive heat in his gaze. "I didn't know what to expect. I remember being worried that I might do it wrong...and that I ought to have brushed my teeth after lunch."

His masculine chuckle eased her embarrassment. "Nothing could detract from your sweetness, love." He grazed his knuckles against her cheek. "And you're a natural at kissing. You couldn't do it incorrectly if you tried."

"At least I'm good at something," she said jokingly.

Her reply was met with a curious silence.

"You are good at many things." His intensity was a bit unnerving. "When it comes to being a wife, mama, and lady, no man could ask for more."

"That's ever so kind of you to—"

"Gabby." The steeliness in his tone cut off her protests. "I'm not being kind; I'm being honest. And I won't have you discounting my compliments as if they are meaningless."

"I'm not discounting them..." She trailed off, frowning. *Was* she? Her response had been so habitual that she hadn't stopped to think about *why* she'd said it.

"Then do you hear what I'm telling you? Do you believe me?"

His eyes bore into her, his keenness thrilling and scary at the same time. There was no escaping him, his words, the force of them deepening the fissure inside her. Self-doubt oozed from the crack, leaving in its wake a relief deeper than pain. More profound than pleasure.

"I believe you," she said, her voice trembling.

"Good."

She didn't know why his firm reply stirred her so. Or why it gave her courage.

"When you kissed me that first time, I knew that you were the husband I always dreamed of," she admitted softly. "That you would be...my everything."

I love you. I've always loved you. Could you love me back?

His nostrils flared. An instant later, his mouth slammed onto hers. And she returned his kiss with all the desperate hope thrumming in her heart.

21

THEY REACHED THE HUNTING LODGE BY MIDAFTERNOON. IT had taken Thompson's discreet knock to alert Adam to the fact that the carriage had stopped. His wife had proven quite the distraction; the hum of unrequited lust still buzzed pleasantly in his veins as he alighted first, turning to help her down.

As her hand quivered in his, her eyes hazy with feminine need, he knew he'd made the right decision to delay their mutual gratification. Waiting, allowing the anticipation to simmer and build, would make their reunion all the more explosive—and from what he'd sampled in the carriage, Gabby was already the female equivalent of a Roman candle.

Cold-natured, his arse.

Behind her shyness and inhibitions lay a hot little wanton, praise God.

As he told her, he wanted more than her body. The ride over had answered some of his questions about the intricate—and sometimes convoluted—workings of Gabby's mind. It was her insecurities, not lack of interest, that had led her to shy away from his initial advances. He didn't know the root of these anxieties that blinded her to her own worth, but he meant to find out what they were this week and eradicate them for good.

One of the most frustrating aspects of his amnesia was not knowing why he hadn't tried harder to build up his wife's self-confidence in the past. Why he'd let walls stand between them. Since Gabby seemed to idealize who he was before, not even recognizing that he'd failed her, these were questions that no one but his forgotten self could answer.

I knew that you were the husband I always dreamed of. That you would be my everything.

Her words had tapped into a vein of consciousness deeper than memory. In it flowed his soul's secret yearning: to own a woman's complete surrender. To have her entrust her body, her loyalty, and her love to him. To have her yield control to him, to trust him, to know that he would do everything in his power to protect and cherish her.

He didn't want this with just any woman—he wanted this from Gabriella.

His wife.

Just thinking those words roused a swell of possessiveness. And a physical swell too, which wouldn't do since Thompson and the guards that had accompanied them stood nearby. A line of servants was also waiting on the steps of the Tudor-style manor house.

Adam bridled his desire; he had the next five days to convince his bride that her price was beyond rubies and that she belonged to him. Unwilling to relinquish the pleasure of her touch, he tucked her hand into the crook of his arm and led her over to the entrance of the lodge.

"Do we have an army of servants at all our properties?" he murmured.

"You haven't seen the country house in Berkshire." Her smile had a hint of mischief. "When it comes to hiring help, your motto is, *The more the merrier.*"

Shaking his head at his extravagance, he went to meet the legion for whom he was apparently providing gainful employment. The well-trained staff didn't blink an eye when he had to ask for their names. Beside him, Gabby greeted everyone with her natural warmth, eliciting genuine smiles in return.

After the introductions were done, Gabby gave him a tour of the place. The manor was medium-sized and renovated to serve its purpose of masculine enjoyment. The public rooms included a billiards room, library, and a sparring room to practice boxing. A theme of rich oak paneling, buttoned-leather furnishings, and trophies of the hunt lent the rooms a rustic yet elegant ambiance.

In her bubbly, enchanting way, Gabby told him the history of the house.

"The manor was owned by an aristocratic family for centuries. By the time the last owner inherited it, the place was in such disrepair that he decided to put it up for sale. He wanted an exorbitant sum, claiming that a king had stayed here because the hunting was so fine. But you were ever so clever and told him that it would take the ransoms of *several* kings to pay for the repairs," Gabby said with such wifely pride that he had to grin. "You negotiated ten thousand pounds off the asking price."

"And spent it on the restoration, no doubt." He cast an admiring glance around the present room, a richly outfitted study. Whatever he'd spent, it had been worth it. The space was luxurious and inviting...just like the house in London. And he remembered what she'd said earlier in the carriage. "You oversaw the decoration of the manor?"

"In consultation with the architect, of course," she said diffidently. "You had business matters to attend to, and I was happy to pitch in where I could."

"You did a splendid job."

She gave a modest shrug. "I relied on the architect's judgement."

"And the London house? Did you have a hand in that too?" He

knew the answer: their home's comfortable, warm style was quintessential Gabriella. But he wanted to hear it from her.

"Well, yes, but I asked for your opinion quite a bit. You have a refined sensibility when it comes to such matters, and I wanted to—"

"Gabriella."

He used the firm tone that had gotten her attention earlier in the carriage. She blinked, comprehension flaring in her eyes. Along with chagrin.

She pressed her hands to her cheeks. "I'm doing it again, aren't I?"

If the matter hadn't been so vital to her well-being, he might have smiled at how endearingly flustered she looked. Instead, he nodded.

"Truly, I hadn't noticed how I discounted compliments before." She sounded befuddled. "What an ungracious habit. I'm ever so sorry."

"I'm not the one who is owed an apology."

Her brow furrowed. "You mean to say…"

"You do not give yourself credit where credit is due. Who does that hurt, if not you?"

"I've never thought of it that way." Biting her lip, she said, "I don't know how I got into the habit of it, but I shall do my best to stop."

"I have a suggestion."

"Yes?"

"When I next pay you a compliment," he said gently, "simply say, *Thank you*."

"That seems like a simple enough solution," she agreed.

"Gabby?"

"Yes?"

"You've made our home and this property the envy of any man," he said gravely.

After an awkward pause, she said with obvious effort, "Thank you."

"Was that so difficult?"

"No."

"Then try this one. Thank you also for making *me* the envy of men with your beauty, strength, and sweetness."

Her bosom surged; he could see her fighting her instincts to deny the praise.

"Thank you," she said with such reluctance that his lips quirked.

Firming them, he said, "Last, but not least, thank you for the kisses in the carriage. You make me so hard that I ache, my sweet, passionate wife, and more eager than a newlywed bridegroom for his wedding night."

"Adam."

He lifted his brows. "What do you say, pet?"

She looked equal parts scandalized and stirred. She moistened her plump lips. He had a sudden image of her kneeling before him, employing that soft, wet swipe over the tip of his cock, and he had to bite back a groan.

"Thank you," she whispered.

"You're welcome." He curled his finger beneath her chin and felt her tremble. "Now I want you to go upstairs and refresh yourself so you'll have energy for this evening. We'll have supper in our chamber, if that suits?"

"That sounds lovely," she breathed.

"Good." He allowed himself a brief kiss on her brow. "Go on, sweetheart. I'll see you soon."

Two hours later, Gabby paused at the door of the shared sitting room between her and Adam's chambers. She felt more like a breathless virgin than a married lady of eight years, butterflies swarming in her belly. After a long bath in the luxuriously updated bathing room, she'd taken a refreshing nap. As befitting an intimate evening with her husband, she'd had the maid dress her in her favorite wrapper, which was made of white silk and embroidered with a motif of pagodas and birds. She'd left her hair down, the maid brushing the long strands until they shone.

After the steamy interlude in the carriage, Gabby knew what would transpire tonight. Truth be told, she ached for it, for the passion that Adam had always brought forth in her...and for the newfound intimacy that heightened all her desires. In the past, she'd always felt safe in her husband's virile thrall. Now she sensed he wanted more from her, a deeper connection that was both exciting and terrifying. It would alter their marriage, but hadn't their marriage already changed?

Yet she was still standing, still breathing, still desperately in love with her husband.

Thank you also for making me the envy of men with your beauty, strength, and sweetness.

She heard Adam's praise, but more than that, she truly *felt* it for the first time. It challenged her long-held assumptions about herself. His words made her feel beautiful and strong and fed her burgeoning confidence.

Inhaling, she opened the door and crossed the threshold.

Adam was waiting for her. He, too, had forgone formal attire, wearing a deep sapphire smoking jacket over his shirt and grey trousers. He'd left off his cravat, the strong column of his throat rising from the open collar. The vee also gave a tantalizing glimpse of the coarse hair that lightly furred his chest. He surveyed her like a sultan viewing his prized treasure, and every part of her quivered in response.

"How ravishing you are, my dear," he said.

"You look rather fine yourself," she managed.

He came to her, lifting his hand to her hair. He captured a strand between finger and thumb, rubbing gently.

"Like firelit silk," he murmured. "I'm torn between my desire as a man to see you thus always and my desire as a husband to keep this beauty all to myself. For my viewing pleasure alone."

Even without the constriction of her undergarments, she couldn't breathe. The proprietary heat in his gaze summoned her arousal, blood swelling the tips of her breasts. Need gnawed at her belly, and she wetted her lips.

"Hungry?" he asked.

Not only for food. The thought popped into her head, but even her newfound confidence couldn't compel her to say it. The knowing gleam in Adam's eyes made her intimate muscles clench. She felt herself sway toward him, physically drawn to his charismatic force...

A growl broke the reverie...and it came from her *belly.* Her cheeks pulsed with embarrassment.

Lines crinkled around Adam's eyes. His lips curved into that new and irresistible grin. "There's my answer. I'd best feed my beautiful wife before indulging in other appetites."

His wink teased a chuckle from her. Then his hand engulfed hers, leading her to the table by the roaring hearth. It had been set for two, the firelight twinkling in the ruby depths of the wineglasses. A tiered cart beside the table held several covered dishes.

"I requested a simple repast, one that we could serve ourselves," Adam said as he seated her. "I hope you do not mind."

"I like this very much. It's ever so cozy." She smiled at him. "And that smells delicious...is it hotchpotch?"

He lifted the lid of an earthenware pot, releasing a confirming puff of savory steam. Her mouth watered as he served them each a plate of the rich stew made from local game and vegetables. A rustic oval loaf sat on the table, along with a pot of butter.

He raised his wineglass to hers. "Bon appetit, pet."

With sudden hunger, Gabby dug in. She savored the chunks of tender meat braised with onions, carrots, and parsnips, the homey mélange specked with parsley and sage. She slathered her crusty slice of bread with creamy butter, her eyes closing briefly at the pleasure of that humble yet timeless pairing.

She realized that Adam was watching her, wineglass in hand, his plate mostly untouched.

Feeling like a glutton, she swallowed her mouthful. "I must be hungrier than I realized."

"I like watching you eat. Seeing you enjoy a sensual, natural pleasure." His husky tone made her hunger for other sensual pleasures as well. "Tell me about another time we shared an intimate supper like this, sweetheart."

Remembering their game from the carriage, she took a sip of wine before answering. "This one is rather difficult. We didn't dine alone often. And due to the demands of your business, you were frequently away from home."

He frowned. "I didn't take my meals with you and the children?"

"We usually breakfasted together." Heat rose in her cheeks as she thought of other aspects of their regular schedule. "And you were always home on, um, Wednesday nights. We usually supped as a family then."

Afterward, you came and made love to me. I looked forward to each and every Wednesday.

"Out of seven days, I only supped with you on one of the nights?" he said, brows drawn.

"You're a busy man, as I said." She found herself defending him. "And most fashionable couples do not live in each other's pockets. We each had our own social functions to attend, although some of them overlapped." Beneath his inscrutable gaze, she felt compelled to add, "It is common for husbands and wives to maintain separate schedules."

"On the topic of schedules, I've gleaned from various people that I'm a man of routine."

Not knowing what to make of the swift turn in the conversation or the edge in his voice, she nodded warily. "You're an organized, disciplined sort of person. You told me once that you hated surprises."

"I'm so organized and disciplined that I only made love to you on Wednesdays?"

Her pulse spiked. "How...did you remember...?"

"You told me, Gabriella. The night you drank too much champagne you said that I wouldn't make love to you because it wasn't Wednesday," he said grimly. "Is that true?"

"Well, yes. That was the routine," she admitted.

"Why the bloody hell did I only make love to you once a week?"

"I don't know. It was just the way it was," she said helplessly. "Ever since we were married."

"Did you want it that way?"

Her heart thumped as his gaze probed hers. The flickering firelight deepened his predatory intensity. She felt like a cornered rabbit, the instinct for self-preservation coupled with a paradoxical thrill. That of being...seen.

"It is what you wanted," she ventured.

"Is it what *you* wanted? For your husband to make love to you once a week, per the schedule?"

"I wanted to be a good wife." She moistened her lips as the truth seeped from the cracks in her heart. "To please you."

His smoldering gaze caused her pulse to race with alarm and longing.

"What would please me most is to hear what *you* want, Gabriella," he said. "Are you satisfied with supper once a week, each of us going our own merry way? A once-a-week bedding on a specified schedule?" A pause. "A husband who tells you he doesn't believe in love?"

Her breath caught on a jagged edge. "How did you...?"

"You told me. When you were drunk."

Her temples tightened. "I shouldn't have said—"

"I wanted the truth from you then, and I want it now." He

didn't blink. "Are you happy with the way things were?"

Confronted, panicked, with nowhere to run, she stilled—and the answer flashed in her head. She saw fully, for the first time, the price she'd paid for security. For eight years, the limits and routines of her marriage had kept her safe, but those walls she'd hidden behind had also been a cage.

"I want more." In her admission, she heard the click of a key, felt the tremble of something shifting, opening within herself. "I always have."

"How much more?"

Is he really going to make me confess my deepest desires?

He would, for she recognized his focused calm. She'd witnessed him in this state throughout their marriage. When he was about to close a difficult business deal or when the children got too rambunctious. Or the time when she'd been overtaken by despair after Max's birth.

This was the way Adam got before he stepped in and conquered the chaos. Before he made everything all right. Because he'd always done that for her, even when he'd been clear that romantic love wouldn't be part of the equation for him.

Yet Adam now wasn't the same as Adam then. He seemed less god-like and more human. He'd pushed for intimacy between them, had even helped her to realize a truth about herself. He made her feel beautiful and wanted, not just because of her wifely aptitudes, but simply for being...herself.

"I want all of you." The words welled up, unstoppable as her tears. "I want a marriage of hearts and minds and bodies, too. I want nothing between us. Nothing."

"Then we are in accord, my sweet wife." In a lightning-fast move, he was by her side, thumbing away her tears. Then he scooped her up in his arms. Her hands landing on his rock-hard chest, she was captivated by the ferocity of his expression. "Because when it comes to our marriage, I won't settle for less than everything."

22

ADAM CARRIED HIS WIFE TO HER BEDCHAMBER, HIS HEART pounding with wonder and pride. She was a fantasy come true, and she was his. Whatever the reasons behind their prior stupid arrangement—not for the first time, he wanted to knock some sense into his old self—he planned to erase it from her mind, replace it with what he wanted from her now.

What she'd so bravely admitted she wanted too.

Everything.

He set her on her feet by the bed, tipping her chin up.

"Tonight, we start over," he told her. "I don't give a damn that it's not Wednesday. From now on, I won't limit my desire for you in any way."

"I don't want you to. I want to please you, Adam. It's...it's all I've ever really wanted."

Her sweet submission swelled his cock with lust, his chest with tenderness.

"Your trust is a gift, sweetheart," he said, his voice hoarse with reverence. "But if I ever do something you don't like, you will tell me, hmm? I want honesty between us at all times."

She nodded, then sighed with pleasure as he ran a possessive hand through her hair. The lamplight turned her tresses into molten copper, and he reveled in the satiny slide between his fingers. When he got tangled, the slight tug on her scalp made her neck arch, her eyelids growing heavy. He made note of her reaction, the way he made note of everything where she was concerned.

Because she was his. His to pleasure and enjoy in any way he wished.

His to honor, protect, and cherish.

Curling his hand in her hair, he pulled gently. Her head tilted back with the loveliest gasp, and he swallowed it, thrust his tongue deep inside her mouth. She was delicious.

Sweet and savory. Womanly, wet, and warm. His Gabby.

He took his leisurely fill of his wife's mouth before being lured away by her other charms. Lucky bastard that he was, he had plenty to choose from. Plump earlobes just begging to be suckled, the soft, soft curve of her neck. He rested his lips against the flutter of her throat, absorbing her fragility, his desire fed by the savage thought that if anyone tried to take her away from him, he would tear them from limb to limb.

Impatient with the barriers between them, he untied her wrapper, pushing it off her shoulders. The nightgown beneath was thin, teasing him with the hint of her bountiful curves. Unfortunately, the line of tiny mother-of-pearl buttons stretching from her throat to her toes was as long as the bloody Great Wall of China.

"How much do you like this nightgown?" he asked.

Her brow pleated. "It's quite comfortable. Why?"

He let the sound of ripping cloth serve as his reply.

"*Adam.*" Her eyes rounded with shock. "That was expensive and—"

"I'll buy you another. On second thought, no I won't." His voice thickened, his gaze drawn to her breasts—by God, they were perfection—then to her shapely limbs and pretty pussy. "I don't want anything to stand between me and your beautiful self."

Before she could say anything, he lifted her onto the bed, laying her across it horizontally so that her legs dangled off the edge. Standing between her spread thighs, surveying the feast, he knew what he wanted to sample first.

A moan broke from her as he ran his tongue through the deep crevice between her breasts. He savored the way her rounded mounds overflowed his palms, squeezing them as he buried his face in her fragrant flesh. He avoided her nipples, teasing her with leisurely licks and soft nips, gauging what pleased her. She began squirming, her hands clutching at his shoulders.

"Adam, *please*," she said, her voice breathless and sweet.

He traced the rosy perimeter of her areola with the tip of his tongue, watching as her nipple swelled to new heights.

"Ask for what you want, love. Better yet, show me." Catching her right hand, he kissed the fingertips. "Touch yourself where you want my mouth."

Her fingers trembled, and he wondered if she was too shy to obey. Then, after a heartbeat, her hand left his and moved to her right breast. The sight of her ladylike fingers feathering over her straining red nipple was the stuff of male fantasies.

"With pleasure," he said huskily.

Lowering his head, he laved his tongue over her taut bud. She whimpered as he flicked the sensitive nub, wetting it thoroughly, then blowing softly. He alternated that with deep sucking, drawing her into the heat of his mouth. He went back and forth between her luscious mounds, and her moans escalated, making him wonder if he could make her come just by licking her tits.

He touched her pussy, and lust bolted through him. *Devil and damn*, she was wet. Dripping with honey. He searched out her pearl, frigging her with firm strokes...and that was all it took to send her over the edge. She cried out, her thighs clamping around his hand as she climaxed.

He kissed the plump underside of her breast, the smooth valley of her belly, enjoying her aftershocks of pleasure. When her thighs slackened, he withdrew his hand. Holding her passion-dazed eyes, he licked his fingers, the taste of her making his cock weep.

"Delicious," he murmured. "But everyone knows nectar is sweetest from the source."

He placed his hands on her legs, spreading them wider to expose her glistening pink slit, prettily framed by her fiery nest. His hunger broke its tether, lunging for what it craved. His nostrils flaring, he bent his head.

"Adam, oh my goodness...merciful *heavens*..."

Gabby didn't know what she was saying, words leaving her like a chant. She was simultaneously floating and drowning in bliss as her husband put his mouth to scandalous use. The only other time he'd kissed her there he'd been drunk, and she'd always wondered if the spirits had caused his behavior. If the brandy had been responsible for his one-time enjoyment of this lewd act.

Given that he hadn't remembered that night, she hadn't had the courage to bring up the topic. For months, she realized, vague worries had floated in and out of her consciousness.

What had prompted the introduction of this outrageous act to his repertoire? Where had he learned it? (A question that had been promptly relegated to the *Bin of Blissful Ignorance*). Was it...*normal*, what he was doing? Why had he done it only once? Had he not enjoyed it? Was it wrong and immoral of *her* to enjoy such depravity?

Right now, he was answering some of those questions.

Because he wasn't drunk, had only had a glass of wine. And he showed every sign of enjoying what he was doing to her.

"I love eating your pussy," he said thickly. "In fact, it's destined to become my favorite meal of the day."

His wicked words caused her hips to arch in helpless need. He held her spread, licking her, doing mind-melting things with his lips, tongue, and, goodness, *teeth*. He searched out her throbbing peak, lashing it with hot, liquid strokes, compressing it against his teeth, leaving her shaking and desperate for more.

"What do you want, love?" He blew softly on her sensitized flesh. "Tell me."

Heavens, could she say it? "More of...what you're doing."

He playfully nipped the crease of her thigh. "Don't be shy, sweet wife. I want to hear the naughty words from your beautiful lips."

His gleaming eyes compelled her to obey. To say the words he'd taught her, that until now she'd only repeated in the safety of her thoughts.

"Please...eat my pussy," she said, her cheeks flaming.

"With pleasure." The growl in his voice told her how much he liked hearing those words from her. "Your cunny is like a boiled sweet, pink, shiny, and mouth-watering. I want to lick it, suck on it, have your honey coat my tongue and throat."

Heavens.

He made good on his word. Gabby gripped the bedsheets, twisting them as he left no part of her cunny uncharted, laying claim to every quivering inch. He sucked on her pulsing pearl, working it with his tongue until she was gasping his name. Then he buried his face fully in her wet pussy, his tongue tracing her opening and stabbing *inside*.

"Move your hips," he growled. "Fuck yourself on my tongue until you come in my mouth."

Desire became a frenzy, her hips moving mindlessly to his command. The heat inside her built and built, incinerating thought and inhibition as she gyrated against her husband's masterful kiss. Pleasure erupted, a molten gush from her core that he greedily consumed.

As she lay there, boneless with bliss, he straightened. His lips glistening with her essence, his eyes feral with lust, he was a beast who'd only begun feeding. His gaze pinned hers as he stripped, her pulse skipping as she took in his male grace.

She gazed in awe at the muscular breadth of his shoulders, the granite slabs of his chest with its wiry furring. For a moment, she was drawn to his injury, the sight of that knitted flesh a potent reminder never to take life, this real and breathing moment, for granted. Swallowing, she returned her attention to the path of hair on his sectioned abdomen, not an ounce of fat there or on his narrow hips. He was taut and sinewy everywhere, with no excess bulk...except between his thighs.

Her breath puffed through her lips. Sweet heavens, his male equipment was large.

She'd felt his cock in the past, of course, and snuck glances at it. But he'd never stood before her as he did now, with his shoulders back, encouraging her to look her fill. His message was clear: nothing was to be hidden in their pursuit of marital pleasure. A tingle reawakened in her center as he wrapped his fingers around his rampant member, the slow stroke up and down inviting her to watch.

The thick pole strained in his casually pumping fist, the engorged tip nearly reaching his navel. A prominent vein snaked along the underside, feeding into his stones, which hung heavy and swollen in a cloud of dark hair. She remembered all the times she'd taken that big cock inside her, felt it stretching her open and filling her up, and need flared in her pussy.

"You do this to me, wife. Make my cock hard and ache to be inside you," he said silkily.

"I want you inside me." Her voice sounded as breathless as if she'd run for miles.

"Then spread your legs. Show me how much you want me."

Heart thumping, she obeyed his command. He stepped between her thighs as if he had every right to be there, a sultan claiming his prize. Grasping her hips, he drew her to the very edge of the bed. He fisted his cock again, and she moaned as he ran the fat head up and down her cleft.

His eyes glinted down at her. "Another time, I'll put you on your knees and wet my cock between your sweet lips."

As that erotic image trembled through her, he entered her in a swift, hard thrust. The fullness made her mewl with delight. Even as her body clenched, trying to hold onto him, he withdrew. He plunged again, deep and deeper still. Gripping her hips, he pulled her into his pounding thrusts.

"*Christ*, you were made to take my cock. So wet and tight." Arousal stained his slashing cheekbones, his jaw taut with masculine demand. "You want me deeper, don't you?"

"Yes," she gasped.

"Then take me. All of me."

With a growl, he slammed into her deeper and harder than before. Her calves clung to the notches of his hips, his muscular buttocks flexing beneath her heels. As she felt the heavy siege of his balls against her tender entrance, the truth blazed: she would take whatever he gave her—his cock, his tongue, and sweet heavens, please, his heart—because she loved him.

Then and now and always.

Tears slipped from her eyes, words from her lips. "I love you so much."

"My sweet Gabby." His eyes burned with the fierceness of a dark star. "I don't know what I did to deserve you. But from the moment I awakened, I started falling in love with you."

Her soul spasmed with ecstasy. With a whole and complete joy that she'd never felt before. That only love could give.

She heard him groan as her fulfillment rippled through her flesh, binding her to the source of her pleasure. He curved over her, his furious shoves lifting her off the bed. Thump, thump,

thump. Her back pounded against the mattress as he took her with merciless force, prolonging her rapture as he sought his own. His formidable body shuddered, and he buried a hoarse shout against her neck as he exploded inside her, melding them with his volcanic heat.

Afterward, he moved them both under the covers. He tucked her into his side as if she'd always belonged there. Safe in her husband's arms, his thudding heartbeat beneath her ear, she smiled and drifted into a deep, peaceful sleep.

❧ 23 ❧

SOMETHING TICKLED ADAM'S NOSE, MAKING IT TWITCH. HIS eyelids slowly slid up, and he found his face pressed into a coppery waterfall of silk. Memories of the night returned, and his lips curved. He buried his nose deeper, inhaling the flowery scent of his wife's hair.

The light seeping in through the curtains suggested it was early yet. He should probably let Gabby rest, especially since, after a short doze last night, they'd had a second round as lusty as the first. Now he was lying on his side, his wife nestled against him like a spoon. His arm was slung around her waist; even in sleep, he'd been reluctant to let her go.

Who could blame him? When a man was married to his lady love who also happened to be a hot little wanton, he'd be a fool not to claim her at every opportunity.

She mumbled something in her slumber, her plush bottom shifting against his morning cockstand and testing his good intentions to allow her to rest. He shuddered as his erection landed in the crack of her arse, nestling between the soft hills. He couldn't help a slight lunge of his hips.

Ah, God, that felt fine.

Beneath the covers, his hand moved up, cupping one plump breast. He squeezed the firm globe, teasing the budding tip between finger and thumb. She sighed, and he leaned forward, tracing the rim of her ear with his tongue. Her sleepy shiver ratcheted up his lust.

They were on vacation. They could always take a nap later.

Pushing aside the heavy curtain of her hair, he kissed her nape. Her skin flowed like silk beneath his lips as he followed the elegant ladder of her spine, his fingers still playing with her nipple. He felt the instant she came awake, the tiny jolt coinciding with the nip he placed just above the split of her pretty arse. He delved lower, his tongue seeking out her sweet pucker, teasing the secret rim.

"*Adam.*"

Her scandalized reprimand told him this was new to her. Last night, he'd witnessed her inhibitions unraveling one by one under his command, and he knew this would be no different. While he lived like a gentleman, he had no intention of making love like one. Gabby brought out the uncivilized beast in him: the part of him that wanted to mark every part of her as his.

If her reactions thus far were any indication, she was not only willing but *eager* to submit to his darker desires. His need was to dominate, hers to surrender: they fit together like pieces of an erotic puzzle. But...he didn't have to fall on her like a ravening animal now. They had plenty of time to explore his deeper fantasies and hers. Hell, they had a lifetime.

For now, he could yield to his wife's modesty.

He slid back up. She relaxed against him, clearly thinking that she was getting her way and he was giving up on his carnal plot. Pushing her top leg forward, he drove his cock into her pussy, adoring her startled little gasp.

"Good morning, love," he murmured into her ear. "One day, I will have everything I want from you. But for now, I'll settle for a proper morning fuck."

This time, she moaned his name.

Even though he'd done little to prepare her, she was still moist and slick from their prior couplings. Primal, visceral satisfaction gripped him as he felt how thoroughly he'd sprayed her with his seed. It made him plow her harder, driving his essence even deeper into her womb. It didn't take long for her to catch up, and he helped her along, strumming her pearl in time to his vigorous shafting. Her back arched in that telling way, and he turned her head toward him, covering her mouth with his own. He drank her cries of culmination and fed her his own groans of pleasure as he detonated, flooding her again.

He collapsed onto his back, pulling her with him. He tucked her head beneath his chin, and closed his eyes, enjoying the hum of aftermath. "I've just found my favorite way to wake up."

"Me too."

His lips quirked at the dreamy quality in her voice. "Capital. Since I seem to like schedules so much, we'll put a morning tup as every day's top priority."

"Oh, I wasn't referring to our lovemaking."

At that, he cracked his eyes open to look at her.

"Or not *just* that, anyway," she amended with a gratifying blush.

"Then what were you referring to? What is your favorite way to wake up?"

"In your arms," she whispered.

"Surely you've woken up here before..." When her gaze broke from his, he caught her chin; the shadows in her heavenly blue orbs made him say in disbelief, "Haven't you?"

The quick shake of her head felt like a punch to his solar plexus.

He forced himself to inhale. "We didn't sleep together? *Ever?* Not even on those bleeding Wednesdays?"

"No," she said quietly.

Outrage and incredulity seared through him. "Why the bloody hell not?"

"We just...didn't." She sat up, wrapped her arms around her raised knees. Her posture made her look young, a bit forlorn. "Most fashionable couples have separate bedchambers and don't sleep together."

"I'm not talking about most people; I'm talking about us." He settled his back against the headboard, trying to understand the past he didn't remember. Trying to keep a rein on his frustration and anger at himself. "Hell, Gabby, we set the sheets aflame together. More than that, I cannot fathom not wanting you beside me every night, even if we're not making love."

"Truly?"

The hope in her eyes was more than he could stand. "Sweetheart, didn't you hear me? I'm falling in love with you." He cupped her face in his hands and felt the preciousness of what he held. "Christ, I'm not falling—I'm bloody *there*."

"I love you." A tear slid down her cheek. "I always have."

"I'm not sure I deserve it." He thumbed the moisture away. "What kind of a bastard did you marry, Gabby? What in blazes was wrong with me?"

"Nothing was wrong with you." That was his wife, loyal to a fault. "You were just...different back then."

"I was an idiot," he said flatly.

"No more than I was." She let go of a breath. "There were two of us in this marriage. I could have said something, tried to change things...but I didn't."

"What stopped you?"

She bit her lip. "I've been asking myself the same thing. Why didn't I ask for what I wanted? Why didn't I try to have these conversations that we're having now? I don't think I know all the answers yet."

"You don't have to have the answers." He tucked a wayward tress behind her ear. "Just tell me what you're thinking."

Her eyes, so big and pure, searched his face. As if reassured by what she saw, she gave a quick nod, her hair rippling over her shoulders.

"When you asked me to marry you, I was ecstatic. In shock, truth be told, because I never, ever imagined a man like you would be interested in someone like me."

He frowned, about to interrupt, but her rueful smile stopped him.

"You wanted to know what I'm thinking, and this is it," she reminded him.

"Go on, then."

"You were so handsome, powerful, and rich...you could have had anyone you wanted, but you chose me. A wallflower who was shunned, even at her own house party. Not only that, but you were kind to me. You listened to my silly woes and made me feel... important. I think I fell in love with you at that moment." Her throat rippled. "When you proposed to me, you said you wanted a virtuous, trustworthy, and loyal wife. And I knew I could be those things—that I *wanted* to be those things more than I'd ever wanted anything in my life. Because you were the kind of husband I'd always dreamed of having."

The sincerity of her answer tautened his chest. He forced himself to remain quiet and listen, to let her release what she'd clearly been keeping to herself for so long.

"The only catch was that you said you didn't believe in romantic love. I told myself it didn't matter, especially because you offered other things that were just as important. Your affection, protection, and care. I have always felt those things from you, Adam. Always."

He gave a terse nod, knowing that she was trying to reassure him. To lessen his responsibility when it was as clear as day that he'd had his head stuck up his arse. To his further frustration, he had no idea why.

"You were a good husband to me and father to our children. I was content. And even if I knew my love wasn't returned, you were never cruel about it. Never made me feel stupid or awkward. On the contrary, you were ever so nice when I blurted out my feelings."

"*Nice?*" He shoved a hand through his hair. "Christ, Gabby, you deserve so much more."

"You gave me more than I've ever had in my whole life." Her fervor hit him deep in his gut. "When I was a girl, I was... awkward. My mama died giving birth to me, Papa was busy with the bank, and I don't think I ever really learned how to, well, get on with other people. My experiences at finishing school confirmed what I knew about myself: that I hadn't much in the way of looks, charm, or accomplishments. That the only hope I had of making friends was to be as pleasing as I could, hide any unpleasant feelings, and always keep a cheerful demeanor."

He knew it cost her to reveal these things to him. Her fingers were tightly clasped around her knees, the delicate knuckles white. A primitive part of him wanted to avenge her: to give whoever had hurt her what they deserved. But that reaction was selfish, for his own satisfaction. Knowing what his wife needed, he bridled his anger.

"You do not need to hide your feelings from me," he said. "You don't need to be cheerful if that isn't how you're feeling."

"I know." Her smile, bright and genuine, peeped out suddenly, like the sun from behind clouds. "Even though I've tried, I've never been able to hide my feelings from you. You've always seen through me...and what is more, you've accepted me. My tendency to worry and talk too much, all my different moods."

He stroked her hair, feeling her tremble of pleasure. "You are perfect the way you are, love."

"After Max was born, I fell into a period of doldrums. I was overwhelmed, bursting into tears over the slightest thing. Many men would have run from their wives at that point, but you didn't." She gave him a tremulous smile. "Do you know what you did?"

He lifted his brows.

"You made me a schedule."

"That's bloody romantic, isn't it?" he muttered.

"It *was*. That schedule showed me that you were thinking of me, taking care of me. You were attentive to my needs even when I, myself, was not." The adoration in her eyes halted his breath. "You made sure I ate, slept, took time for leisure. You hired more staff to relieve me of household duties. You even scheduled a time every night when you came into my chamber and we discussed the goings-on of the day and the agenda for the morrow. Even with the demands of running an empire, you have always made time for me."

His chest tight, he didn't know what to say.

"And about our Wednesday rendezvous," she said in a soft yet fierce tone. "While it's true that I didn't awaken in your arms, after you made love to me, you always held me until I fell asleep. And I always slept well those nights, feeling your affection and care."

He wished he'd given her more. Wished he knew why he hadn't.

But wishes were a waste of time, and a man in love had better things to do.

"From now on, you'll wake up in my arms every morning," he said. "And you'll wake up knowing that you hold my heart. Do you hear me, Gabby?"

"I hear you." Her shining eyes clogged his throat. "And I love you."

She tilted her head back, and he took her invitation, sealing their new vows with a kiss.

❧ 24 ❧

THE LAST DAY OF THEIR VACATION, GABBY WENT THROUGH THE manor in search of her husband. Happiness hummed through her as memories of the past four days flitted through her mind. Days and nights of such discovery and intimacy that she'd come to think of this trip as their second honeymoon. Indeed, since they'd never taken a wedding trip—Adam's business had been too demanding for him to leave London for long—perhaps this counted as their first.

No matter how one counted it, this time with her husband was magical.

Adam had taken her into the village, where they visited the shops looking for presents for Fiona and Max. He'd bought her countless gifts too, including the soft-as-a-cloud blue cashmere shawl she was wearing. When he'd seen her examining the expensive accoutrement at the milliner's, he'd insisted on buying it for her...in every available color. She'd teased him for overindulging her; he'd murmured in her ear that she deserved to be spoiled, and he planned on pampering her further...in bed.

He'd made good on that promise too.

With each walk through woods, shared meal and, yes, session

in bed, she felt the closeness between them growing. She'd shared more with Adam than she'd shared with anyone. Encouraged by his genuine interest, she told him more about her childhood, the feelings of loneliness and isolation she'd experienced. She told him about her father, how much she loved him and tried to be the child he wanted. She'd even told him about her management system for her worries, which he'd seemed to find highly amusing.

He also seemed to enjoy hearing her stories about how she'd met the Kent family and the adventures she'd shared with the intrepid family. When she candidly revealed that he'd been the suspected villain in some of these adventures, his brows rose...and for an instant, she feared she'd offended him. There was such a thing as being *too* honest.

Then he'd pretended to twirl an imaginary mustache, as if he were some villain from a very bad play, reducing her to giggles. He'd hauled her off as if he were kidnapping an innocent maiden and proceeded to debauch her thoroughly. Of course, she loved it.

Surrounded by the warmth of Adam's attention, she felt herself unfurling like a flower in the sun. It wasn't easy to open up, to break old habits, but she was determined to try. The time for hiding had come to an end. Even though Adam insisted that he bore the brunt of responsibility for the previous state of their relationship, she knew she was equally at fault.

Two people lived in a marriage. She saw now that her own lack of confidence and self-worth had contributed to the walls between them. Together, they were tearing down those barriers and rebuilding their union, with love and intimacy as their brick and mortar.

If anything, she wished she could provide the sort of insight to Adam that he'd given to her.

With his amnesia unchanging, she saw him struggle with frustration, with not knowing why he'd done the things he had or what had motivated him to set emotional boundaries in their marriage. To distance himself with schedules and routines. Since she knew so little about his past, she couldn't tell him either. Not for the first time, she wished she'd been brave enough to dig deeper, to get to the heart of the man she loved.

But as her father had been wont to say, *If wishes were horses, beggars would ride.*

Wishing wasn't going to change anything, but actions would. From here on in, she would try to have more confidence in herself. She would ask for what she wanted, work for the relationship she wanted—fight for it, if need be.

A frisson shivered through her as a ghost of the past flitted through her consciousness. It hovered like a moth drawn to the glow of her newfound happiness.

Jessabelle.

Gabby told herself it should no longer matter. She had her husband's love now, the thing she'd always wanted but had been afraid to ask for. She couldn't change the past...and Adam couldn't even remember it. What was the point in bringing up a problem to him that couldn't be resolved and would only mar the joy of the present?

She told herself she wasn't hiding; she was just being sensible.

Besides, Tessa was already looking into Jessabelle's identity. Dread quivered in the pit of Gabby's stomach, and she took a calming breath. Whatever Tessa discovered would determine her own next steps. If Jessabelle wasn't amongst those killed in the brothel fire, then Gabby would let go of her suspicions about Adam's infidelity once and for all. But if Jessabelle *had* worked at The Gilded Pearl...

I'll cross that bridge when I get there.

Such was her faith in her marriage, in who she and Adam were becoming, that she could put all those worries aside for now. She continued her search for him and found him in the sparring room. The sight of him set her pulse aflutter.

Goodness, she'd married a potent man.

He was working on his pugilistic skills, a delight she'd never seen first-hand since he practiced at a boxing saloon when they were in London. He was in the padded rectangular ring, the perimeter marked off by four posts connected by rope. His fists jabbed the air in a hard, rapid sequence.

His outfit was designed for ease of movement: he wore a linen shirt open at the collar and loose white trousers that hung low on his narrow hips, kept up by a colorful striped belt, the kind worn by prizefighters. The wide ends of the belt flapped as he moved lightly on his feet, shifting balance, feigning left and right as he threw punches.

She wetted her lips, arousal spilling through her.

In his present attire, he looked exactly like the sultan of her fantasies.

He caught sight of her, the alertness of his gaze sending tingles over her skin. When he exited the roped ring and came toward her, she saw the expanse of hair-dusted muscle revealed by his unbuttoned shirt, the sweat-dampened fabric clinging to his ridged torso. His shirtsleeves were rolled up, revealing his sinewy, veined forearms. An ebony wave fell across his brow, completing the image of an exotic prince.

When he bent to kiss her cheek, the smell of his clean, male sweat made her pussy quiver.

"Did you have a nice nap?" he murmured.

"Yes," she managed. "It was quite refreshing."

"I'm glad. I would have stayed with you, but after all those weeks as an invalid, I couldn't stomach being in bed any more than necessary."

Given the disproportionate amount of time the two of them had spent in bed in the last few days, she had to lift her brows.

His smile was lazy and all male. "Making love to my wife is necessary."

Since she wasn't about to argue with that, she asked, "How did your practice session go?"

"I know the basics." He looked pleased with himself. "My form's not bad, actually."

She glanced at his taut, muscular form. *It's not bad at all.*

As if he caught wind of her thoughts, he gave her that slow, toe-curling smile again.

"What are you thinking about, my dear wife?"

"Nothing." The reply was habitual, the way she always responded when she was afraid, embarrassed, or uncertain about sharing what was really going on in her head. And, truly, she couldn't be expected to say her wicked fantasy aloud.

The reproving heat in his eyes made her heart thump faster.

"Did you just file something away in the *Bin of Blissful Ignorance?*" he asked softly.

Dash it, maybe she oughtn't have divulged quite so much of her inner life. "It's nothing, truly."

"You have a tell-tale sign when you're lying. A pretty blush that rises from here,"—he brushed his index finger on the bare skin just above the neckline of her gown, causing her nipples to tighten—"all the way up here."

She shivered as his fingertip feathered up her throat, over her lips, to her eyebrows.

"What aren't you telling me, hmm?"

Not fooled by his mild tone, she mumbled, "I'm just, um, happy to see you."

Hedging wasn't the same as lying, was it?

After a pause, he said, "I suppose there is another explanation for your blush other than lying."

Thank heavens. Thinking quickly, she cast a look at the roaring hearth.

"It *is* rather warm in here," she said brightly.

"I don't think that is the kind of heat you're responding to."

Uh oh. In that instant, she knew she'd been snared. Her breath came faster as he cupped her jaw, his eyes holding her fast.

"I know this blush because I see it spread like a sunrise over your beautiful skin when I make love to you. When you're aroused and hot and all you can think about is how empty your pussy feels. How much you want my cock to fill you, to take you, to make you come."

Held captive by his words, by her own clamoring desire, she couldn't speak. Need spiked, her pussy clenching on emptiness just like he said. Wanting him...just like he said.

"Let's try this again," he said silkily. "What are you thinking about, Gabriella?"

"I was thinking that you remind me of a sultan," she blurted.

His eyes flickered, his expression unreadable. When he said nothing more, she realized that he was waiting for her to explain what she meant. Now that the horses had bolted, there was no use closing the barn door, was there?

She swallowed. "You're going to think I'm silly."

"Let me be the judge. Go on."

Since it wasn't really a request, she sighed and gave him what he wanted.

"When I first met you, I happened to be reading *Arabian Nights' Entertainments*. Not the, um, modified version the children are reading. The original translation which has the sultan marrying a new virgin bride every day and killing them after one night so that they couldn't betray him as his first queen had done." Squirming under his scrutiny, she said, "You reminded me of him. Of how I pictured him in my mind, that is."

His eyebrows drew together. "I reminded you of a wife-murdering lunatic?"

"No, not that part. See? I knew this would be difficult to explain."

"Try anyway, pet."

Her hands twisting the ends of her shawl, she said, "It was your power, your absolute command of yourself and the world around you that made me draw the comparison. You have a confidence, an animal magnetism that is ever so compelling. Whenever you looked at me, I felt...special. As if I were being seen for the first time." She lowered her gaze to his chest; it was too difficult to say the rest to his face. "I wanted to be granted an audience with you. Wanted to do anything to please you. To win your love and be your cherished queen."

His finger curled under her chin, tipping her gaze up to meet his.

"A fitting fantasy," he said softly, "since you remind me of Scheherazade."

"Because I talk so much?"

His lips twitched. "I like the way you talk. It's charming and unique, just like you. But that is not the only way you resemble Scheherazade. Like her, you have strength and courage that might be easily overlooked, that have helped you survive hurt and pain without ever losing your smile. Like the queen who married a tyrant to prevent the murder of more innocents, you are kind and caring...too often putting the needs of others before your own. Not to mention, you're as beautiful, loyal, and intelligent as the heroine of legend."

Her heart felt full to bursting. "Oh, Adam, that's so—"

"If you say *kind*, I may throttle you."

"I was going to say beautiful. Wonderful," she said ardently. "The most *romantic* thing anyone has ever said to me."

"I should hope no other man has spoken to you in that way."

His stern tone gave her a pleasant shiver. "Of course not."

"And no other man ever will because you're *mine*, Gabby. My wife, the mother of my children, the woman I love. Which means you can trust me."

"I do trust you—"

"Then why did you lie? Why didn't you tell me what you were thinking?"

"Because, well, it was...*embarrassing*."

"What was?"

"How fanciful I was being." Cheeks flaming, she met his gaze nonetheless. "When I saw you there all...sweaty and manly, in that outfit with that sultan-ish belt...I started having thoughts of a rather, um, indecorous nature. Not the sort of thoughts a virtuous wife should have."

His brows arched. "What makes you think I want a virtuous wife?"

"You told me you did. When you proposed."

"I think we already established that the old me was an idiot." He reached out, rubbing his thumb over her bottom lip. When he did that, she experienced the strange and wanton urge to open her mouth...to lick him. "And surely my lovemaking during this trip has shown you that I have no interest in carrying out polite conjugal duties."

He was right. He'd been many things—passionate, tender, demanding—but not polite.

Thank heavens.

"I want *you*, Gabby. A marriage of body, heart, and mind, remember? In order to have that, you'll have to trust me, to trust that I won't belittle or discount your thoughts or feelings, that I'll do everything in my power to make you happy."

"You're right, and I'm ever so sorry," she said with true contrition. "I should have trusted you not to make fun of my flight of fancy."

"I'm glad we got that out of the way. Now pertaining to your little fantasy, I wouldn't make fun of it because it also happens to be mine. "

She blinked. "You fancy...being a sultan?"

"Not precisely." The gleam in his eyes made her pulse leap. "But I fancy the idea of being your lord and master. Of you serving me, pleasing me in any way I wish. In fact, I think we ought to have a sampling of that now."

❧ 25 ❧

HEARING HER DEEPEST SEXUAL FANTASY UTTERED IN ADAM'S sensual baritone set off tremors of desire in Gabby. Her knees wobbled, but he swept her up in an easy movement. To her surprise, he didn't take her toward their bedchamber but into the boxing ring.

"Here?" she asked breathlessly.

"Here."

He set her down on the soft mats that padded the ring and began to undress her with a cool efficiency that further stimulated her senses. In a matter of heartbeats, she was naked, her unpinned hair cascading down her back. She trembled beneath his appraising gaze and instinctively moved to cover her breasts. He stopped her with a calm command.

"A queen doesn't hide herself. If you want to please me, you'd best show yourself to an advantage." He stepped back from her, circling her slowly, a sultan assessing his carnal prize. "Let me see all the alluring parts of you—tempt me with your charms."

Even as she squirmed at the notion, excitement thrummed in her veins. A part of her understood that this wasn't just about sex: this was about changing old habits and taking a risk. She'd said she no longer wanted to hide, and Adam was inviting her to reveal her true longings...in a bold and naughty way.

The familiarity of the fantasy made it easier to let go of her inhibitions. How many times had she dreamed about this very scenario? As she slipped into the twilight pool of her imagination, she shed the skin of the awkward, rejected girl she'd once been. Beneath Adam's approving gaze, she became a beautiful queen, his willing slave.

For his pleasure and her own, she explored her woman's body, the lush swell of her hips and the inviting softness of her belly. She slid her palms upward, cradling the full curves of her breasts, feeling their sensual weight. Power leapt like a flame inside her when his mouth tightened with arousal.

"Such beautiful tits," he praised. "Do you enjoy petting them, teasing them for me?"

Understanding his instruction, she rolled her thumbs over her straining red nipples, the spark of pleasure intensified by his avid stare.

"Rub those nipples harder. I want them as ripe as cherries when I taste them."

She pinched her nipples between finger and thumb, imagining his mouth there, his tongue. The memory of his hot suckling blazed a path between her breasts and pussy, the tug and pluck of her fingers bringing forth a needy spasm in her sex.

"Is your pussy wet and ready for me?"

The coolness of his inquiry threw kindling on her arousal. Reminded her of the power of the man who'd chosen her to serve his needs.

"Yes," she said throatily.

"Show me."

After a slight hesitation, she slowly placed her hand between her legs. Even as she shyly touched her slippery cleft, a part of her couldn't believe she was doing such a thing. That she dared to perform this wicked deed in front of her husband.

"Is that how a queen pleasures herself, so timidly?" he admonished. "Show me how you really touch yourself, pet. All those nights when you were alone in your bed, wishing it was Wednesday. Thinking of me just on the other side of the door and how I ought to have been in your bed instead, filling you with my hard cock. Taking away the ache in your cunny that your hand could only partially satisfy."

Her breath panted from her lips, desire and shame a combustible mix. How had he guessed what she'd done? Yet the glint in his eyes wasn't one of disgust but hungry desire. Her gaze dropped to the front of his trousers, where his enormous erection tented the fabric. He was aroused by the thought of her touching herself. Of her finding wanton pleasure.

Heady with wanting, she began to stroke herself. Slowly at first, then with increasing confidence, she explored her aching flesh. Finding the center of her sensation, she rubbed there, using that covert rhythm and friction that had eased her lonely nights. Only now she wasn't alone, she was with her master, whose dark, lustful encouragement propelled her rapidly toward her peak.

"That's right, pet. Diddle your pearl, rub your sweet cream all over it."

Gasping, she moved her fingers faster and faster, the muscles of her pussy clenching...

"Come for me," he commanded.

She moaned as her release washed over her, a tide of bliss that made her toes curl against the mat. She would have stumbled had he not caught her against him. His iron-hard cock pressed into her belly.

"So beautiful, my queen," he growled.

He took her hand, the one she'd used to stroke herself, and brought it to his lips. He sucked her fingers into his mouth, the warm, wet pull releasing a fresh wave of need.

"Delicious," he said thickly. "I'll have more of that after."

"After what?" she asked breathily.

"After I enjoy the pleasure of your mouth."

His words from several nights ago flashed in her head. *Another time, I'll put you on your knees and wet my cock between your sweet lips.* The idea had intrigued her, stimulated her, touched upon a nerve of longing that made her lick her lips now.

He caught that movement, his eyes turning darker than midnight. He cupped her shoulders, pressing downward even as her knees bent of their own accord. Kneeling at his feet, she looked up as he pulled off his shirt, revealing the glory of his muscle-paved chest, all that rippling sinew dusted with hair. His long, clever fingers unknotted the colorful sash at his waist. It occurred to her that a sultan wouldn't disrobe; he'd have his slave do it for him.

When she touched his hand, he stilled.

"May I do it for you?" she asked softly.

Her courage paid off; his eyes flashed with approving hunger. At his nod, she went to work, pulling the belt from its loops. She found the fastener behind his waistband, undoing it with trembling eagerness. As she tugged the garment down, her thumbs tracing the steely arcs of muscle on his hips, the fabric caught on his rampant erection.

He shivered as she freed the material from his jutting member. She worked the trousers over his knees and down to his large, bare feet. As he stepped out of them, she was treated to an erotic view of his swaying cock, a long, heavy branch that defied the pull of gravity. His balls hung like a succulent plum, swollen and ripe with juice.

Naked, standing like a proud king, he wrapped his fingers around his mighty scepter. He stroked himself almost thoughtfully as her anticipation spiraled higher and higher. She waited, her eyes automatically finding his as she awaited his pleasure...and her own.

"Have you sucked my cock before?" he inquired.

"No." Her throat convulsed with desire, curiosity...and regret.

All these years, she'd been hiding, choosing to live in a cupboard when her marriage was a palace waiting to be explored. When room upon room of dazzling pleasures had awaited her. How she wished she'd had the courage to discover this intimacy sooner.

"An oversight I intend to rectify immediately."

His forceful scrutiny banished her thoughts of the past, anchored her in the scorching reality of now.

"Take my cock in your hand and stroke it."

With quivering enthusiasm, she obeyed. He leapt at her touch, the feeling of holding his hard vitality giving her an indescribable rush. He strained against the limits of her clasp, her fist barely fitting around him.

"Use both hands to frig me," he said.

Loving the guttural edge in his voice, she did as she was told, using two hands to work his meaty stalk, to drag that velvety skin up and down over the iron core. When her fists descended, exposing his purplish tip, a drop of liquid leaked from the slit at its center. The urge to taste him was a visceral need.

"Lick it off."

His dark permission banished any lingering uncertainty, cocooning her in the present. There was only her and her sultan, the all-encompassing passion between them. She leaned in, swiping her tongue across his burgeoned crown, his essence affecting her senses like a drug. She couldn't help drawing on him, her lips fitting around his thick dome, trying to coax out more of his salty male elixir.

His hands clenched in her hair, a message for her to hold still. She did, and his hips lunged, his cock pressing forward. Pulse racing, she widened her mouth for him, welcoming the strange sensation of him entering her this way.

"Breathe through your nose, love," he said through harsh breaths. "Mind your teeth and relax your throat as much as you can. Give me the gift of your beautiful mouth."

She moaned around the turgid flesh pushing deeper and deeper inside her. Her hands clung to the hard trunks of his thighs as she served him with her mouth the way she had with her pussy. As he owned this part of her along with the rest. She was an eager servant to his desires, his grunts of approval building her excitement. Her cunny wept with need even as she parted her lips wider, wanting more, everything he had to give. She lost herself in the beauty of their perfectly aligned bodies, hearts, and minds.

He reached the end of her, butting the silken wall of her throat, causing her muscles to flex involuntarily. She choked, and he withdrew, panting heavily. His thumbs dashed the tears of strain from her cheeks, tears she hadn't known had fallen.

"I'm fine," she gasped. "Don't stop—"

"Lie back and spread your legs for me." His gaze glowed with savage hunger. "I want to fill you with my seed. Want you to pull it from my cock with your greedy little pussy."

The moment her back touched the mats, he was upon her. Driving into her with a possessive force that made her scream with pleasure. Her orgasm came abruptly, a thunderclap of rapture that began in her cunny and reverberated in the deepest part of her soul. Slinging her knees over his shoulders, her master continued to ram into her, his stones pounding against her sensitive folds, his eyes burning into hers. He took her higher and higher until she was suddenly poised upon another peak.

"Come now," he said. "Take me with you."

Her pussy convulsed at his command, milking his hardness, pleasure bursting in her womb. He threw his head back, groaning as he shoved into her, inundating her with his scorching heat. He collapsed upon her, their bodies still joined, and she wrapped her limbs around him, welcoming his weight. For long moments, neither of them moved, bonded by the sweat of their bodies and the frantic symphony of their hearts.

Finally, he lifted his head. His sated, relaxed expression deepened her bliss.

"My own Scheherazade." He traced her lips with his finger. "A queen who is indeed talented with her mouth."

It amazed her that she could blush after what had just transpired.

"I'm glad you shared your fantasy with me." He shifted his hips, drawing her attention to the fact that he was still hard inside her. His gaze serious, he said, "You don't need to hide anything from me. I want to know what is in your heart, always."

"*You* are in my heart." On impulse—and with great daring—she used her lower muscles to give him an intimate squeeze. "And other places."

His eyes crinkled at the corners. "I may have created a monster."

Since she could feel him burgeoning inside her, her virile sultan rising once again, she took it as a compliment. Smiling, she tipped her lips up for his kiss.

∾

She was sitting at her vanity, one of her favorite places to be. He saw that she'd probably spent a great deal of time on her toilette. She wore another new gown, expensive but vulgar in how much it displayed of her smooth white skin. Her blonde hair was arranged in ringlets that enhanced her angelic features, yet the effect was marred by her heavy face paint. A gold, crystal-encrusted demi-mask lay on the table in front of her.

She met his eyes in the looking glass.

"Let's go to the club tonight, luv," she cajoled sweetly. "I want to please you."

He didn't believe her. Behind her angel's face lay a self-serving heart. Knowing her history, sharing a good chunk of it, he didn't hold it against her. Life in the stews hardened you, taught you to get what you wanted, however you could get it.

He'd wanted her. She'd wanted to be wanted.

And not just by him.

"You want to please yourself," he said bluntly. "Change out of that dress and wash that bloody paint off your face. You look like a whore."

"You used to like me like this."

Her sparkling lemonade voice, which he'd once loved with a young man's passion, soured to a petulance that made impatience gnaw at his gut. He didn't have time for a tantrum; he had a business to build.

"You liked the games we used to play," she said, her pink lips forming a practiced pout.

Perhaps he had, once. He'd been aroused by her lack of inhibition, her penchant for dark, carnal adventures. But the older he got, the less appealing these qualities became. Especially when he realized that what stirred her wasn't the fact that she was sharing the experience with the man she loved but the covetous looks she received from others. She thrived on being the center of lustful attention, on his mounting jealousy.

"I don't have time for games," he said shortly. "I have work to do."

"*Work.*" She spat the word like an epithet, rising from the vanity and whirling to face him. "That's all you care about!"

"You should care about it too. After all, my labor pays for your jewels and gowns, the roof over your head," he said flatly.

Her eyes narrowed. "You don't own me."

"Don't I?" He flicked a glance at the ring on her left hand. An ostentatious cluster of rubies and diamonds that she'd wanted and that had cost him several months of his hard-earned pay. Rubies for his wife...the irony didn't escape him.

"I 'ate you."

Rage rubbed off her polished accents. So much for the blunt he'd spent on their elocution lessons. His irritation grew: he was a man on the rise and, by God, she dragged him down.

The thought stabbed him with guilt. For despite everything,

he still loved her. She couldn't help who she was any more than he could quell his own ruthless need for power and revenge. Unlike love, he thought cynically, those two things might actually bring a man peace.

"I wish me and Garrity 'ad never rescued you from the river. We should've left you to dine wif the fishes!"

"Nonetheless, you will stay put in the house tonight," he said curtly. "If not to respect my wishes, then for your own safety. The war with O'Leary isn't over. He's not going to sit back and let me take over his territory. There will be bloodshed, and I'd prefer it not be yours."

"What do you care what 'appens to me? You leave for your precious work, and I'm stuck in this 'ouse all day. I'm lonely, bored out o' my bleedin' skull!" She hugged her arms around herself. "No one's e'er given a damn about me. I ne'er should've married you, you selfish bastard!"

Despite her lashing words, he saw the shadow of his first love in her vulnerable pose. His sense of responsibility warred with impatience; in the end, the latter won out. She was a bucket that could never be filled. No matter how hard he tried, a new leak sprung. Another night spent arguing with her wouldn't make a difference...whereas the meeting he was already late for could be the next step in building his empire. A step closer to avenging his honor and that of his mama.

Numquam obliviscar. Never forget.

"But you are married to me, which means you will obey me in this," he said firmly.

Her lips quivered, her eyes sheening.

Stifling a sigh, he crossed over to her, curled his finger under her chin. "Tomorrow night, I'll take you somewhere. The opera or a play." When she didn't take his olive branch, he sweetened the deal. "You can buy yourself a new gown for the occasion, hmm?"

Still, she said nothing.

His patience at an end, he left.

The next time he saw her, she was lying in a pool of blood.

"Adam. Wake up." A soft voice called to him. "Wake up, darling."

He surfaced from dark, obscure depths, his lungs straining, his heart hammering with panic...from what he didn't know. As his vision adjusted to the glow of lamplight, he saw her leaning over him, looking at him with worried eyes.

Gabriella. She was safe. His wife was safe.

"You were having a bad dream—"

Her words ended in a gasp because he'd hauled her against his chest. Wrapped both arms around her, pressing her warm, vital softness against his rigid muscles until he was convinced that she was truly there. That his beloved was alive and well.

She murmured softly to him, didn't protest at his suffocating hold.

Only when the tides of fear receded did he loosen his embrace.

She stayed in his arms, caressing his jaw. "What was the nightmare about, darling?"

"I don't remember." Drawing a ragged breath, he searched for details and found none. There was only the remnant of that gut-wrenching terror. "When I woke up, I had this feeling of...panic. That I was going to lose you."

"You'll never lose me." She pressed a kiss on his chest. "It was just a dream."

He tunneled his fingers through her silken tresses, holding her against his heart until it calmed.

"Do you know what I think the dream was about?" she asked.

"What?"

"Our time here coming to an end."

"That's a possibility, I suppose. But as fine a time as we've had,"—he slid his hand down her lush backside, giving her a squeeze—"we have much more ahead of us."

"I know. But things have been so magical here. I just wonder... if they'll stay that way. Once we're back in London, in our ordinary life and regular routines."

Hearing the quiver in her voice, he tipped her head back to look into her eyes. And realized that he was not the only one struggling with the fear of the unknown.

"Nothing's going to change between us," he said.

"I know. It's just that it's taken us eight years to get here." She bit her lip, a telling sign that whatever she wanted to say wasn't going to be easy for her. "When your memory returns, what if you...change back?"

Hearing the heart of her uncertainty filled him with remorse... and tenderness.

"Sweetheart, I love you. Nothing can alter that," he said firmly. "I don't know why I was such an idiot before, but whatever the reason, I won't let it get in the way again."

"Promise?" she asked in an aching whisper.

"I promise." He sealed his vow with a lingering kiss, letting the sweetness of their passion wash away the bitter dregs of his nightmare and her fears.

When they parted, she said breathlessly, "I must admit that, as much as I miss the children, I wish our vacation didn't have to end."

"It's not over yet." He rolled on top of her, his erection pressing into her belly. "We've got a few hours left, and I intend to make good use of them."

❦ 26 ❦

As she stepped over the threshold into the townhouse, accepting Burke's welcome, Gabby had the odd sense that she was entering a new place. Yet nothing had visibly altered; the veined marble floors, tiered chandelier, and sweeping double staircase were the same as when she saw them last. It must be that something in *her* had changed, then, that caused her to see her home with fresh eyes.

The floors gleamed with a deeper shine, the wood accents richer and finer than she remembered. Beneath the twinkling chandelier, the bouquet on the round rosewood table bloomed with colorful magnificence, the scent of hothouse roses perfuming the air. She experienced a fresh, poignant appreciation for this home that she'd had a part in building. That was a symbol of the love and commitment between her and her husband.

As if Adam, too, felt the significance of their return, he slid an arm around her waist.

"It's good to be home, isn't it?" he murmured, his lips brushing her temple. "To be back where we started...but also in a different place."

She was no longer surprised at how attuned he was to her

feelings. Adam had always been perceptive. The difference now was that she felt safe letting her guard down, allowing him to see the parts of her she'd previously kept hidden. He returned her honesty with his own; in some ways, she felt she'd learned more about him in five days than she had in the prior eight years.

"Mama! Papa! You're home!"

The happy cries and stampeding footsteps announced the arrival of Fiona and Max. As Adam swung Fiona in an arc that made her giggle, Max ran to Gabby, who crouched to receive his hug.

"How I've missed you, my lamb." She hugged him close, inhaling his sweet boy smell.

"I've missed you too, Mama. I learned new words when you were gone," he exclaimed. "Miss Thornton taught me how to spell *rainbow*!"

"Too bad you couldn't figure it out during charades," Fiona muttered.

Yet her jibe at her younger brother was good-natured, and she dashed over to receive Gabby's hug as Max went to Adam, who affectionately ruffled his son's dark hair.

"How was your vacation with Papa?" Fiona asked.

Loath to let her firstborn go, Gabby held Fi close for another moment. "It was ever so wonderful. Although we did miss the two of you."

"Maybe next time Fiona and I can go on vacation too," Max said eagerly.

"A splendid idea, lad," Adam said. "We'll plan a family trip next summer. To the Continent, perhaps."

The children's eyes widened.

"Truly?" Fiona breathed.

"Yes, poppet. Your mama informs me that we've never taken a vacation as a family, an oversight that I intend to remedy." Adam's gaze moved up to meet Gabby's. "Besides, I think vacationing agrees with your mama. A change in routine brings out a whole new side of her."

Gabby blushed at the very knowing, very male look in her husband's eyes.

"You do look different, Mama." Fiona studied her with a disconcertingly keen gaze. "Your cheeks are glowing and your eyes are brighter. You look very pretty."

"Mama is always pretty," Max said.

Fiona rolled her eyes. "You are such a sycophant, Maximillian."

Gabby felt her brows rise at the same time that Adam said sternly, "An impressive word, although not one that applies to your brother."

"I'm sorry, Max," Fiona muttered.

"I'm not a sycophant." Max scowled at his sister. "Whatever that is."

"It's a toadying sort of person," Fiona explained.

"Where did you learn the word?" Gabby asked curiously.

"Olivia taught it to me. She learned it from her papa, who was describing members of the Queen's court."

"A word used in its proper context." Adam's expression turned to one of amusement.

"Context is important." Gabby narrowed her eyes at her husband, which only made his lips quirk. "But no matter the situation, it isn't nice to make judgements of others, for no one is perfect. Recall the proverb about glass houses."

"Yes, Mama," Fi and Max chorused.

Relieved and rather surprised by the children's obedience, Gabby smiled at them. "Papa and I brought back presents for the two of you. After our valises are unpacked, we'll bring them to the nursery. For now, run along with Miss Thornton."

The children dashed off.

"I can't believe I'm going to say this, but I actually missed the mayhem," Adam remarked.

Gabby tried out a coy look. "Did I not provide enough excitement for you, Mr. Garrity?"

"Minx." His eyes gleamed. "I really did create a monster. Lucky me."

He was pulling her close when Burke came into the antechamber. At the sight of his master and mistress embracing, the ancient retainer turned a bright shade of red.

"Oh...beg pardon," he said hastily.

"It's quite all right, Burke."

Flustered, Gabby swatted ineffectually at Adam's hands, which remained clamped on her waist. He returned her beseeching look with an amused but unyielding one of his own. His words rang in her head.

From now on, I won't limit my desire for you in any way.

Not even in front of the servants, apparently.

Her embarrassment gave way to her true desire. She and Adam had years of intimacy to make up for. If he wanted to indulge in public displays of affection, who was she to argue?

Relaxing against Adam, she addressed the butler. "Was there something you wanted?"

"A letter arrived for you, madam." Burke extended the silver salver with the note the way one might hold out a steak to a rabid dog. "It is from Mrs. Kent. The messenger said it was important."

Gabby's entire being froze. A message from Tessa...it could only be about one thing. What happiness had pushed from her mind.

Jessabelle.

Aware of Adam behind her, she took the note with numb fingers. "Thank you, Burke."

After the butler took off like the hounds of hell were at his heels, Adam let her go, giving her a curious look.

"What is the matter, love? You look like you've seen a ghost."

If only he knew how close he was to the truth. For an instant, she considered telling him what she'd asked Tessa to do for her...

but she couldn't bring herself to do it. To destroy their hard-won joy over a matter that could be nothing. Moreover, even if Jessabelle had been a whore at The Gilded Pearl, Adam would have no memory of her. What good would it do to accuse him of an infidelity he couldn't even remember committing?

For the first time in my life, I'm truly happy. My husband is a different man now, and he loves me. Whatever he may or may not have done in the past, does it really matter?

"It's nothing." Her hand curled around the note.

"Burke just said it was important."

Although she was terrible at lying, the excuse came with surprising ease. "Tessa is holding a ball next week in honor of Maggie and Ransom's engagement, remember?" she said brightly. "She probably wants to know what I'm wearing."

"Ah. Important ladies' matters."

She was so relieved at her husband's faint smile that she wasn't prepared for his next question.

"So, what are you wearing?"

"Oh, I, um…don't know. I'm certain I have a suitable ballgown lying around. Nell will help me choose something from my wardrobe."

"A special occasion calls for a new gown. We'll visit the modiste tomorrow."

"We?" She tilted her head, confused. "You're coming with me?"

"Don't you want your husband's opinion?"

"You've never gone to the dress shop with me before," she said doubtfully. "It can be dreadfully dull."

"Nothing involving you is dull." As he leaned in to kiss her cheek, her hand tightened protectively around the note. "Make the appointment for late afternoon tomorrow. I'll go straight from the office."

She'd almost forgotten that he'd be returning to work on the morrow.

"Very well," she said.

"I'd better check in on the unpacking of the gifts. Much longer and the children will start a rebellion," he said with a grin.

"I'll meet you up there," she replied.

After he left, she looked at the crumpled note in her hand. How strange that a piece of paper felt as lethal as an explosive device. Delaying wasn't going to ameliorate its impact, however.

Taking a breath, she broke the wax seal and scanned the brief message.

The female of interest was not an employee of a certain place. You may put your mind at ease, dear friend. Now I have a favor to ask: would you please come over at your earliest convenience to help me choose the flowers for my ball? Who knew there were so many varieties of the blasted things?

-Tessa

The sound that escaped Gabby was halfway between a sob and a laugh, but the feeling that flooded her was one of pure, dazzling relief.

27

"This is all I have at the moment, but I swear on my mama's grave that I'll have the rest of the blunt to you next month."

Adam looked at the gold locket on his desk then back at the bedraggled lordling sitting across from him. Evanston had the bleary-eyed look of a man who'd spent the night drinking, gambling, whoring...and God knew what else.

"Your mother's still alive," Adam said, having reviewed the client's file thoroughly. "Which is more than you'll be if you miss another payment."

Murray, who was watching the exchange with his shoulder propped against the wall, smothered his laugh with a cough.

"Have mercy, sir. I won't be late again." Evanston exuded the optimism of a man who believes his own lies.

"If you want mercy, go to your priest." Adam pinned Evanston with a look, long enough for the cove to start shaking in his boots. "Leave the locket. I'll consider it interest for the amount you owe. Which, by the way, has doubled for next month."

"Yes, sir. Thank you, sir." Clearing his throat, Evanston said hopefully, "Would you consider extending some extra credit—"

"Do you enjoy being Kerrigan's punching bag? Get out before I have him throw you out."

"Right-o!" Evanston leapt to his feet, bowing all the way to the door. "See you next month!"

Shaking his head, Murray went to close the door. "*See you next month.* Evanston says that as cheerfully as if you're his best crony. If one didn't know better, one would think he missed you during your absence."

"A moneylender is a gentleman's best friend," Adam said wryly.

"By God, you haven't changed at all." Murray grinned. "Good to have you back, Garrity."

"It's good to be back."

That was the truth. The moment Adam had walked into his spacious, well-appointed office, he'd felt a sense of belonging. A king—or sultan, he'd thought with a private smile—returning to his rightful throne. He'd spent the morning reviewing matters of priority with Murray then transitioned to meeting with clients in the afternoon.

All of it had come as naturally as breathing. The business of being a moneylender, of assessing risk and benefit, seizing upon opportunity and, aye, collecting his just dues, suited his nature. It gave direction to his ruthless ambition and drive, his bone-deep need to achieve success. And he didn't give a damn what anyone thought of it.

Murray sprawled in the chair vacated by Evanston. "How was your trip to Hertfordshire?"

Memories heated Adam's blood. In truth, thoughts of Gabby had been a threat to his concentration throughout the day. As much as he enjoyed his return to work, he missed having her near. Hearing her sweet voice as she chattered on about some domestic matter, smelling her perfume, holding her soft, curvy body against his...

"From the way you're smiling, I'd say you enjoyed the time with your lady very much."

Seeing Murray's waggling brows, Adam quickly firmed his lips. "Stop being an idiot."

"I was wrong before: you *have* changed." Murray studied him with lazy hazel eyes that hid a razor-sharp mind. "Why, Garrity, I believe you are a man in love."

Adam returned the other's stare with a pointed one of his own. "Do *you* wish to have a session with Kerrigan?"

"Love is naught to be ashamed of. Despite his best intentions, no man is immune to it. Take my older brother, for instance," Murray said airily. "Carlisle was a confirmed bachelor, a practical soul who wouldn't know a poem if it smacked him in the nose. Yet one nudge from my lovely sister-in-law Violet—and by nudge, I mean she literally pushed him into a fountain—and he toppled straight into Cupid's arms."

"Is there a point to this soliloquy?"

"A sensible man guards his heart; a smart man knows when to yield it." Murray's brows lifted. "With a wife like Mrs. Garrity, you'd be a fool to withhold your heart—or any of your organs."

"Mention my wife's name in the same sentence as 'organs' again, and I will personally tear you from limb to limb."

"Protective, aren't we?" Murray held his hands up in a placating gesture when Adam began to rise. "All fun aside, may I say how glad I am to see you fully recovered? I know these past weeks have not been easy on you or Mrs. Garrity."

Settling back into his chair, Adam gave the other one last warning look. "My wife has been an angel. No man could ask for more."

"I'm glad you finally realize your good fortune."

Something in Murray's tone made Adam frown. "Are you implying that I did not before?"

Did the other know something about Adam's past? About why he'd kept a deliberate distance from his own wife? He had committed himself to moving forward in his marriage, to not waste time trying to unearth old history when he could spend that energy loving his Gabriella. But if there was something Murray knew...

"Just a feeble attempt at humor," Murray said easily. "Enough about you, let's talk about a more interesting subject: me."

Adam couldn't tell if the other was lying, but he decided to let it go. For now.

He steepled his fingers. "What about you?"

"I've landed us a trio of new clients. All newly come into their titles and all horse-mad, with a convenient penchant for betting on the wrong horse. We're going to make a fortune—"

The longcase clock chimed, alerting Adam to the time.

"Bloody hell, is it three already? I'm going to be late." He rose, striding to the door, grabbing his hat and walking stick from the mahogany and brass stand along the way.

"Late for what?" Murray's forehead furrowed. "You usually don't leave the office until six. At the earliest."

He was damned if he was going to admit that he was headed to a dress shop to choose a gown for his wife.

"It's an urgent matter," he said curtly.

No lie there. Gabby was delectable no matter what she wore, but when it came to fashion, she *was* a bloody emergency. She needed his help...whether she knew it or not.

"In that case, I'll hold down the fort," Murray said. "By the by, Cornish sent a note. Said he would have some report to you soon."

"Excellent. Have the secretary schedule him in the calendar."

With that, Adam strode out.

"Papa, I have to go," Gabby said regretfully.

"You just got here," her father grumbled.

Which wasn't true. She'd spent the day at his bedside. In the short time that she'd been in Hertfordshire, his condition had taken a turn for the worse. Today, she'd kept a fretful vigil as he drifted in and out of sleep; even when he was awake, his mind was foggy from the laudanum the physician had prescribed for his growing pain.

Seeing her father's pallid skin stretch over his increasingly skeletal features wedged a lump in her throat. She could hardly believe that this was the robust, larger-than-life man of her childhood. While his presence might have been limited in her life, she'd always known that he'd held affection for her, in his own way.

She loved him so...and wasn't ready to say goodbye.

She brushed the sparse grey strands off his forehead, placed a kiss on his speckled brow.

"I'll be back tomorrow," she said. "And I'll bring the children. Fiona and Max miss their grandpapa."

"They're welcome to visit as long as they don't perform a play. I might not live long enough to get through another one."

The unexpected flash of her father's dry wit made her smile.

"No play, Papa," she said tenderly. "Just a nice chat."

"Speaking of chat, there is something we must discuss. Help me sit up, Gabriella."

Glancing at the clock on the bedside table, Gabby gnawed on her lip. She would be late meeting Adam at the dressmaker's, and it was too late to send a note. Seeing her father struggle to sit up, however, she assisted him so that he was propped up comfortably against the pillows.

"Now that the damned laudanum is finally wearing off," he said though huffing breaths, "I have something to say."

"Do you need more medicine?" she asked anxiously. "Are you in pain?"

"What I need is a clear head for a blasted second. Stop hovering, girl, and sit."

She returned to the chair, perching warily. "What is it, Papa?"

"For some time now, I've had a gut feeling that something is rotten in the state of Denmark. And by Denmark, I'm referring to your trust."

"My trust?" Gabby blinked. "You set that up years ago, with Mr. Isnard as my trustee. I thought the terms were laid out to your specifications."

"The terms are clear. Upon my death, all my wealth, including property and controlling interest in Billings Bank will go into the trust. Mr. Isnard is directed to oversee the trust for your benefit and that of my grandchildren."

Years ago, before she'd even met Adam, her father had devised the trust as a means to protect her and her inheritance from fortune hunters. Other than her dowry, her husband would have no access to her wealth. All financial decisions would be made by the trustee, whom her father had chosen to act in her best interests.

What had made Adam's proposal magical was that he'd known about the trust...and hadn't cared. He hadn't wanted her for her money but for *who she was*. For the first time in her life, she'd had a taste of what it could be like to be valued and wanted, just for being herself.

Looking back, she knew that that had been a pivotal, life-altering moment for her. It was the foundation for all that had happened since. Adam had seen the promise of her and now, eight years later, they had a loving union beyond her wildest imaginings.

"If the terms are clear, then what is the problem?" she asked.

"The problem is that I've become aware of Mr. Isnard's financial woes," her father said grimly. "Financial problems that he has been hiding from me, problems that could make him vulnerable to corruption."

Gabby suppressed a sigh; she knew where this was heading. Her father had never hidden his distrust of his son-in-law, and the feelings had been mutual. Normally, she tried to stay out of the men's reciprocal animosity, letting them circle one another like suspicious wolves, but the time away had changed her. She felt a new strength and confidence to speak her mind.

"Are you saying that you think Adam would influence Mr. Isnard?" she asked point-blank.

"Precisely." Her father gave a vigorous nod. "I've never trusted your husband. Who knows what he would do if he got his hands on my bank?"

"Adam does not need your money, Papa," she said patiently. "He is an extremely wealthy man in his own right."

"There is no such thing as too much wealth. I'm a banker; trust me, I know. All my life, I've worked with men like your husband, whose ruthless ambition knows no bounds."

"In that respect, Adam is not unlike you." She gave her father a wry look.

He grunted, crossing his arms over his nightshirt. "I came from nothing. I had to earn a living to survive."

"And is Adam any different? He came from the stews and built an empire with his own two hands. And he is not just a business-man, but also a loving father and husband."

"*Is* he a loving husband?" her father asked gruffly.

Secure in Adam's love for her, her suspicions about Jessabelle laid to rest, she could, for the first time, answer that question with confidence.

"He loves me, Papa," she said with quiet conviction. "As much as I love him."

After a moment, her father said grudgingly, "At least Garrity is not a total idiot. That fall in the river did him good."

From her father, this was high praise. Unfortunately, he wasn't done.

"But I still don't trust him. And I won't leave Billings Bank—my legacy and life's work—at the mercy of a moneylender. I'm going to have Mr. Isnard investigated further, to make sure every-thing is on the up and up."

At her patience's end—and seeing the hand of the clock edge

closer and closer to her appointment time—she decided not to argue any further. Her father had always been possessed of a distrustful nature. If he wanted to investigate his long-time, trusted friend, then she couldn't stop him. She was certain nothing would come of it; after all, Mr. Isnard's only wrong-doing was having some financial difficulties. If that was the barometer for guilt, then half the men in England would be culpable.

"Do what you must, Papa." She kissed his cheek. "But I really must get going. I'm meeting Adam at the modiste's."

Her father gave her a confused look. "He's back at work, isn't he? Why the devil would he meet you at the dressmaker's in the middle of the day?"

"Because he wants to help me pick a gown for an upcoming ball." She smiled dreamily. "Because he thinks I'm as important as his work."

"Well, that's just daft." Her father shook his head. "Imagine a man wasting working hours on some frivolous errand."

Love isn't frivolous, she wanted to say. But she didn't because she knew her father would not understand. Instead, she kissed his cheek once more, promised to return on the morrow, and hurried to meet her husband.

28

ADAM WATCHED HIS WIFE IN ACTION IN THE DRESSING ROOM OF Mrs. Yarwood's shop, a fashionable establishment on Bond Street. Anticipating their arrival, Mrs. Yarwood had set up dress forms to display a variety of styles that Gabby could use for inspiration for her own gown. At the other end of the room, a dais surrounded by cheval looking glasses would allow her to view herself from all angles if she wished to try on a garment.

Surveying the selection of gowns, Gabby pointed a decisive finger.

"I like this one," she said.

Predictably, she'd chosen the fussiest, dowdiest frock of the lot. The insipid pink eyesore was trimmed with miles of ribbon and lace, the neckline suitable for a nun. The wide skirts had the most flounces Adam had ever seen on a single piece of clothing.

"May I suggest another gown that might suit you even better?" Mrs. Yarwood asked with the tact necessary for success in her profession. "This green velvet, for instance, has a most flattering shape..."

"I want the pink one," Gabby said.

Mrs. Yarwood looked more resigned than surprised. Adam

imagined the modiste had had more than one argument with this particular customer. As he was discovering, Gabby's sweet nature hid a backbone of polished steel. That strength had enabled her to endure countless hurts while keeping that pretty smile on her face. It could also work to her detriment...the present situation being a case in point.

"For my gown, however, I'd like the neckline raised," Gabby went on.

She was examining the style she'd chosen, her brow furrowed in concentration. As if she were imagining herself in that sack-like garment. Adam could have spared her the trouble and told her what she would look like: a giant iced cake.

His wife's attempts to hide her charms were a damned travesty.

"And my dress should have more embellishment. More ruffles and whatnot." Gabby's face lit up. "Indeed, I recently saw a fashion plate that featured a *cape* as part of the gown. Perhaps you could attach one to the shoulders, have it flow down and cover the entire back..."

Seeing Mrs. Yarwood visibly cringe, Adam decided it was time to step in.

"I think we're headed in the wrong direction with this," he said.

Gabby blinked at him. "Wrong direction? How do you mean?"

"Less is more," he said succinctly.

Mrs. Yarwood was looking at him as if he'd walked across water to arrive at her shop. "Your husband has an excellent point, Mrs. Garrity. The latest fashions are cut more closely to the figure—"

"I don't care about the latest fashions. I know what I like," Gabby said stubbornly.

"If I may have a private moment with my wife?"

"Have all the time you want, sir," the modiste said fervently.

He thought he heard her utter a prayer as she fled the dressing room, her assistant on her heels.

"As much as I value your opinion, I know what I want," Gabby said the instant the door closed.

"I'm certain you do. But that doesn't mean you know what looks best on you."

She narrowed her eyes. With her rounded cheeks, golden freckles, and lush mouth, she looked like an adorable yet annoyed faerie. On a deeper level, he was heartened by her increasing willingness to speak her mind in front of him. He loved her growing confidence and wanted to encourage it...even if he had to rouse her ire in the process.

Admittedly, there were other reasons why he liked his wife riled up. Her irritation was causing her breasts to heave in a most delightful way.

"Who has more experience shopping for dresses, you or me?" she asked.

"Who spends more time looking at you, you or me?" he returned.

Her cheeks turned rosy, but she raised her chin to a mutinous angle. "If you must know, dress shopping is one of my least favorite activities. It's ever so tedious, and you're not helping by prolonging the experience. It has taken me years to find a style that I'm comfortable with, one that suits me—"

"Your clothes don't suit you."

Her jaw slackened. He didn't like to be the cause of the pain flashing across her features, but being direct was the best way to make her understand.

"Gabriella, you are beautiful no matter what you wear," he said. "But the way you hide your gorgeous body in dowdy dresses is a damned crime."

"You think I'm *dowdy*?" Her poise wilted, her gaze lowering.

Hell, her vulnerability destroyed him.

He closed the distance between them. "Sweetheart, you're the most desirable woman I've ever laid eyes on."

To prove his point, he caught her hand and brought it to his groin, holding it there. Her eyes lifted, her fingers trembling against the ridge of his erection; beneath his thumb, the pulse in her wrist quickened, making him even harder.

"I want you all the bloody time," he murmured. "Over breakfast, at my office, anywhere I happen to be, I think of fucking you. The moment when I'll next taste your sweet lips, feel your tight quim clenching my cock, hear those delightfully breathy sounds you make when you come. There isn't a minute that passes when I don't thank my lucky stars that you're mine."

Her lips formed a lush "O," her gaze darkened not with pain now but feminine desire.

Taking advantage of her agreeable state, he led her over to the dais.

"Stand here for me, love." He began to unfasten the hooks of her dress.

Her startled eyes met his in the looking glass. "What are you doing?"

"I'm going to show you how I see you."

He deftly stripped her down to her undergarments. As tempting as she was with her maidenly blushes, her toes curling against the carpeted platform, he had another objective in mind. He crossed over to the line of dresses and selected the ruby satin that had caught his eye from the start. Returning, he helped Gabby into the gown.

Even though the garment was loose on her, its potential was undeniable. The rich hue brought out the fire in her hair, the purity of her rounded blue eyes. The deceptively simple cut showcased the perfect hourglass of her figure. The neckline left her shoulders bare, dipping to a daring vee between her ripe breasts. The vee was repeated at the bottom edge of the bodice, lengthening her torso...and drawing the male imagination to the sweet, feminine place where that arrow pointed.

Holding the fabric together between her shoulder blades to give an approximation of the fit, he said huskily, "Tell me what you see."

"I suppose...the gown looks well enough," she said reluctantly.

"Let me tell you what I see, pet."

His gaze holding hers in the reflection, he ran a possessive hand over her. From the silky slope of her bared shoulder to the plump swell of her breasts above the neckline. He trailed his fingers down the bodice, feeling the quick, shallow surges of her breath. Then he gripped her cinched waist.

"All of this is mine," he said softly against her ear as she shivered. "Mine only to touch and enjoy. But I want the world to know what a lucky man I am and, most importantly, I want *you* to know your own worth. To know that women look at you and wish they had half your beauty, that men look at you and envy me because I'm the one who will be taking you home. I'm the one who will be making love to you, worshiping your body with mine."

He brushed his lips against the side of her neck. She let out a shuddering sigh, raising her arm so that her fingers brushed his nape, her head tilting back for his kiss. He obliged her, a heated swirl of tongues. Then he broke off the kiss, nodding toward the mirror.

"Look at you," he said. "What do you see?"

The image *he* saw dampened his smalls with pre-seed, his heart and cock pounding in unison. They were man and woman, twined together in a pose as old as time. Lost together in the garden of desire.

"I see a woman in love," she whispered. "A wife who knows she is beautiful because her love is returned by her husband."

"I want you to be as proud to be mine as I am to be yours," he murmured.

"I am proud." Smiling, she turned to face him. "And you're right. I adore this dress."

"Good, let's summon Mrs. Yarwood and have her take your order as quickly as possible."

"Why the rush?"

"The sooner we're done here, the sooner I can have my way with you in the carriage."

His wife lowered her eyes demurely. "I'll have my gown ordered in less than ten minutes."

✢ 29 ✢

IN THE PAST, GABBY HAD DREADED BALLS BECAUSE THE CRUSH
of people made her nervous. The disparaging glances and snickers
behind fans had always struck an unpleasantly familiar chord,
causing memories to rattle within the *Humiliating Experiences I'd
Like to Forget* category. Being in the public eye put her on edge;
when she was on edge, she tended to chatter in a mortifyingly
inane manner that increased the withering looks and closing of
circles as she passed, thereby feeding the cycle of her anxiety.

Yet tonight was different: Gabby was actually enjoying Tessa's
ball. When the other had asked for decorating advice, Gabby had
given a few suggestions. She was happy to see how well the ideas
had worked.

The "midnight garden" theme created a romantic atmosphere
in the mirrored ballroom, apropos for celebrating Ransom and
Maggie's engagement. Gabby had suggested bringing in large
potted plants to create "hedges" at different parts of the room,
which provided intimate areas for conversation. The jasmine and
gardenia plants did double duty, filling the room with their sweet
fragrance. Tessa had even had a small white gazebo constructed in
one corner; the champagne fountain was housed within, and

guests were clearly enjoying the novelty of entering the latticed structure to have their glasses refilled.

It wasn't just the ambience that Gabby was enjoying. For the first time, her dance card had been full and not just due to the kindness of her friends' husbands. She'd twirled on the dance floor with admiring gentlemen, and what made that experience special was knowing that Adam was there, watching with possessive pride. His presence gave her confidence, calmed her, and allowed her to carry on a normal conversation.

At present, she stood in a circle of friends. Tessa was chatting in her animated way with Maggie, Polly, and Emma joining in. The hostess wore a stylish emerald shot-silk gown that brought out the unique green of her eyes. The guest of honor's dress of bronze velvet flattered her voluptuous figure and lustrous cinnamon curls. The duchesses were both buxom visions, Polly in blue taffeta and Emma in grey Gros de Naples with an overlay of sparkly silver netting.

For once, Gabby felt equal to her lovely companions. Despite the rush order (or perhaps *because* of the exorbitant price Adam had paid to get the dress made in time), Mrs. Yarwood had outdone herself. The ruby gown exceeded Gabby's highest expectations. When Nell had completed her toilette, she'd hardly recognized herself. The dress revealed more than she'd ever dared to reveal before...and the improvement was *shocking*.

Curves she'd thought too abundant now appeared alluring. Her bare shoulders and the hint of cleavage between her breasts was the right balance between sensuality and decorum. Her coloring, which she'd once believed to be vulgar, looked regal against the deep red satin. She'd found a new jeweler's box on her dressing table, and when she'd opened it, her heart had stuttered, Nell letting out a low whistle. Fashioned of heavy gold, the brooch had an egg-sized ruby at the center, the peerless gem ringed by flawless pearls.

A brief note had accompanied the gift. *For a wife beyond rubies.*

Nell had pinned the magnificent brooch at the dip in Gabby's décolletage. Standing before the cheval mirror, Gabby had seen her own beauty for the first time. It was as if a weight had been lifted off, allowing her to stand taller, her shoulders back and posture proud.

Her confidence had only grown at her children's reactions.

Watching as Nell had arranged soft braids over Gabby's ears, completing her simple coiffure with a few fresh blooms, Fiona had breathed, "I want to look just like you when I'm grown up, Mama!"

"You're the prettiest lady in the world," Max said.

Gabby had had to discreetly dab at her eyes.

And if her children's admiration had bolstered her self-esteem, then her husband's had sent it into the stratosphere. His appreciation hadn't just taken the form of words. Before leaving for the ball, he'd crowded her against her dressing room wall and planted the proof of his approval deep inside her.

"I want you to feel me all night. Here, in your pretty pussy," he'd rasped in her ear. "I want to know that while other men ogle what's mine, you'll bear my claim where it counts."

Just thinking of that deliciously debauched interlude heated Gabby's cheeks.

"Gabby, you're looking overheated." Tessa's observation stirred her from her risqué thoughts. "Do you think it's too stuffy in here? I could have the footmen open the balcony doors—"

"The temperature is fine," she said quickly.

"Then why are you redder than an apple?" Tessa demanded.

"I was, um, just thinking about..."

As she desperately searched for an acceptable excuse, Maggie and Emma exchanged looks, their mouths quivering.

"What's so amusing?" Tessa wanted to know.

"I think Gabby's glowing for a reason other than the room temperature." Maggie's tip-tilted emerald eyes were warm with understanding.

"Was it the dress?" Emma asked knowingly. "Husbands always like a new dress."

Polly aimed a mischievous look at her older sister. "Is that why Strathaven buys you a new wardrobe every month?"

At least now Gabby wasn't the only one blushing.

"Are we talking about you-know-what?" Tessa broke in.

At that, all the ladies pealed with laughter, Gabby included.

When they all quieted, Maggie reached over and gave Gabby's hand a conspiratorial squeeze.

"Love is nothing to be ashamed of," she said in her quiet, wise way. "Having waited so long for Ransom, I, for one, believe in seizing the moment."

"Especially when our respective moments are so very fine," Tessa said.

Everyone blinked at her.

"What? I can be sentimental." Their hostess's slim shoulders moved up and down. "I mean, look at our gentlemen: finer specimens you'll not find elsewhere."

Their gazes shifted to their husbands—in Maggie's case, her fiancé—who were having their own conversation near a row of potted plants. Gabby had to agree that their male counterparts were an exceedingly virile bunch, each man in his own unique way.

With his spectacles and tall, muscular figure, brown-haired Harry Kent was an intriguing mix of scholar and athlete, his fierce intelligence a match for his lady's cleverness. Maggie's fiancé Ransom had the exotic look of a pirate prince with his dark hair and dashing trimmed mustache and beard, his charm the perfect foil for Maggie's steady nature. Nor was there any arguing with the wicked appeal of Strathaven's cool jade eyes or Acton's Adonis looks, the way both men kept looking over at their wives the most appealing of all.

And there was Adam. To Gabby, the most magnificent of the group (she was a bit biased). It was good to see him at ease with the other husbands. He didn't speak often, yet his sultan's gaze missed nothing, the faint curve of his mouth conveying his enjoyment of the male camaraderie.

"Goodness, Gabby, you *do* have the look of a newlywed tonight." A smile tucked in Emma's cheeks. "I take it matters with Mr. Garrity have improved?"

"Beyond my wildest dreams," Gabby said fervently.

"It shows, you know." Polly's aquamarine eyes out-sparkled the gems in her exquisite necklace. "You've always been lovely, Gabby, but tonight you're glowing inside and out."

"The look of a woman in love...and who knows she's loved in return." Maggie's smile included the whole group. "We all have that special glow, don't we?"

"My glow is because I'm increasing," Tessa grumbled. "Why doesn't anyone tell you that being with child makes you hotter than a blasted steam engine?"

∼

"What the devil do you think they're giggling about?" Harry Kent asked.

Adam stood with Kent and the Dukes of Strathaven, Acton, and Ranelagh and Somerville. They were observing the merriment of their respective ladies.

Strathaven's brows lifted. "How are we to guess what transpires in the minds of females? We'd have better luck catching fish with our hands."

Seeing Gabby's blush, Adam was certain he knew the cause of it. She always got charmingly flustered when it came to things of a sexual nature. She'd had that blush after he'd tupped her in her dressing room, after he'd waltzed with her, and she had it now... which pretty much told him the topic of conversation.

"Garrity's got a smug smile." Behind the wire rims, Kent's eyes were acute. "I think he has a guess."

"Well, he is an old married fellow," Ransom drawled. "He's had more time to develop his husbandly powers of deduction. Tell us, what are our lovely ladies plotting?"

Although Adam didn't remember the time when Ransom had been a client who'd owed him a great deal of money, Gabby had filled him in on the details. The part he'd played in saving Ransom's daughter had apparently dissolved the contention between him and the duke. When Ransom had visited during Adam's convalescence, he'd been sincere in his well wishes but wary. Adam had sensed a similar guardedness from the husbands of his wife's friends.

Tonight, however, he noticed a subtle shift in their attitude toward him. From politeness to something friendlier. If he'd had to put a name to it, he'd call it acceptance.

Adam didn't much care what anyone thought of him—with the exception of Gabby. Her opinion mattered. Yet the male company wasn't unwelcome, and there was something to be said for husbands banding together. Especially when their wives were likely up to no good.

"Should we be worried, Garrity?" Acton arched a brow.

"They're women. We should always be worried," Adam said succinctly.

"Spoken like an experienced husband." Despite Strathaven's grimace, there was amusement in his jade eyes. "Emma's 'hobby' of being an investigator has given me more grey hairs than I care to count."

"At least Emma only takes on the occasional case." Kent directed his gaze heavenward. "My wife runs a territory in the bloody *underworld*."

Yet there was unmistakable pride in his voice, and he snuck a glance at his lady. She waved her fingers at him, blowing him a kiss, and he winked back at her.

"You have it easy, Acton," Strathaven said. "Polly being the most docile of the Kents."

"Oh, my kitten has claws." Acton's grin was slow and altogether male.

"Say no more." With a mock shudder, Kent held up a large hand. "That's my sister you're talking about, and what's heard cannot be unheard."

"I suppose I shouldn't tell you about how Emma surprised me on my last birthday..." Strathaven drawled.

When Kent clapped his hands over his ears, his brothers-in-law guffawed.

Even Adam felt his lips twitch.

Kent turned to him. "Garrity, you're not married to one of my sisters—*thank God*. Let's talk about the lovely Mrs. Garrity. How do you keep your lady out of trouble?"

"By giving her everything she needs and wants," Adam said.

The group went silent, the men staring at him as if he'd sprouted another head. He wondered why his words surprised them when it was obvious that every one of these fellows was devoted to his lady and would do everything in his power to make her happy.

Ransom cleared his throat. His shocked expression had turned into one of...respect?

"I do believe that is the best advice of all for this husband-to-be," he said in solemn tones. "And precisely what I intend to do with my Maggie."

"We should toast to that." Kent waved over a footman bearing a tray of champagne.

The men took glasses and raised them.

"To our ladies," Kent declared. "May we be everything they deserve."

After they drank to that, Adam heard the orchestra start up again. The lilting melody he'd been waiting for filled the room.

"If you'll excuse me, gentlemen," he said, "I'm going to claim my wife for our second waltz."

With a bow, he strode away, but he caught Ransom's murmured words to the others.

"I never thought I would say this...but, devil and damn, I actually *like* the new Adam Garrity."

Flushed from dancing and the pleasure of being in her husband's arms, Gabby felt giddy as Adam led her off the dance floor. In the past, if they were at the same function, he had usually stood with her for one dance. Tonight, he'd claimed *two*, both of them waltzes. And while he had always been her favorite partner, their newfound intimacy added another dimension to their dancing.

He led flawlessly, and she followed with equal grace. Their bodies swayed together in perfect, sensual synchrony, one that reminded her acutely of how well they moved together in bed. Or against the wall. Or in the carriage...

"I can't wait to get out of here," Adam muttered.

She blinked, seeing the taut edge of his jaw above his crisp cravat. "I thought you were enjoying the evening?"

"I was. But dancing with you,"—he slanted her a meaningful look—"is enough to make a saint hard. And I'm no saint. How much longer do you want to stay?"

"We ought to bid our host and hostess farewell before we leave," she said decorously.

"Excellent, there they are now."

She smothered a giggle at her husband's virile impatience as he tugged her toward their friends.

There was a newcomer in the group, she noted, a man to whom she'd never been formally introduced but whose wheat-blond hair and piercing dark eyes were instantly recognizable. Sketches of him appeared regularly in the papers, and a recent caricature had shown him sitting astride a golden locomotive, a crown atop his head and scepter in hand.

The caption had read, *Midas Rules the Railways*.

"Ah, here are my dear friends, the Garritys," Tessa said. "May I introduce Mr. Anthony De Villier? Although I'm sure he needs no introduction. He does us an honor, gracing this ball despite his busy schedule."

The industrialist was rumored to be in his sixties, yet he had a young man's vigor, his body ruthlessly fit. His light hair, dark brows, and unlined face gave him an oddly ageless aspect. When De Villier took Gabby's hand, she noticed his heavy signet ring, the gleaming bloodstone carved with his initials.

"A pleasure, Mrs. Garrity," he said in deep, silky tones.

"Likewise, sir." Something about the man's hawkish stare made her uneasy. His hand gripped hers with a bit too much pressure; flustered, she pulled away. "I've, um, been reading about your latest successes in the papers. I understand your steam-powered design is to be the fastest in the world?"

"My steam engine, once completed, will revolutionize the industry." De Villier's charisma and confidence were potent; Gabby could see why so many people had invested in his ventures. "We have orders already from all major railway interests. Our business is booming—but your husband is no stranger to that." He turned to Adam, his gaze assessing before he inclined his head. "Garrity, I hear you are quite a successful...entrepreneur in your own right."

Gabby did not miss De Villier's subtle slight. She narrowed her gaze at him.

"I'm a moneylender," Adam said bluntly. "Have we met before?"

"I don't believe so." De Villier's smile was condescending. "But then, our circles aren't exactly the same, are they?"

This time, the snub wasn't subtle, and Gabby felt her hackles rise. How *dare* the blighter look down upon her husband? De Villier might be rich, but so was Adam, and both were self-made men who'd found success in their respective trades. Why did people feel the need to push others down in order to make themselves feel superior? Why couldn't everyone just be *nice?*

A lifetime of held-back emotion surged in Gabby. Boxes and bins toppled in her head, thoughts and feelings breaking free. Restraint gave way to blazing indignation.

"If you do not like the present company, sir," she said in trembling tones, "then you are welcome to go elsewhere."

The words shocked her as much as her friends, who went wide-eyed. The men stilled, their postures tensing, as if they were readying to deal with the aftermath of her cut direct.

De Villier stiffened, his dark eyes flashing. A pair of burly men emerged out of nowhere to flank him. They were dressed like footmen, but she knew what they were for Adam had guards too. De Villier's men looked especially brutish: one had an angry red scar that ran from his ear to his chin, his beady gaze focused on Adam.

Sweet heavens. The consequences of her outburst hit her. *What have I done?*

"Actually, stay if you like, De Villier." It was Adam who broke the silence, his voice calm and controlled. "My wife and I were on our way out. Our thanks to you, Mr. and Mrs. Kent, for your hospitality. And felicitations to the happy couple."

"As our dear friends, you're welcome any time," Tessa said, with a cold look at De Villier.

Numbly, Gabby let Adam steer her away.

"I can't believe I did that," she said in shock. "That I just insulted one of the most powerful men in England."

"The prat deserved it." Adam flashed her a grin. "Next time he'll think twice before insulting me in front of my fierce and loyal wife."

30

A FEW DAYS LATER, GABBY ENTERED ADAM'S STUDY WHILE HE was at work. She was in search of her son's missing book. Max was inconsolable at its disappearance, and the staff had combed the house from top to bottom to no avail. The study was the only place they hadn't looked, and since Adam often read to Max, Gabby had high hopes for finding the lost volume in here.

She checked the seating area by the hearth first, even peering beneath the furnishings. She didn't find Max's book but did recover one of Fiona's hair ribbons. Heavens, the pair was like Hansel and Gretel, leaving a trail wherever they went. With a rueful smile, she continued onto Adam's desk. She sat in his chair, the feel of the studded leather and faint whiff of his spicy musk giving her a pleasant shiver.

She scanned the surface of the desk, which included a tray of writing implements and an ornate wax jack. Burke had left a large stack of the day's correspondence on the leather blotter, and she started there, triumph sparking when she spied the missing book beneath the pile.

A mama's intuition is never wrong, she thought with a touch of smugness.

As she dug out the book, a letter slid from the stack, the flowy, feminine handwriting catching her eye. After a moment, she set down the book and picked up the note. The paper was creamy and thick; coolness feathered over her nape as the scent of cloying perfume reached her nostrils.

The letter was addressed simply to Adam Garrity with no return address. Turning it over, she found a red wax seal that bore an odd stamp. She examined it more closely and saw that it depicted two crossed swords—no, not swords...riding crops? The chill spread to her insides, her fingers curling around the sealed note.

A private note, one that she had no right to open.

She broke the seal. Unfolding the paper, she read the short lines:

My dearest Adam,

It has been weeks since I've heard from you. Know that I've been thinking of you, praying for your speedy recovery. And hoping that I shall see you at the club soon on our usual Friday.

Yours fondly,

J.

J...Jessabelle.

A crack split open in Gabby's heart, the pain making it difficult to breathe. She stared at the note, willing the voluptuous loops of handwriting to change, to somehow rearrange itself into something less damning.

But it remained exactly as it was. Proof of her husband's infidelity.

A hammer poised to smash her happiness to smithereens.

Yet as despair pushed hotly behind her eyes, another feeling surged alongside it. A similar but stronger version of what she had experienced when she'd stood up to De Villier. It took her a moment to label it as...rage.

Our usual Friday.

Had Adam kept this...this *harlot* on a schedule too? How long had he been carrying on this affair? Was he in love with the blasted lightskirt?

In the past, she would have tried to hide from the pain. To ignore or block out the evidence of Adam's betrayal. To try to move on from it the best she could.

But that was before.

She was different now. The *Bin of Blissful Ignorance* was no more, and she would accept nothing less than honesty in her marriage. With bitter irony, she saw that love had changed her. Afterward, she would nurse her broken heart, but first she wanted the answers to her questions—*deserved* them. Because of his amnesia, her husband, damn his eyes, couldn't give them to her... and now she didn't know if she would even trust what came out of his lying lips.

No, she would have the truth from the source.

Her hands shaking, she inspected the note again. Perfectly discreet, no address, no clues except for the stamp on the seal and the fact that the meetings took place at "the club."

Our usual Friday.

Adam had to get to the meetings somehow. If this was a regular visit as the note implied, then there was someone who'd transported his master to that place time and again. Someone who would now take Gabby there—or else.

She marched out of the study to find the groom.

Adam stared at the report on the desk in front of him. Cornish had presented it to him a half hour ago, and as he'd looked at the summary of his failing investments, he'd heard a strange buzzing, like a fly trapped in his ear. The buzzing got louder and louder, as if the invisible insect was trying to burst out of his skull. For a terrifying instant, he'd wondered if he was going mad. Then the noise turned into a megrim, a pulsing vise that gripped his entire head.

He'd dismissed Cornish and washed down a packet of birch bark with a swallow of whisky. As he waited for the pain to subside, he kept looking at the report. Kept turning Cornish's conclusion over and over in his head.

The banks in question are failing, sir. No question about it. I would recommend that you cut your losses immediately. Indeed, I don't know why you refused to do so before now...unless it was because of Anthony De Villier.

Anthony De Villier. The throbbing in Adam's temples increased. There'd been something familiar about the man.

These banks have one thing in common: all have sizeable loans out to De Villier. It's possible that, like so many others, you were betting that his latest venture will pay off in spades, and these banks will be the beneficiaries. But being a conservative sort myself, I must caution against gambling on speculative interests. Recall the fiasco of the South Sea Bubble. Anthony De Villier may appear to have the Midas touch, but beneath that veneer of gold, there may lay a core of lead.

Anthony De Villier. What was it about him? Why would Adam invest so heavily to support his schemes? By nature, Adam was a man who took calculated risks...not foolish or reckless ones.

On a positive note, it appears that De Villier has been paying off some of his debts recently. In the week that it took me to compile this report, he has discharged his commitments to two of the banks you own.

On a gut level, Adam knew he'd had a reason for extending credit to De Villier, one that didn't necessarily involve profit. A reason that had to do with De Villier himself. God, he could sense it, like a word on the tip of the tongue, a memory just beyond reach...

The knock at the door made him growl in frustration.

Kerrigan entered, the expression on the guard's face setting off alarm bells.

"What is it?" Adam demanded.

"A message just arrived for you, sir." Kerrigan ran a hand over his shaved head; he had the look of a messenger who's afraid he's about to get shot. "It's from Thompson."

A message from his groom? Adam frowned. "What does he want?"

"Apparently, Mrs. Garrity...er...ordered him to take her to..."

"Spit it out, man," Adam said impatiently.

"Mrs. Wilde's Club," Kerrigan blurted. "She somehow found out about your, er, visits there. She cornered Thompson, insisting that he take her to the club. He wouldn't have done it, but then she threatened to get a hackney by herself. To go to every bawdy house in the city until she found the right one..."

The room began to spin, overtaken by a vortex of images.

Mrs. Wilde's Club, a smiling blonde...

Whips, orgies, another blonde dead in a pool of blood.

The banks, the banks, the banks.

Anthony De Villier.

He jolted as the past slammed into him.

As everything came back in a single, blinding burst.

"Er, sir? Are you all right?"

He turned to Kerrigan, once again the man he'd known for years. His loyal retainer.

"I remember," he said hoarsely. "Everything."

Kerrigan's good eye lit with relief. "Bloody hell, sir, that's the most welcome news—"

"Let's go." Adam was already on his feet, striding to the door. "I have to get to my wife."

31

GABBY ARRIVED AT MRS. WILDE'S CLUB JUST BEFORE DUSK.

The place was situated on a private lane in Covent Garden, and its Italianate façade looked innocuous enough from the outside. Pulling the hood of her cape more securely around her face, Gabby took a breath and headed for the front door. It was locked; apparently the club wasn't yet open. Picking up voices from the side of the building, she followed them, arriving at another entrance around back, one cordoned off by a velvet rope.

The burly guard posted by the door looked her up and down, his brows lifting.

"Certain you're at the right place, dove?"

"I wish to see your mistress," Gabby said crisply. "You may tell her Adam Garrity sent me."

The flash of recognition on the guard's face when she said her husband's name drove a blade into Gabby's heart.

"Wait here. I'll check with Mrs. Wilde," he said.

He returned a short time later, unhooking the rope and ushering Gabby inside. Her pulse raced as he led her up two flights of stairs, passing flocks of women whose scantily clad bodies and painted faces left no doubt as to the roles they played at the club. As he took her down a hallway lined with rooms, she couldn't help but look inside the open doors.

Merciful heavens.

In one chamber, she glimpsed a cross with manacles hanging from the horizontal ends. A whore wearing a leather corset paced in front of the cross. She selected a birch from an umbrella stand, testing its pliability before giving it a testing slash through the air.

In another room, Gabby saw a massive bed, so huge that it could occupy at least a dozen people. On the ceiling above was an equally large gilt-framed looking glass. Her cheeks blazed as she imagined the lascivious view that it would provide to the occupants below.

By the time the guard took her into a suite at the end of the hall, Gabby's respiration had been reduced to quick, shallow pants, her palms sweaty and trembling. Left alone to await the mysterious Mrs. Wilde, she took in the opulent surroundings, recognition slamming into her.

Good Lord, this place was decorated like...a sultan's seraglio.

It was as if her secret imagination had been brought to life with stunning, lush eroticism. The *trompe l'oeil* murals on the walls depicted white columns and intricate arabesque latticework, sheer waving curtains giving glimpses of the surrounding azure sea. The visual effect of the painting was startlingly real: for an instant, Gabby was transported to a luxurious chamber of the Near East, the breeze blowing through the balcony, her nose filled with the scent of incense and the ocean.

In the antechamber where she stood, there was a round table and chairs, as well as a low red sofa, all of it in an Oriental style. The room was connected to a much larger space by an arched entryway that framed the main piece of furniture on the other side: a round mattress covered in peacock-blue silk. Jewel-toned pillows with gold tassels were scattered over it, inviting a queen to stretch out in sensual abandonment as she awaited her sultan's pleasure...

Gabby's heart spasmed, her fantasy snuffed out by the reality of where she was and why. Her husband wasn't a sultan. He was a traitorous, black-hearted infidel.

The door opened, and Gabby steeled herself as a blonde woman entered. The newcomer was probably in her early forties, tall and statuesque, her thin black robe clinging to her curves and nipped-in waist. With a sinking feeling, Gabby registered the woman's beauty, the exotic appeal of the amber eyes outlined with kohl and the lushness of that painted mouth.

"I'm Mrs. Wilde." The blonde's husky tone had a hard edge to it as she looked Gabby up and down. "You didn't say who you were when you used Adam Garrity's name to gain entry."

Gabby straightened her shoulders, pushing off the hood of her cloak. "I am his wife."

She saw the shock in the other's feline eyes. "You're Gabriella...I did not realize..."

Hearing the woman say her name was a slap to the face. Humiliation burned through Gabby. Adam had told his mistress about his wife? What else had they talked about, done together...?

"You are Jessabelle, I presume?" Gabby said tightly.

A spasm crossed Mrs. Wilde's features. "I am not." She exhaled, running a hand through her loose gold locks. "Would you care to sit down? I can have tea brought in."

"I do not want tea. I want answers," Gabby said fiercely. "How long have you and Adam been lovers? How many *Friday visits* has he had?"

"I am not, and have never been, your husband's lover, ma'am."

The blonde's quiet statement had the ring of truth.

Or perhaps that was just wishful thinking on Gabby's part.

"Then who was he visiting here at your club? Is Jessabelle one of your whores?" Gabby removed the note from her cloak, slapping it onto the table. "She sent my husband this note."

"I sent that note," Mrs. Wilde said.

"You just said that you're not Jessabelle."

"I'm not. My name is Jeannette."

"Then who is Jessabelle?"

"She was my sister, and she's dead."

Taken aback, Gabby stared at the other. Mrs. Wilde—*Jean-nette* Wilde, apparently—returned the look with a steady one of her own.

"What is Jessabelle's connection to my husband?" Gabby finally asked.

"That is not my story to tell." The bawd's tone was firm but not unkind. "I cannot imagine how confusing this is for you, Mrs. Garrity, but I think you must have a conversation with your husband. Indeed, I have been urging him for years to unburden himself to you."

"Why...why would you do that?" Gabby whispered painfully. "What right do you have to discuss *my* marriage with *my* husband?"

"No right, save that of a friend who has known him for a very long..."

The opening door cut off Mrs. Wilde. A handsome, ginger-haired man entered, his gaze shifting alertly between Gabby and the bawd.

"Is everything all right, love?" The man directed the question to Mrs. Wilde. "Ronald mentioned a friend of Adam's was here."

Gabby frowned in confusion. This man knew her husband as well?

"Everything is fine. This is not Adam's friend; she's his wife," Mrs. Wilde told him.

"Oh." The man did a credible job of hiding his shock and bowed courteously to Gabby. "Beg pardon. I did not think Adam mentioned us at home."

"He didn't," Gabby said.

"Ah. Pardon my manners, I'm Thomas Pender. Jeannette's husband."

"You're *married?*" Gabby blurted to Mrs. Wilde...or Mrs. Pender, rather?

"We'll be celebrating six years next month." The blonde regarded her husband fondly. "Adam introduced us."

"Garrity and I had done some business together," Pender explained. "That is, he lent me money, and I was one of the few smart coves who paid him back on schedule. We became friendly. He knew I was a widower and introduced me to Jeannette. She'd always been too busy with her club to bother with a husband. But Adam played matchmaker. I think he knew marriage would add to our happiness, the way it added to his."

"Not that Adam would ever admit it in so many words. When it comes to emotions, you know what a clam the man can be." Mrs. Wilde's look of understanding deepened Gabby's bewilderment. "But I've known him for far too many years, so he could not hide his contentment from me. The happiness and peace you brought him was plain to see. He's been a changed man ever since he married you."

"I don't understand." With roiling frustration, Gabby said, "If Adam isn't having an affair, then why didn't he tell me about the two of you? Why did he keep your existence a secret from me? And what does Jessabelle have to do with all of this?"

Mrs. Wilde and Pender exchanged looks.

"As much as I'd like to oblige you," the bawd said regretfully, "it's not my place to answer those questions—"

Adam's voice cut through the room. "No, that responsibility is mine."

As Adam accepted the greetings from his old friends, he kept his gaze on Gabriella. He saw the way her lips trembled, the pain and confusion in her expressive eyes, and he hated himself for it. Cursed himself for letting things get to this point. For letting down his guard and allowing her to get hurt...for not protecting her as he ought to have done, regardless of the blasted amnesia.

The throbbing on the side of his head vied for his attention. It was as if the sudden return of his memory had retriggered the wound. Although the tissue was healed, the muscles remembered the pain, gripping onto it.

He fought to concentrate, to get himself under control. He felt as if there were two disparate halves of him warring with one another, the past and present colliding with jarring dissonance. He was who he'd always been, and he was his new self: neither was prepared to deal with the present situation. A situation that his old self would never have let come to pass and which his new self found more than a little appalling.

You lost control, and you hurt her, his old self said.

Why did you keep so many secrets from her? his new self asked in disgust.

Regardless, there was one thing he knew with his entire being: he had to minimize the damage. To protect Gabriella from further pain. Christ, that look of shattered betrayal upon her face...it destroyed him. He'd rather take a knife to the chest than cause her hurt.

"Are you certain you're well?" Jeannette's voice reminded him of her and Pender's presence. His old friends were watching him with concerned expressions.

"I'm fine," he said. "I would like privacy to speak with my wife."

"Of course, old boy," Pender said. "Good to see you back."

As Pender ushered Jeannette to the door, she touched Adam's arm as she passed.

"Be gentle with her," she murmured.

Annoyed that she felt he needed that advice, he gave a brusque nod.

Then the two were gone, leaving him alone with his wife.

They stood on opposite sides of the table. The tension in the room was thicker than the fog on the Thames.

Gabby's head tilted. "You remembered them," she said acutely.

"I remember everything," he said. "It came back to me. All of it, today."

He saw relief ripple across her sweet face, the wifely devotion she could not hide despite her anger, and he was filled with profound gratitude. Despite her justified doubt and suspicion of him, she cared about him still. He could work with that.

"Then you will have the grace to explain what is going on." Her voice quavered with the force of her emotions, yet she held her head high. "Why didn't you tell me about Mrs. Wilde and your Friday visits?"

Even as he calculated his response, he registered that he wasn't the only one who'd changed in these past weeks. Gabriella's new confidence and composure were remarkable. Now that his memory was back, he could fully appreciate the difference between past and present. He saw with pride his wife's revealed strength, the fire she'd kept hidden from him and herself.

You can trust her to handle the filth of your past, a voice inside him said. *Tell her the truth.*

As much of it as she needs to know, another voice cautioned.

He pulled a chair out from the table. "Perhaps you'd like to sit for this."

"I'd like you to tell me the dashed truth," she shot back.

He gripped the back of the chair. "I didn't tell you about Jeannette because she's part of a past that I'm not proud of. It happened a long time ago, before I met you and, as such, has nothing to do with you."

"Let me be the judge of that." She narrowed her eyes at him. "Were the two of you ever lovers?"

"Christ, no. I have never thought of her in that way," he said with emphasis. "She is a friend, nothing more. We have...a shared history that bonds us but not in a sexual way. I have never been unfaithful to you, Gabriella. From the moment I met you, I've never wanted any other woman in my bed."

It was the absolute truth. He saw the yearning in her eyes, how much she wanted to believe him. Yet distrust shadowed those pure blue depths, and it felt like a blow to his gut, one that he deserved.

She lifted her chin. "Then who is Jessabelle?"

Although he knew he would have to address the issue, he still reeled from hearing his wife say the name aloud. For so long, he'd fought to keep these two worlds apart, and now they were crashing into one another like planets gone off course. The damage couldn't be prevented; the best strategy was to minimize it by giving his wife the necessary facts.

"She was my wife," he said.

He heard Gabriella's sharp intake of breath, saw her stiffen with shock.

"You were m-married?" she stammered.

He gave a terse nod. "For a brief time, long before I met you. I was a young man, in my early twenties. I'd known Jessabelle—and her older sister Jeannette—since I was a boy. All three of us were rescued from the streets by the same man, Oswald Garrity. When Garrity found out that I had no family, he gave me his surname and protection. I chose the name 'Adam' to symbolize my fresh start."

Taking in Gabriella's wide-eyed expression, he decided there was no need to delve into his history before Garrity. His mind wasn't fully clear, and his emotions were a tangled mess. He thought of De Villier, of meeting the man face-to-face just several days ago, and panic clawed at his gut.

Had De Villier guessed who he was?

Up until then, he'd taken care to avoid direct contact with the bastard; he hadn't wanted to trip the snare. He had the trap laid out precisely in his head: he would reveal himself to De Villier at the moment of the other's destruction. Only then would De Villier know why he'd been ruined and by whom.

From the age of nine onward, revenge had anchored Adam. It had motivated him, given him the will to survive and become who he was today. Remembering his purpose was like finding a port in the storm.

His confusion, the agonizing conflict within himself dissipated as he sought and found his harbor. The voice that won out was calm, collected. As the familiar feeling of control flowed through him, he felt the tension ease in his temples.

Everything will be all right. You'll figure out what to do about De Villier. But first you must win Gabriella back, convince her that she belongs to you, by any means necessary.

She was his wife, and he loved her—he saw that now. Accepted it as one accepts that the sun rises in the east and sets in the west. If anything, he regretted that he'd not realized it sooner. He'd let his history with Jessabelle spook him, make him afraid to recognize what was in his heart. What had been there for years.

But he wouldn't run from love any longer.

Over the last weeks, things had changed in his marriage, yes... and he would use that to his advantage. Arousal stirred as he considered ways to stake his new claim. Now that he knew the passion that burned inside Gabriella, he would use it to bind her to him. Instead of his prior *stupid* plan of swaddling his marriage in routine, propriety, and restraint, he would use desire and the strength of their bond to protect her.

She would obey him when it mattered; he wouldn't let anything happen to her. Wouldn't let the darkness of his world touch or harm a single hair on her head. This time, he wouldn't let love end in pain and bitter regret.

With that in mind, he continued his story.

"Garrity led a gang of children. He was not a bad sort: he provided a roof over our heads, food for our bellies, and in return we helped him with various tasks. Scavenging and petty thievery, mostly. He did not abuse us, and he taught us the necessary skills to survive.

"Even as a boy, I was infatuated with Jessabelle," he went on. "She was two years younger than me, a pretty blonde angel who could charm a bird from a tree. It was a useful skill when it came to swindling. She never learned to pickpocket for all she had to do was spin some Cheltenham Tragedy about why she needed money, and strangers would shower her with coins."

Gabriella's throat worked. "When did the two of you...?"

"I was twenty when I proposed to her. She accepted, but Garrity was against our union. In his eyes, we were his children and therefore brother and sister, although there were no blood ties between us. In the end, he kicked us out." Adam recalled his mentor's expulsion with bittersweet acceptance. "Jeannette left with us because she'd always been a protective older sister to Jessabelle. The three of us started over. Jessabelle and I got married, and I found work as a guard for a moneylender named Helmsley. He saw my potential, and I moved up the ranks quickly. My star was beginning to rise at the same time that my marriage began to sour."

Gabriella bit her lip. "What happened?"

"Jessabelle grew bored with the long hours I spent away from her. She accused me of abandoning her, of infidelity, though I never broke my vows."

He saw Gabriella's teeth sink deeper, worrying her bottom lip, and knew that his sweet, sensitive wife had noted the parallel between her behavior and Jessabelle's. It was a deliberate, ruthless move on his part to gain her empathy. In truth, there was no comparing the two situations. Jessabelle had been spoiled and demanding, using tantrums to manipulate him and get her way. Gabby gave everything of herself and only asked for what was rightfully hers in return.

Even as that new, raw part of him balked at using her tender-hearted nature against her, he steeled himself. It was necessary. There was more to share, the ugly part of his life that he'd never wanted Gabby to know. Yet she had to know it in order for her to understand and accept his actions. Thus, as he ventured forth onto the explosive-laden battlefield of his past, he needed the upper hand.

"We fought constantly," he said, keeping his tone matter-of-fact, "and we made up just as often, just as...intensely."

He saw the stain rising up his wife's cheeks and wished he could protect her from the hurt he was inflicting. If he'd had to listen to her talk about another man touching her, he'd put his fist through a goddamned wall. But this was required history, and the best thing he could do was get it over with as quickly as he could.

"Jessabelle enjoyed carnal games. Coming from the stews, she was exposed to the variety of ways that pleasure could be found, and she was adventurous by nature." He exhaled before continuing. "In particular, she was aroused by displaying herself in front of other men. Letting them see and lust after her while we fornicated."

Gabriella's jaw slackened. "You *allowed* that?"

He understood her shock. Because he'd kill any man who so much as *looked* at her askance, and he was gratified that she knew that. That she knew he'd never allow anyone to share her pleasure. That she was his and his alone.

"I was a young man, and she was my first lover. I wanted to please her. And it was titillating at first," he admitted. "Her sister worked at a club that specialized in bacchanals, and Jessabelle and I would go there sometimes and...join in. But the novelty soon wore off for me, and I realized that I'd never really wanted what she craved. I put my foot down, told her we wouldn't be going back. I wanted us to settle down and start a family."

"Did she agree?" Gabriella asked quietly.

"She paid lip service to the idea. But her discontent was there, festering, and I chose to ignore it. It's no excuse, but I was dealing with a territorial war at work. Helmsley's growing success was encroaching on that of O'Leary, a competitor, and the clashes became deadly and personal. Several of my colleagues were killed; I was part of the team that retaliated, taking down our enemy's son. With that move, I sealed Jessabelle's fate."

Even now, the embers of guilt flared. *I should have protected her. She was my responsibility, and I failed her. I had no business marrying her when I cared about my vengeance more.*

A powerful man couldn't let sentiment get in the way. De Villier had been right. Adam's love for Jessabelle had weakened him, prompted him to make the wrong choice. If he hadn't married her, she might still be alive today.

"What happened?" Gabby's voice guided him back, mooring him in the here and now.

"We had one of our usual fights. I told her to stay put in the house because my enemies were everywhere. Then I left. I left knowing that she was angry, that in that state she was capable of anything." He raked a hand through his hair. "There was a masquerade that night at the club where her sister worked, and Jessabelle went in disguise. She participated in the bacchanal until Jeannette recognized her, told her to go home to her husband. She never made it that far. I found her in a nearby alleyway.

"O'Leary and his men had raped her before they stabbed her. Before they left her to die in a pool of her own blood." He met his wife's eyes steadily as the old, helpless rage swirled inside him. "Even when I avenged her, when I slaughtered the men who'd done this to her one by one, I knew they weren't responsible for Jessabelle's death. I was."

❧ 32 ❧

SEEING THE HAUNTED LOOK IN ADAM'S EYES, GABBY COULDN'T help herself any longer. She crossed over to her husband, reaching up and taking his face in her palms.

"You didn't kill Jessabelle," she said firmly. "Those evil men did."

"I shouldn't have left her. Shouldn't have *married* her." Pain and guilt creased his features. "At that time in my life, I wanted power more than anything...even her. I let my infatuation fool me into thinking that I could have both, and she died because of it."

"You don't bear all the blame. She knew who you were. She made the choice to marry you, to go out that night despite the dangers," Gabby whispered.

His hands covered hers, gripping them and bringing them to his chest. She felt the fierce pounding of his heart, knew what it had cost him to tell her all this. Even as she grappled with the knowledge of how much Adam had kept from her, she couldn't stem her flooding relief. In spite of his many omissions, he hadn't lied to her.

He'd been faithful. Since their marriage, he'd wanted only her.

"Why didn't you tell me about your past?" she asked softly.

"I didn't want to taint our marriage. You were a new beginning for me, Gabriella. Everything I wanted." His burning gaze told her this was the truth. "You were so innocent and trusting, so willing to give me everything I needed. Your love is, and has always been, the sweetest thing I've ever known. I didn't want my past failures to change the way you saw me."

Comprehending his unspoken fear, she said, "I could never stop loving you."

Even as she saw the lines around his mouth ease, she had an uneasy flash of intuition. She pulled herself from his grip, and he let her go with obvious reluctance.

She took a step back, wrapping her arms around herself. "Is what happened with Jessabelle why you kept a distance from me all those years? Why things were so different before and after the amnesia?"

"Yes." His admission was gruff, but his eyes never left her face. "As stupid as this sounds now, I was afraid of allowing our marriage to go down the same path. I blamed myself for not curbing Jessabelle's recklessness. I told myself that if I'd done my duty as a husband, if I'd kept her and her excesses in check, she'd still be alive. I convinced myself that the only way to protect you was to always be in control. To keep my head clear and not let you get too deep under my skin."

The breath that Gabby drew in felt jagged, like splintered glass.

"The reason you only came to me once a week, that you kept your distance, that you never told me you loved me...was because you thought I would betray you like Jessabelle did?"

Did he think her so faithless?

"*No.*" In a heartbeat, he reached for her. Hauled her against him and held her there despite her struggling. "Listen to me, Gabriella. Not for one moment did I think you were anything like Jessabelle. It wasn't you I didn't trust but *myself*. Because love had always led to pain in my past, I was afraid to love you. Or, more accurately, afraid to *admit* that you captured my heart since the first moment we met."

She stilled. "You don't have to say that. You didn't love me when you proposed."

"Maybe it wasn't love at first sight," he allowed, "but it was certainly lust. The moment I laid eyes on you, I remembered a painting my mama took me to see as a child. Titian's portrait of Venus. The goddess of love was so pure and sensual that she stole my breath, even as a boy. Every time I look at you, Gabriella, I see that beauty."

He thought of her as a *goddess*?

"Truly?" she asked, her breath hitching.

"Truly. From our first meeting, I knew that I wanted you all for myself. That I'd stop at nothing to make you mine." He paused, and when he spoke again, his voice was rough with emotion. "You are still, aren't you? Tell me that despite everything you now know, you are mine. My wife, my true partner, the only woman who has ever held all of my heart."

How could she deny him when his every word spoke to her own heart?

Yet there was something she still had to know.

"A few months ago, there was that fire at The Gilded Pearl." As she spoke, she felt his arms bulge, hardening around her, but she forged on. "Someone important to you died that night. If it wasn't Jessabelle, who was it?"

When he said nothing, she began to push away.

He held her fast.

"It was a woman by the name of Drusilla Wiley," he said in flat tones. "Before I met Garrity, she and her husband Roger, a sweep, kept me and other children as 'apprentices,' although 'slaves' would be a more apt term for how they abused us. We were forced to clean chimneys and commit countless crimes for them. We were beaten within an inch of our lives for any infractions...or merely for the Wileys' sadistic pleasure. I swore to myself that when I had the opportunity, I would see justice done. Roger died in a knife fight, robbing me of my revenge. But there was still Drusilla."

Even as his cold detachment sent a shiver down Gabby's spine, the knowledge that her husband had suffered further atrocities tore at her heart.

"What did you do to her?" She wasn't certain that she wanted to know.

"She did it to herself. She got into debt with me—not knowing who I was, of course. When she couldn't pay me back, I had her work off her debt. At The Gilded Pearl."

"Doing...what?"

"Whatever was asked of her," he said coolly. "Given that she was a toothless old trull, I'm sure most of it involved scrubbing chamber pots and the like. When she died in the fire, she still owed me five years. She got off too easily."

Her husband's mercilessness ought to have shocked her. But it didn't. She'd gone into the marriage with her eyes wide open when it came to his origins and profession, the nature of the man she'd married.

An eye for an eye—that was who Adam Garrity was.

He was as fierce in his loyalty to his friends as he was in his hostility to his enemies. Did she agree with his ruthless methods? No. Was she going to waste time feeling pity for Drusilla Wiley, a woman who'd enslaved and abused helpless children? Also, no.

In the end, Gabby understood that the world that had birthed her husband was a place where street-level justice and survival went hand in hand, and she accepted it...because she loved him.

In truth, there was only one thing she couldn't accept.

"Have I finally succeeded in shocking you?" he inquired.

Despite his indifferent tone, she heard the underlying tension. Felt it in his body. His arms were steel bands around her, as if he feared she might try to leave him.

Tipping her head back, she looked into his dark, fathomless eyes.

"I know who you are," she said quietly. "Nothing you've said changes my love for you."

A shudder ran through him, his nostrils flaring. "My sweet wife—"

"You will always have my love. And my loyalty." She returned his fierce gaze with one of her own. "As long as you don't lie to me. I won't tolerate you keeping any more secrets."

His eyes smoldered with emotions she couldn't name. But she felt their intensity in the way he was staring at her, as if he wanted to snatch her up and carry her away to his own private den and keep her there forever. Her own emotions pulsed dangerously close to the surface. Her skin tingled, as if it couldn't hold in all that she was feeling. Energy swelled between them, around them, morphing with startling swiftness into physical need.

Her pussy clenched, already wet, already wanting.

"You're my wife, Gabriella, the love of my life," he said with a cool emphasis that made her fires burn hotter. "I will *never* let you go."

Before she could catch her breath, he swept her up in his arms.

There's more to tell her. Another secret she doesn't know.

Adam shut out the voice as he carried his wife into the adjoining room. He knew he wasn't fully in control of himself: between the sudden return of his memories and the baring of his past, he felt a volcano of emotion roiling within him. He wasn't ready to tell Gabby about his plans for vengeance. Hell, he didn't even know if they were still in play.

What he did know was that De Villier was onto him. That explained why De Villier was suddenly paying off some of the loans, loosening the noose that it'd taken Adam *years* to place around the other's neck. The meeting at the ball hadn't been a coincidence, either. Likely the bastard had been sizing him up, trying to discern what he wanted and why. Had De Villier figured out that Adam was the son he'd tried to murder all those years ago?

Christ, Adam wasn't ready to face the possibility that a lifetime of working, planning, and strategizing had been laid to waste. During his amnesia, had he somehow tipped De Villier off? He'd been so bloody close to achieving his goal...

Maybe he could salvage his plan yet. He needed time to regroup. To evaluate the situation rationally, from all angles. After he ascertained where matters stood with his enemy, he would tell Gabriella what she needed to know. Right now, he, himself, didn't know the state of affairs; he could hardly explain it to his wife.

Tomorrow, he'd assess the damage. In this moment, he had a different kind of fire to put out.

He found that it wasn't difficult to push all thoughts of De Villier aside. To allow his burning need for Gabriella to eclipse all else. He'd bared himself to her in a way he'd never done with any one. He felt exposed—and he'd be damned if he was the only one who would feel that way.

He set his precious burden down by the peacock-blue mattress, untying and discarding her cloak. Her hands caught his.

"Here?" she whispered.

"You're mine. Without limits, remember?" Deliberately, he added, "Perhaps I am in need of reassurance that this still holds true."

He was taking advantage of her sweet nature, and he didn't care. In acknowledging his love for her, he'd accepted the depth of his need for her. He could hear her say the words a million times, and it would never be enough. He'd always be greedy for what she gave him, what he'd never received from anyone else.

"I'm yours," she whispered. "Always, Adam."

Her devotion soothed the darkness in him. She was nothing like Jessabelle. She was incapable of betrayal and playing games; loving her wouldn't end in pain. Not that he could stop loving her even if he tried. He'd been a fool to let his past come between them, to waste years of their marriage. He wouldn't waste a single minute more.

"Then you'll obey your sultan's wishes and let him do with you as he pleases," he said.

He saw her eyes widen at his stern tone, her lips parting on a sensual breath. By some stroke of luck, Jeannette had put them in the seraglio, the heart of his wife's sexual fantasies...and his own. For he yearned for her surrender as much as she yearned for his claim.

Especially now. When his world was in chaos, he had to know that he could be certain in this. The need to establish his control, to feel her submission, burned in him.

To his everlasting satisfaction, her hands fell obediently to her sides.

He took off her clothes, layer by layer, stripping her bare. Doing to her what she did to him. When she was as naked as he felt, all thoughts save pleasure fled his mind. He looked at his treasure with covetous eyes and knew he was the wealthiest man alive.

He ran his hands over her silken curves, her sensual shiver pumping blood into his already stiff cock. So responsive, his queen. When he touched her pussy, his satisfaction grew.

"My slave is already drenched with dew," he said silkily. "Do you want to come, Gabriella? Ask me nicely, and I might help you."

Charmingly flustered, she asked, "Please, would you make me come?"

She gasped as he spun her around, pulled her generous backside against his hard, clothed form. With one hand, he swept aside her hair, his lips skimming the graceful curve of her neck.

He'd discovered how much she liked to be stimulated there, his kisses, licks, and nips eliciting throaty moans. With his other hand, he rubbed her cunny, alternating feather-light caresses with sinuous circles upon her sensitive nub. She was so close he knew she wouldn't last long.

Sure enough, her thighs began to quiver. He drove two fingers into her tight passage. Her quim sucked at him, fierce hungry pulls that caused his prick to jerk in envy. He stirred his fingers inside her, setting his teeth on the tender juncture of her neck and shoulder, holding her captive as she came to a trembling climax.

He wound her fiery hair around his fist and said in her ear, "Now that I've seen to your pleasure, you will see to mine. With your mouth, I think. That warm, wet hole that takes my cock so nicely."

Her shudder of excitement matched his own. Since that first time in the sparring room, Gabriella had performed fellatio upon him regularly, showing a wanton enthusiasm for sucking his cock. A good thing since he was an equally enthusiastic recipient. She turned to face him, sinking slowly to her knees upon the blue mattress, her eyes never leaving his as he disrobed.

When he was naked, he fisted his rearing shaft. He frigged himself slowly, pre-seed dribbling from his flaring crown as he looked upon his wife's uplifted face. She glowed with love and passion, his adoring goddess and eager queen.

"Place your hands on my thighs," he said huskily. "Open your mouth for me."

This was a little different from what they'd practiced before, but tonight he wanted full control. His desire to claim her transcended rationality and emotion. Pure need burned in the part of him that, if he were a spiritual man, he'd call his soul.

When her red lips parted, he slid himself home.

God, *God*, this was fine.

His hands tangling in her hair, he held her still while he

thrust himself through heaven's gates. He went deeper with each pass, judging how much she could take since she'd yielded that privilege to him. Her palms twitched against his thighs, the wet sounds of her sucking adding to his lustful frenzy. He shoved more aggressively, and she moaned not in protest but encouragement, her throat relaxing even more. Tears gathered and fell from her shining eyes, the jewels of her commitment and effort.

He buried his full length into her giving warmth, grunting when he butted her throat. Her muscles surrounded him, the spasming reflex that never failed to drive him mad. But he was too close now to enjoy more of that decadent squeeze and release, his stones swelling with unstoppable pressure. He loosened his hold on her hair, intending to pull out before it was too late.

To his surprise and bloody delight, her hands shot to his buttocks, holding him where he was. Her delicate fingernails bit into the steely ridges of his arse, telling him that she wanted him to continue, that she wanted *all* of him. With surging pride, he gave her what she wanted. As he thrust deeper and deeper, his mind blurred with pleasure, with the dawning recognition of who of the two of them was truly enslaved...

His spine bowing, he groaned as he shot thick, scalding jets down her throat. She took it all, continuing to gently suck and lick while he emptied his seed. When he withdrew from her, he was still hard, glistening with her kisses, and nowhere near done.

He tumbled her onto the mattress, fusing his mouth to hers. The taboo taste of his seed upon his lady's lips sent a jolt up his spine. Gripping her hips, he drove inside her, grunting when her pussy closed around him like a silken fist.

"You're ready again?" she asked in breathless surprise.

Her hair was a fiery fan against the peacock silk. Her arms were splayed above her head, a pose of sweet surrender. Her eyes shone with the purity of her love, her lips with the wantonness of her desire. Her beauty branded itself upon his brain; even if he lived to be a hundred, he knew that he'd never forget this moment.

"Again and again," he growled. "I'll never get enough of you, Gabriella."

She moaned as he set about proving the truth of his claim.

❧ 33 ❧

THE NEXT DAY, GABBY AWOKE ALONE IN HER OWN BED. SHE had a moment's disorientation before she remembered how she'd arrived there. After their intense lovemaking at Mrs. Wilde's, Adam had brought her home. He'd carried her up to bed...and taken her again. And again. He'd been insatiable, leading her through a sexual marathon, and she'd loved every moment of it.

Yet now that the bliss had faded to pleasurable twinges, reminders of the night's excesses, she found herself unsettled. She couldn't put a finger on why she felt that way: Adam had declared his love for her and demonstrated it with ardent virility. Even so, a part of her was still reeling. From what she'd learned about her husband's past...and the fact that he'd kept all those secrets hidden from her for *years*.

Now that Gabby knew about Jessabelle, she understood why her husband hadn't wanted to divulge the tragedy of his first marriage. The experience had left him scarred and made it difficult for him to trust again. Truth be told, she ought to count herself lucky that she'd somehow broken through the fortress that guarded his heart.

Nonetheless, in the light of day, questions assailed her.

How could I have been so ignorant, so blindly trusting all these years? Would I know if he kept other secrets from me? Now that his memory is back, will he revert to the way he was before?

Her anxiety was fed by Adam's absence from her bed. Since their fresh start at the hunting lodge, he'd slept with her every night. Not only that, he'd kept her close, their bodies in constant contact. She'd become used to waking up entangled with him, sometimes even with him inside her, her favorite way to start a morning. These last weeks, she'd had the most restful sleep of her entire life.

But sometime in the early hours of this morning, she'd felt him leave. Exhausted from their tempestuous lovemaking, she'd dozed on fitfully. Now, looking at the empty place where her husband ought to have been, she felt uncertainty slither through her belly.

Don't be silly, she chided herself. *Now that he's recovered from his amnesia, he must have plenty to attend to at work. Knowing Adam, he'll want to catch up on everything immediately.*

She told herself it wasn't a reflection of his regard for her. This was simply who her husband was: a driven and ambitious man. Tonight, when he returned from the office, they would have time to converse further. She decided to plan a cozy supper with his favorite dishes. She'd have it served in her sitting room, a setting that encouraged intimate conversation. And she'd wear one of the risqué negligees that Adam had commissioned from Mrs. Yarwood.

Feeling better, she rolled over and buried her face in her husband's pillow. The familiar scent of his spice and musk reassured her. Sitting up, she was reaching to ring the bed when a knock sounded on her door. It was Mrs. Page, her grave expression making Gabby's fingers clutch the coverlet.

Pulse skipping, Gabby asked, "What is it?"

"Your papa's physician sent word. I'm sorry, ma'am, but he says your father has taken another turn for the worse."

"Gabriella, you're here at last," her father said from the bed. "I've been waiting for you."

Despite the tightness in her chest, Gabby managed a smile. The physician had informed her that her father's wasting disease was entering its final stages. Nonetheless, Papa still managed to give her his customary peremptory wave, his tone brisk and businesslike.

"How...are you feeling, Papa?" As she bent to kiss his cheek, she couldn't help a tear from escaping, a trace of wetness clinging to his papery skin.

"What's this? Are you crying?" Despite his words, tender awareness glimmered in her father's eyes. "We'll have none of that, Gabriella. Death comes for everyone, and there's no use wasting tears over the inevitable. Besides, we have urgent business to discuss."

The physician had told her that, in these final days, the patient's mind could become surprisingly clear. This was the case for her father, who sounded so much like his old self that she couldn't suppress the irrational hope that somehow the doctor was wrong. That despite Curtis Billings's frail state, he could somehow beat this disease...the way he'd conquered everything in his life, through sheer will and determination.

She picked up the bowl of beef tea from the bedside table. "Why don't you have some of this, Papa?"

"I don't have time for sickroom mush," he said impatiently. "I'm dying, so what's the point? And you're not listening: we have a pressing matter to settle."

Sighing, she set down the bowl. "What is it, Papa?"

"I was right about Isnard."

A cool feather brushed over her nape. "Right about what?"

"He's being paid off. By your husband."

Panic warred with denial. *It has to be the illness talking. Papa isn't in his right mind. Adam would never do such a thing. He told me he didn't marry me for money—he's never lied to me...*

Last night's revelations wound through her like an icy river. While her husband might not have told her lies, he hadn't been fully honest either. In some ways, his sins of omission had been as impactful as outright deceit. Nevertheless, he'd had his reasons, and she felt compelled to defend him.

"I know you've never liked Adam, Papa, but—"

"It's true that I regret agreeing to Garrity's offer for you. The persuasive bastard has always had a way of getting what he wants. At this point, however, my feelings are inconsequential. I have proof, Gabriella."

The chill inside her spread. "Proof of what?"

Her father reached over to the bedside table. Opening the drawer, he removed a stack of paper.

"It's all here." He slapped the papers onto the bed. "My investigator discovered that Isnard is up to his ears in debt to Fratelli & Sons Bank. It took some digging, for there were obvious efforts made to hide the true ownership of the bank through legal maneuverings, but do you know who ultimately holds the deed to Fratelli & Sons?"

Gabby didn't want to believe it. After all they'd been through, if Adam was lying to her...if he'd been manipulating her this entire time, their marriage based on deception from the start...

"Your husband." Papa's index finger stabbed the papers like a nail into a coffin.

"That...that might mean nothing..." She hated herself for her own stupidity, for holding onto hope when there was none to hold onto.

But that was her. Stupid Gabriella and her stupid *Bin of Blissful Ignorance*.

She thought of all that Adam had kept from her throughout their marriage. How he'd changed as soon as he'd recovered his memory, left her this morning for what had always been more important to him. His business, the demanding mistress that she'd never been able to compete with. That she hadn't *thought* to compete with...until he'd made her believe that she could. That she could hold his attention, his passion, his desire more than power and money.

What a fool I've been.

"I confronted Isnard with my findings this morning. The bastard broke down in tears and admitted that Garrity has been pulling his strings for years. Once I'm dead, Garrity apparently intends to take over my bank." Rage took away her father's pallor. "Isnard had the gall to beg for my forgiveness—forgiveness, hah! If I wasn't dying, I'd ruin the traitor worse than your husband ever could. As it is, however, I need to save my energy to get us out of this mess."

"How will you do that?" she asked dully.

And why did it matter? Nothing mattered if her happiness had been built on a lie. If Adam hadn't wanted her for herself, if he'd been a fortune hunter after her inheritance. Why, oh why, had she let herself believe that anyone could love her?

Everything that had happened since seemed to disintegrate, her joy smashed into glittering ash. Perhaps it had all been an illusion anyway. Dash it all, she thought with mounting rage, why did Adam have to make her believe that her love was returned? That she was beautiful, desirable? If he'd left things the way they were before his amnesia, she might have found some way to survive.

But he'd laid siege to her defenses. One by one, she'd relinquished the *Bin of Blissful Ignorance* and her other shields, believing she no longer had need of them. She had no walls left, nowhere to hide.

Which made reality all the more devastating.

"The obvious course of action is to replace Isnard. This has to be done immediately for I haven't much time." Papa drummed his fingers against the papers. "I've been trying to think of who I can trust to oversee your future and that of Billings Bank. The problem is this man must be so rich and powerful that he would be impervious to your husband's corruptive influence; that doesn't leave us many choices."

"I don't care." The words were bitter on her tongue. "Let Adam have what he wants."

What could Adam do to her that was worse than what he'd already done? Despite her spiraling despair, she didn't think he'd throw her out on the street. He would continue to provide materially for her and the children the way he always had. But what she truly wanted—his heart—might forever be out of reach... because she wasn't even sure he had one.

"It's not just your future at stake: it's the future of Billings Bank. My legacy," her father said in outrage. "Isnard admitted to me that Garrity wants to call in the loans secured by De Villier. We're talking nearly a million pounds; there's no way De Villier will be able to pay back that amount immediately. Not until his railway venture is fully operational and that could take years. If Garrity gets his way, De Villier will be ruined—as will my bank. I've bet heavily on De Villier, and if he falls, I fall. I will not let that happen."

"What do you want me to do, Papa?" she asked helplessly.

"I want you to take pride, Gabriella. For Billings Bank is your legacy as much as mine." His gaze was fierce. "You've sacrificed as much for the business as I have. Because of the bank, you, a motherless child, grew up without a father, too."

His recognition resonated through her. And the regret that briefly flashed over his wan features pressed upon her battered heart. She couldn't let him part this world believing that he failed her.

"Despite all the burdens you carried, you provided for me, gave me the best that money could buy. Sweet heavens," she said in an attempt to lighten the mood, failing when her voice cracked, "you bought a country estate and hosted the most infamous house party of all time in an attempt to find me a husband."

"I wanted to land you a fat title. Instead, I got you a shark," Papa said sourly.

Although she cringed at the aptness of the metaphor, she managed a smile. "Regardless of the results, you've always had my best interests in mind. You are the best of fathers."

"I'm not. But somehow I raised a good girl." He cleared his throat. "A woman of whom I am very proud."

"Oh, Papa." This time, she couldn't stop the heat from over-flowing her eyes. "I love you so. I don't know how I'll get on without you."

"Nonsense." He reached out, giving her hand an awkward pat. "You got on fine without me all these years, I don't see why anything should change. You're a late bloomer, just like your mama. You have her beauty and patience...her quiet strength, too." His gaze grew faraway, as if he were recalling some sweet bygone moment. "I can't recall your mama ever raising her voice or being disagreeable. She just went her way, spreading her sunshine, making life brighter for those around her. Truth be told, I look forward to seeing her again."

Gabby heard the longing in her father's voice. He'd so rarely spoken of her mother, and she'd believed it was because he was a practical man, one who didn't dwell in the past. Now she wondered if the opposite was true: if he'd avoided talking about his wife because he'd felt *too* much.

"But before I go," he said, his eyes flaring with the brilliance of a flame nearing the end of its wick, "I need to find you a new trustee. The devil of it is that I can't think of anyone who meets all the necessary criteria—"

"I know someone," she said.

The idea had been germinating since her papa brought up the problem. She knew someone incorruptible, who wouldn't be afraid of Adam, who believed in doing the right thing. She even thought that he'd help her if she asked.

But could she defy Adam in this way?

The old Gabriella would have never considered it.

It was a bittersweet testament to how the last month had changed her. She could no longer ignore, deny, or spin some cheerful tale to cover up the problems in her marriage. There was only one way left to deal with her troubles: head-on.

You must find out the truth once and for all, the voice inside her said. *Does Adam love you...or has everything been a lie? Only then will you know whether or not your marriage is worth fighting for.*

"Who?" her father asked eagerly.

"Before I ask him, I need to know, Papa...do you have faith in me?" She clasped his age-spotted hand in both of hers. As she contemplated the step she was about to take, one that would change her marriage forevermore, she needed to know that she was doing the right thing. "Do you believe that I have the wherewithal to do right by you—by myself and my children?"

"If I ever gave you reason to doubt your worth, that failing is mine and not yours." Although his squeeze was weak, his gaze remained steady. "But what I think isn't what counts. You, Gabriella, must have faith in yourself."

34

It was nearing midnight when Adam returned home the following evening.

Climbing the steps to his bedchamber, he lacked his usual vigor. He felt like a bloody wrung rag after collecting and reviewing the latest figures on his banks.

At least now he had his answer: the game was up.

Somehow, De Villier had gotten wind of Adam's plans. In the past fortnight, the bastard had been methodically paying off his debts to the smaller banks. He'd probably pulled in the additional capital from personal investors, using the skyrocketing price of his stocks as bait to lure them in.

With every minute that passed, De Villier was slipping farther out of Adam's grasp.

Adam didn't know how De Villier had discovered that he'd been slowly and systematically buying up all of De Villier's debts over the years. His best guess was that it had happened during the course of his amnesia; devil take it, he'd taken his eyes off the prize for a *single bloody moment*...and now everything was falling apart. Coming down around him like a house of cards.

He had no one to blame but himself. He felt a rush of impotent fury. He'd been carrying on like a bloody mooncalf, cavorting on vacation with his wife, when he *should* have been keeping tabs on his vengeance.

A powerful man isn't blinded by sentiment, De Villier's voice taunted him.

His hands fisted as he reached the floor of his suite. *I'm not going to lie down and accept failure like the damned weakling De Villier thinks I am. I'll fix this. Numquam obliviscar—never forget.*

All hope wasn't lost. There was still De Villier's debt to Billings Bank: it amounted to nearly a million pounds, a sum that even De Villier couldn't immediately raise. Speculative frenzy would only take him so far, especially when he wouldn't be able to unveil his much-heralded steam engine: according to Adam's inside source, the machine was still not viable. Despite De Villier's threats and bribes, his engineers apparently couldn't deliver the promised product.

Thus, if Adam managed to call in the debt soon, De Villier would have his throat exposed. With no locomotive to back his promises, his adoring public would abandon him. He would have no means of paying off the debt, and Adam would *own* him at last.

Only one thing stood in Adam's way: Curtis Billings.

Christ, it was just like his father-in-law to be a thorn in his side. Why couldn't Billings just cock his toes and depart gracefully into the great beyond? But no, the stubborn bastard had to cling to life like a goddamned leech, rendering Adam's options a great deal messier.

If Billings had just passed away, Billings Bank would have been under the control of Gabriella's trust. Since the trustee, Isnard, was Adam's puppet, Adam could have maneuvered the strings with no one the wiser. Now he'd have to go to his father-in-law, who detested him, and try to broker a deal.

He knew Billings would refuse. Not only to spite him, but because he would want to preserve his precious bank. That meant Adam might have to consider a radical move: to have Billings declared incompetent because of his illness. That would trigger the transfer of all of Billings's assets, including the bank, into the trust...and, ergo, into Adam's hands.

But what would that do to Adam's marriage?

He'd arrived at his wife's door. Pausing, he saw the light that seeped beneath, telling him that she was still awake. It was late, yet she'd waited up for him. He hadn't seen her in nearly two days, the urge to be with her gnawing inside him. He yearned to leave the darkness behind and lose himself in her sweetness.

But that's what caused this whole mess, a voice inside him sneered. *You got distracted, got soft. That's why De Villier's gaining the upper hand.*

His temples throbbed with frustration. He couldn't deny that his feelings for Gabriella were muddying his thinking. As he'd contemplated the best way to get his plans back on track, he'd wrestled with his conscience. How would she react if he had her father declared incompetent? What would the implications to their marriage be? Would he lose her love forever?

She's your wife. Her first loyalty is to you, the old, familiar voice in his head stated.

She loves her father, a newer voice argued. *You'll break her heart with this betrayal.*

He dragged a hand through his hair, his eyes closing for a brief instant. The warring inside him was driving him mad. He didn't even know who he was anymore.

Get a hold of yourself, man. Don't be the weakling De Villier thinks you are.

Inhaling through his nose, he continued on to his own room. As much as he wanted to see Gabriella, he wasn't in a good place to be with her. He needed time to align his thoughts and emotions, to regain control of himself and his life.

Entering his room, he dismissed his waiting valet and poured himself a whisky. Sipping meditatively, he couldn't help but glance at the door that connected to Gabriella's chamber; beneath it, light still shone through, which meant she was either awake...or she'd fallen asleep with the lamp on. With a pang, he remembered what she'd confided to him, that she'd been a restless sleeper until he started spending the night with her, and the impulse to go to her tore at his gut.

He didn't know if he could trust this part of himself. It was one thing to have no limits in their sexual activities: he was all for that. Just thinking of stripping Gabriella of her inhibitions made him hard as rock. Emotions, however, were another matter.

He loved her, yes. More than he'd loved anyone.

But he couldn't let himself be controlled by love.

He was about to pour himself another drink when the door to Gabriella's room opened. His wife entered, and his exhaustion fled in the wake of rising lust. Given the success of her ballgown, he'd helped her to choose a new wardrobe, one designed to show off her magnificent figure. At present, she wore a sleek robe of sapphire silk. The garment revealed the deep crevice between her breasts and clung to her curves. With her fiery tresses cascading down her back, she looked every inch an exotic queen.

His prick throbbed with anticipation. Maybe what he needed wasn't to stay away from his wife but to ride her good and hard. Maybe that would clear his head.

"I heard you come home. Why didn't you stop by to say good night?" she asked.

Her tone had an odd edge to it...but he was tired. He could be imagining things.

"It was late, my dear, and I didn't wish to disturb you." He set down his glass with a click. Prowling over to her, he ran a finger over her shoulder, the beast in him savoring her shiver. "Since you are awake, however, I would be happy to entertain you."

"We need to talk," she said.

He dropped his hand. He hadn't imagined it then. Gabby's voice and expression had a hardness that was foreign to her nature and therefore impossible to miss.

"What about?" he said, with the wariness of a man who isn't stupid.

"The fact that you're bribing my trustee to do your bidding."

Her words sliced like a scalpel. Shock bled through him. Cornered, he reacted on instinct.

"Where did you get that idea?" He shaped his lips into a quizzical smile. "Has your father been spouting his paranoia again?"

"I know about Mr. Isnard's debts to you," she said steadily. "I know that you want him to call in Mr. De Villier's debts and destroy Billings Bank in the process. What *you* need to know is that I will not allow that to happen."

Shock turned into something else. If she'd come to him in another way, if she'd asked him why he'd done what he'd done, he might have reacted differently. But she was confronting him, *threatening* him. Threatening to take away the one thing that he'd worked for his entire life, that defined him, that kept the chaos at bay.

His already tenuous grip on his self-control slipped. He responded how he always did to intimidation: he pushed back.

"How do you propose to stop me?" he asked with silky menace.

"It's already done." She folded her arms over her chest; the belligerence that flashed in her eyes was a lightning rod to his own volatile emotions. "Mr. Isnard has been removed from his role as my trustee. That role now belongs to Harry Kent."

Her words sunk into him like a knife between the shoulder blades. The betrayal momentarily cut short his breath, his vision turning red. His wife—the woman he loved and who professed to love him in return—had ruined his chances of achieving his life-long goal?

No *bloody* way would he allow that to happen.

"We'll get it changed back," he said through his teeth.

"You can't. The deed is done, with three witnesses testifying to my father's sound state of mind. Whether or not you like it, Mr. Kent is now my trustee, and he will take his direction from me, acting in my best interests. And you know as well as I do that you cannot bully or intimidate him into doing your bidding."

Lungs straining with rage, Adam knew she was right. If there was one person in the goddamned world whom he couldn't buy, it was Kent. Not only was the bastard morally incorruptible, he was married to the King of the Underworld's granddaughter and brother-in-law to a host of powerful aristocrats. He was protected, out of Adam's reach.

If this were a game of chess, Gabriella would have claimed checkmate.

Fucking hell, Adam had been beaten...by the person he had least expected to betray him.

But that was the best type of deception, wasn't it?

Unholy fury blazed as he took in the tight seam of his wife's mouth, her composed blue gaze. Where was the sweet, biddable wallflower he'd married? His adoring queen who'd pledged her loyalty to him? In her place stood a woman he didn't even know.

Once again, he'd let love distract him, deceive him. Now he was paying the price: the woman he loved had single-handedly ripped away his control and demolished his life's work.

That bastard De Villier got one thing right: only a fool lets himself be blinded by love.

The darkness in Adam swirled, his vision blackening with wrath.

≈

"Why did you do this? To preserve your father's legacy?" Adam asked tightly. "Your first loyalty should belong to me, your *husband*. All your talk of love is meaningless otherwise, you traitorous bitch."

"*I'm* the traitor?" The unfairness of his accusation fed

Gabby's anger. "*You're* the one who betrayed our marriage by lying from the outset. You told me you didn't care about my money, that you wanted *me*. But that was all a ploy so that you could get your hands on my father's bank. To play out whatever Machiavellian schemes you have brewing in your moneylender's brain."

"You have no idea why I'm doing this, woman," he roared.

"And I don't give a damn." It hurt to breathe, to live, to look at this man to whom she'd given her soul. "Nothing you could say would justify your deception, and I wouldn't believe you any way."

I'm tired of being a fool. Tired of wanting what I can't have. Tired of hoping, always hoping...

"I don't have to justify anything to you. I'm your husband. According to the law," he said acidly, "I bloody *own* you."

His words confirmed that it was futile to hope. During the course of her marriage, she'd accepted the ruthlessness in her husband's nature as part of who he was, a product of surviving a childhood in the stews. Yet that acceptance had been tempered by her faith that he'd never be ruthless toward *her*. Even before the amnesia, when he'd been stoic about his feelings, he'd treated her with tenderness and care. After the amnesia, he'd convinced her that he truly loved her...

All of it *lies*.

Now her blinders were ripped off, and she was seeing her husband for the first time. Cold-blooded, callous, willing to sacrifice his marriage and family for more money. More power. The only things that mattered to him.

You mean nothing to him. You're only the means to an end.

"Legally, you may own me but not my trust." She saw her riposte hit home, his eyes burning with rage. "That was rather the point of my father's planning. In truth, you have two choices, Adam. You can accept the reality that Billings Bank and my wealth are out of your reach, and we will find some way to muddle on in this marriage."

"Or what?" he said dangerously. "You should know that I do not respond well to ultimatums, Gabriella."

Refusing to be cowed, she marched up to him. She saw his gaze veer to the throbbing pulse of her throat and knew that she'd roused his darkest instincts. But she didn't care because he'd done the same to her.

Gabby had never fought with anyone, didn't know how to. All her life, she'd tamped down her hurt and pain, and now it exploded from her like a cannon. She was *done* with being nice. Anger took over her voice, her body, her every impulse. She, who'd rarely raised her voice in the past, now had a rabid desire to draw blood.

"Or it's going to be war between us," she said fiercely. "From here on in, I am taking charge of my future. I won't let you—or anyone—take away my father's legacy."

His fingers curled and uncurled at his sides. "You are making a grave mistake, Wife."

"Actually, I'm rectifying the one I made when I married you."

The muscle in his jaw ticked.

"Get out," he said softly. "Before I do something I regret."

"What could you possibly do to me, Adam, that is worse than what you've already done?" Her voice shook, but she held his merciless gaze. "For years, I've been telling myself stories about our marriage, making it seem like a faerie tale. Well, I'm out of stories. Out of faith. Out of *love*. Now I see what really happened: I worshipped you, gave you my heart, and what you gave me in return is as worthless as your honor."

The muscle on his jaw stilled, standing out in stark relief. His muscles bunched, quivering like that of a beast about to spring.

"If you won't leave, then I will," he gritted out.

"Go ahead and leave," she said bitterly. "I'm used to being alone in this marriage anyway."

With a look of impotent fury, he stalked out, the slam of the door shaking the walls.

❧ 35 ❧

IT TOOK A BOTTLE OF WHISKY TO CALM ADAM'S RAGE. AND even that wasn't enough to bring about the oblivion he craved. Hours later, he was still wide awake, sitting at his desk in his office, watching the cool grey light of morning blanket the city below.

Usually, the bird's-eye view of the city gave him pleasure, a symbol of the heights he'd achieved, but now all he felt was bleakness. It was as if all he'd worked for, all his triumphs and successes...meant nothing. It had taken the whisky and hours of brooding contemplation to understand why.

I'm out of stories. Out of faith. Out of love.

If he lost Gabby's love, he lost everything.

Since the age of nine, he'd taught himself to think that revenge was the only thing that mattered. That love only brought disappointment and pain. Perhaps all that had been true—until Gabby had burst unexpectedly into his life.

From the start, his heart had known what his head had been afraid to believe. That there could be more to life than *an eye for an eye*...that there existed a kind of love so pure and beautiful that it would never let him down. That would give meaning to his existence, explain the suffering and pain, and conquer the chaos inside him in a way that no amount of control ever could.

His wife had given him that love.

In return, he'd given her duplicity.

She was right: he'd betrayed their marriage first, by not being honest about his intentions regarding her father's bank. In his fury last night, he hadn't even told her about De Villier, hadn't corrected her erroneous assumption that he hadn't deceived her for money and power, but for...his honor. The honor she accused him of not having.

Perhaps she was right. He hadn't been honorable toward her, had taken her love and devotion for granted. He closed his eyes briefly, the heat of remorse prickling his eyelids. Tears he hadn't cried since age nine.

A knock sounded on the door, and he quickly swiped his sleeve across his eyes.

Clearing his throat, he said hoarsely, "Come in."

Murray sauntered in, looking as fresh as a damned daisy in his grey suit and yellow cravat, his bronzed hair gleaming. He sprawled into the chair on the other side of the desk and flicked a glance at the empty whisky decanter. "Looks like someone dipped too deep last evening."

The chipper tones made Adam aware of his splitting headache.

"For God's sake, keep your voice down," he said tersely.

"That's your pickled brain shouting at you not me." The other slid a silver flask across the desk. "Here, try this."

Taking the flask and uncapping it, Adam grimaced at the released fumes. "What is it?"

"A personal remedy that I keep handy at all times. Wickham Murray's Cure for All Ails—or Cure *for* the Cure of All Ails, rather. Drink up like a good lad."

Adam would have refused the cheeky bastard, but he needed to clear his head. He needed to find a way to fix things with

Gabriella. But what if she couldn't forgive him for his years of neglect, for the secrets he'd kept, for scheming to take over her father's bank? His gut clenched. If he tried to explain to her why his retribution was important to him, would she understand? What if he had lost her trust and her love for good?

"For God's sake, it's the hair of the dog, not a visit to the tooth-drawer," Murray said, clearly misinterpreting the cause of Adam's expression.

Adam downed the concoction; it blazed through his system.

"I'd wager your head feels better already, doesn't it?"

He coughed, surprised when fire didn't come out of his mouth. "Only because the hole your 'remedy' burned in my throat is distracting me from the headache."

"Whatever works, I always say." Murray studied him. "Do you want to talk about it?"

"About what?"

"About why you're wearing yesterday's clothes and clearly spent the night at the office getting as soused as a sailor on leave."

Adam managed a quelling stare. "Mind your own bloody business."

"Fine." The other man shrugged. "Then I'll just have to come to the obvious conclusion. The one that every single clerk in the office has also arrived at."

"What conclusion is that?" He wondered if he had the where-withal to strangle the other.

"That you're in hot water with your lovely wife."

The accuracy of the statement struck Adam like a flaming poker to the chest. He was in more than hot water, he thought with burning despair. He was drowning without her.

"Holy hell, how bad is it?" The humor faded from Murray's voice, his hazel eyes turning serious. "Did she really kick you out of the house?"

"What part of *'mind your own business'* don't you understand?"

Christ, he wished Murray would stop prying. He felt as if his self-discipline had abandoned him. He needed to be left alone, to think things out. How was he going to satisfy his honor without losing his wife?

"When have I ever minded my own business? Admit it, my nosiness is part of my charm, and why I've grown on you despite your futile efforts to find me annoying."

"Who said my efforts were futile?"

Murray smiled, but his gaze was earnest. "I should hope that, after all these years, you know you can trust me."

In the stillness that followed, Adam realized that the other man *had* earned his trust. Despite Murray's raffish ways, he had proved himself a good business partner, had never let Adam down, and had always been true to his word. Hell, he'd even had the bollocks to confront Adam about the visits to Mrs. Wilde's, to try to make Adam see what a gift Gabriella was.

Adam was used to keeping his own counsel. But look at where that had gotten him. Maybe another's opinion might help him figure out what he needed to do.

"I've wronged my wife," he heard himself say hoarsely. "I have to find a way to win her back."

He gave Murray the necessary details. About De Villier, Gabby's trust, the fight he'd had with her last night. As he spoke, he heard his own perfidy more clearly than ever. He hated himself for hurting her, for making the wrong choice time and again. Murray listened, his expression somber and without judgement.

"She said that…she'd run out of love for me," Adam concluded tightly.

"And you've never said anything that you didn't mean in the heat of anger?" Murray shook his head. "Look, I've never been married, but I know women…at least in the biblical sense. Trust me, one can learn a lot about ladies in intimate situations—"

"Is there a point to this philosophizing, or are you just bragging about your prowess?"

"My point is that women, as a whole, tend to be forgiving

creatures. They have to be, don't they, in order to deal with us hardheaded bastards. And your wife, in particular, is one of the sweetest, most devoted ladies I know. She loves you, and she's not going to stop loving you overnight, even if you've had your head up your arse." There was compassion in Murray's eyes...and empathy. "I've made my share of mistakes. Ones I couldn't undo. The next best thing was owning up to them and accepting responsibility."

"I accept full responsibility for my actions." His throat worked. "But how do I convince Gabriella to give me another chance?"

"Just go to her and explain things. Bare your soul, if need be. If that doesn't work, try groveling...although your lady is far too nice to let you suffer for long." Murray regarded him with a small smile. "I'm sure the two of you will come to a compromise."

Clarity struck Adam. Suddenly, he *knew* what he had to do. To prove to Gabriella what she meant to him and hopefully win her forgiveness.

"There will be no compromise," he stated.

"See here, if your marriage is important to you..."

"It is the most important thing in my life." Everything else— his past, his anger, even his vengeance—paled in comparison to what he had with Gabriella. The gift she'd given him. "Which is why I won't stand in the way of Gabriella's wishes. If she wants control of her trust, it's hers. I'm not going to fight it. I'll prove to her that I married her because I wanted her...because I love her."

"You never do anything in half measures, do you?" Murray murmured. "And your revenge against De Villier?"

"Either I'll find another way to take the bastard down or I won't. But I won't sacrifice my marriage doing it."

He rose with single-minded purpose, the desire to see his wife eclipsing everything else. Once he saw her again, everything would be all right. Because *she* made everything all right for him... had been doing so for years. His thirst for revenge had blinded him to what had been in front of his face all this time. What his amnesia had helped him to realize.

The peace he was looking for...he already *had* it.

Now it was time to show his wife that he was worthy of her love.

Murray stood, offering his hand. "Good luck."

"I'll need it." Adam shook the other's hand and added gruffly, "Thank you."

"You gave me a second chance all those years ago. I'm just returning the favor."

With a nod, Adam headed to the door. It swung open, narrowly missing him.

Kerrigan stood in the doorway.

"We're leaving," Adam said to his guard. "Get the driver—"

"Something's happened, sir."

The look on Kerrigan's face sent a chill through him.

"What is it?" he demanded.

"Mrs. Garrity was ambushed. In broad daylight, on the way to her father's house," Kerrigan said, his voice low. "She had three guards with her, but they were outnumbered—killed."

"Where is my wife?" Adam said as the iciness spread and spread.

Please, God, no. Don't let anything happen to her. I'll give anything, do anything...

"They took her. Left this in the carriage."

Adam snatched the piece of paper from the guard.

If you want to see your wife alive again, await my instruction.

36

GABBY CAME TO, BLINKING GROGGILY IN THE DIMNESS.

Where am I?

She managed to rise to her feet. When she swayed, she steadied herself against the wall, felt cold, powdery brick beneath her fingertips. Smells tickled her nose: coal smoke, sulphur, and brine. Where was she, how did she get here...?

The attack returned in a flash. The carriage jerking to a stop. An army of ruffians—*oh God*, they'd shot her guards, killed them. Even as shock and grief pervaded her, she bottled it, forced herself to recount the rest of the events. The blackguards had dragged her out, smothered her scream with a soaked handkerchief, the chemical choking her lungs...then nothing.

Who did this? Why? How will I get out of here?

Frantically, squinting in the gloom, she tried to map out her prison, find a way to escape. Hand over hand, she felt her way along the walls, solid and thick, no way of getting through. Her palms scraped against wood.

A door.

She fumbled with the knob. Jiggled it desperately but it would not turn. She pounded on the door and screamed for help until her fists and throat were raw.

No aid came. She was trapped. Held hostage by some murderous and mysterious villain.

She sat, her back against the door, the reality of the situation sinking in. Her first thought was of Adam: how frantic he'd be, how he'd do everything in his power to find her, once he knew she'd been taken. Sweet heavens, for him it would be like losing Jessabelle all over again.

She thought she was out of tears, but they leaked down her cheeks once more. Following Adam's departure last night, she'd given into a fit of weeping. She'd cried for the loss of her girlhood dreams, for her shattered heart in the present, and for the uncertainty of her future. Her sorrow had felt like a dark and bottomless well, one from which there was no escape.

This morning, she'd awoken from an exhausted sleep. Her eyes had been puffy, her chest and throat tender. Even so, she'd known that staying in bed would do her no good and, after freshening up, she'd gone to bid good morning to Fiona and Max.

Her babes. Hers...and Adam's.

Looking at Max, she'd seen a miniature replica of his handsome father, down to his unruly forelock. Listening to Fiona's happy chatter, she'd felt the confidence and ambition her daughter had inherited from Adam.

And Gabby had realized something important: she wasn't out of love.

She would *never* run out of love because of who she was. She might not have Tessa's cleverness, Maggie's fortitude, or Emma's determination, but she did have her own strength: when she gave her heart, she gave it completely. She loved with everything that she was. For right or wrong, she'd given her love to Adam...and he would have it, forever and always.

Thus, as hopeless as the future seemed—she had no idea how they could repair the damage done to their marriage—she had her love to guide her. It reminded her of the intimacy and passion she and Adam had shared in the last month, how far they'd come. It told her to be patient: Adam had suffered greatly in his past and his recovery from amnesia must have come as a shock. Most of all, it reaffirmed the vows she'd given him and that he'd given her in return.

For better or worse. Love was a commitment. Despite everything Adam had done, if he was willing to work to change things, to make them better, then she would fight for their marriage too.

Those had been her thoughts when she'd been attacked. Now she didn't know if she would have the chance to tell Adam how she truly felt or to see their beautiful children again. As despair swamped her, she heard footsteps.

Scrambling to her feet and out of the path of the opening door, Gabby was momentarily blinded by a shock of light. A lamp...held by a man. She blinked as his features became clear, as she saw the unmistakable gleam of wheat-blond hair.

Shock bombarded her. "*Mr. De Villier?*"

"Good afternoon, Mrs. Garrity," he said in his smooth-as-silk accent.

Her shock gave way to fury when he executed an elegant bow...as if they were in a dashed ballroom. *This is madness. The man is mad.*

She drew herself up. "I do not understand what is going on. Regardless, I demand that you release me at once."

"Hidden fire, as I suspected." He hooked the lantern on the wall, revealing the room's spartan interior. "To match that lovely hair of yours."

When he reached toward her, she instinctively retreated until her back collided with brick. Her skin crawled as he captured a lock of her unpinned hair, stroking it between finger and thumb. His eyes were hard, reptilian.

"My son has apparently inherited my taste in women. I've always had a fondness for redheads," he said with a smirk.

It took her a moment to comprehend what he was saying.

"Your son?" She stared at him in astonishment. "You can't mean Adam..."

"Your husband didn't tell you? I'm not surprised. The man is good at keeping secrets." De Villier released her hair and stepped back. "I, myself, did not know that he still lived until recently."

An icy hand gripped her nape. "I don't understand."

"In my impulsive youth, I married his mama, a beautiful opera singer named Seraphina. My papa didn't approve of the match and disowned me. I took Seraphina to Italy; it didn't take long for me to realize the mistake I'd made. I wasn't cut out for living in poverty, for being a powerless nobody. Luckily, my papa offered me a way out. He'd found me an heiress to marry, one whose dowry would add considerably to the De Villier fortune. If I wanted back into the family fold, all I had to do was have the marriage annulled and return to London. The annulment was a bit tricky, given Seraphina's resistance to the idea, but..."

His casual shrug conveyed his callousness. "Money makes the world turn, as they say. I bribed a few officials, got my annulment, and there was naught Seraphina could do about it. The matter was settled—or so I thought. Imagine my surprise when a sweep named Wiley and his wife came to me some years later, claiming that they had my six-year-old son in their custody. They'd met the boy on a boat from Italy, they said, his mother dying before they reached the shore. The boy had told them that he was coming to London to find his father, Anthony De Villier. Out of the goodness of their hearts, Wiley and his wife had taken the boy in and would return him to me...for a handsome reward, of course."

De Villier paused, but Gabby already knew what he would say next. A man who'd so cruelly abandoned his wife wasn't likely to show mercy toward his child.

Feeling ill, she said, "You didn't pay the Wileys, did you?"

"Oh, I did."

Gabby couldn't hide her surprise, and De Villier's smile

widened, the look of a predator who enjoyed playing with his food.

"I paid the Wileys...to keep the brat out of my sight," he said with relish. "As long as he didn't cause me any problems, they could do with him as they wished. They operated a flash house and had other young boys they were training to be climbing boys and thieves. From what I understand, the brat fit right in."

The notion of Adam being forced to labor as a climbing boy and to do worse things, things she could not even imagine, tore at Gabby's heart. She'd always admired her husband's drive and success, but knowing where he'd started from, the odds he'd beaten, pushed tears from her eyes. Then a new thought struck her. Her father had said that once Adam gained control of Billings Bank, he meant to call in De Villier's loans: surely this could be no coincidence.

"Did Adam know that you'd paid the Wileys to keep him?" she blurted. "That you'd consigned him to this life of hell?"

"If the Wileys had done their job, everything would have been fine. But good help is hard to find, isn't it?" De Villier sighed like a hard-pressed lord of the manor. "When he was nine, the brat escaped and made his way to my doorstep. He didn't know, of course, that I'd paid for his maintenance with the Wileys; he thought I would take him in. Him—a dirty, ill-bred guttersnipe." De Villier shuddered. "Worse yet, since he was conceived before the annulment, he might have a legitimate claim to my wealth, if he could prove the relationship. My family and in-laws would never have accepted him as my heir, especially with my wife being barren. I couldn't let the brat destroy everything that I'd worked for."

Premonition tightened Gabby's throat. "What did you do?"

"I had Wiley take care of him. For good."

"You ordered the murder...of your own son," she said numbly.

"Twice, actually." De Villier's smile curdled her insides. "It came to my attention several months ago that someone was methodically gaining control over my debts. It took a while to peel away the layers of legal claptrap, but I finally discovered who owned all the banks that were so willing to give me money: one Adam Garrity. Why would this moneylender be so interested in my business, I asked myself? I had him investigated; once I learned his origins, I guessed his true identity. The damned Wileys had failed me once again, and somehow the brat had survived.

"This time, I hired a professional to take care of the problem. He followed Garrity to a skirmish, intending to make Garrity's death look like the result of a clash between cutthroats. But my assassin failed too." De Villier shook his head. "Luckily, your husband didn't emerge entirely unscathed. His amnesia was nearly as good as having him dead and saved me the trouble of hiring yet *another* killer. But, of course, good things never last. When I went to check up on Garrity at that ball, my gut told me he was a loose end I had to tie. Once he had his man-of-business digging into my affairs again, I knew I had to act. Which brings us to now."

Understanding flooded Gabby, horrifying and relieving at once. The reason Adam wanted control of her trust wasn't for money or power: it was for justice. He wanted to avenge his honor and that of his mama, rightly so. Moreover, knowing that his father—the man he'd crossed an ocean to find—had ordered his death, how could Adam trust anyone again? And then Jessabelle, his first love, had cuckolded him, her death burdening him with pain and guilt.

With growing wonder, Gabby realized what a miracle Adam was. After everything he'd gone through, he'd been a faithful husband to her and loving father to their children. And who he'd been during his amnesia...that had been real. The Adam unburdened by his horrific past, the one who knew how to love, who taught her to believe in herself: he'd been real. His love for her was real.

She remembered their fight:

You have no idea why I'm doing this, he'd said.

She'd responded, *And I don't give a damn.*

With thrumming remorse, she realized how she'd misjudged him. If only she'd responded differently, perhaps he would have told her about De Villier, perhaps she wouldn't be where she was now. And she did give a damn because she loved Adam and always would. God willing, she'd have the chance to tell him that.

"Now that you have the facts," De Villier said smoothly, "I hope you'll understand this inconvenience. Your husband is a dreadfully dogged and Machiavellian fellow. He's waited and planned all these years to pounce and get his revenge...which, of course, I cannot allow. But your visit shan't last much longer. After I've finished setting up the trap, I'll send word to Garrity to come forthwith—mustn't give him time to prepare, after all. Knowing his fondness for you—his sentimental nature always was his weakness—he'll come straightaway, and I'll put an end to this, once and for all."

She knew De Villier meant to kill Adam to protect his interests. And he'd kill her as well. Adam was clever and would know that De Villier had set a snare for him, but she knew in her heart that he would come anyway.

Because he loved her. She understood that now.

And she couldn't let him be hurt again by love.

"You don't have to do this," she said in what she hoped was a reasonable voice. "I've regained control of my trust, replaced the trustee that Adam had in his pocket. I give you my word that Billings Bank will not call in your loans until your project is complete. I will honor my father's pledge to you."

De Villier studied her, his head cocked. "Hmm, an interesting notion. But I'm afraid I cannot leave my fate up to a stranger, no matter how pretty she may be. Now you'll have to excuse me, Mrs. Garrity, for I have to prepare for the evening's festivities."

He collected his lamp, went to the door. Desperation gripped her. She couldn't do nothing, be the bait for Adam's trap. Powered by sheer determination, she ran full-tilt toward the open door, toward De Villier's retreating back...

A hand shoved her in the chest. She flew backward, sprawling on the ground. Head spinning, she looked up at a scarred and menacing face—the guard from the ball.

Her limbs shook as he scowled down at her and barked, "Stay put."

He slammed the door, sealing her in darkness.

37

NEARING DUSK, FOG CLOAKED THE THAMES, OBSCURING everything but the black water beneath the stealthy trio of lighters. Scanning the environs from the prow, Adam was grateful that Mother Nature was on his side. The dense grey miasma would provide excellent cover for his siege.

For the greatest battle of his life, one he could not lose.

Wait for me, my love. I'm coming.

With a nod to Kerrigan to keep watch, he descended into the ship's cabin, shutting the door to prevent the leakage of lamp-light. The faces that greeted him were somber but determined. Once again, he was thankful that his wife's sweet nature had won her so many friends. Despite the danger of the night's mission and the short notice, Kent, Strathaven, and Ransom had offered their assistance, their men following in the other boats. Murray joined them around the table.

"We're almost at the foundry." Too on edge to sit, Adam remained standing. "The good news is that we'll have surprise on our side. De Villier has no idea that I have a man on the inside who tipped me off to this location. The bastard thinks he has hours to prepare for our meeting. When we attack, he won't be expecting it."

"How many men does De Villier have?" Strathaven asked.

"Close to a hundred, according to my man. De Villier apparently hired some additional cutthroats for the occasion," Adam said grimly. "Given that we didn't have time to do the same, we will be outnumbered."

"My devices will make up for any disadvantage." Kent's spectacles glinted.

The other had brought along an arsenal of smoke-emitting canisters and explosive devices. When Adam's brows had lifted at the stockpile Kent's men loaded onto the ship, Tessa Kent, who'd come to see them off, had given her husband a fond smile.

"Harry likes to be prepared," she'd said impishly.

Adam had to admit that it was damned useful to have a scientist on his side.

"Before you start tossing detonating devices pell-mell," Strathaven said wryly to his brother-in-law, "we'll have to ensure Mrs. Garrity's safety first. Garrity, did your man mention where De Villier is keeping her?"

Adam gripped the table's edge. "He didn't know at the time when he sent the message. He was with De Villier when their guards arrived with Gabriella. He barely had time to get a note off to me before De Villier ordered them all to the foundry."

"One of my colleagues in the Royal Society toured the foundry and was able to give a rough idea of its layout. I made a sketch." Kent unrolled a drawing on the table. "There are four main buildings, one facing each direction. Each building is accessible with a door to the outside—a precaution should there be a fire or any other need for escape. The doors will likely be bolted, but one of my milder explosives ought to do the trick."

"Who needs a key when one has explosives?" Ransom drawled.

"We can each lead a team to search a building," Murray put in.

"We need a signal," Adam said. "To let the others know when Gabriella is found."

"I brought fireworks," Kent said. "The blue sparks will be visible even with the fog, and the devices make a sound like a thunderclap that can't be mistaken."

Despite his grim mood, Adam felt a prick of humor. "Anything else in your pocket, Kent?"

Kent lifted his brows. "What do you need?"

"I'll take the northern building," Murray said.

"East," Ransom said.

"South," Strathaven said.

"West." Kent looked at Adam. "Unless you want it?"

"Gentlemen, I will entrust you to find Gabriella and bring her to safety." Inhaling, Adam looked into the faces of his allies and prayed he was doing the right thing. "She is everything to me, and I need to know that she is in good hands...no matter what happens."

"We'll look after Mrs. Garrity." Ransom's promise was delivered with a wry smile. "Or our *own* ladies will have our heads."

As the others nodded in agreement, Murray asked, "What will you be doing?"

"There is only one surefire way to protect Gabriella and my family. I have to eradicate the root of the problem." Cold rage flowed through Adam. "I'm going after De Villier."

Gabby started at the loud *boom* that shook the walls.

Was that an explosion? Her ears pricked. She thought she heard men shouting...what were they saying? Their voices neared, becoming more distinct...

"Mrs. Garrity, where are you?"

"I'm in here!" She stumbled to the door, pounding on it with both fists. "It's me, I'm here!"

More booming, more shouting, the fracas so loud that she became panicked that her rescuers couldn't hear her. She continued yelling, her lungs straining, her fists beating a desperate drumbeat against wood.

"I'm here, Mrs. Garrity, I've got you."

Relief filled her as she recognized the voice filtering through the thick barrier. "Oh, Mr. Murray, thank goodness—"

She heard the key turn in the lock. Her eyes adjusting to the sudden flood of light, she saw...*the scarred face*. De Villier's guard had returned.

She backed away. "Get away from me—"

"Not to worry, Mrs. Garrity." Mr. Murray appeared behind the villain. "Livingston here works for your husband. He's been spying on the enemy for us; he sent us word so we were able to spring a surprise attack on De Villier. He led me to you."

She looked at Livingston, whose brutish face was transformed by a toothy grin.

"Beg your pardon, ma'am, for pushing you earlier," he said solicitously. "I had to make it look real so as not to rouse De Villier's suspicion."

"Thank you, sir," she said gratefully. "Where is my husband?"

"He's going after De Villier." Mr. Murray took her arm. "Come, we have to get you to the boat—"

"I'm not leaving without Adam." Fear for her beloved made Gabby dig in her heels. "You don't know De Villier, he's capable of anything—"

"Believe me, so is your husband when your well-being is at stake. The sooner I get you to safety, the sooner he can focus all his energies on vanquishing his enemy."

Although she understood the logic, she couldn't bring herself to leave Adam. Not when he'd been left to survive on his own so many times. "The three of us can find him together—"

"I was hoping it wouldn't come to this," Mr. Murray muttered.

"Come to what?"

"Your husband anticipated that you might be reluctant to leave without him. If that were to happen, he gave us a message to convey to you."

Seeing the ruddy color on the other's face, she asked curiously, "What message?"

"*Go to the ship, Gabriella.*" Murray cleared his throat. "*Your sultan commands it.*"

38

SEEING THE BLUE SPARKLES SHOWER THE COURTYARD, ADAM felt the knot in his gut ease.

Gabby is safe. Thank God, my beloved is safe.

He let himself enjoy that blissful instant of relief...before picking up the scent again. Knowing that Gabby was out of harm's way, he gave the hunt for De Villier his full attention. As he stalked through the courtyard scattered with wooden crates, tools, and assorted machinery, De Villier's men were stumbling from the adjacent buildings, smoked out by Kent's devices. The choking, gasping men were easily subdued by Adam's allies.

Others of De Villier's army were still battling fiercely. Aiming his pistol, Adam took down one who was grappling with Ransom by a pallet of metal rails. From the other side, a brute came charging at Adam, and he pulled out another pistol, ending the attack with a bullet. He strode on, scanning the brawling throng for De Villier.

Having searched the other buildings, he was about to enter the western building to continue his search when Kent came running out of its doorway, a handkerchief tied over his mouth, his arms gesturing wildly.

"Run."

Adam turned and sprinted, Kent at his heels. They managed to find shelter behind a stack of crates just as a deafening blast tore through the air, the ground shaking. When the debris stopped raining, Adam looked around the edge of the makeshift shield, his eyes widening at the demolished building and rising blaze.

He gave Kent an incredulous look. "What the bloody hell happened?"

"I may have, er, accidentally tossed one of my devices into a cupboard full of fog signals." At Adam's blank look, Kent said abashedly, "Fog signals contain gunpowder."

Christ. Adam was shaking his head...when he saw his quarry.

"De Villier." He was on his feet, on the trail. "He just ran into the eastern building."

Kent followed him into the long, cavernous space. The flickering glow of lamps revealed that this was the workshop where the locomotives were assembled. A metal behemoth sat unfinished, its iron skin gleaming. At the opposite end of the building, Adam saw the flash of De Villier's pale hair...disappearing into the ground?

"Trapdoor," he and Kent said at once.

They raced over as the trapdoor slammed into place. Adam reached it first, pulling at the metal ring. The door didn't budge.

"It's locked from the other side." Giving Kent a glance, he took a step back. Then a few more steps, just to be safe. "Try not to blow us up."

With a rather maniacal grin, Kent set to work. In a matter of minutes, they climbed through the jagged hole where the door had once been and found themselves on an underwater dock. Adam spotted De Villier: the blackguard was in a boat being rowed by one of his brutes, and they were nearly out of the underground passage. If he reached the Thames, the fog would give him cover, and he might easily escape.

There was only one boat left tethered to the dock: a small rowboat with a single oar.

Adam ran over and jumped in. "I'll be faster alone."

"Good luck, Garrity." Kent helped him untie the rope. "See you back at the ship."

Adam plowed his oar through the water, his transport gaining speed. De Villier had reached the river, but Adam wasn't far behind.

"Row faster, you imbecile!" De Villier's roar sounded close.

Adam squinted, trying to see the other's boat lamp in the fog. A glimmer just a few lengths ahead, a movement...

He threw himself down on the bottom of the boat just as a bullet whizzed by, puncturing the starboard side. *Christ.* Water began pouring in. Muscles bunching, sweat pouring down his brow, he rowed toward his target. Water swirled around his calves. He closed in just as De Villier was reloading his pistol.

In a single motion, Adam rose and sprang onto the other boat.

He tackled both men as he landed, hearing their surprised grunts, the sound of De Villier's weapon splashing into the river. He was already reaching for his boot when De Villier's brute rolled him over. The man's beefy hands circled Adam's throat at the same time that Adam's blade struck home. Adam withdrew the knife and kicked his foe over the side.

Crouching, dripping blade in hand, Adam faced De Villier.

Weaponless, the other scrambled back against the opposite end of the boat.

"Don't do anything rash." De Villier's chest heaved. "I can give you anything you want. Wealth beyond your wildest dreams—"

"I don't want your money." Adam advanced, keeping his balance as the boat swayed.

"My name then. You want that, don't you?" De Villier held out his hands, a placating gesture. "It's what you always wanted, and I'll give it to you. You were conceived before the marriage was annulled...I will attest to that, make you my heir. Here, take this."

He tugged on his finger, removing the bloodstone signet, holding it out like an offering in his palm. "It belongs to you. Along with all the De Villier holdings, including Grand London Northern—"

"I want nothing from you," Adam said in disgust. "If I could, I would erase your blood from my veins."

"But you can't. Because you're like me." De Villier's eyes darted side to side. "Deep down, you understand why I did what I did. A powerful man can't let sentiment get in the way. True power is within your grasp now, Son, don't do anything foolish..."

The bastard hurled the signet at Adam. On instinct, Adam dodged the projectile, and the other used that moment of distraction to lunge. A lifetime's training made Adam twist, evading the attack, kicking out. His boot connected with De Villier's chest, sending the other over the edge with a splash.

De Villier thrashed in the water, his eyes bulging with panic. "Help me! I can't swim!"

"That's one of the many differences between you and me." Adam regarded the other coolly. "I learned to swim at an early age."

"I won't die this way," De Villier gasped. "I'll give you anything...money, power..."

Adam watched the dark waters close over his past. When the last surfacing bubbles were swept away by the waves, he returned his gaze to the boat...and saw the glint of the signet ring. He scooped it up and contemplated it for long moments, running his thumb over the Latin inscription, feeling the weight of what he held.

Then he threw the ring over the edge.

Picking up the oar, he headed to shore.

❧ 39 ❧

THE LIGHTERS BROUGHT EVERYONE BACK TO THE DOCK WHERE their carriages were waiting. Safe in the circle of Adam's arms, Gabby bid farewell to their assembled friends.

"Thank you all ever so much," she said, emotion clogging her throat. "I don't know how we'll ever repay you—"

"Just put in a good word with our ladies." Strathaven bowed over her hand, his eyes warm. "I'm certain Emma will be paying you a visit on the morrow. It's a miracle I was able to convince her to stay home tonight."

"Tell me about it," Mr. Kent said with feeling. "Tessa will insist upon a full accounting the minute I get home."

"Gentlemen, I am in your debt." Adam spoke, his words gruff with sincerity. "If I can ever be of assistance, I am at your service."

"We'll call it even, shall we?" Ransom's lips curved below his dashing mustache. "No debts between us. Just friendship."

"Speak for yourself," Mr. Murray said. "Garrity owes me a raise."

Enjoying the blessed normality of the male banter, Gabby smiled...but it turned into a yawn.

Adam's arm tightened around her waist. "I'd best be getting my wife home."

The men departed, and Adam swept her up in his arms.

"You don't have to carry me," she protested. "I'm perfectly capable of walking."

"If you think I'm *ever* letting you go, you can think again," came her husband's reply.

Since she felt the same way, she looped her arms around his neck, snuggling closer, letting his familiar scent and warmth soothe away the terrors of the night. Once in the carriage, he settled her on his lap. She would have been content to remain there forever, tucked up against him, feeling the steady thump of his heart.

"Can you forgive me, Gabby, for the way I've treated you?"

At his guttural words, she jerked her head up, nearly hitting him on the chin.

"Adam, there's naught to forgive." Her gaze found his; in the dimness of the carriage, his eyes were as dark and fathomless as the river they'd just crossed. "De Villier told me everything. About your history, what he'd done to you...that he was your father. I understand why you wanted to destroy his company. An eye for an eye: the villain *deserved* to be punished for his evil acts."

He cupped her cheek, his eyes no longer unreadable but burning with emotion. "I should have told you the truth from the start. About De Villier and my past. I should not have kept secrets—any secrets—from you."

"Last night, when we...fought," she said hesitantly, "I was angry at you."

"I deserved your anger. Christ, if I could take back what I've done—"

"Let me finish," she said.

He nodded, his jaw taut.

"I was angry because when my father told me that you had Mr. Isnard in your pocket, I thought you'd married me only to get your hands on Billings Bank. That money and power were what you'd been after all this time, that you'd never really wanted me."

"That's not true," he said vehemently. "Gabriella, I—"

"When I confronted you, I was so angry and hurt that I didn't bother to ask *why* you wanted my father's bank; I simply assumed the worst. I attacked you, and that wasn't fair of me. In retrospect, my reaction wasn't only about discovering what I felt was a betrayal: it was about my own fear that I wasn't worthy, that I'd fooled myself into believing that you could be in love with me."

"I *am* in love with you." Adam's tone was fierce, unyielding. "That night we fought, I acted like a right bastard. It's no excuse, but I think I was still reeling from the sudden recovery of my memories...the confusion I felt over who I'd become. I lashed out at your 'betrayal,' which is rich when I deceived you first with my underhanded actions. My reaction stems from my own past, my fear of once again being duped by sentiment, the way I'd been fooled by De Villier, Jessabelle, and others."

"I understand," she said gently. "Anyone who'd gone through your harrowing journey and survived would feel the same way."

"By morning, I already realized what a complete arse I'd been. I was on my way to apologize to you. To tell you that I didn't give a damn about your trust or revenge: if I lost you, then I had nothing. Then the news came that you'd been taken." He let out a ragged breath. "That was the worst moment of my life, Gabriella. Bar none. Worse than finding Jessabelle dead, worse than everything De Villier has done to me. In those other instances, I could go on, but Gabby...I couldn't survive without you."

At her husband's stark declaration, heat surged behind her eyes. To hear this strong, fearless man say that he couldn't live without her shook her very foundations, breaking down the remnants of those old, imprisoning walls. Seeing herself reflected in his darkly adoring sultan's eyes, she knew she was worthy and beautiful. Loved.

"I love you," she said tremulously.

"Thank Christ," he said with a hoarse reverence that curled her toes. "You say my journey has been harrowing, but I regret none of it since it brought me to you. You are my reward, and loving you is my true purpose, what gives my life meaning. My heart is yours until it stops beating and beyond."

Even as she absorbed his words, letting their beauty sink into her marrow, she felt a shiver.

"Don't even talk about your heart not beating," she whispered. "When I think about how close I've come to losing you...oh, heavens, I almost forgot. De Villier, that *bastard*, told me that he hired an assassin to shoot you during the battle with Sweeney. He caused your wound, your amnesia."

"I know. Livingston told me during the boat ride back. He apologized for not discovering that plot and the one to kidnap you before they happened."

"It's not his fault. When I think about all the evil De Villier has done—"

"Don't think about it." Adam brought her into the shelter of his body once more, stroking her hair. "I'm here. We're both here. Together as we're meant to be."

When she finally calmed, she lifted her head to look at her husband. The lines had eased from his handsome face, his eyes warm and intent as he regarded her. Was it her imagination or did he look younger, more at peace?

"Do you still feel confused about who you've become since the amnesia?" she asked.

"No," he said immediately. "Tonight helped me to realize that who I am now is who I've been becoming since I first met you. By taking away my past, the amnesia took away my blinders, allowing me to see that revenge, the goal I'd worked toward all my life, wasn't really what I needed. When De Villier died, I thought I'd feel something...some sort of resolution. And do you know what I felt?"

"What, darling?"

"Nothing. He had no power over me, nothing I wanted. *You* have already given me everything I need: the peace I'd been searching for was mine all along." Adam's eyes eclipsed all else, burning into her soul, melding them as one. "I started falling in love with you the moment we met, but I was too stupid to realize it. Too afraid to open my heart. De Villier told me once that a powerful man isn't blinded by sentiment, but he was wrong. A man is *made* powerful by the love of a good woman and the love he gives her in return."

"Oh, Adam," she said tearfully, "that is the most romantic thing you've ever said to me."

Tenderly, he thumbed away her tears. "More romantic than *your sultan commands it?*"

She gave a watery giggle. "That comes as a close second. You should have seen how mortified poor Mr. Murray was when he gave me the message."

"I knew my brave and loyal queen would insist on staying otherwise."

"I'll always be by your side," she promised.

"On my lap is even better." His arms circled her, his eyes holding her just as securely. "I may be your master, but you own me, Gabby. I'm yours, every part of me: my heart, my soul...and other assorted wicked parts."

"I love you and all your wicked parts." She wriggled against him, smiling when she felt his virile response. "After we get home and give the children a good snuggle, I'll show you how much."

"How about a sampling of it now?"

"Is this my sultan's wish?"

"Yes. Love me, Gabriella." His eyes smoldered. "Don't ever stop."

With a blissful sigh, she obeyed her heart's command.

EPILOGUE

FLORENCE, ITALY

"Are we there yet?" Gabriella asked.

"You sound like Fiona and Max," Adam said, amused.

Below the black silk blindfold, the rueful curve of his wife's beautiful mouth acknowledged his observation. Just a week into their three-month tour of Italy and the children were already proving to be impatient little scamps. Today, whilst walking across a magnificent piazza, surrounded by views of the stunning terra-cotta-tiled rooftops and Renaissance buildings and sculptures, Fiona had started up the chorus of "Are we there yet?" and Max had promptly joined in.

"Children, you are where you are," Adam had said severely. "I suggest you enjoy it."

Fiona and Max had looked at one another. Then at him.

"Yes, Papa," they'd said obediently.

Then they'd started whining for *gelato*, their newly discovered treat.

Thank Christ they were currently with their governess and the army of nursemaids that he had had the foresight to bring along. As much as he loved the rambunctious imps, he wanted time alone with his wife. To give her the surprise he'd planned.

He continued to lead her down the long corridor, their footsteps echoing against the diamond-checked tiles. Priceless art filled the passageway: busts, intricate tapestries, a brilliant fresco covering the ceiling. Because of the blindfold, Gabby couldn't see any of it, but he'd arranged to have the entire *Galleria degli Uffizi* to themselves for the evening. There would be time for her to explore the museum's riches after his surprise.

"Can you give me a *hint* about what you've planned?" his better half asked.

"I could, but that would ruin the surprise, impatient minx." He tightened his arm around her waist, murmuring against her ear, "I ought to make you practice waiting more."

Her cheeks turned rosy against the black silk. He knew she was thinking of a recent interlude when he'd used velvet ropes to tie her to their bed. He'd enjoyed every inch of his lovely slave's body, teasing her until she was panting, writhing helplessly against the sheets. He hadn't let her come until she'd begged him for it, pleading with him using the hot, naughty words he'd taught her.

Thinking of that decadent encounter made him harder than rock, and the festivities had just begun. When his wife had allowed him to blindfold her in the carriage, her sweet trust had made his chest throb along with his prick. She was the finest gift a man could wish for, a treasure he couldn't believe was his, and that he would never again take for granted.

In fact, he'd planned on taking her on this trip sooner, but several events had delayed his plans. First, Gabby's father had passed. She'd needed time to grieve, and Adam was determined to give her everything she needed. For her sake, he'd even mended fences with his father-in-law before the other's death, giving his word that he would look after Billings Bank. Billings had passed away peacefully, with Gabby, Adam, and his grandchildren by his side.

The second delay was business related. After De Villier's death, Adam had inherited the lion's share of Grand London National Railway, not because of the blood relation, but because he owned Villier's debt. He'd planned to let the venture run its natural course—that is, to let it fail. Gabby, however, had asked him to try to save it for the sake of the ordinary folk who'd invested their life savings in the scheme.

Because he could deny his wife nothing, Adam set about reviving the company. He took on partners to oversee various aspects of the business: Harry Kent, in particular, had expressed interest in the scientific side of things and Murray had always dealt well with the public. Adam himself managed the financial matters. It had taken about eight months and a complete restructuring of the business, but GLNR had recently unveiled the world's fastest steam engine, and the value of the company had shot through the roof.

Now that GLNR was a success and Gabby was out of mourning, the time had come for Adam to take his family on a vacation...and to give his wife a special treat. Hence, he navigated her into the present chamber. Noting that everything had been arranged to his specifications, he steered her into place.

He stood behind her, his hands on her shoulders. "Ready for your surprise, love?"

Her nod sent ripples through her flame-colored tresses. Per his instructions, she'd left her hair loose, and it flowed down to the waist of the ivory silk gown he'd chosen for her. Time to reward his good little wife...and himself.

He untied the blindfold.

Gabriella blinked, her jaw slackening as she saw what he intended for her to see.

"Goodness," she breathed. "This is the painting? The one you think...*I* resemble?"

"Titian's *Venus of Urbino*," he said with satisfaction.

The goddess was as he remembered her: her naked curves

lush, her eyes warmly sensual, her reclined pose on the red couch coyly come-hither. Her body was tilted toward the viewer, her front elbow resting upon a pillow, a bouquet of flowers dangling loosely from that hand. Her other arm was draped across her body, that hand resting over her sex, hiding it...or deliberately drawing attention to that shadowed cove.

As stunning as the painting was, it was Adam's real-life goddess who consumed his attention. He'd had full-length looking glasses placed in a semi-circle around the artwork, giving him views of his lovely wife from various angles. Behind them was a wide crimson couch, a replica of the one Venus was reposed upon. As in the portrait, fluffy white pillows were piled at one end.

Gabby was staring at the painting as if transfixed. He couldn't blame her. The likeness between her and Venus was uncanny.

"She's so beautiful," Gabby said in a hushed voice. "You truly think I look like her?"

He couldn't resist teasing her. "I'm not absolutely certain." Seeing her crestfallen expression, he said silkily, "You're over-dressed compared to her, and one ought to compare apples to apples, don't you think?"

He cupped her nape, loving her shiver of awareness, which turned into a deeper trembling when his fingers continued onto the silk-covered buttons on the back of her dress. He'd chosen the garment because it resembled a tunic gown of the Far East, gathering beneath her bosom and flowing down in a graceful column... and because it was easy to remove.

As he unhooked the last button, the garment slid down, pooling at her slippered feet. His nostrils flared as he saw she'd followed his instructions to the letter: no corset, no petticoats, not even a chemise to hide her beauty from him. The only thing she had on were sheer white stockings held up by frilly garters and her slippers.

He stepped back. "Take off the rest."

When she bent over to comply, presenting him with her

peach-shaped arse, his erection strained against the fall of his trousers. By God, she was delicious and so willing to play out their mutual fantasies. There wasn't a woman in existence who suited him better than his own wife.

Straightening, she whispered, "Now what should I do?"

"Lie on the couch the way Venus is doing," he said huskily. "So that I may fully judge the resemblance, hmm?"

Looking flustered, Gabby did as he bade. She reclined against the pillows, and he had to smother a grin as she awkwardly flopped this way and that, trying to emulate Venus's seductive, side-lying pose. Although Gabby's self-confidence had grown by leaps and bounds, she was still sweetly shy by nature. He didn't mind. In fact, he enjoyed unraveling her inhibitions strand by silken strand.

Posed on the couch, she bit her lip. "Will this do?"

God, yes. His cock heartily approved the picture she made. But the game was just beginning, and he liked to draw out their marital pleasures.

He went over and casually tapped her hand where it lay on her top hip. "Is this where Venus has her hand?"

Her gaze slid to the painting, her cheeks growing rosier as she shook her head.

"What part of herself is Venus touching? Use the proper word, the one I've taught you," he said in a deliberately strict tone.

"Which word do you mean?" She peered at him with guileless blue eyes. "Because thus far I've learned a few. There's *pussy, cunny,* and *quim.* And let's not forget *hot buttered crumpet...*"

Perhaps his wife had come along farther than he realized. Saucy minx.

Then it occurred to him.

"I've never called it a hot buttered crumpet," he said with narrowed eyes.

"It must have been someone else then." At his pointed stare, she added with a laugh, "One of my *female* friends mentioned that she overheard a footman use that term. We found it ever so amusing."

In recent months, Gabby's circle of ladies had become even more tightly knit. They bonded regularly over tea and mischief, to the amusement and exasperation of their husbands.

"Kent was right: we husbands ought to plant a listening device when you ladies get together." Adam's lips twitched. "Now, Scheherazade, stop diverting me with your fascinating vocabulary and tell me where Venus has placed her hand."

"On her pussy."

Christ, he loved hearing dirty words uttered in his wife's sweet voice.

He arched a brow. "So where should your hand be?"

"On my pussy." After a moment, Gabriella moved her hand over the gentle swell of her belly to her sex. Her fingers hovered over the coppery nest like birds poised to take flight.

"Good," he allowed. "Now tell me, do you think Venus is being modest...or naughty?"

Her eyes went first to the painting, then to a reflection of herself.

"Naughty," she said, her voice breathy.

"I agree. Now show me exactly how naughty you can be."

He watched, his jaw taut with arousal as his wife's delicate fingers dipped between her thighs. She was always shy when she did this for him, which was why he loved having her do it. The sight of her petting her pretty cunny made his cock weep. She was similarly aroused, her fingers and slit glistening with her honey.

"So beautiful and you're all mine." He placed a hand gently over her throat, feeling the rapid flutter, the warmth of her pleasure flush. "Say it."

"I'm yours."

The affirmation expanded his chest with lust and love. He got down on one knee. "Then keep frigging yourself while I avail myself of my queen's delights."

He kissed her, long and hard and deep. It was a conquering kiss, and she yielded in that way of hers that drove him wild, made him burn to have all of her. He found a sensitive spot on her neck, claiming it with a savage suction that would leave a mark.

He made his way to her breasts, pure male greed taking over. God's blood, her tits were a masterpiece. He kneaded and squeezed, his thumbs grazing the stiff cherry tips. He licked around her wide areola, spiraling toward the peak. As he suckled her, she moved her arm faster, diddling herself with lovely desperation.

He nuzzled the inviting softness of her belly, his hands roving possessively. Such bounty and all of it was his. When he arrived at her sex, breathing in the scent of her arousal, her fingers stilled.

He glanced back at her face. "Did I tell you to stop pleasuring yourself?"

"No."

"Then why did you cease?"

Her eyes were wide, earnest. "Because my sultan does it better."

Devil and damn. She knew exactly how to incite the beast in him.

"Does my slave wish for me to take care of her?" He had to fight to keep his voice calm in the face of his raging desire. "To frig and eat her pussy?"

"Yes, please."

"Tempt me with a taste, then."

She brought her hand to his lips. Holding her delicate wrist, he slowly sucked two of her fingers into his mouth. Her flavor intoxicated him, a drug that made him crave more.

He licked his lips. "Your cream is delectable, a meal I shall enjoy." Her hand trembled in his grasp, and he brought it to her sex, positioning the index and middle fingers on her nether lips. "Spread your cunny for me, love."

His nostrils flared as her slim, ladylike fingers exposed her dewy secrets for him. He leaned in, running his tongue up her plump seam. He took his time worshipping her femininity. She chanted her pleasure as he feasted on her. As he swived his naughty queen with his mouth.

When her thighs tightened in that telling way, he commanded, "Come for me now."

With a tremulous cry, she obeyed, her completion gushing upon his greedy tongue.

Breathing heavily, he rose and tore off his clothes. His wife's face was radiant with love and insatiable sensuality worthy of the goddess she resembled. When he was naked at last, he curled one hand around the base of his thick, straining cock and gave her a meaningful look. She needed no further prompting, moving to kneel gracefully at his feet.

Her palms resting on his hard thighs, she swallowed his prick with mind-obliterating enthusiasm. As her mouth serviced him, her eyes stoked his flames ever higher. Those blue depths glowed with the pleasure of pleasuring him. With the knowledge that she was his equal in passion and in life.

Everything he wanted—love, loyalty, tender playfulness—swirled in his wife's gaze. He couldn't resist the emotions she invoked in him or her selfless sucking. He gave himself over to the joy, the sheer carnal bliss of spending betwixt his beloved's lips. She took all of him as she always did, and he grunted with approval as her throat caressed and coaxed out the last drops.

Still hard, still hungry, he lay on the couch, hauling her on top of him. He teased her by rubbing his crown along her cleft until her cream coated them both, her eyes beseeching him.

He tucked a wayward tress behind her ear. "Do you want my cock, sweetheart?"

"Ever so much," she breathed.

"Then sit on it."

Her palms pressed against his chest as she impaled herself, inch by inch, on his up-thrust rod. He loved her initial struggle to accommodate him, the way she wriggled and stretched around his invading shaft. They both groaned when she took him to the balls, her sheath surrounding him like a hot, tight glove, every part of her made to fit every part of him.

She slid up and down, her movements torturously slow.

He placed his hands on her hips, urging her on. "Tell me how it feels to ride my cock."

"It feels...so good." Her neck arched as she sank down again.

"Surely my Scheherazade can do better than that."

"You're so big and thick, filling me up. Sometimes it feels like too much...but at the same time not enough." Her passion-slurred voice revealed how close she was to coming. Her fingers tangled in his chest hair as she rose up. "There's this place...deep inside. When you push into it, it feels like a Roman candle going off..."

"Like this?" He slammed her down on his cock, thrusting his hips up at the same time.

She cried out as her crisis hit her. He let her ride out her peak, then flipped her onto her hands and knees, plowing into her from behind.

"It's never enough," he said through harsh breaths. "I'll never get enough of you, Gabby."

She looked back at him, her red hair streaming over her shoulders, the sweetest smile tucked in her cheeks. Only she would look at him so tenderly while he speared her cunny with his veined meat. The recognition unraveled the rest of his control. Unleashed his limitless wanting for this rare, glorious woman who was his mate, his heartbeat. His everything.

"I'll never get enough of you either," she whispered.

"Good because you're getting more," he vowed. "All of me, love."

He thrust harder, deeper, his balls grinding against her folds. Her beautiful arse jiggled, the tiny pucker between her cheeks calling to his primal need to claim every part of her. Coating his thumb in her abundant wetness, he brought his slickened digit to the virgin entrance. Pushed gently but firmly inside.

She jolted, her muscles clamping down on him, a dark and visceral delight. But that was reflex, and he needed to know what his lady wanted. After a moment, she pushed back, taking his finger and cock deeper inside her, her back arching at the dual pleasure.

With a growl scraped from the depths of his soul, he screwed himself into his wife's holes, taking all of her, giving all of himself in return. He pushed her into climax, the clasp of her pussy summoning his own release. Ecstasy roared over him as he poured himself inside his wife, a scorching, shuddering affirmation of their bond.

Sated and spent for now, he sprawled onto the couch, tucking her against his side. Contentment hummed through him, a peace he felt down to his marrow. There was a veritable treasure trove of art to explore...but all he wanted to do was cuddle with his wife.

Her cheek on his chest, Gabby was studying the painting. "I do look like her, don't I?"

"With one exception," he said.

She lifted her head, her gaze curious. "And that is?"

"You have better tits."

He grinned when she wrinkled her nose at him.

"Is that the only thing men think about?" she asked.

"I thought I was rather creative with other parts of your anatomy this eve."

That earned him the blush he adored. "That was depraved, Adam."

"It was." He gave her bottom a satisfied, proprietary pat. "We'll do it again soon."

"You're wicked." She smiled, snuggling against him. "Thank you."

"For being wicked?"

"For making all my dreams come true." The love in her eyes was tender and strong, enough to last a lifetime and beyond. "For making me feel special and loved every single day."

"Just returning the favor, love," he said softly. *"A heart for a heart and a soul for a soul.* That's the kind of justice worth living for."

AUTHOR'S NOTE

Arabian Nights' Entertainments, which may be better known as *Thousand and One Nights* to modern readers, is a collection of ancient Arabic tales, many Persian in origin. The stories first appeared in Europe in the eighteenth century, translated from Arabic to French by orientalist Antoine Galland into twelve volumes he titled, *Les milles et une nuits*. The version that Gabby would have read in *Regarding the Duke* would be the English translation of Galland's work, either the "Grub Street" version (published anonymously in the early 1700's) or the translation by Jonathan Scott in the early 1800's. Of course, Gabby's naughty and romantic take on Schahriar and Scheherazade is entirely her own.

More information about *Arabian Nights' Entertainments* can be found on Wikipedia and in the extremely informative introduction by Robert L. Mack in the Oxford World's Classics 1995 Edition.

Another historical point of interest concerns Titian's *Venus of Urbino*. This painting has been part of the *Galleria degli Uffizi's* collection since the 1700's. I last visited the Uffizi as a back-packing college student and, alas, cannot recall if I actually saw this work of art (it was a long time ago, and there were a lot of competing masterpieces!). Nonetheless, I chose to use this painting in the book because it is an allegory of marriage, and the journey of marriage is one of the themes in *Regarding the Duke*. According to the *Uffizi* website, the painting was a gift from a duke to his young wife, and symbols within the painting are intended to be "lessons" about the importance of eroticism, fidelity, and motherhood in marriage.

ABOUT THE AUTHOR

USA Today & International Bestselling Author Grace Callaway writes steamy and adventurous historical romances. Her debut book, *Her Husband's Harlot*, was a Romance Writers of America Golden Heart® Finalist and a #1 Regency Bestseller, and her subsequent novels have topped national and international bestselling lists. She's the winner of the Passionate Plume Award for Historical Novel, and her books have been honored as finalists for numerous awards, including the National Reader's Choice Awards, the Maggie Award of Excellence, and the Daphne du Maurier Award for Excellence in Mystery/ Suspense.

Growing up on the Canadian prairies, Grace could often be found with her nose in a book—and not much has changed since. She set aside her favorite romance novels long enough to get her doctorate from the University of Michigan. A clinical psychologist, she lives with her family in Northern California, where their adventures include remodeling a ramshackle house, exploring the great outdoors, and sampling local artisanal goodies.

Keep up with my latest news!
Newsletter: gracecallaway.com/newsletter

f facebook.com/GraceCallawayBooks

BB bookbub.com/authors/grace-callaway

instagram.com/gracecallawaybooks

a amazon.com/author/gracecallaway

ACKNOWLEDGMENTS

To the readers and fans who take my characters' journeys with me: from the bottom of my heart, thank you. You make it possible for me to dream big and keep on dreaming. I hope my stories inspire the same spirit in you.

To my retreat groups: you gals are the best. Learning and laughing with you is as essential as coffee to my writing (that is no faint praise!).

Special thanks to my editor Ronnie Nelson and my cover designer Erin Dameron-Hill for making my books shine, inside and out.

To my family: I love you. You're the inspiration for everything that I do.

Made in the USA
Coppell, TX
04 November 2024

39607356R10204